dis.

In
Dahlia's
Wake

Also by Yona Zeldis McDonough

The Four Temperaments

DOUBLEDAY

New York   London   Toronto   Sydney   Auckland

In Dahlia's Wake

a novel

YONA ZELDIS McDONOUGH

PUBLISHED BY DOUBLEDAY
a division of Random House, Inc.

DOUBLEDAY and the portrayal of an anchor with a dolphin are
registered trademarks of Random House, Inc.

Book design by Nicola Ferguson

Library of Congress Cataloging-in-Publication Data
McDonough, Yona Zeldis.
In Dahlia's wake : a novel / by Yona Zeldis McDonough.—1st ed.
p. cm.
1. Accident victims—Family relationships—Fiction.
2. Children—Death—Fiction.
3. Married people—Fiction. I. Title.

PS3613.C39I5 2005
813'.54—dc22   2004056157

ISBN 0-385-50362-8

PRINTED IN THE UNITED STATES OF AMERICA

May 2005
FIRST EDITION

1   3   5   7   9   10   8   6   4   2

For my mother,
Malcah Zeldis,
and in memory of
my grandmother,
Tania Brightman

In Dahlia's Wake

1

Coffee Break

On a Friday morning in early December, Naomi Wechsler walked up Seventh Avenue, head bent slightly forward, umbrella positioned in front of her like a shield. It was wet and sleety and the umbrella kept getting pulled inside out by gusts—brief but sharp—of winter wind. Still, Naomi prevailed. She was on her way to Holy Name of Jesus Hospital for her morning in the pediatric ward, and she didn't want to get soaked. The three mornings a week she spent at Holy Name had become the scaffolding on which her days were precariously balanced. Naomi was scrupulous about honoring her commitment there; in some small way, it was what kept her going.

Rick, her husband, didn't understand why she wanted, no, needed to go to Holy Name. He had asked her about it repeatedly, and when her answers failed to satisfy him, he had begun a quiet but penetrating campaign of reproach: small, exasperated sighs and looks, a certain clipped tone when he asked if she was "going up there—again." But, then, it seemed that there were so many ways in which she had failed Rick these days. So many ways she could hardly count them. And he had failed her too. Still, she had resolved not to think about that today. She would not let herself.

As Naomi came to the corner of Sixth Street, she checked her watch. Only a little past nine. She was not due to arrive until nine-thirty. She decided to duck into Barnes & Noble to buy a cup of coffee from the café. There was free coffee on the ward and coffee sold in the hospital cafeteria, but Naomi knew from experience that the former was flavorless and cold; the latter, flavorless and hot. She had a little extra time this morning. She could indulge.

Shaking the excess water from her umbrella, she folded it up before stepping inside the double doors of the bookstore. Quickly, she made her way to the café and got on line. To her left was a table with a large display of Godiva chocolates: gold boxes tied with red ribbon and adorned with pinecones, the same gold boxes tied with blue ribbon and adorned with silver stars. Christmas and Hanukkah, the December twins, had arrived in New York. There were also foil-covered chocolate Santas with rouged cheeks and abundant white hair meant to resemble confections of a hundred years ago and mesh sacks of chocolate coins wrapped in silver and gold foil. Naomi picked up six sacks of coins and six Santas. She knew that several of the children on the ward had dietary restrictions forbidding them to eat chocolate, but surely there would be some who would be allowed to have it. And there were always the nurses. Her hands full, she stood patiently in line waiting for her turn.

There was a man ahead of her wearing a greenish-gray raincoat and a ridiculous-looking yellow rain hat, the kind of thing fishermen wore and was now found in J. Crew and L.L. Bean catalogs. The hat seemed to be too large for him and resembled, in some vague way, a hen that had come to roost on his head. When he ordered his coffee— a double hazelnut latte with whipped cream and cinnamon—she thought she could detect something familiar about his voice. When he turned around, she recognized him. Michael McBride, the head of the pediatric unit at Holy Name. The man who, last summer, had told her that her seven-year-old daughter, Dahlia, was dead.

McBride stood there, a cup of steaming, fragrant liquid in his hand. She saw at once that he knew who she was.

"Mrs. Wechsler." It was not a question. "It's been a while."

"Only five months, two days, and about ten hours," she wanted to say. But she didn't.

"I hope everything has been . . . all right . . . with you. And your husband."

"We're fine," Naomi said and moved past him. She could sense him still standing there as she ordered, but she didn't turn around again. Instead, she paid for the coffee and the chocolate and accepted the bags with which to carry them, all without looking at him a second time. She went over to a high, circular table to retrieve napkins, a stirrer, and a packet of sugar. It wasn't strange to run into him, of course. He worked in the hospital and now she did too. The only strange thing about the encounter was that it hadn't happened sooner.

Back outside, the wind was still blowing the sleet around in wet, angry gusts. Naomi reached the hospital's wide, automatic doors with relief. As she stepped inside, she opened the lid of the coffee, took a sip and then another. She saw McBride, yellow hat now collapsed under his arm, talking to a doctor right next to the large, lavishly decorated Christmas tree in the hospital's lobby. She stayed out of sight, so that she wouldn't have to speak to him. But even McBride's presence, painful as it was to her, wouldn't stop her from coming here. If she ran into him again—and she knew she would—she would find some way of being, or acting, that didn't rip her heart out. She knew she would be able to do it. Hadn't she managed to live through the last five months? If she could do that, she could do anything.

Although they had never discussed it, Naomi suspected that Rick avoided the hospital entirely. She could imagine him walking along Seventh Avenue, toward that well-stocked secondhand bookshop that had opened on Seventh Street, or toward Two Little Hens, the bakery he liked up on Eighth Avenue, always making sure that he was on the other side of the street.

Naomi herself wasn't entirely certain why she was drawn here. She told herself it was better than spending her days on the couch, her eyes tracking the progress of the light as it filtered into the front windows of the house in the morning and, later in the day, through the dining room windows in back. But that was only part of it.

This was the year she had planned to return to graduate school, for her PhD in English literature. Dahlia was getting older; Naomi thought that she could comfortably leave her with Rick when she took her classes or spent time in the library. After Dahlia had died, though, Naomi lost interest in pursuing an advanced degree. Yet she didn't want to go back to teaching either.

For the last three years, she had been employed at a small, tony private school in Brooklyn Heights. The neighborhood—elegantly maintained homes of brick, brownstone, and limestone; tall, graceful windows with a glimpse of a chandelier through one, a sheer, patterned curtain at another—was lovely. She liked the other teachers and the headmaster, the orderly routine of her days that included classes in the mornings, prep periods in the afternoons, and lunch with her husband when he could take a break between his appointments. And Dahlia had been enrolled there as well, in the lower school, so that Naomi's morning and afternoon commute dovetailed nicely with the dropping off and picking up of her daughter. But the teaching itself had worn her down, the room of jaded fifteen-year-olds, surreptitiously making calls or playing games on their cell phones, the girls exchanging notes or examining their hair for split ends.

And what girls they were. The leader of the pack, Cordelia Cox, was tall and thin-faced, with a cascade of black hair, a jeweled navel ring, and an uncanny ability to cow both her friends and enemies. Once Naomi had found her in the girls' bathroom, taunting Meg Stanton, one of her less popular classmates, with a handful of tampons. Cordelia had used lipstick to color their tips red; when Naomi had walked in, Cordelia was holding one of the besmeared tampons aloft by its short, white string.

The other girls were visibly frightened when they saw Naomi. Not Cordelia. The tampon was swaying a bit, as if she had been shaking or flicking it with her finger.

"What's going on here?" Naomi had said, looking back and forth from Cordelia's cool, composed face to Meg's tense, uncomfortable one. "Are you conducting a hygiene class?"

"I was just explaining to Meg about the differences in tampon sizes." She pointed to her selection, fanned out on the sink. "Super, regular, light." Some of the other girls couldn't help snickering.

"And the lipstick?"

"To make them seem more realistic. Aren't you always telling us to use realistic details, Mrs. Wechsler? To make our writing 'come alive'?"

"Well, class is over," Naomi said in a clipped, furious voice. She abruptly knocked all the tampons off the sink. "Clean this up. Now." The other girls quickly knelt down and began gathering tampons. "There's lipstick on the floor and on the sink. Someone will have to clean that up too."

Cordelia hadn't moved, though Meg had managed to inch away toward the door. Naomi looked over at her. "That's all right, Meg. You can go."

When the room was tidied again, Naomi dismissed the other girls but asked Cordelia to remain behind. The audacity of that girl. And the cowardice of the others.

"Throw that out," Naomi said, indicating the tampon Cordelia still held. Cordelia complied, but nothing seemed to penetrate—or to alter—the controlled, condescending look on her face.

"Was that fun?" Naomi asked when the tampon was at last in the trash.

"Was what fun?"

"Tormenting Meg."

"Meg." Cordelia looked bored. "Meg can take care of herself."

"Evidently, so can you." Naomi sent Cordelia back to class with the others. Had she stayed any longer, Naomi thought she might have actually slapped her. Instead, she ran the cold water and splashed it on her wrists and face. She was so angry she was shaking. Later, she mentioned the incident to the headmaster, who commiserated and called Cordelia into his office. There had been a detention and some community service that the girl had been asked to perform. But somehow, Naomi didn't feel vindicated, only disgusted. She had had enough of these entitled girls, this school, this work. She needed to immerse herself in something altogether different. And after Dahlia had died, she found that something at Holy Name.

Here was a place, a world really, where time was told by the intravenous drip that administered medication, the distance from a room to an operating lab, the buzz and whir of the X-ray machines as they recorded their mysterious internal data.

Naomi did a little bit of everything: she wheeled picture books around on rolling carts, read *Curious George Goes to the Fire Station* six times to a boy waiting his turn for the dialysis machine, held the basin into which a fourteen-year-old girl vomited after her chemotherapy treatment.

"Good morning," said Pat Ryan, the volunteer coordinator, as Naomi came into the Volunteer Services office and hung her wet coat and umbrella on a hook on the back of a door.

"Hi, Pat. Did any new toys come in since Wednesday?" Now that the holiday season was here, Naomi had been put in charge of wrapping and labeling gifts for the children on the ward, most of which had been donated by local schools and businesses.

"There's a bag over there. See it? The big brown one with the handles?" Naomi found the bag and peered inside. On top were three Beanie Babies: a whale, a kitten, and an elephant. Adorable but hard to wrap. Below she saw several boxes of Crayola crayons, some thick pads of paper, a coloring book featuring the Power Puff Girls. "Do you have wrapping paper?" Naomi nodded. "Then you can work in here. I'm at a meeting for most of the morning. God help me." Pat walked by and eyed Naomi's coffee. "That smells good. You didn't get it here, did you?"

"No." Naomi smiled at Pat, who lingered for a moment in the doorway. "But when your meeting is over, I'll run over and get you a cup."

"It's so miserable outside."

"The store is just across the street." Naomi shrugged off the minor inconvenience. "What do you take in it?"

"Milk, sugar, the works." Pat smiled back. "Thanks, Naomi. You're an angel."

An angel. Naomi repeated the phrase in her mind. Rick wouldn't think so. Neither would her mother, Estelle, whom she had not long ago placed in that Riverdale nursing home. How was it that she managed to disappoint each of them, in such different yet equally damning ways? But here, at Holy Name, she was effective, competent, in control. Everyone seemed to like her, and to her own grateful amazement, she liked everyone she had encountered here: Pat Ryan, the beleaguered parents, overworked nurses, the army of physicians, the technicians and janitors. And the children. The children were what made the whole thing worth doing.

Naomi went to a cupboard behind Pat's desk, where she had stored the wrapping paper and ribbons she had purchased. There were two packages of red tissue. Good, she could use some of the sheets to wrap the Beanies, then she would find a way to secure the lumpy bundles with ribbon. Pulling the long tubes out of the bag, she surveyed paper with snowmen, with dreidels, with candy canes, paper that was nothing but a roll of shining, metallic green. Pat kept a small radio in her office; Naomi turned it on to an oldies station, and the strains of the Beach Boys—that creamy, California sound—filled the office.

For over an hour, Naomi unfurled and snipped, wrapped and labeled. Mets Monopoly and Scrabble Junior. A plastic-boxed kit containing four bottles of nail polish, a nail buffer, polish remover, and ten snowflake decals, one for each fingernail. As she looped a length of gold ribbon around the wrapped kit, Naomi found herself thinking that Dahlia would have loved such a thing. She could endure this thought only within the confines of Holy Name; had she been at home or anywhere else, such an observation would have caused her to convulse with sadness, with weeping. But here, she was relatively safe.

She thought of the girl who might well receive this gift, Holly Munsford. A little younger than Naomi's former students, Holly was someone they nonetheless would have dubbed "all that." Which meant that Holly seemed to have everything: a lithe, athletic body, a blond braid that dipped down to her waist, a straight-A average, a boyfriend who was a high school senior. Oh and lymphatic cancer; she had that too.

"Pat?" Naomi looked up. There stood Michael McBride. Again. She had been working at Holy Name since the end of September and had not run into him until today. When she happened to see him twice.

"Pat's in a meeting. She told me I could use her office."

"I see." McBride stood in the doorway. He was as disheveled as she remembered, with the buttons on his white doctor's coat fastened incorrectly and several creases in his tie. "You're volunteering here now?"

"Since September." Naomi was still holding a pair of scissors in one hand, the spool of gold ribbon in the other.

"I hadn't realized."

"Why would you?" Her voice sounded colder than she meant it to; still, why was he here, taking up her time?

"I'm sorry." McBride's face reddened slightly. "I just meant that if I had known—"

"If you had known, then what?" Naomi put down the scissors, the ribbon. This man should not be here talking to her, stirring things up that she didn't want stirred.

"I would have talked to you sooner." His voice was firm, authoritative. She wasn't surprised. He was the head of a department after all. She couldn't have been the first mother of a dead child with whom he had spoken.

"And what would you have said?" An angel. Pat had called her an angel. But would an angel have used such a bitchy voice to someone who was, in his fashion, trying to be kind?

"I would have told you how sorry I was. Am."

"You said that already. In July."

"I would have said it again."

"Why? It won't change anything."

"Because it's true. I'm always sorry when we lose a patient."

"Dahlia was never your patient." It was a good thing she had put the scissors down; she had a mad but electrifying impulse to hurl them across the room, as if she were a turbaned and bejeweled knife thrower with deadly aim.

"As soon as she came through the doors of this facility, she was our patient," said Michael McBride. "They all are. Every single one of them." Despite the wrinkled tie—Naomi saw there was a blurred, dark smear on it too—and the crooked buttons, he seemed, in that moment, enormously dignified.

"Now I'm the one who's sorry." Her anger suddenly dissipated and left her drained and even a little weak. Coffee. She wanted another cup of coffee. And she had promised to get one for Pat, who would be back in the office any time now. Naomi stood and reached for her coat.

"Are you leaving?" Michael McBride fixed his dark, blue eyes on her face.

"Just for another coffee. Then I'll be back."

"I'll come with you."

"But you don't have a coat."

"It doesn't matter. It's not far." He took her elbow and guided her through the corridor and toward the doors on Sixth Street. As the doors slid open, Naomi saw that although the wind still whipped the wet leaves and bits of debris up the street, the rain itself had stopped, and the heavy gray clouds showed an improbable streak of sunlight between their large and threatening shapes. It was only when they reached the Barnes & Noble store and his hand left her elbow to open the door that she noticed she had not once recoiled from his touch.

2

Playmate of the Month

Rick Wechsler was horny. Horny in the way he had not been since he was sixteen and smuggling his father's stack of *Playboys* into the room over the garage, frantically working at himself as he gazed— slack jawed and rapt—at the succulent array of tits and thighs, bellies and asses of the girls featured in the centerfolds. April, June, November, January. Straight black hair with a feathering of bangs across the forehead, tan nipples, long legs. Strawberry blond, a light dappling of freckles across the cheeks, downy covering of hair on the smooth slope of stomach. Corkscrew curls, lips pink as the nose of a kitten, nipples even pinker than that, butt shaped like a perfect heart. One image more desirable than the next, all impossibly out of his reach, now and seemingly forever.

But Rick was no longer that hormonally charged boy of sixteen. He was a guy pushing forty, a podiatrist, with an ever-receding hair-line, a still-decent though hardly formidable physique, and a seven-year-old daughter he and his wife had buried last summer in the verdant expanse of Green-Wood Cemetery.

Why was he possessed like this? It was distracting, it was frustrat-ing, it was humiliating, for God's sake. He and Naomi had always had plenty of sex, first in their courtship, then in their marriage. Since Dahlia had died, however, he had not had the temerity to approach her, though they slept, as they always had, side by side or nestled in the queen-size bed that looked out over their small backyard. If she did not show the inclination, he could not bring himself to initiate anything. It had to come from her first.

Still, just because he didn't have the courage to suggest to his wife that they begin making love again, it didn't mean he had lost the urge. His days—and nights too—were populated with fantasies the likes of which he hadn't had since— No, he had never had such fantasies, even back then. He hadn't had the language for them. Now he did. Instead of the chaste images of *Playboy*—he remembered with an almost quaint affection that no pubic hair appeared in those pages—he now had the Internet, where pornographic images could be had—enjoyed, lusted after—any time he wanted. Of course, he had to choose his times. Never at work, where Lillian Acevedo, the office manager, or Helene Newmann, the chiropractor with whom he shared the office, could easily stumble onto his cache of private longings. And at home could be risky too, as Naomi was apt to wander without notice into the narrow upstairs room that he used as his office.

But since Naomi started her volunteering at Holy Name—a totally baffling and even irritating activity as far as he was concerned—he could count on her being gone three mornings a week, as punctual as the clock with its illuminated red hands that topped the tower of the Williamsburg Savings Bank. She started early, and it was an easy matter to schedule his appointments a little later than usual on those mornings. Lillian had been particularly solicitous since Dahlia's death. So if he let her know that on some days he preferred not to come in until ten-thirty or eleven, she was happy to make the necessary adjustments to his daily appointment book.

This left Rick with a brief, giddy hour, three mornings a week, to log on to sites that promised wet hot chicks, horny housewives, girls who wanted to make it with other girls while guys looked on, girls who let you blindfold them, piss in their faces, who would take it up the ass and smile the whole time. Stuff he couldn't have imagined at sixteen, though he sure was having a good time imagining it now. God, it was too bad he hadn't had all this at his disposal years ago. No matter though. He could make up for the time lost. He already was.

As the weeks slipped by—he thought of those girls of the month, long ago, Miss December in an elf's hat and little black boots, Miss July pressing a pair of match-thin firecrackers into the plump pillows of her naked breasts—he grew impatient with the cybersex in his upstairs office. He wanted the real thing. But with whom?

The girls and the women he saw on the streets of his neighborhood, some pretty and young, others less so—might have been the playmates of three decades ago for all their accessibility. How was he to approach them? And did he in fact even want to? He loved Naomi, still grew stiff at night as he watched her slip out of her jeans, her white blouse. But she had shunned him, and he could even understand why. He was tainted for her, as she was for him, tainted with the acrid taste of Dahlia's death. So here he was, randy as a dog sniffing in crazy circles while longing for release, and wishing he could howl, long and hard, at the moon.

He thought many times of hooking up with someone he had met on the Internet, someone who began her e-mail to him with the words, "Hi, you sound kind of lonely. I'm lonely too. Maybe we could get together . . ." But he didn't know if he could really do it, the cataloging of qualities and desires, the first meeting, all of it so hopelessly awkward, so filled with expectations that were almost guaranteed to remain unmet. Maybe an old-fashioned, straightforward prostitute was a better a idea: he could find a woman whose face and body pleased him, who would do what he wanted for a price, with no lasting consequences. But when he really imagined it—the negotiating over money, the sterility of a motel room—the thought of paying to fuck some woman, any woman, made him so mournful it was like burying Dahlia all over again.

Rick had pretty much resigned himself to a fate of longing, frustration, and self-recrimination when a solution, wholly unexpected and as tantalizing as the apple Eve offered Adam in the garden, fell ripe and ready into his lap.

One cold and icy Thursday in December, a day Naomi did not go to the hospital, Rick left the house on Carroll Street early, intending to see the four patients Lillian had scheduled for him that morning. At one, he planned to have lunch with his sister, Allison, who had promised to come in from Manhattan to meet him over on Smith Street. When he got to his office, though, he found that the first two patients of the day—Mrs. DiStefano and Mr. Baer—had already called in and canceled their respective appointments. And his sister had left a message saying that she had to postpone their lunch; could they reschedule the following week? So Rick had some unexpected time to himself. He had a brief urge to log on to Slit, which was currently his favorite sex site. But he was stopped by the thought of Lillian, whose movements—the efficient smack of a file drawer as she pushed it closed, the staccato sound of her black high heels on the parquet floor—he could hear just outside his office door.

Instead of the computer and all its enticements, he forced himself to address some of the paperwork that always awaited him. There was a sizable pile of insurance claims to sift through and sign. He pulled the top form off the pile, lifted his reading glasses to rub briefly at the bridge of his nose, which had already, even this early in the day, started to hurt, and then, settling the glasses back on his face, began to read.

Lillian was on the phone now. She might be rescheduling DiStefano and Baer. Or confirming tomorrow's appointments—she was good that way. In all ways, in fact. The office had never been so well organized or well run as it had in the two years that she had been in control of its daily workings.

But something about her voice—a slightly escalated pitch, a tense pause between words and then a great rush of them followed by a silence—made him think that this was a personal and not an office-related call. No matter. He knew she was divorced and was raising her eleven-year-old son, Jason, by herself. It was not easy, but she was, at least in his view, doing a good job of it. So if she needed to make a few personal calls during the workday, he certainly wasn't going to give her a hard time over it.

There was a silence. Rick paused, unsure of what to do. Then he heard the sound of Lillian's muted crying, and he put down his pen and walked into the waiting room.

She was seated at the desk, bent over the phone, with her face down and covered by her arms. Her shoulders were shaking. She hadn't yet realized he was there, and not wanting to catch her off guard or seem as if he were spying, he said her name.

She looked up, and Rick saw the tears puddled in her eyes. Then she put her head back down again and continued to sob, only louder this time.

"Lillian," he repeated and moved so that he was standing right next to her, close enough to smell her shampoo. "What's the matter?"

"Everything. Everything's the matter." Her words were muffled by her arms, and he had to strain a bit to hear her.

"Can you tell me?" Rick was aware that she had been having trouble with her ex-husband, who frequently missed child support payments and was erratic in visiting their son.

"It's Ramon. Again." She lifted her head and looked around for the box of tissues she kept on her desk.

"Not paying?"

"Not paying, not telling the truth, breaking his promises. You know."

"I know." And he did. Lillian tried to keep her personal life out of the office, and mostly succeeded. But she had confided in him on occasion, like the time when Ramon had promised to take the boy to a Yankees game, and Jason had sat, dressed in his Yankees jacket and Yankees hat, clutching his baseball glove for three hours on their front stoop in Sunset Park before accepting that his father was not going to come. "What happened?"

"He was planning to take Jason to San Juan for the holidays. To his grandmother's. So I go out and buy him all this stuff: new bathing suit, goggles, flippers, a beach ball, a portable CD player. A new CD to go with it. I told him they were all early Christmas presents. He's spent the last week packing and unpacking his suitcase, making sure that everything was going to fit in. He was so excited."

"And?" Rick was interested; he had met Jason before and thought he was a sweet boy, a little slow in school, but with big green-gold eyes and a diffident, appealing smile. But he was equally interested in looking at Lillian, dressed in her red silk blouse and slim-fitting black skirt. She was wearing red lipstick too, and he found himself gazing back and forth, from her red mouth to the division between her breasts that was just visible at her neckline.

"The trip's off."

"Ramon's not going?"

"Oh, he's going all right. But he's not taking Jason. He says he's met someone," Lillian said and blew her nose in disgust. "He's taking her instead. So the kid is out, and the chiquita is in."

"Is Jason disappointed?"

"I haven't even told him yet." Her eyes filled with tears again. "What am I going to say?"

Rick didn't answer. But to his own surprise, he reached out his hand, wanting to touch her shoulder, encased as it was in the red silk shirt. There was a moment of hesitation, and then he let himself do it, realizing as he did that the touch was as much a comfort to him as he hoped it was for her. First just one hand, tentatively, then the other. He gently kneaded her flesh, whose warmth emanated up through the shirt and into his fingers.

She said nothing at first. Then she abruptly stood up and faced him. Rick stopped massaging her shoulders but let his hands remain where they were. She didn't move them.

"I'm sorry," she said, looking hard into his eyes.

"Sorry for what?"

"For going on and on about my problems with my ex and my kid, when—" She stopped.

"When my kid is dead, right?"

"When your kid is . . . dead." The word hung there for a moment, and painful as it was, he was strangely grateful to her for just saying it. So many people seemed to avoid the topic, their reticence and hesitation only compounding his isolation, his sorrow.

Rick was ready to step back when she unexpectedly kissed him, her tongue just dipping inside his mouth for a fraction of a second. The blood went rushing to his face, his ears. The feel of her lips, the softness of them. But she had turned away and was picking up the telephone again. "Hello, Mrs. DiStefano? This is Dr. Wechsler's office calling to reschedule your appointment. We have an opening next Tuesday at one . . ." This was all happening so quickly, he didn't have a chance to keep up. Lillian, Jason, Dahlia. The kiss. He looked at her again as she jotted down something in the office appointment book. When the call was finished, she punched in another number.

The rest of the day passed in a kind of haze. Rick retreated into his office, where over and over he replayed the sensation of Lillian's leaning forward, the tiny darting motion her tongue had made, the scent of her skin and hair. He saw three more patients—a bunion that would require surgery, a persistent case of toenail fungus that was resisting treatment, a child who had bruised his foot during a basketball game and had been limping for a week.

At lunchtime, Lillian popped her head into his office to tell him she was going out, but she didn't meet his eyes. When she returned, she left him a container of soup—tomato rice—with a white plastic spoon poised over the lid. It was hot and comforting, though it didn't have much taste. Maybe that was him, though. Ever since the summer, he had had trouble really tasting, or certainly savoring, anything he ate.

Finally, at the end of the day, when he was ready to get his coat and go home to his house on Carroll Street—where Naomi would have made some dinner and perhaps rented a movie for the two of them to watch—Lillian came into his office and, to his surprise, locked the door, although they were the only two people there. He watched, with utter amazement, as she undid the buttons on the red blouse, then unzipped the skirt, taking the time to fold and hang both of them on the back of his chair.

In her white half-slip, white bra with deeply scalloped, lacy edges, and high heels, she could have been a Playmate of the Month from decades earlier, Miss June, in snowy bridal attire. Without saying anything, she walked over to where he stood, incredulous and waiting. She stood looking at him for a moment before she put her arms around him and kissed him again, this time more slowly and deeply. Rick felt the unfamiliar plushness of her breasts as they pressed into his chest. He put his arms around her, hesitantly at first, but then with increasing ardor. It had been so long. And it felt so good. Dahlia was dead and Naomi was a zombie. He had been a zombie too, every minute, every second since he had lost his daughter, until today, when Lillian had kissed him, and now, to his shock and his unutterable relief, he was kissing, kissing, kissing her back.

3

Room with a View

From the window of her small room, Estelle Levine could see the water but the sight confused and even angered her. Sitting on the twin bed or the uncomfortable leatherette chair, she had an excellent view of it, down at the end of a grassy incline that unfurled from the sprawling, low building. But the color of the water was wrong, all wrong. In Miami, where she and Milton had gone to live after he'd retired, the water she saw from the terrace of their tidy, two-bedroom condominium was aquamarine, a clear, tranquil color that seemed to match the sky overhead. She had loved that color, and the way the sunlight randomly hit the water's surface, causing it to glitter.

But the water here, the water she saw from the window of this place—she was not entirely sure where she was, though she didn't want to ask, it was too humiliating—was generally gray or brown. The few times it had been anything like blue, the blue was nonetheless wrong, dark and murky looking, without the brightness she had come to expect. There was wind blowing on the water and she imagined it would be cold. Very cold. It was not water in which you could swim or even wade.

Of course, the water was the least of her problems. There were so many other things she detested about this place. The clotted mashed potatoes, for instance, that appeared day after day on her plate. The potatoes sat there growing cold and less appealing as she looked at them; she would sooner have eaten a sponge. She had never cared for mashed potatoes; why didn't they know that, why was she given them over and over? Estelle also detested the heavy woman on her left, who smelled strongly of a cloying perfume, and the birdlike man with the shaking hands on her right. Who were these people, why was she subjected to their company?

She missed Milton, though she was angry at him too, angry at him for dying, for leaving her. She remembered him as he lay in the hospital, the tube of the respirator—a clear and lovely blue, so like the water, she remembered thinking at the time—making it impossible for him to speak, but there had been a mute entreaty in his eyes that seemed to be saying, "Let me go, let me go." As if she had any control over it. Over anything.

After Milton died, Estelle sat in her Miami Beach apartment for a month, shades drawn, scarcely going out, subsisting on packaged dry cereal straight from the box and ginger ale. Then she learned that one of her best friends in Florida, Norma Klein, had been diagnosed with breast cancer. Estelle was galvanized by the news, and she shook off her torpor to appear at Norma's bedside every morning for the entire length of her hospital stay, bearing freshly baked muffins, flowering plants, paperback novels. Each morning, after leaving the hospital, she went to Norma's apartment, fed the cats, wiped the counters, gathered the mail, and swept the floors. When Norma came home, she was overwhelmed with gratitude for Estelle's help. But Estelle knew that it was actually Norma who had helped her.

She resumed something of the life she had had before Milton's death, volunteering at a local thrift store three days a week—she was given first dibs on everything that came in, and enjoyed the modest thrill of scouting out a leather handbag from Ferragamo, a silk scarf from Hermès—and the voting site on Election Day, where she patiently directed voters to the correct line. There were walks along the beach, where she collected shells and sea glass that she kept in a large copper bowl on her kitchen table, and more volunteering, at the local blood drives, and collections of canned goods to send to homeless shelters. Cards and bingo had never appealed to her, but some of the women in her building met for Scrabble once a week, and there were matinees at the movie theater, the occasional trip to the Miami Performing Arts Center for a concert or the ballet.

But then she'd had the stroke, and later this thing had come over her, she didn't know what to call it, and she had been unable to continue with her life in Miami. The young one came, small, not beautiful but crisp and fine as the first fall apple. Naomi, the girl. Her girl. Estelle could remember, though it was with difficulty. Still, the girl came, wrung her diminutive hands, cried a bit, kept saying, "Mom? Mom? Are you there, Mom?" After a time, she took Estelle away, but not to live with her again. Instead, she brought her to this place with the mashed potatoes, the fat woman, the skinny man, and the water outside the window that was the color of mud.

The days had a new rhythm now: She got up, was washed and helped to dress by a series of young women whose names she could not learn. There was breakfast—oatmeal, bruised fruit, sometimes an egg, always cold—in the big room downstairs. Certain mornings she went down some stairs to a place where young men—why was everyone here so young?—did things to her arms, to her legs. "To make them walk better," they said, though where was there to go? Could anyone tell her that?

Other mornings she went upstairs to a big, sun-filled room where she was expected to make things with felt, with feathers, with clay. Ridiculous, she would have none of it, and she sat at the table, mute and glowering. One day she took the Styrofoam tray filled with beads—some wooden, some glass—and dumped them all over the floor. Now that was satisfying, watching the bright little shapes roll and scurry across the tiles. One of the young ones came hurrying over, saying, "Now, Mrs. Levine, you really shouldn't dump the beads like that, someone could trip, someone could get hurt."

"Hurt? Really? Maybe it will be you," Estelle said, pinning the girl with her gaze. She was Oriental, pretty, with chin-length black hair and painted lips. Her dark eyes opened very wide when Estelle delivered this remark.

After that, Estelle didn't go to the big room anymore, but went to a different room at the end of a hall where she was asked to say what various inkblots on cards looked like to her. Inkblots! Imagine! Did people still believe in this sort of thing anymore? Why not read tea leaves or coffee grounds too?

"Nothing. It looks like nothing."

"I see," said the man, not so young, a white coat, a salt-and-pepper beard, who showed her the picture.

"How about this one?" He turned the first card down, showed her another.

"Nothing."

"And this?"

"Nothing. How many times do I have to tell you?"

"I understand," the white-coated man said, putting all the cards aside and stroking the beard. "You see nothingness here. Emptiness. A void."

"No." Estelle looked at him, assessing the seriousness of his response. And he was supposed to be a doctor. "I see an inkblot. And it resembles nothing but an inkblot."

He was quiet momentarily but then began talking again, pelting her with pointless questions about her childhood: Had she had a pet? Loved her mother? Harbored a suppressed desire to kill her sister? Been sexually molested by her brother/father/uncle/cousin? Estelle was now sorry she had dumped the beads on the floor. Going to the sunny room would have been preferable to this.

The best time of the day, the only time she could really bear, came later, when she went to another big room, but this one was not sunny, it had no windows, and there were a lot of seats, like a movie theater. And in fact, movies were shown here, but not the sort of movies she had gone to see with her friends in Miami. Although Estelle would reluctantly join Norma and Grace, Dottie and Bev at the matinees where seniors were admitted for half price, she privately disdained the sort of the films in which the men said "fuck" and "shit" right out loud and the women bared their beautiful breasts.

No, these movies were much better than those, no color other than the rich blacks and sparkling whites and all the nuanced shades of gray in between. The women had a look then. They didn't need to expose their bodies to be desirable. They could do it with a glance. A smile. And the men didn't need to curse to be strong. Estelle sat by herself in one of the seats, away from the others, many of whom insisted on chattering during the film. She gave herself over to the images on the screen. They didn't disappoint her.

Bette Davis. Joan Crawford. Barbara Stanwyck, her favorite. Olivia de Havilland. Jimmy Stewart. Now there was a man who could say "gosh" and still be a mensch. Where had they all gone, these actors and actresses who were her truest friends in this place? Why couldn't she find them anywhere but in this room? She wanted that one, the young one who called so often, Naomi, that was it, to take her away from this place to someplace where she could find Bette and Barbara, Montgomery and Errol. But the girl wouldn't do that, she was as bad as that doctor, with her ceaseless questions: "Are you all right, Mom? Are they treating you well? Do you know me?" Know her? Did anyone really know anyone else? All along she had thought Milton was dependable, steadfast. Instead, he had looked at her with the puppy dog eyes and then abandoned her by dying. Knowledge, the kind of knowledge that says, This person will or will not do this or that, was a sham. Better to watch movies.

The sky outside the windows grew increasingly dismal and gray; the water Estelle saw was nearly black. Inside the place that she could not name, the heat was turned way up and the rooms were hot and smelled slightly of old food, old bodies. No one else seemed to mind. There was a big, artificial Christmas tree in the lobby downstairs, red plastic balls the size of grapefruits on the branches, and an electric menorah with multicolored bulbs. Cardboard signs, some red and green, others blue and white, appeared on the walls. Happy Holidays, Peace on Earth.

A package came for Estelle. She struggled, futilely, with the thick padded envelope, trying to pry out the staples from one end. Tears of frustration formed in her eyes. One of the young ones came over, took the package without even asking, and pulled a thin, red strip to open it. But when Estelle saw what was inside—a large, glossy book entitled *Old Hollywood Lives Again*—she forgot her anger and her impatience. Inside the book was photograph after photograph of all her friends. Look, here was Barbara, and Lana, and Veronica too. Estelle ran her fingers over the smooth surface of the pages, as if she could absorb the images they contained through her fingers. Now she did not have to wait for the movies, which only happened sometimes. Now she would have this book to look at whenever she wanted. She turned back to the beginning and began again, more slowly this time.

Rain drummed hard against the windows of Estelle's room. The water, down at the bottom of the hill, was not visible, but Estelle could feel its presence, gurgling, alive, anyway. Seated on her bed and covered with a small mohair blanket—a pedestrian plaid in putrid shades of green and brown and scratchy besides—she looked at the pages of the book. She didn't bother to consider where it had come from; she was merely content to lose herself in its still, silvery images. Marlene Dietrich. Edward G. Robinson. Even Donna Reed, so lovely and becoming before she had been turned into television pudding, innocuous and bland.

Now here was one, a child. Shirley Temple. Estelle was familiar with the trademark characteristics—the dimples, the curls, the starched dress and shined shoes. Talented. Cute too. But something was bothering her, and Estelle couldn't figure out what it was. The child. The child was reminding her of something, someone. Not the girl, Naomi, who came sometimes and other times did not, offering not herself but her useless questions. No, it was someone else, yet Estelle couldn't think of who it might be. She turned the page, trying to disengage her mind from the frustrating, unanswered question. She looked at the Marx Brothers, and Buster Keaton with that sad, sad face. Mae West. W. C. Fields. My God, the nose on him. Orson Welles, and his soulful, penetrating look. Yes, she could have fallen in love with Welles. Easiest thing in the world. Still the child, and the unanswered question, bothered her.

She turned back to the page where Shirley Temple stood in the center of the picture. She wore a polka-dot dress with lace bordering the hem. With her two hands, she spread the dress out wide, like a fan. Her head was tilted, her eyes were looking up and out at something beyond the camera. There was a bow, a dark one, in her tightly coiled ringlets. Dimples, she had, two of them, perfectly placed as if by design.

Dahlia. The thought burst in Estelle's mind like a sudden flame. Dahlia was the one she had been trying to remember, couldn't remember at first and now could. Dahlia. She was connected, Estelle vaguely remembered, to that other one, Naomi. But really and truly, Dahlia was hers. Only Estelle hadn't seen her in the longest time. There was something unsettling about this absence, something she could not identify but was still aware of, the way you are aware of a paper cut or a splinter. Why hadn't she seen her? Had she been sick? Had they told her something about the child, something significant and essential, which she had failed to remember?

Estelle closed the book and pressed her fingers firmly against the two covers. She had to summon up everything it took to find her way back there. To reach the one called Naomi, so that she could find her way back to the real one, the small one, the true one, named for the extravagant, showy flower. Dahlia.

4

Carols

Michael thought about her all the time, Naomi Wechsler, that woman he had met in the summer, the one whose little girl had died before she had even gotten to the hospital. He wasn't sure why she stayed on his mind; there were other situations, children who had died, where he had felt more deeply involved, more deeply responsible. This child had not even been alive when she had been brought in.

A gallingly stupid accident, of course, one brought about by a cell phone, awful devices, people yammering away on them all the time, wherever they were, in the street, behind the wheel. Just last week when his wife, Camille, had asked him to pick up a jar of olives at D'Agostino on his way home, he saw a young woman talking into a cell phone. "I'm standing in front of the chopped meat," she had said. Did anyone want or need to know that information? If his own cell phone had been turned on—he had to have one; these days all doctors did—would he have used it to call Camille and relay that particular bit of minutia to her?

But even so, the driver of the offending vehicle hadn't been reckless, hadn't been going very fast at all. If the child—what was her name?—had not chosen that precise moment to lean down and tie her shoe, then the impact, gentle as it was, would have done nothing more than rock the car and elicit a small curse or two from the child's father, the whole thing relegated to the status of minor irritation by the time they got home.

Instead, the girl—her name was Daisy? Dawn? No, Dahlia, that was it—had seen the untied lace, leaned down to retie it. And so the rest had unfolded on that summer day, just the way he remembered it, and there was that woman, that Naomi, lodged in his head—and in his heart too—ever since it had happened. Odd that he had even encountered her, been the one to tell her the news. Usually, it was one of the ICU or ER doctors, not the department chair, who performed the task. But that day, Boris Vishniyak, from ER, had stopped him in the hallway.

"Mike," Boris had said. With his thick Russian accent, it came out as "Mik." "I need your help."

"What's up?" Michael scanned Boris's face, which looked unusually troubled, the brows pulled together in a brooding, heavy line, the mouth tight and cheeks pale.

"I've got another DOA in the ER. Little girl."

"How old?"

"Six or seven. The father's in there with her."

"He's all right?"

"No injuries at all. Freak accident. The car wasn't even moving." Boris went on to describe the incident with the cars, the girl bent over her shoe, the horrific outcome.

"What do you need, Boris?" Michael had asked gently. There had been two DOAs in ER that week, and one of them involved a three-year-old who had eluded his harried father's hand and walked straight into the oncoming traffic on Union Street. It had been up to Boris to break the news to the mother. She and the father had recently separated, and when Boris told her what had happened, she dropped to the floor, sobbing and shouting in such a stricken way that the security guards had come running over. As they attempted to help her up, she kicked one, hard, in the shin, and bit the hand of the other. Before she could be subdued, she slugged Boris in the stomach and then spit lavishly into his face.

"The mother," Boris said, and the color seemed to bleach out of his cheeks even more, leaving him ashen and unhealthy looking. "She'll be here in a few minutes. But I can't tell her, Mike. I can't."

"That's all right, Boris," Michael had said. "I'll do it. Just tell me her name."

"Wechsler," said Boris, who was now taking Michael's hand and pumping it in gratitude. "Naomi Wechsler."

For months he had thought about how furious Naomi had been that day in his office and how little he blamed her. Sometimes, he would imagine running into her and try to devise kind, wise things he could say. Things that would if not heal her, then at least offer her a momentary reprieve from her sorrow. He knew she lived here in Park Slope, the same neighborhood where he and his family—Camille and the twins Mackenzie and Brooke—had a house on Ninth Street just off Prospect Park. Later, after the funeral, he and Adelaide, the head pediatric nurse at Holy Name, had actually gone to Naomi's house down on Carroll Street. Spoken with the girl's father. Looked for Naomi, but when she saw him, she had run out of the room. He could not forget the way she had stared at him before she took those stairs, as if his presence was so wounding, so repellent, that she could not endure it at all.

He had other fantasies too, even more confusing and troubling than those of simply encountering and comforting her in the streets of the neighborhood. Her face came into his mind when he was making love to Camille or kissing one of the girls good night. In Michael's fantasies it was always summer and Naomi wore something light and airy, a skirt that whipped around her slim ankles, a top with spaghetti straps that revealed the delicate clarity of her collarbones, her neck. So when he did run into her at the coffee bar in Barnes & Noble, he was almost thrown off by her heavy coat and long scarf. Almost, but not quite.

He knew her at once, and had offered what he hoped was a subdued and sympathetic greeting. She cut him, of course, cut him and he wasn't even surprised. What had he really thought would happen if he saw her again? Still, he was curious enough to watch as she moved ahead and out the doors, curious enough to see where it was that she was going next. She turned up Sixth Street and—now this was a surprise—entered the hospital. He had seen the chocolate Santas she was holding; was she visiting someone there? Quite possible, but that was a lot of chocolate for a single patient.

He followed her slowly and was aware of her again in the lobby, but this time, he pretended he didn't notice her as he stood there chatting with Cliff Rothschild, from Anesthesiology. But later, in his office, he made a few inquiries and found out that she was volunteering in Pediatrics. And he hadn't known a thing about it. Until today.

He spent the first hour making his rounds, checking on a girl who had had an emergency appendectomy the previous night, and another who had dropped a bowling ball on her foot and crushed two toes. But then mid-morning he found an excuse to go to Pat Ryan's office. Pat coordinated the efforts of the volunteers throughout the hospital, and through her, he might be able to find out where Naomi was. It was just pure luck that he found not Pat but Naomi herself.

She started out with the same hostility he had encountered before and come to expect from her. But somehow, something changed, and she allowed him to accompany her back to Barnes & Noble, where he bought and carried three more cups of coffee—one for him, one for her, and a third for Pat—back to the hospital. He wanted to suggest that she come into his office for a few minutes while she drank it, but he sensed that this was the wrong move, the wrong time. She would not want to be back in his office. The fact that she had allowed him to walk her to the bookstore for the coffees, let him pay, was enough for a single day. Best to leave it at that for now. Noting the attention with which she had approached the gift wrapping, he was confident that her tenure as a volunteer would be a long one. She would be around. And so would he. He wasn't sure why he was looking forward to their next encounter, only that he was. There was nothing explicitly sexual

28

in his feelings for this woman. Nothing that he would have felt compelled to confess in church on the odd Sunday that he accompanied Camille and the girls to Mass.

Michael was a not-entirely-lapsed Catholic; instead, he was one who had been marked by his early experiences in parochial school—first the Immaculate Heart of Mary, later Bishop Ford—and still found reassurance in the trappings of Catholicism if not in its essence. He couldn't, for instance, tolerate the Church's position on abortion, homosexuality, or contraception. Yet the mornings that he went with Camille and the twins to church on the corner of Carroll Street and Sixth Avenue, he felt comforted by hearing Mass—sadly enough no longer in Latin—by the smell of the incense, by the look of the apse, painted its celestial shade of blue and pocked with gold stars. He also liked, perhaps mostly for its nostalgic waft of reassurance, the feeling he got when he stepped into the small confessional and unburdened himself of his sins—the impatience that might have prompted him to snap at an intern, the petty jealousy he might experience at the success of a colleague—and receiving the gentle penance—the Hail Marys, the Our Fathers—that such transgressions elicited.

He remembered how Brooke had been shocked the first time she saw him go into the confessional. "Daddy," she had said, pulling on his jacket in an effort to keep him from actually entering the small booth. "You can't go in there."

"Why not?" he had asked.

"Because you're perfect. Aren't you, Daddy?" Michael had looked at Camille and shaken his head as if to dislodge the hyperbolic notion, even as it was being articulated with such conviction by his child. Camille had merely smiled indulgently.

Michael had not actually been to church in some time, but when he remembered that their church, St. Francis Xavier, was literally up the street from Naomi Wechsler's house, he decided to start going more often. Not too often, as he did not want his behavior to seem unsual to Camille. But often enough so that he might just happen to see Naomi coming up the street some Sunday morning, headed for

Keyfood or the hardware store or the flower stand on Garfield Place, and seeing her, stopping to say hello, how are you.

So there was something illicit about the way he was dwelling on her. Something he did not want his wife to detect or question. But how could he characterize it, even if he tried, to the priest behind the metal grille? "You see, Father, there's a woman I met last summer. Her daughter died at the hospital. Actually, she didn't die there, she was dead when they brought her in, but that's where the mother, this woman, Naomi, learned that the child had died. And now I want her forgiveness, the mother whose child's death I did not cause. Her forgiveness and something else too. Only I don't know what it is." No, he couldn't say any of that to the priest. It was too vague, too ridiculous even.

Instead, he looked for her in the hospital, in Barnes & Noble, on the streets of their shared neighborhood. He often saw her in the halls of Holy Name, smooth, dark hair pulled back into a low ponytail, tiny pearl earrings lending their luster to her sad but lovely face. Sometimes she just nodded, and while she didn't actually smile, he thought he saw a thawing, a subtle softening in her eyes when she looked at him. Other times she would actually stop to talk about the progress of a patient or some piece of hospital business. She seemed to have a personal, even proprietary interest in the place and was concerned about all aspects of its operation.

One evening, shortly before Christmas, he ran into her in Possibilities on the Slope, one of the newer gift shops on Seventh Avenue. Brooke and Mackenzie had wanted his help in picking out a gift for their mother. While Mackenzie sniffed scented candles and Brooke admired a turquoise choker, he let his gaze drift around the densely packed shop. When Naomi walked in—gray coat, dark scarf hooded over her head—it was as if he had actually summoned her, so frequently did he find himself conjuring her image.

"Last-minute shopping?" Michael said, unable to contain his smile.

"There's always someone I've forgotten." She shook the scarf off her head and let it rest around her shoulders.

"You don't seem like the kind of woman who forgets anyone."

"Well, remembers at the last minute then. I need to get something for one of the aides in the nursing home up in Riverdale. Where my mother is living. That is, if you can call it living." She started looking around the store, picking up a crystal paperweight, a bottle of foaming bath gel.

Michael was about to offer a comment—about Naomi's mother, the nursing home—when Brooke came rushing up to him.

"Dad, Dad, you have to see this." In her excitement she stepped on his foot. Michael moved back.

"Can you say excuse me first?" he said patiently, but with the expression of someone who had made this same request many times before.

"Excuse me, Dad, there's something I just have to show you. Mom is absolutely going to go crazy, and I mean crazy, over this. It's right here, you just have to—"

"Brooke, this is Naomi Wechsler."

"Oh. Hi. I mean, nice to meet you Mrs. Wechsler."

Naomi stared at her for a moment before replying. "Nice to meet you too."

"I'll just be a minute," Michael said as Brooke pulled him to where her sister stood.

"That's all right." Naomi settled the scarf back over her head and started moving toward the door.

"But you didn't get your gift." Michael wasn't moving quickly enough for Brooke, who kept tugging on his arm.

"I'll find something," she said. And then she was gone.

Michael pretended to study the music box—white, with small painted flowers around its edges—that his daughters insisted they had, absolutely had, to buy for their mother. But he kept thinking of Naomi, how she had looked when she saw Brooke. Still alive, she must have thought. Still alive, still thinking of Christmas, of presents, still wanting her father's attention, her mother's approval.

"And it's lined with velvet inside, Dad," Mackenzie was saying. "Black velvet."

"Well, show him," Brooke said. "Let him see."

The jewelry box was opened, its black velvet interior, many compartments, tinkling music, and round mirror eagerly pointed out and exclaimed over.

"Dad," said Mackenzie sternly. "You are not paying attention. And this is important—it's Mom's Christmas present."

"He's still worrying about that woman," said Brooke.

"What woman?" Mackenzie leaned down to scrutinize her face— or what she could see of it—in the small mirror.

"Naomi what's-her-name."

"Who?"

"That woman. The one Dad just introduced me to."

"Oh." Mackenzie, bored by this conversation, used her fingers to fluff out her hair. "Anyway, what do you think, Dad? About the music box? Isn't it just perfect? The thing is, we don't have quite enough money for it and we were wondering, that is, hoping you would—"

"Why do you say I'm worried?" Michael interrupted, looking at Brooke.

"Huh?"

"You said I was worried. About that woman. Mrs. Wechsler. What makes you think that?"

"Well, she works at the hospital, doesn't she? As a volunteer?"

"Who told you that?" Michael felt exposed, angry.

"Mom," Brooke said meekly.

"Oh." He ran his fingers over the surface of the music box. The girls had chosen well. Camille would love it. He could imagine it on the dresser in their room, filled with her necklaces and earrings, bracelets and rings. Trinkets he had bought for her. "Did she?" He tried to keep his voice cool, noncommittal. "What else did Mom tell you about her?"

"That her daughter died in a car accident."

"That's true," Michael said, scrutinizing his daughter's face, but Brooke looked away from Michael, toward Mackenzie, as if trying to enlist her support. Mackenzie had wandered off, though, and was examining a pair of gloves with a border of maribou feathers at the cuff.

"She said you always worry about the parents of the kids who die," Brooke said.

"Your mother is right," Michael said soberly. "I do."

"I know that, Daddy," Brooke responded softly.

"So," he said, summoning up his most enthusiastic, most hearty tone. "How about that music box? Should we have them gift wrap it?"

On the way home, they ran into two of the nurses from the hospital, a neighbor from down the street, one of Brooke's classmates, two of Mackenzie's, and the coach of Mackenzie's basketball team. All in the little village that was Park Slope. Michael greeted them, said Merry Christmas to everyone, but he was still thinking of Naomi. "If you can call it living," she had said about her mother. And then the conversation with his daughter. Camille's acute observations from the mouth of a girl. "Everyone knows everything, all the time," his mother used to say. He hadn't known what it meant, back then. But now he did. Camille knew all about Naomi working at the hospital, although he was sure he had not mentioned it. She also knew about his lingering sense of guilt, of sorrow, for the children who were lost and the parents who were left to trudge through the rest of their lives without them.

So, if he suddenly started going to church more often, Camille would notice that too. Notice and draw her own conclusions. Still, very soon it would be Christmas. And Michael always went to church with Camille and the twins on Christmas. Camille would wear a red wool suit, with a pin shaped like a wreath on her lapel; the girls would have on new holiday dresses, gifts opened just that morning and put on for the first time. Michael wore a suit that Camille wouldn't let him put on until five minutes before they were ready to leave the house.

"I don't want you going to church with egg on your jacket," she would say. "Or toothpaste on the pants."

He had always liked the ritual, but this year, he was looking forward to it even more than usual. Walking along Prospect Park, past the bare, black trees and hardened ground. Turning down Carroll Street and walking down the hill until they reached the church. There were other Catholic churches closer to where he lived. But Michael liked St. Francis Xavier and Camille had not protested. Xavier was his namesake after all. Michael Xavier Thomas McBride.

The church doors would be open Christmas morning and people would be streaming in. The floor, though regrettably covered in linoleum, would be freshly waxed. The heavy marble columns, some mustard yellow, others brick red, would gleam a welcome. With his wife and his daughters he would enter, take a seat in a pew, wait for the service to begin.

Afterward, he and his family would go back home for Christmas dinner. He and Camille had been hosting the meal for years; at last count, twenty-seven people would be at the house that afternoon. Camille had begun her preparations for this dinner two solid weeks in advance, shopping, cooking, freezing, labeling, just so she could accompany her family to Mass. She would make turkey, chestnut stuffing, and three bean salad, which his relatives would expect; she would also make lasagna, meatballs, and prosciutto bread to please her own.

He wouldn't even see Naomi. But knowing that she was just down the street, sitting at home with her husband—he didn't really know what Jews did on Christmas—made him feel closer to her somehow. If, after leaving church he turned right instead of left, walked down the hill instead of up, he would come, as he had last summer, to her house.

He imagined himself climbing the steps, ringing the bell. Her husband would answer the door. Or maybe even Naomi herself. She might be a little puzzled as to the purpose of his visit, but this time she wouldn't be so angry, she wouldn't run up the stairs as soon as she saw him. No, she would invite him in, maybe ask him to sit down.

What would he say to her? All he could think of were words from the carols that Camille had been playing in their house for the last three weeks. Tidings of comfort and joy. Away in a manager. Silent night. Have yourself a merry little Christmas. One more sentimental and saccharine than the next. And yet. The hope contained in such facile lyrics. Be near me, Lord Jesus, I ask you to stay / Close by me forever, and love me, I pray / Bless all the dear children in your tender care / And fit us for heaven, to live with you there.

Yes, that was it. All those silly, foolish words stood for some kind of hope. That was what he wanted to bring to Naomi. Hope. Hope that Michael wanted to grasp tightly in his hands and bring, without crushing or dropping it, to her. "Look what I have," he would say. "And it's all for you."

5

Red Balloon

Dahlia had been prone to tantrums. Frequent tantrums. Extravagant, full-blown tantrums, the kind that had caused her to stretch out on the floor, sobbing and wailing, or to hurl her toys and shoes around a room. They could be set off by seemingly small incidents like being told that she couldn't have M&M's until after lunch or that she would have to wait her turn for the pony ride at the President Street Block Party. The reaction, though, was anything but small. Other people—mothers mostly—would look at Dahlia, and then Naomi, sometimes with pity, as if they too had been there, but sometimes with scorn. "Why can't you do something?" those looks seemed to say. "Aren't you the mommy?"

Yes, Naomi was the mommy, but sometimes that didn't seem to count for much. Dahlia faced her own small life with an intensity that left Naomi wondering where the child had actually come from. Neither she nor Rick seemed to share their daughter's ability to descend, so deeply, into a well of self-created despair. But neither, perhaps, did they share the fierce joy Dahlia had taken in things. A new container of bubbles, an encounter with a friendly beagle on the street, getting her favorite color of gumball—orange—from the machine at the pizza place, all these were occasions for the kind of happiness that was commensurate—in some inverted, looking-glass world—with her sorrow.

The good memories Naomi had of her life with Dahlia—and there were so many—wounded her daily. But the bad memories, the times when Dahlia's storms had caused her to become exasperated and furious, to lose her temper and her goodwill, well those memories tore her heart out. She could still recall, if she let herself, a certain Monday morning on which Dahlia had insisted on changing her clothes three times. They were already running late and Naomi was trying to remain patient, even though these clothing changes were accompanied by drawers banging shut and were peppered with various complaints leveled against her. "You didn't buy me those embroidered jeans, and those are the only jeans I want," and "Why is the blue shirt in the wash?" Even when Dahlia was finally seated at the breakfast table in what Naomi hoped was the final combination of the morning—bell bottoms, fringed Gap top—and managed to pour maple syrup all over her lap, Naomi, who had read *How to Talk So Kids Will Listen, How to Listen So Kids Will Talk* several times, underlining and making copious notes each time, just said calmly, "There's syrup all over your clothes. I guess you'd better go up and change." In response, Dahlia had sent the plate of French toast across the table and onto the floor. It landed facedown, where the thick, wool pile of the rug soaked up the sticky fluid.

Still, Naomi didn't let her rising anger consume her and commented with some effort, "I can see that you're very angry. But French toast is not for throwing. It needs to be cleaned up." That book was a godsend; Naomi thought she really ought to write the authors a fan letter. And she would. Today, if she could ever get this child readied for school and out of the house.

"I won't," Dahlia said, belligerently. "And I'm not going to school today either."

"You don't want to go to school?"

Dahlia had a wonderful teacher that year and was usually eager to see her.

"No, because I don't have anything to wear. And it's all your fault, Mommy!" That's when Naomi lost it, started shouting, calling her names. Dahlia seemed uncowed and actually called her mother a bitch—imagine being called a bitch by your seven-year-old!—right to her face. To which Naomi had responded with a resounding slap across the girl's denim-clad behind. Naomi probably cried as much as Dahlia had, Naomi who had sworn to herself that she would never hit her child, who believed that women who did ought to be fined, even jailed. So much for *How to Talk.* Its authors, a pair of middle-aged women she fairly idolized, would probably come to her house and demand back their book. Clearly all its compassionate and well-reasoned insights were wasted on the likes of her.

Mostly Naomi willed herself not to think of these things, not to relive them with the awful precision and thoroughness her own mind could summon. But sometimes the memories crept up on her, stealthily, waiting for the right moment to reveal themselves, and when they did she was undone all over again, consumed by guilt, by shame, for which there was no relief, no end because she couldn't make it right with her daughter, not in this life, ever again.

"I'll take her for a bagel. You can get some more sleep." Naomi would never forget Rick saying those words on that day last summer. She had turned over when she heard his voice, nestled her face back into the pillow. He had known that Dahlia had been up several times in the night—she had had a bad dream, was wearing an uncomfortable pajama top, needed a drink of water, a trip to the bathroom—known that Naomi was tired and could use another hour in bed. Such a good husband, she had thought sleepily as she closed her eyes again. Such a good father.

Though the day would be hot, the morning was still cool. She had turned off the air conditioner during the night, and now, through the open window, she could hear the early-morning sounds of birds: sparrows, blue jays, and the low, plaintive sounds made by the pair of brownish-gray doves that nested somewhere in the small yard. She awoke about an hour later. The sky was bright now, the air warmer.

She stretched, located her flip-flops kicked under the bed, and went to close the window. They would need the air conditioner today.

The kitchen was quiet; Rick and Dahlia were not back yet. Coffee was ready and she poured herself a cup, looking out into the backyard as she sipped it. The birds were quieter now; she'd fill the birdbath when she watered her flowers. This year she had planted some daisies, a few black-eyed Susans, and some very gaudy zinnias in addition to the petunias and impatiens that were her summer garden's staples. Usually Dahlia liked to help her with the watering. Naomi decided to wait until her daughter had returned. She finished the coffee and rinsed the mug. She took a shower, washed her hair using a new mango-scented shampoo she'd bought for Dahlia. Ever since Dahlia had announced her goal of growing hair down to her behind, there had been the predictable struggles about its maintenance and grooming. The new shampoo—and the scented cream rinse Naomi had bought along with it—were her effort to make hair washing fun instead of a battle. When she emerged from the shower, hair smelling fruity and sweet, Naomi's husband and daughter were still out.

She didn't worry, though. Why would she? They had probably gone to the bagel place on Avenue Z. Even though Park Slope had plenty of places to buy bagels, Rick preferred the place out near Coney Island, maintaining that its bagels were chewier, its cream cheese fresher. Dahlia agreed. Coney Island was, even on the best day, a twenty-minute drive from their house. Maybe they had run into traffic. Ocean Parkway could be slow going, with all those stoplights.

Or maybe they were back in the neighborhood and had decided on an impromptu trip to the playground or a stop at a stoop sale. Since the blocks and blocks of row houses had yards without street access, sales were conducted on the front stoops. Naomi often shopped at such sales herself, looking for books, housewares, and clothes. Nor was Dahlia immune to a stoop sale's charms. Though she had recently decided that secondhand Barbies were no longer acceptable, she was more tolerant about the matter of their outfits and was willing to paw through the gaping Hefty bags in search of sequined, strapless gowns and pink, faux-fur-trimmed parkas if they hadn't been too rudely handled by their owners. Naomi looked again at the backyard and the flowers. God knows it was hot enough to water twice today. She and Dahlia could do it again together in the afternoon.

It wasn't until the flowers were soaked, birdbath filled, a load of laundry washed, dried, and folded, and the entire paper read that Naomi began to feel concerned. Well, not concerned actually, but annoyed. Rick could have given her a call to let her know where he was, just so she could make some plans. Wasn't that the point of paying an extra forty dollars a month for the cell phone? So they could keep in touch if they needed to?

Naomi folded the newspaper neatly and left it by Rick's chair in the dining room. She would go to the supermarket; she really needed to do that today. She'd leave Rick a note. Then, after lunch, she and Dahlia could spend the afternoon together. Maybe they would go to Prospect Park, where the abundant trees and open spaces would provide some relief from the heat. Or the playground up at Third Street; the sprinkler would be on, no doubt, and Dahlia could run, shrieking, tossing her hair back and forth, through the cold, refreshing spray. Naomi had just uncapped one of Dahlia's markers—Hot Rockin' Pink—when the telephone rang.

But it wasn't Rick on the other end of the line, calling to tell her where they were, asking her to fix grilled cheese sandwiches, and wanting to know if she already had pickles or should he pick up a jar on his way back. Instead, it was a woman named Adelaide Peters who identified herself as the head nurse of the pediatric unit at Holy Name Hospital up on Seventh Avenue. Rick and Dahlia were there with her. There had been an accident and they wanted Naomi to come right away.

Naomi put down the phone very gently, as if she were afraid she might injure it. She found her keys, her sunglasses, and her handbag and was outside in minutes, striding up the hill like a giant in seven league boots, toward Seventh Avenue and Sixth Street. It was only when she arrived at the wide, glass double doors that she realized she was still holding the hot pink marker, Dahlia's favorite color. She looked at the marker and remembered all the pictures Dahlia had drawn with it: schematically rendered flowers, lopsided hearts, an oversized ice-cream cone dotted with confetti-like sprinkles. Then she slipped it into her handbag, a talisman against harm.

Inside the hospital, Adelaide Peters was waiting for her at the reception desk. She was a competent-looking black woman with a headful of dark braids that covered her scalp evenly, like so many rows of corn. A line of gold earrings traveled up the outer curve of her ear, and in the V of her white hospital scrubs was a large gold cross. Next to her stood a man who looked to be in his early fifties. He was as disheveled and untidy as Adelaide was neat: white hair that stood from the side of his head like wings, tie loose and askew under the scrubs. His stethoscope seemed to wind round his neck like a snake, impossibly large and menacing. As soon as Naomi saw them she knew she was going to hear something awful.

"Mrs. Wechsler?" the man said, hand extended. "I'm Michael McBride. Head of the pediatric unit." Head of the pediatric unit. That was bad. Very bad.

"Where is my daughter?" Naomi asked, ignoring the hand.

"In ER. With your husband."

"Is she all right? Is he?"

"Let's go and see them now," said Adelaide. "You can follow me." The hospital was cool, too cool. In her haste to get there, Naomi hadn't thought to take a sweater and now she wrapped her hands around her own bare arms. When they reached the ER waiting room Naomi heard a terrible, strangled sound. Several other people in the waiting area heard it too, and they looked up, momentarily roused from their own pain and illness to register their unease. That awful sound. Naomi suddenly understood. It was Rick and he was howling.

"She's dead, isn't she?" Naomi said, pausing in the unbearable chill of the hospital corridor. In the merest second before the response came, she still hoped for a miracle, a reprieve: Dahlia wasn't dead, only hurt, badly hurt. But she was resilient and strong. Think of the energy with which she ran, turned cartwheels, jumped from the highest rung of the jungle gym at the playground. She would get well; this immaculate woman and her sloppy companion would save her. Then Adelaide Peters put her hand on Naomi's left shoulder and Michael McBride put his hand on her right one. The momentary reprieve evaporated and she knew.

Nothing could ever prepare you for the shock of seeing your child's corpse. Naomi looked down at the small body, the body she had brought into the world, and felt the tears rise up and spill from her eyes. Though she was aware of some noise that emerged from her throat, she didn't really hear it. Nor did she really hear Rick, still sobbing in the background. It was as if all the ambient sound had been turned down, muted, and what unfolded now was on a purely visual plane.

There was Dahlia on the gurney, stark white sheet emphasizing the summer brown of her skin, though Naomi could see how, already, the cheeks under her tan had gone gray. Her straight brown hair was pushed to one side and her eyes, those clear, aquamarine eyes both Naomi and Rick had loved so much, were closed. But it was the strange twist of her head, the impossible angle at which it lay, that revealed what had happened: her neck had been broken in a car accident only a few minutes away from their house. There wasn't even any blood.

Rick had come over to join Naomi as she stood looking at Dahlia, and he began to tell the story. He and Dahlia had gone to the bagel place on Avenue Z, just as Naomi had surmised. It had been crowded, but they decided to wait anyway. Dahlia was hungry; she ate two entire bagels, one raisin cinnamon with cream cheese, the other plain and slathered with butter. A whole container of chocolate milk.

Naomi knew Rick included these details because Naomi worried—frequently, irritatingly—that Dahlia didn't eat enough. He wanted her to know that he had succeeded, even if it was for the last time, in feeding their daughter well.

After the bagels, they drove by the carousel in Coney Island, and Rick had stopped to let Dahlia take a ride. He bought her a balloon, a red one, but she had accidentally let it go and it shot through the hot summer sky, its bright red globe growing smaller and less distinct as they watched. He would have bought her another, but the balloon vendor had by this time left. He had carried her to the car, and she had stared upward the entire time, as if the force of her gaze might summon the errant balloon back to earth once more.

Just as they reached the car, Dahlia saw another vender, this time selling pinwheels with multicolored metallic stripes. Rick bought her one, in consolation for the balloon, and she played with it during the ride back to Park Slope, which was uneventful. They came to an intersection at the corner of Third Street and Eighth Avenue. Rick was planning to make the left turn and go down to Fourth Avenue, where he would swing around and head up Carroll Street to their house. But the light turned red and he had to stop. Dahlia's shoe had become untied and she wanted him to tie it. "Wait until we're home," he told her from the front seat. "I'll do it when we get back. Or you can do it yourself." Even though Dahlia was old enough to tie her own shoes, she often still asked one of her parents to do it. Rick had probably been annoyed by her asking; Naomi would have been too.

Dahlia had sighed loudly, registering her displeasure. Then she laid the pinwheel on the seat beside her and bent down, her hands straining for the laces over the seat belt that bisected her body. As she was bent over, a bloated silver SUV came up behind them. The driver was talking on a cell phone and trying to control a small white dog that was jumping around the passenger seat beside her. Rick could see the SUV getting closer in the rearview mirror. Way too close for comfort. And then it hit him. Not all that hard, either, just enough to set the car rocking for a moment. Had Dahlia been sitting upright in the seat, nothing would have happened.

But Dahlia had not been sitting up. She was bent over, and the impact, combined with the odd, vulnerable angle at which her head was inclined, had broken her neck instantly, like snapping the bud off a perfectly straight, vibrant tulip will suddenly end its life. Rick had pulled over, gotten out of the car, knelt on the hot pavement, and stared in disbelief at what he saw in the backseat.

The driver of the SUV had gotten out, and when she came to stand beside Rick, began to dial 911 on her cell phone. Rick ignored her and instead got back behind the driver's seat and sped to Holy Name Hospital, which was only blocks away. They had rushed Dahlia into the emergency room, where three doctors and a team of nurses descended. But Dahlia was already dead.

"That's not possible," Naomi said, looking back and forth from Rick to Michael. "That's so . . . so . . ." she groped for a word, because words seemed to be deserting her, fleeing all at once from her brain, "stupid," she finished lamely. "Such a stupid way to be killed." She reached up to wipe the tears that coated her face, accepted the fresh wad of Kleenex Adelaide proffered as the tears started falling again.

"Yes, it was," said Michael McBride. He put his hand on her shoulder again. Naomi looked down as if it were excrement deposited from a passing pigeon, and he withdrew it.

"Mrs. Wechsler," he began once more, arms folded across his chest and hands tucked into his armpits, "why don't you and your husband come up to my office? Please?" Naomi wanted to say, "What for?" but there was Rick, shuffling along behind McBride. Adelaide Peters followed them at a slight distance.

Michael McBride's office was large and filled with light; clearly the good doctor rated a corner office. But a corner office and all the prestige and rank it implied hadn't been able to save her daughter. Naomi laced her fingers together so tightly that her knuckles paled.

"I want you both to know how deeply sorry I am. Truly, deeply sorry." Naomi let her eyes scan his face, taking in the two lines that framed his mouth, the eyebrows, still dark though the hair was white, the blue eyes. The plastic name tag he wore said Dr. Michael X. McBride. What kind of middle initial was X anyway? It sounded made up, invented. Like his sympathy. How sorry was he? And even if he was being sincere, what did she care? It wouldn't make the events of the last few hours reverse themselves and vanish, would it?

Naomi looked over at Rick, who was staring at the doctor and nodding his head very slightly as he listened. His mouth was slightly open. Naomi realized that she and Rick had not actually touched since she had arrived here. As if he had read her mind, Rick reached over and put a hand on her leg. Without meaning to, she flinched. She looked at the hand on her thigh as if it were the hand of a stranger, and she wished she could push it away. Still, this was Rick, her husband, Dahlia's father, her partner in life and now in death. She let the hand remain, though it felt heavy and alien.

To distract herself, she looked around the office, which was as sloppy as its occupant. The rug on the floor was of some abstract pattern: tipsy blue triangles, buoyant circles of red, yellow, and orange. There were plants, easily a dozen, lining the floor near the window. Walls filled with diplomas, a poster of a Matisse cutout, diagrams of the human body. A big basket of toys stood in one corner, and next to it a pink and purple Fisher Price castle. Naomi recognized the castle as something Dahlia had vigorously lobbied for but had not convinced her parents to buy. That memory stabbed Naomi now, and she kept her eyes moving, to the shelves, which were filled not only with medical texts but children's books—she saw *Goodnight Moon*, *The Cat in the Hat*, and *Pippi Longstocking*—and novels, books of poetry, and several oversize art books. The desk was filled with papers, more toys—a big plush panda bear sat on one corner—and a clear plastic model of a heart. A covered crystal dish was filled with jelly beans and another with Hershey's chocolate Kisses.

Naomi's eyes roamed the clutter, settled finally on a cluster of small snapshots in silver frames: McBride without the scrubs, at the beach, his arms around a pair of young girls, twins from the look of them. Naomi studied the photo. McBride seemed younger, as if the picture had been taken a while ago. The girls appeared to be about twelve, the buds of their breasts, so clearly visible in their tank tops, just beginning to swell. Dahlia would never be twelve, would never accompany Naomi on a trip to buy her first bra, her first strapless dress, her first pair of high heels. Naomi stood abruptly, pushing aside Rick's hand and knocking the photograph to the floor.

"I'm sorry," she said curtly, though she was not sorry, not at all. She was in fact glad she had knocked the photograph down and was only sorry that she had not broken the frame, the glass, or both. Looking at it, she made no move to pick it up.

McBride stood too. "It's nothing," he said quietly. "Don't worry about it."

"I won't," Naomi said belligerently. "I won't worry about it at all. I'll just worry about my daughter, my dead daughter. The one you couldn't fix." She was aware of Rick staring at her, and of Adelaide Peters's liquid, pitying gaze, but she didn't care. She left the doctor's office and started walking quickly down the freezing corridor. There were a pair of double doors up ahead, and beyond them, the elevator. She had no thought further than that. But her progress was halted by Adelaide's fine dark hand on her arm. She resisted the impulse to shake her off too. Why was everyone touching her today, when she couldn't stand, couldn't bear to be touched?

"It's been a shock, I know," Adelaide said kindly. "But you'll need to fill out some forms before you go."

"Forms?" Naomi echoed.

"So that we can release the body." She looked at Naomi, who found she could not return the look.

"Let my husband do it," she croaked. "I have to get out of here." She pushed through the doors, and closed her eyes in the elevator as it descended. Feeling the heated air outside was a relief after the hospital's chill. She began to walk but had no idea of where to go, so she went once, twice, and three times around the block. By this time she had grown hot and started sweating. Her cotton shirt stuck to her skin. She slowed in front of the hospital doors, not wanting to experience that frigid air all over again. But suddenly, she was hit by the realization that Dahlia was still in that building, Dahlia whose motionless brown body was growing colder with each passing moment. She realized that she hadn't actually touched Dahlia, laid her hands, for one final time, on her face, kissed the thin, vein-laced skin of her eyelids. The knowledge hit her like a blow, and propelled her back through the hospital's handprint-smeared doors.

Months later, Naomi was still walking through those doors, although her purpose now was very different. She was not there to say good-bye to her daughter, but to try to offer comfort to other people's children, children who were, blissfully, enviably, still among the living. There was also something else that drew her here, something that she tried to hide from herself, much as she tried to hide from the memories of her less-than-perfect daughter and her less-than-perfect self.

She had known from the start, from the first awful day when she saw Michael waiting for her in the hospital lobby, that he was not responsible for Dahlia's death. But it was easy to blame him anyway, to let some of her rage and her sadness spill over onto him. He could take it. Mr. Big Shot, as her mother, had she been fully there, might have called him. Mr. I'm-the-Head-of-the-Pediatric-Unit-and-Have Seen-It-All. He came with that nurse of his to her home, for a shivah call, but she wouldn't even look at him. She banished him from her thoughts, which wasn't at all hard; there was so much else, after all, to consume her.

But that was before she had started running into him at the hospital. Months without seeing or thinking about him and now it seemed that every time she turned around, there he was. Maybe it wasn't just a coincidence either, at least not after that first time. Maybe he was seeking her out. Somehow she thought he was, and she derived some small and perverse comfort from it. He had known other women who had lost their children, other women with stories even worse than her own. She wanted him to tell her those stories; she wanted him to help her put her own grief into a larger context, one that she could somehow bear.

It started over coffee. She had gotten into the habit of buying coffee for both of them at Barnes & Noble and bringing it to his office. There wasn't a lot of time because he was so busy and there were always interruptions—cell phone, pager, Adelaide Peters hurrying in and hurrying back out again.

But even with all that, there were moments when she could ask him something about what he'd seen and what he knew.

"What's the worst thing you've ever had to tell a parent?"

"Depends on what you mean by worst." He blew lightly on the coffee before taking a sip.

"The thing that made you feel you couldn't say it, no matter how hard you tried."

"Well, I once had to tell a woman that her thirteen-year-old daughter had been hit by a bus while she was bicycling to school."

"The daughter was killed outright? Or did she die at the hospital?" Naomi felt her interest was macabre; still she needed to know, and Michael—she thought of him as Michael now—was willing to indulge her.

"Killed outright. It was the bus that runs along Prospect Park West. The girl had gotten too close to the rear. The driver never even saw her when he backed up. The poor mother went totally to pieces."

"But why is that the worst?" No worse than what happened to me, Naomi wanted to say, though she didn't. It seemed too mean to utter, though clearly not to think.

"Well, I had been told that this woman had had another daughter, a little older than the one who died in the bus accident, who had also been killed by a bus."

"You're kidding." Naomi tasted the coffee, let the sweet warm liquid move around her mouth before swallowing.

"I wish I were. That first time, though, there was no bicycle. The bus—it was a school bus—veered off the highway and into a divider when her class was coming back from a trip to Philadelphia. Some of the other kids were hurt, but she was the only one who died. They had gone to see the Liberty Bell."

"You remember that?"

"I remember a lot." Michael put the coffee down for a moment. "Too much, maybe. At least that's what my wife says."

"Your wife," Naomi echoed, feeling a strange uncomfortable twinge when he said those words. But then her thoughts snapped back to the woman who had lost two daughters. Two. "You're right," she said, "that must have been awful." She paused, looked around the office she had come to know quite well. She had bought a few more of those chocolate Santas for Michael, and he had them lined up on a shelf like a row of foil-covered soldiers. "What happened to the mother?"

"I'm not sure," Michael said. "I do know that she and her husband divorced not long after losing the second girl. He stayed in Brooklyn; I've seen him once or twice since then. I heard the woman left the city altogether."

"No wonder." Naomi stood and dropped her empty coffee cup into the wastebasket. "What did she have left to stay for?"

6

Miracle Baby

Estelle knew she had to find her way back to the child. It was essential that she do so. But how? There were so many impediments. First, she would have to hack her way through the ruined thicket of her memory to find out where Dahlia lived. She could see pieces in her mind: a house made of bricks, a room painted pink. White curtains. A green table. But where were these things?

Estelle did not want to ask any of the attendants here or, even worse, the doctors. The more she let them know about her true condition, the more vulnerable she became. No, she would have to retrieve the information some other way, conceal her objectives and her plans from everyone here. For they—the doctors, the attendants, all the busy and active people who moved with such purpose through the long halls and small rooms of this place—were among the chief obstacles between her and her plan. To find the child. To reclaim her.

She began laying the groundwork, piece by tiny piece, an elaborately constructed mosaic of cooperation, good behavior, docility. It began in the morning, when one of the girls came to dress her.

"How are you today?" Estelle said. She stretched her lips into a facsimile of a smile as the young, strong hands pulled the nightgown over her head, mussing her hair. She hated to have her hair mussed; why couldn't the girl manage to undress her without doing that?

"I'm just fine, Mrs. Levine." Now the nightdress was being replaced with a slip and then a flowered blouse. Estelle studied the name tag the girl wore pinned to her smock. Taneesha. She went over the letters in her mind a few times. Reading was tricky. Sometimes, she remembered everything and could make her way through the Metro section of the newspaper with no trouble. But other times the letters swam across the page, morphing into a perplexing trail of dark squiggles and angry blobs whose meaning she could no longer decipher. Today she was lucky, though. She recognized the tapping sound of the *t*, the nasal humming of the *n*, the elongated sound of the double *e*. Ta-neesh-a.

"Glad to hear it. Taneesha." There, she had said the girl's name. She was sure this would get a reaction. She was not disappointed.

"You seem very alert today, Mrs. Levine. That's just great." Taneesha finished dressing Estelle and wrote something on the chart that was attached with a yellow elastic cord to Estelle's bed.

When Taneesha had left, Estelle studied the chart. "Resident was well behaved and cheerful today. Knew my name and used it in an appropriate way." Estelle was pleased, even proud. She had known what to do and done it. If she had dared, she would have made an addition to the chart, but she did not think she could replicate Taneesha's neat writing; her own hand either shook too badly or else it took a direction wholly unknown and unexpected once the pen made contact with the paper.

Instead, she walked to the big room, where they all ate, by herself. She said good morning to the fat woman on one side, the skinny man on the other. Neither seemed to notice, but the attendant serving the gummy oatmeal gave her a friendly nod. The oatmeal was perhaps even more offensive than the potatoes, but Estelle gamely stuck her spoon in and lifted it to her mouth. It didn't have much taste, but she discovered there were raisins, dark and plump as beetles, concealed in the tannish muck and they sweetened it somewhat. Estelle swallowed and was grateful that the food went down without protest. She ate another spoonful and then another. Soon it was gone.

"You have quite an appetite today, Mrs. Levine," said the attendant who came around to collect the empty dish. Estelle just stretched out her mouth again—no one could seem to tell that this was not actually a smile—and folded her hands in her lap. She had discovered that doing that helped her resist the urge to slap or pinch someone, anyone, whose irreparable stupidity frayed her nerves beyond endurance.

All day long, she continued the charade. The grimace that was mistaken for a smile, using someone's name, returning to the big room with the beads and, this time, pasting square glazed tiles into a small, iron frame. She was making something whose name was eluding her, but just barely. She knew that if she didn't insist on recalling the word, but just let herself be lulled by the pattern of the tiles—two whites, a blue, two more whites, a red—it would come to her. Trivet. There, just like that, she remembered. "Trivet," she said out loud, to no one in particular.

"What's that, Mrs. Levine?" said the young occupational therapist with pale, strawlike hair.

"I'm making a trivet. For my daughter." Estelle couldn't read her name tag from over here, but she responded anyway.

"That's so thoughtful of you. I'm sure she'll love those colors." The occupational therapist walked over to survey Estelle's work. Estelle looked up to see the name tag. Cora. That was an easy one.

"Thank you, Cora." Her voice sounded loud, even offensive to her own ears, but Cora seemed pleased. She stood looking over Estelle's shoulder while Estelle applied more glue and more tiles to the frame. It looked pitiful, she thought, something a child would make. And not even a talented child. But she would keep doing it, because it was going to help her find her child. Dahlia. Who was waiting, in the pink room, somewhere that Estelle had yet to locate.

Back at the dawn of the exuberant and optimistic 1960s, Estelle had had trouble not getting but staying pregnant. Conceiving was not the obstacle. But as pregnancy after pregnancy ended in miscarriage, both her confidence in the future and her hopes for a baby began to wither.

On a cold, wet morning in December, she took the three subway trains from her Brooklyn neighborhood to the Upper East Side, to the plush offices of a Dr. Cunningham, a renowned fertility specialist.

Once there, Estelle sat in the waiting room for over an hour, impatiently flipping through back issues of *Life* magazine—pictures of President Kennedy in Hyannis Port, of Marilyn Monroe in Hollywood—and surreptitiously glancing at the other, well-dressed, well-coiffed women in the waiting room. When she was finally ushered into Dr. Cunningham's inner sanctum, her initial annoyance melted away. She took in the fine, silver hair brushed back from his broad forehead, the silk tie, and the gold watch as flat and round as a half-dollar and knew that she had found a man who could help her. He listened attentively as she spoke, taking notes all the while in a large, leather-bound book whose open pages spread across his desk like wings. When she had finished, he took both her hands in his and said, in the quietest, most reassuring voice she could imagine, "I think you've come to the right place."

It was those words she kept replaying in her mind during the examination, which, thanks to his dexterous touch, she barely felt. She didn't know what the bill would be, but she didn't care. Milton would have to understand. She knew this man was worth any price, any price at all.

Dressed and seated across from him in his office once more, she smiled and nodded when he told her about the new miracle drug, the one that she would take—completely free from any side effects—to keep her unborn baby safe and snug within her womb until the hour of its birth. "Think of him—or her—as a little sailor," Dr. Cunningham had said. "It will be our job, yours and mine, to see that little sailor safely to port." He withdrew his hand from hers only long enough to write the prescription and to give it to her. Estelle folded it carefully and tucked it into the zippered pocket of her handbag. All the way back to Brooklyn, she was highly aware of the scrap of paper. Though invisible now, she felt its aura, as if it radiated a secret heat only she could detect.

Dr. Cunningham had not lied to her. Shortly after her visit to the esteemed doctor, she became pregnant for the sixth time. But now she was armed with the tiny red pills, cheery as valentines when she shook them out into her palm. This time, instead of the pregnancy terminating in a bout of cramps and a rush of blood, Estelle swelled and thickened. Unlike her friends who bemoaned the weight gains, the puffy ankles, the new and unfamiliar veins popping up everywhere, Estelle reveled in all of it. These were the tangible signs of Dr. Cunningham's promised miracle: she was having a baby. And that was what, on a hot September night at Lenox Hill Hospital, she did. Naomi Louise Levine was six pounds, six ounces, and she filled Estelle's heart utterly, to the brim. When she was back home and back on her feet, she wrote to Dr. Cunningham, who had come to see her almost every day that she had been in the hospital. *Thank you for everything. Milton and I couldn't be any happier.*

It wasn't until Naomi was about ten that Estelle first read, in the New York Times, about a rare vaginal cancer that occurred in the daughters of women who had been given DES, the medication she had taken while pregnant with Naomi. Estelle finished the article and put the paper down. The buttered toast, the cup of tea were left unfinished. It was Tuesday morning; Naomi was at school. Estelle had to restrain the impulse to shed her bathrobe, pull on her clothes, and rush off to Naomi's fifth-grade classroom in search of her, just to see her, make sure that she was all right. Maybe she would even whisk her off to the hospital that very day for tests. But it wouldn't have helped. The article said the cancer did not manifest itself until later on, until the DES daughters were in their teens.

Instead, she called Dr. Cunningham's office. She had not been to see him in almost a decade and found that he had retired about five years earlier. Estelle's current gynecologist, Dr. Kahn, on Plaza Street, was not terribly helpful. He finally referred her to the New York State Medical Society office in Albany. She waited on hold for nearly twenty minutues before she spoke to another doctor who told her that really, nothing could be done until Naomi had reached adolescence.

When Naomi was fifteen, Estelle scheduled an appointment with a doctor at Sloan-Kettering Cancer Center in Manhattan. If, God forbid, Naomi did have this rare disease, Sloan-Kettering was the best place to have it treated. Estelle thought that was reason enough to begin there. All the tests came back negative; Naomi showed no signs of abnormality. The doctors at Sloan-Kettering were pleased and optimistic. She should continue to have annual Pap tests and pelvic examinations. The cancer did not strike each and every DES daughter. It looked like Naomi had been spared.

It was only when Naomi was in her twenties and married to Rick that Estelle found out otherwise. Like her mother, Naomi could get pregnant easily enough. But the insidious path taken by the drug finally revealed itself. She had what Dr. Agharian, the snippy and intimidating young gynecologist from Iran, said was an incompetent cervix. She kept losing baby after baby, despite the precautions, the bed rest. Early miscarriages, all of them, were disappointing but not devastating. Naomi was still young and otherwise in good health. There was every reason to think that she would be able to bear a child. Finally, after the seventh miscarriage, Rick was ready to quit. So they wouldn't have a baby. Or they would adopt. It was just too painful this way. That's what Naomi reported to Estelle.

"But you still want to try again," Estelle said, looking at her daughter, remembering her own sadness and how it had all melted away when she held Naomi in her arms for the first time.

"Yes," Naomi said. "I do."

Naomi became pregnant again. This time, she was put on complete bed rest for nearly the entire pregnancy, and her cervix was stitched shut. It was maddening, it was enervating, but it also seemed to work. The fetus stayed inside her and grew into a baby. Estelle watched her daughter's stomach rise, like the swell on the pan of Jiffy Pop when the popcorn was finally ready. With her feet up, her head propped by pillows, she looked expensive, fragile, easily broken.

Rick and Estelle alternated their visits so that one of them was there every day. Friends stopped by with books, cards, a Barbie-type doll that had a plastic addition to its body and could give birth to a small plastic baby. Dahlia was born in the summer, small and perfect in every way. After all the lost fetuses—her own and her daughter's—Estelle could not get over the fact of her, the fuzz of golden hair, the balled fists, the mouth as self-contained and prim as a knot.

Later, Dr. Agharian did the internal examination. She took a long time with it, probing her latex-clad fingers and various instruments up and inside Naomi's body while Estelle waited outside the closed curtains. Down the hall was Dahlia, in the hospital nursery. Estelle listened, as if she might actually be able to hear—and identify—her cry from this distance. Finally, Dr. Agharian called Estelle inside so she could speak to both of them at once. "Think of her as your miracle baby." Dr. Agharian was speaking to Naomi but looking at Estelle. "You shouldn't try for another."

Late in the afternoon, Estelle went back to her own room. The light was fading, but she could still see the water—brown, dulled—down at the end of the hill. And suddenly it came to her. Water. The place where Dalia lived was somehow connected to, or by, water. She had had to cross water to get there. Not the turquoise ripples and waves she remembered, longingly, lovingly, from the days by the beach with Milton. No, the water she associated with Dahlia was more like this water: dark, cold, impenetrable. But there was a lot of it. And to cross it she had gone over . . . Just be calm, Estelle told herself. It will come to you. And it did: a bridge. Yes, she felt it all flooding back now, the big bridge with the high spires and proud steel webbing that stretched across the water to . . . someplace, someplace that would come to her if she just waited patiently, like she did when the words *trivet* and *bridge* came floating back into her consciousness.

The light was going quickly; there was just the slightest band of brightness near the horizon before the darkness overtook everything. Estelle stood by the window, watching for as long as it remained. The surface of the glass was cold, which surprised her. Inside these rooms it was always hot.

She turned to the closet and opened the door. Inside were all sorts of garments from another life: cotton shifts in bright prints and colors, capri pants she used to wear when she and Milton strolled along the shore, a linen jacket. Nothing that would help her now. If she were to go out, she would need different clothes—warm clothes—to protect her.

But wait, here was something. A black wool cardigan. She rubbed the material between her two fingers. Suddenly the name of the wool—merino—jumped into her consciousness. What a funny word. She said it aloud, trying the emphasis on different syllables: *mer*-in-o, mer-*een*-o, mer-ee-*no*. That wasn't the way it was pronounced, but Estelle liked the sound of it and began to repeat it like a chant, mer-ee-*no*, mer-ee-*no*, until she remembered that such digressions were not only not helpful they were dangerous, they would distract her from her true goal, which was to find Dahlia. Stop it, she said to herself firmly. Stop it right now.

She reached for the sweater. It was soft. And warm. Warm enough to take her all the way to Brooklyn. That was it. Dahlia and the brick house and the pink room were in Brooklyn. The bridge she had remembered—broad, expansive, grand—was the Brooklyn Bridge.

Estelle slept deeply and well that night and for many nights after. Now she knew exactly what she had to do. Every morning, she had a smile for Taneesha; in the big room she ate her breakfast—a tepid, runny poached egg and slightly burned bagel, more oatmeal, pancakes with the texture and appeal of plastic doilies—with gusto and thanked the attendant for bringing it. So cooperative and so benign did she seem, so well in control of herself and her faculties, that she caused no alarm, required no special attention. This went on for a while, though how long Estelle was not entirely sure. Sometimes, she felt like her old self and could watch the progress of the day—morning, afternoon, evening—and measure her success in the different parts of it. Other times, she lost track of how the hours and days slipped by and confused one morning with another, or with the night before.

But she was getting somewhere, she knew that much. The doctors and all the others trusted her more now. They knew she wasn't going to cause any trouble, so they could relax their guard. Just a little of course. Yet it was enough. More than enough—it was all she needed.

One morning, after she had eaten, she stayed seated a little longer than usual, chatting amiably with the attendant who wiped down the tables and refilled the wire holders with the little paper packets of sugar. Then she slowly rose and walked through the wide double doors into the hallway. It was easy, so easy to leave the big room and head right, not left. No one seemed to notice that instead of walking to the place where they rubbed and pounded her legs or the other one where they offered her loops of cotton to fashion into pot holders, Estelle went back upstairs, to the room she could barely bring herself to call her own.

She closed the door and went straight to the closet. Today she was wearing a striped cotton shirt and some pants with an elastic waist. Taneesha had been so pleased that Estelle remembered and used her name that she hadn't even tried to persuade her to wear a skirt, which was easier for her to get on. Her shoes were all right too—sneakers with soft, cushioned soles. Good, because she planned to do some walking. Quite a bit, in fact.

The striped top had long sleeves, but she added the black sweater she had found. The coat would be trickier. Did she own a winter coat anymore? She pawed through the clothes, unearthing a beaded silk cocktail dress she had worn somewhere important, she could not think where, and the black suit she had worn at Milton's funeral. So many clothes, so many lives lived in them. But here, way at the back, was a well-tailored burgundy wool coat bought more than a decade earlier. Perfect. She wrestled it off the hanger and stuffed it into the nylon bag meant for dirty laundry, the laundry quickly being emptied onto the floor and shoved under the bed.

In the bureau drawers, Estelle found a beret, a scarf that must have once belonged to Milton, a pair of gloves, and perhaps best of all, a twenty-dollar bill. It had been some time since she had handled money, and she did not know if she could remember how to deal with the numbers—marching along relentlessly in columns, they were like the implacable troops of an invading army—but she would have to make the effort. She knew it would take money to find her way from this water to that, from this place to the bridge and the house and Dahlia waiting inside it.

The hat, scarf, and gloves she placed in the bag; the bill she folded into a small square and stuck into her sneaker. She opened the door to her room and looked up and down the corridor. Empty. She walked quickly to the stairs and descended one, two flights. No one in the stairwell; everyone here used the elevator. By the time she had reached the bottom, she had started to sweat and her breathing was labored. The door had some sort of red sign at the top. Emergency Exit Only. Alarm Will Sound If Door Is Opened.

Estelle sat on the bottom step, trying to decide what to do next. She looked from the door to the floor and back again, as if she ex-pected the red letters to have disappeared when she looked away. They did not. But there was another flight of stairs. Where did they lead?

She got up and, holding on to the railing, continued going down. At the bottom was yet another door, another sign with red letters. But there was also a small half-window. She peered out. She saw a concrete enclosure and several large trash cans. Above, and not very far above, she saw light. It was an easy matter to open the window and push the nylon bag through it. It was harder to maneuver her own body through the small space, but she was little and thin, like all the women in her family. It took a few uncomfortable minutes, but when they were over, she was out.

Estelle stood, trying to orient herself. Once the heat from her exer-tions faded, she was shocked by the cold, cold like a smack, that hit her from every direction. She fumbled with the bag, pulled on the coat, the scarf, the hat. She couldn't manage the gloves; to hell with them then. She was just about to drop them in the trash when she hesitated.

The bridge was far away. She knew that, could feel it. She stuffed the gloves into her pockets. Maybe later she would be able to negotiate the complex task of fitting them over her fingers. In back of the trash cans was a short flight of concrete stairs. At the top, she found herself at ground level. There was the hill, the water that lay at the bottom of it, and the sky beyond that.

She had done it. She was free. Staying close to the side of the building, she wound her way around until she saw the grove of trees. Trees, even those without their leaves, were a welcome sight. They would help to conceal her as she made her way out of this place. "Dahlia," she said out loud. The sound of her voice in the open air was reassuring, grounding. She sounded like someone she remembered. Someone she knew. "Dahlia my sweet girl, I'll be there soon."

7

Liar, Liar

Five o'clock on a Friday afternoon. The sky had already turned a thick, velvety gray, not a glimmer of light left in it. Rick was looking out the window in his office. He had just gotten off the phone with Naomi, just told her the first of what he knew would be an increasingly complex series of lies, each one more intricately knotted and tightened than the next.

"I won't be home for dinner," he said to his wife. "I'm meeting Jon Liebowitz."

"How is Jon?" Naomi asked.

"I don't know; I haven't seen him yet." Rick heard the peevishness in his tone. It was caused by guilt, pure and simple.

"You don't have to get so testy," Naomi said. "I was just wondering."

"Sorry," he said. "I'm tired, that's all." *Tired* was their code word. Tired meant: I didn't sleep well, I was thinking or dreaming or crying over Dahlia. Tired meant depressed, despairing even. But even as he said it, he knew it wasn't true. He was anything but tired these days.

"I know," she said gently. "I won't wait up then."

"I won't be too late." He was trying to make amends now, trying not to be such a prick.

"That's okay." There was a pause. "Where are you meeting?"

"I don't know." The guilt rushed back. He hadn't actually thought about a place. But he'd better. She might ask what he'd eaten. "We're meeting for drinks first. Then we'll have dinner." Okay, now that was two lies. Fictional drinks, followed by fictional food. Plus later there would be some fictional stories about Jon, what he had said and what Rick had answered, where Jon and his wife Cindy were planning to go on their vacation in February.

"All right, then. Say hello to him."

"I will."

"And to Cindy."

"Sure thing." Rick knew that Naomi couldn't stand Cindy. This was the chief reason the two men got together on their own, providing Rick, in this instance, with a convenient alibi. So if Naomi was sending her regards to Cindy, she must really be trying hard. "Love you," he added. And he meant it. He did love her. But loving her was not going to stop him from leaving the office with Lillian, getting on the R train and taking it back to her apartment, where he planned to fuck her on the floor, the bed, the sofa, the kitchen table, and anywhere else that seemed appealing. Would any of this have happened if Naomi hadn't been so closed to him, so cut off? He couldn't say. But ever since the summer, since Dahlia's death, he had been trying in vain to get her attention, in bed and out. She was lost to him. Not lost in the way Dahlia was lost, but still different, strange, unmoored.

Rick thought back to the day Dahlia had died, and the days that followed. He remembered the rude and insulting way Naomi had spoken to that doctor, and how she had abruptly left his office and then the hospital. When she had finally returned, Rick found her engaged in an argument with the morgue attendant, berating the man for the "callous and insensitive" way he had handled Dahlia's body. And Rick could feel her anger toward him, a cold, dense cloud that kept her shrouded from him, just when he needed her most. Along with the grief over Dahlia's death and his guilt at his own, albeit unwitting, role in it Rick tried to make some sense of Naomi's anger, but he couldn't. Anger seemed to require too much energy. Ever since that moment in the car, when the SUV banged into him and he immediately swiveled around to Dahlia and heard that small, sickening sound that turned out to be her neck snapping, he hadn't had energy for anything. Nor could he imagine ever having it again.

He had focused all his meager reserves of concentration on making all the necessary phone calls. His parents had died years earlier, but he had two brothers, the younger one living just outside of Denver; the elder, in Atlanta. His sister was in New York, just across the river in Manhattan. He called Helene Newmann, the chiropractor who shared his office in Brooklyn Heights, and Lillian, so that she could cancel all his appointments. When he had finished recounting the story half a dozen times, he called Jon Liebowitz, with whom he'd been friends since the fourth grade, and asked him to take over.

Jon's list of people to call did not include Naomi's parents. Her father, Milton, had died some time earlier and her mother, Estelle, had been suffering from sudden and frightening episodes of dementia. The last time Naomi had phoned the nursing home where she had been placed, her mother hadn't seemed to recognize her.

"Naomi?" she had said suspiciously. "I don't know anyone named Naomi. Are you sure you're not Joan?"

"Joan?" Naomi said, puzzled. "Who's Joan?"

"Joan Crawford," Estelle had answered. "Good actress. But a class-A bitch. So was Bette Davis. Good actress, that is. Not such a bitch. But Barbara was the best."

"Barbara?" Naomi said, growing more confused.

"Barbara Stanwyck of course," Estelle had said. "Now, there was a lady. She used to show up early to the set. She would greet the technicians and soundmen by name. Ask about their wives. And children." There was a long pause. "Are you sure you're not Barbara?" Estelle finally asked in a small voice.

"Yes, I'm Barbara, that's it," Naomi said on impulse.

"Well, why didn't you call sooner?" Estelle replied peevishly. "I've been waiting." And then she hung up, leaving Naomi staring, astonished, at the phone she still held in her hand.

Rick had comforted Naomi after that call, mourning with her the loss of the mother who had routinely broken four hundred at Scrabble, could correctly multiply three digit numbers in her head, and who had sent Naomi a dozen white roses on her birthday every year. But when Dahlia died, Rick revised his thinking. Maybe his mother-in-law's condition was a blessing of sorts. He certainly didn't know how he would have told her about Dahlia and was grateful he didn't have to.

The hardest call turned out to be the one Rick placed to Bloom's Funeral Home on Newkirk Avenue. He sensed the pity—real, palpable, even over the phone—from the smooth-voiced salesman who had answered. Ordering a casket was one thing. Ordering a casket for a seven-year-old girl was another. Rick asked for the cheapest, plainest one available, not because he didn't want to spend the money on a more expensive one, but because he couldn't bear the conversation about the embellishments that came with the higher price. It turned out he had to hear them anyway. The salesman, whose name was Hal, insisted on offering Rick the deluxe model for the price of the economy. So Rick listened, phone positioned away from his ear, about the white enamel finish, the brass handles, the tufted pink velvet lining. Dahlia had loved pink, he thought, nearly choking on the memory.

At the funeral, the service was led by a rabbi so young it looked as if he had just celebrated his own bar mitzvah. The man had an earnest, concerned expression and blinked so often Rick decided it must have been a tic. At one point, Naomi pulled Rick aside and gestured to the young man, whose white knitted yarmulke was secured snugly to his hair with bobby pins.

"I hate him!" she said, and not too softly either.

"Naomi, don't," Rick pleaded.

"Don't what?"

"Don't make a scene."

"Well, it better be over soon."

"It will be," he soothed. "I promise."

After the service, there was the burial at Greenwood Cemetery. Buying the plots—he had gone ahead and without asking Naomi purchased three, since where else would they want to be buried but beside Dahlia?—had been almost as bad as buying the casket. But somehow he got through that too, and so found himself standing, on that blistering day, by the large hole that was waiting to receive Dahlia's body in its velvet-lined casket. He had let Naomi take care of dressing her. "No makeup," she had hissed at the funeral director, and then had given him a shopping bag containing one of Dahlia's favorite outfits, a long skirt with a ruffle at the bottom and a ribbed top. When Dahlia was presented to them in this garb, Naomi leaned over the open casket and tucked a hot pink marker inside. Later, Naomi stood next to him, dark hair pulled up and off her face, leaving the bleached-looking skin of her cheeks, her chin, nowhere to hide. His sister, Allison, was on the other side, holding his hand tightly in the way he wished Naomi would. Allison was crying quietly, and Rick's older brother, Scott, was patting her shoulder. Allison cried harder. But where was Naomi in all this? Naomi whose comfort he wanted so badly and yet who seemed so estranged, so distant from him.

Later, they went back to their house on Carroll Street. They had never put in air conditioners on the parlor floor where their living room was, and even with the ceiling fans spinning at top speed, the room was hot. Rick went upstairs to change out of his dark suit. Although he was normally an orderly man, he left it crumpled in a heap on the floor of the bedroom he and Naomi shared. He would get rid of it, immediately. He never wanted to see that suit again.

Although neither he nor Naomi had been particularly religious, they sat shivah for the requisite seven-day period, and Rick took some solace in the ritual. The house, with its covered mirrors, was full day after day. Neighbors from up and down the block—they had lived here for nearly fifteen years—friends, cousins they hadn't seen in a decade. People came with food, and the kitchen filled with soups and salads, cookies and coffee cake. None of it interested Rick, though he was touched by the enormous bowl of paella made by Lillian and ate a little in her presence just to thank her. Later, he overheard some of Naomi's cousins complaining that it contained both sausage and shrimp—distinctly *trafe* foods—and was therefore insulting to bring into the home of Jews. Rick marveled at their pettiness. Although it had no taste for him, he ate another helping, and then another.

To his surprise, Dr. McBride from the hospital came to the house. With him was a black woman, that nurse who was there that day. What was her name? He was aware of Naomi's hate-filled look when they walked into the living room. She pushed her way past without acknowledging either of them and hurried up the stairs. A door slammed above.

"I'm sorry," he told McBride. "She isn't taking it well."

"How could she?" McBride said. "I've seen people lose children before. Believe me when I tell you I understand." Rick did believe him. It was kind of him to come here. And the woman too. Adelaide. That was her name. Adelaide Peters. He turned to her, but she had already gone into the kitchen. Rick followed.

"Thank you for coming," he said. Adelaide was busy cutting the string off a bakery box. She looked up.

"You don't have to thank me," she said. "I wanted to come. We both did." Rick nodded. Adelaide carefully lifted her offering—a fruit tart from Cousin John's up on Seventh Avenue—from the box and set it on a plate. Peaches, berries, grapes, and plums were arranged in concentric circles, all covered by a thick glaze. Rick stared at the profusion until his eyes blurred and then watered. When he finally blinked, both Adelaide and the tart were gone.

The worst, though, was seeing the parents of Dahlia's friends and classmates, the chastened, sad mothers, the embarrassed fathers, whose grief, though genuine, was undercut with relief: Thank God it's not us, their eyes seemed to say. Rick found he couldn't look at them. He had to leave the room as soon as they came in. He went out to the garden, which, since Dahlia had died, had been neither watered nor weeded. The flowers looked dry and brittle. But even in the heat, the bindweed, with its large, vaguely star-shaped leaves, was thriving, getting into the zinnias, snaking through the rosebushes. Rick didn't think he ought to mention this to Naomi; she and Dahlia had been the ones to tend to the plants and flowers out here. His only job in the yard was grilling, something he certainly had no interest in now.

Through all this, Naomi was there but not there. She sat, she cried, she took the hands of the women who came in sympathy. But to Rick she was sealed off; she barely looked at or spoke to him. She had not come back to their bedroom since the accident, but had slept every night in Dahlia's room, swaddled in the Groovy Girl sheets, stuffed animals ringed around her. Rick didn't think this was a good idea, and when he mentioned it to his sister, Allison agreed.

"Maybe you should start, you know, dismantling the room," Allison said hesitantly. She had joined Rick in the yard and had both hands clutched around a tall glass filled with what appeared to be iced tea.

"Dismantling the room?" Rick said. How was he going to do that? He hadn't even showered in two days.

"I could help you," Allison offered. She reached over to put a hand on his arm. Her fingers were so cold. Then he remembered the iced tea. Allison had neither husband nor children; she was a good deal younger than all her brothers, having been born when Rick was twelve. Even though Allison was unplanned, Rick's mother had been so happy to have a girl at last. The boys, Rick included, were beyond the age of rampant jealousy, at least toward her. All the rivalry, the fighting, the name calling, were reserved for one another, but from which Allison, their new baby sister, was exempt. She had grown up the coddled only daughter in a houseful of adoring big brothers. Rick knew he was her favorite.

He looked at her, eyes rimmed with tears that she was trying not to shed.

"What about Naomi? Shouldn't I ask her first?"

"Why?" Allison said. "Don't make her go through it."

Rick thought it over but didn't say anything.

After the shivah was over, Rick had returned to work. The familiar bike ride to Brooklyn Heights and the routine of seeing patients and office mates gave him comfort. Only a little comfort, but a little was something. Naomi's days were without structure. He'd hear her very early in the morning, clattering around the kitchen, making coffee. She didn't seem to be eating much; normally small and slim, she had become gaunt.

Some mornings Rick would hear her go out, with no note, no indication of when she would return. Rick would leave for work, periodically calling home during the day but only getting the answering machine. It still had Dahlia's chirpy little message on it, asking the caller to leave a message and to "have a really, really nice day." He hadn't been able to bring himself to erase it.

On one of these days, however, he did not leave for his office. He had told Lillian he wouldn't be in that day; she had rescheduled or arranged coverage for all his appointments. Allison showed up before ten, wearing denim shorts and a black T-shirt that said BABE in rhinestone letters on the front. She was carrying a big box of garbage bags.

"I don't know about this," Rick said as they mounted the stairs together. "Maybe I should have asked Naomi first."

"We've been through this," Allison said. "Don't you think this will make it easier for her? If you ask, she'll have to think about it. This way, it will be done. Taken care of. One less thing for her to deal with."

"She's still sleeping in here," he said. They were standing in front of the door to Dahlia's room. "Every night." He didn't add that he wanted to join her, wanted to curl up next to her, see if he could smell his daughter on the pillowcases, on the sheets. But Naomi's grief, which had hardened into a forbidding carapace of accusation and blame, made him too frightened to ask.

"Don't you think it's time she stopped? And started sleeping with you instead?" his sister replied. Rick hesitated for a moment, but Allison marched into the room. He followed her and sat on the bed, awed by his sister's aura of command. She was a fast and efficient worker. She didn't ask what she should do with this sweater, those boots, the stuffed unicorn that she, in fact, had given Dahlia for her last birthday. She quickly established separate bags for different categories: clothes, books, toys, bedding.

"What are we going to do with everything?" Rick asked. Allison continued piling and tossing, tossing and piling. Dahlia lived only seven years and look what she had acquired: Barbie dolls by the dozens, a collection of plastic horses, another of crystal figurines—a rose, a snail, an elephant, a swan—purchased in the kinds of midtown Manhattan shops that were perpetually going out of business. He wanted to tell Allison to slow down, that he needed a chance to touch the things his daughter had touched, to feel her love for them, one last time. But he didn't have the energy. Easier to let her get on with it.

"I've already thought of that. I hired a guy with a van. He'll be here at four."

"He will?"

"I thought it was better than waiting to get an appointment with the Salvation Army. He'll take the furniture too, though he might need to make two trips. But they're open late tonight. I checked. So it all can go."

"You've thought of everything," Rick said. All around him, the pieces of Dahlia's life were tumbling and hurling: the stretched-out leotard she wore to dance class on Saturday mornings; the crown and the boa from last Halloween's costume; rocks and acorns gathered on walks in the park; a single shoe covered with red glitter, from a pair that she had called her ruby slippers. Rick closed his eyes, let the sounds of shuffling and thumping lull him if not into sleep then into a kind of grief-induced trance.

"What about the hamsters?" Rick opened his eyes. There, in a duplex cage, lived Dahlia's three beloved hamsters—Rosie, Shiny, and Sunny. One of the two males—their gender evident from the enormous, even superfluous size of their testicles, so outsized on their tiny bodies—was spinning in the stationary wheel. The other male was burying something in a corner and the female was curled up in a corner. A bowl of seeds, a tube of water, and a thick carpet of cedar shavings completed their environment.

"The hamsters? I don't know." Dahlia had owned these animals for the last several months; since he had brought them home, there had not been a day she hadn't stroked, kissed, or held one. "We can keep them. I guess." Rick wasn't certain he wanted to do that. But he wasn't certain he wanted to get rid of them right away either.

"Pet shops are usually happy to get them," Allison said. "Isn't there one around here we could ask?"

"It's on Ninth Street." He capitulated easily. "Would you take care of bringing them there, though? I can't face it."

Allison looked at her brother, seated on the floor and hugging his knees. "Why don't you get out for a while? Take a walk or something?" She held a pristine-looking Raggedy Ann doll in one hand—Dahlia had been given the doll as a gift and had never liked it—and a Slinky in the other.

"It's too much work to do on your own."

"You're not helping anyway," Allison pointed out.

"All right. I'll get us something to eat. What do you want?"

"A sandwich or a muffin, I don't care. Just as long as you bring me an iced coffee. A big one."

Rick went down the stairs, hand running along the banister. How many times had Dahlia slid down its smooth wood? Even if Allison cleaned out her room, vaporized her belongings, Dahlia would never be gone from this house, her imprint was on it everywhere Rick looked. He made his way up the hill as far as Fifth Avenue. When he and Naomi had first moved here, there was a pizza place on the corner that sold no pizza—he later learned it was a Mafia front—and a funeral home opposite that. A few doors down, past the empty shops, was a bodega that specialized in incense and garishly painted statues of Jesus and a C-Town Supermarket whose dust-coated shelves were virtually empty. Now occupying those same retail spaces were stores selling lingerie from Italy, soap from France, handcrafted cards from

San Francisco, and a bistro-style restaurant with a raw bar up front. Things had certainly changed.

He turned left, headed past Union Street to Press, one of the new lunch places, where he ordered two grilled vegetable and mozzarella sandwiches, along with the iced coffee his sister had requested. Not that he cared what he ate, but Allison was working hard and would be hungry. A couple of times he had brought Dahlia here for a sandwich made with Nutella, one of her favorites. How to escape the persistent memories of his child? Not only did she inhabit the house, but the streets of the neighborhood bore her stamp too. He would no doubt remember places they had gone, things he had bought her, everywhere he went. Maybe he and Naomi should sell the house, move elsewhere, though where on God's earth that would be he had not a clue.

Back home, he brought the sandwiches and the iced coffee into the dining room.

"Allie?" he called up the stairs. "Allie, can you hear me?" Allison came to the top of the staircase.

"Did you get the iced coffee?" she asked. "I'm so thirsty."

"Got it."

Allison came downstairs. She had pulled her hair into a high ponytail, and he could see tiny dots of sweat on her upper lip.

"Are you all right?" she asked, looking at him carefully.

"All right? Yes. No. I don't know. I guess I'm as all right as anyone who killed his kid can be."

"Rick, you didn't kill her." Allison squeezed his arm tightly. "It was an accident. A freaky, horrible accident. You've been all over that already. The coroner's report, the doctors at Holy Name. They all say the same thing. 'Cause of death: accidental.' You have to stop talking like that."

"But if I'd pulled over. Tied her shoe like she asked."

"You didn't know, Rick. No one could have known what was going to happen."

"That's not what Naomi thinks," he said.

"Did she say so?"

"She didn't have to. I can tell. She barely speaks to me."

"Rick, I can't tell you what Naomi's going through. I can't even imagine it. But I know you aren't responsible for Dahlia's death."

"I was behind the wheel of the car, wasn't I?"

Allison had no answer for that.

They ate in the dining room, or rather, Allison ate and Rick watched her. His own sandwich sat untouched on its wrapping of waxed paper. He took a bite and then put it down. No taste, no taste at all. He was hungry, he could tell by the gnawing sensation in his stomach, the growls it made. But when he tried to eat, the result was the same. The lack of taste frightened him. It was like the taste of nothingness, of death. Would that be his life from now on? Naomi was barely eating either. Maybe both of them would just stop altogether like his mother had at the end of her life. No gun to the temple, no noose fashioned from a belt or curtain sash, no great dramatic gesture of any kind. Instead, just the quiet renunciation of a life that had become too painful to bear.

He remembered once, years before, reading a small item in the *New York Times* about a Long Island couple whose only son had drowned while on a school trip. The bereaved parents had gone into their garage and closed the door. Then they had gotten into their car and turned on the ignition. The police later said they were found holding hands. The idea held some appeal for him, though he and Naomi did not have a garage and instead coped with the complicated New York City choreography of alternate-side-of-the-street parking regulations and inexplicable tow-away zones. And he seriously doubted his wife would want to hold his hand.

"You're not eating," Allison observed. She had finished her sandwich and was draining the last of the iced coffee. He was sorry he hadn't thought to bring her two.

"No, I'm not."

"You should eat something."

"You're right. I should." Rick picked up the sandwich. It was now cold and the cheese had congealed into something rubbery and unappetizing. Still, he took a bite, slowly chewed, and swallowed it. "There. Not so bad." But in fact the absence of the taste scared him more than he wanted to tell his sister. He stood up, put his hands on the table. "I'm going out again."

"Okay." Allison looked at Rick's mostly uneaten sandwich. "What about this?"

"I guess you could wrap it and put it in the fridge."

"Where will you go?"

"I don't know. But I'll take my bike."

"Don't forget Henry is coming at four."

"Henry?"

"The guy with the van. Remember?"

"The van. Right." He looked at Allison then. "I don't think I can be here for that. Can you manage it by yourself?"

"Sure. Just make sure you leave me a set of keys so I can lock up." She wadded the napkins and sandwich papers and stuffed them into her empty plastic cup. "I'll be fine."

"Good." He turned to go, but then stopped and faced his sister again. "Thanks, Allison," he said, hugging her tightly. "Thanks a lot."

"It's all right," she said. "Just go."

"There's one more thing."

"What's that?" She pulled away and tilted her head back slightly to look up at him.

"If you find any pictures, you know, photographs in her room, don't throw them out, okay?"

"What made you think I would?" she said.

Outside, the day was hot but not humid. Pedaling along the quiet streets, Rick found he liked the feeling of the heat on his arms, his face. He wore neither hat nor sunglasses and the sun made him squint, but he didn't care. Instead of cycling toward the park, he headed in the other direction, down Carroll Street, past the stink of the Gowanus

Canal, through Carroll Gardens, and eventually into Brooklyn Heights. He considered riding past his office on Monroe Place but decided against it. Instead, he rode toward the Promenade that skirted the Hudson River. There were people walking by, as there were at most times of the day or night: a group of girls on Rollerblades; an elderly couple wearing straw hats; women pushing strollers; a guy about his age, only with lots more hair, with a baby in a Snugli. He looked away, toward the water and the buildings of lower Manhattan beyond that. He hadn't brought Dahlia here very often; only a few times, when she had visited his office, which was something she didn't like to do all that much. It reminded her of the pediatrician she visited, and those visits in turn made her think of shots or of having a long swab poked down her throat, as she was prone to frequent strep infections. Had she lived, they probably would have had her tonsils removed in the fall.

Rick pedaled on and on, in an effort to wear himself out. It was no use; he seemed to have built-up secret reserves of strength for just this moment. He kept riding, without feeling tired or thirsty. Having neglected to put on his watch this morning, he didn't know what time it was, but he was aware of the sun's progress over the city. He wanted it to get late and then dark. He didn't want to be anywhere near his house on Carroll Street when Harry—Henry?—came with his van to get Dahlia's furniture: a white bed and chest of drawers; a pink, green, and black rug shaped like a large wedge of watermelon that had come from the Pottery Barn catalog; a round table and pair of chairs from IKEA. He looped around the Promenade several times, then back toward the movie theater on Court Street. He locked his bike on a parking meter, paid for a ticket, walked into the theater in the middle of some action film that he would have loved as a kid.

The hero, a muscular, unshaven actor Rick did not recognize, punched, slapped, kicked, and bit his way out of every danger or enemy he faced. What would he have done about the SUV and the little girl sitting in the backseat who just happened to be tying her shoe at the wrong moment? Would he have pulled the driver—in this case the older woman with the puny, insistently yapping dog at her side—out of the car, pummeled her bloody and senseless?

Rick sat quietly mesmerized in the cool, nearly empty theater. He had bought a large tub of buttered popcorn, not to eat but simply because the smell, another reminder of his own childhood, was comforting. By the end of the film, the hero, whom Rick had still not been able to identify, was left standing alone, backlit against a vast and cloud-streaked sky. Without waiting for the credits, Rick stood and left. He deposited the popcorn in the trash and unlocked his bicycle. Dahlia's glittery pink Barbie bike had been downstairs in the hallway; he wondered whether Allison would have remembered to have that taken away too.

He pedaled back toward Park Slope. The sun had lowered and the sky had turned one of the pale, rosy colors that come before nightfall. He almost enjoyed not knowing the hour, being forced to guess and gauge from the quality of the light, the air. He rode back past the Gowanus over the Union Street Bridge, cut over to Carroll on Fourth Avenue.

His house was quiet and dark when he returned. Allison's guy with his van must have come and gone. Rick checked downstairs—the bicycle with its tasseled streamers on the handlebars was gone. She had thought of everything. He didn't want to go upstairs, to confront the reality of the stripped space above him, but he forced himself to do it anyway. He climbed the stairs slowly, waited for a few seconds in front of the closed door—who had thought to close it?—before putting his hand on the knob.

Rick had not been prepared for the jolt he would feel when he saw the empty room—its walls and windows bare, its floor naked. He was shocked to realize how much rage had fueled this act—rage at fate, rage at the SUV and its driver, rage at Naomi for leaving him to face this alone.

Naomi. It was the first time he had thought of her in hours. How the hell was she going to react when she saw not what he had done but what he had authorized? She would understand the violence implicit in his act. And she would understand, too, that she was, at least in part, its target. He had wanted to anger her, he realized, looking around the room, unfamiliar in its austerity, had wanted her to feel the anger he now felt. He didn't care what the consequences were; he was ready to take them on.

Rick turned and left the room—he did not close the door behind him—and took his time going down the stairs. He sat heavily on the couch and leaned his head back. Then he closed his eyes, and while he didn't actually sleep, he drifted, mercifully, to some other place where his daughter was not necessarily alive, but not dead either. He opened his eyes only when he heard the key—Naomi's key—turning in the lock.

Ever since that day when Lillian had first put her arms around him, Rick had felt like a time traveler who had discovered an alternate world existing alongside the one he had previously inhabited. That world seemed to mimic the one he had left behind, and its features were superficially the same. But underneath, in its secret, pulsing core, everything was different. The office, once his refuge and his haven, was now buzzing with an electrical charge, filled with the most insanely tantalizing sexual tension that kept his mind and his body humming.

He got hard the minute he walked in the door and saw Lillian's profile facing the computer screen, and he stayed that way for most of the day. Thank God for the white doctor's coat that he liked to wear over his shirt and tie; at least he could conceal himself. Their exchanges were muted and casual, for the collective benefit of his office mate, Helene Newmann, the patients, the UPS and FedEx deliverymen, but each word, each glance had a magnetic, even propulsive effect. He was hyperaware of her: talking on the phone, typing at the keyboard, showing people into the examination room. He inhaled the cologne—kind of sharp, musky, wholly unfamiliar—that she wore, tried to find moments to brush up against her or put his face close to her head of dark, wavy hair, the rough texture of which was so unlike Naomi's.

But despite the constant state of arousal in which their workdays put them, there had been only two subsequent occasions on which they had been able, like that first time, to go into Rick's office and lock the door behind them for a brief, heated interlude. Tonight, though, they would have more time. Tonight Jason was sleeping at his father's—since the aborted Christmas trip, Ramon was trying hard to heal his son's bruised affections—and Rick had lied to Naomi about having dinner with Jon, so they would be able to go back to Lillian's apartment and be alone together for at least a few hours.

On the crowded subway, Rick deliberately stood apart from her. He knew the address and would get off at the Forty-fifth Street station, just like she did. But he didn't want to run the risk of being seen with her in public; this seemed like a sensible precaution to take. After a few stops, she got a seat, and he watched covertly as she pulled out a copy of the *New York Post* from her bag and began to read. Her face was broader at the top, narrowing to a small, pointed chin, with dark, widely spaced eyes, a long, elegant-looking nose, full lips and a pair of beauty marks, one on each cheek.

She apparently treated each morning as if she were preparing for a Las Vegas casting call: bronze eyeshadow covered her lids, false lashes often fringed her eyes. She painted her lips cherry, scarlet, orange, or crimson, and she darkened the beauty marks that framed her lush-looking mouth. Rick was fascinated by her desire for artifice and for display; she wore leopard-print bras, satin panties, slips of magenta or teal, fishnet stockings with seams down the back. All things Naomi disdained.

But this wasn't about Naomi, Rick told himself. This was about survival, his own, for the moment, because that's what Lillian offered him: a reason to feel, to be alive, in the wake of Dahlia's idiotic death.

So he watched as she licked her finger to turn the page, and hooked a lock of hair back behind her ear. He thought about what she might have on under her clothes—she had promised him a surprise—and what he would do to her, with her, once they were alone together.

But when he actually was in the apartment—in a brick row house not unlike his own, except Lillian and her son occupied the top floor only—his desire suddenly wilted. In the office, Lillian was a three-dimensional fantasy, dressed in a midnight blue thong and risen from the pages of his boyhood magazines or a present-day Web site. Lillian in her own apartment was different; both more and less real to him. Through an open door was a glimpse of a narrow room that must have been Jason's. Posters of Derek Jeter and Sammy Sosa were on the wall; a hat rack held baseball caps from what looked like twenty different teams. Rick's throat suddenly ached. He didn't think he could stand to get any closer.

Instead, he looked around at the cheap sofa, the television that sat across from it, the ugly glass-topped coffee table, the thin, acrylic rug. He was ashamed of himself for noticing and judging these details, ashamed to think that such things might matter to him, that the disparity in their backgrounds was something he would care about. What a cliché his lust for her seemed at this moment. White, well-educated professional screwing the hot Hispanic office manager. Maybe he was using her after all, whatever else he may have told himself.

Lillian seemed not to notice his misgivings. She kissed his earlobe and helped him out of his coat. Her touch was instantly arousing; he relaxed a bit. Then she pulled him—gently—toward the kitchen, where a small round table was set for a meal. Tablecloth, white napkins, bud vase with a single, predictable, red rose. But her effort touched him.

"What's all this?" he asked, gesturing to the wineglasses, the flatware neatly flanking the gold-trimmed white plates.

"You're having dinner out tonight, right?" Rick nodded. "Well, then, you have to eat, don't you?"

"Are you going to cook? Now?" She had taken off her coat and the sight of her breasts in the tight pink sweater made him remember why he was here, what he had come for.

"It's all ready. I just have to heat it up." She turned to the refrigerator and pulled out a large, foil-covered bowl. "Paella," she said, smiling shyly. "You said you liked it."

"I do," said Rick. He watched as she transferred the contents of the bowl to a pot and placed it in the oven. Her movements in the kitchen were as efficient as those in the office.

"There. That won't take too long. And while we're waiting, we can just go into the bedroom."

He was all over her in a minute, yanking the sweater over her head, which caused her hair to rise up in wild, static-driven waves. Underneath, she wore a black bra made of shiny, stretchy material and sheer black panty hose with nothing underneath. They did not make it to the bedroom.

Shuddering as he lay over her, he kissed her forehead, her nose, her lips, and her chin. The cheap furnishings, the cliché of their situation, none of it mattered. She was keeping him alive, that's what she was doing. And Rick wanted to live.

Later, she gave him a flannel robe to wear while they ate the paella. He found he was hungry, starving in fact, and he ate two large platefuls of food. They went into the bedroom after dinner, and this time it was less frantic, more leisurely. Still, he was conscious of the time, of needing to return to Naomi, waiting patiently at home.

"It's getting late," he said, reluctantly pulling away from her and starting to dress. He wondered if he should shower; would he smell different somehow after having been with Lillian? But then how to explain his wet hair on a cold December night?

"I know." She sat up, pushed her hair away from her face. The makeup was somewhat smeared now, but she still looked good. Really good. "Your wife is waiting." That was the first time either of them had spoken out loud about Naomi.

"She'll be asleep." He checked his watch. "She usually is by this time."

"Am I the first?" She had relaxed back into the pillows and put her arms behind her head.

"The first?"

"The first person you cheated with."

"Yes," Rick said, eyes still on her recumbent form, the silky white robe she wore. He could stay here all night, stay here forever.

"And you've been married how long?"

"Sixteen years."

"She's lucky then. Ramon was screwing around by the end of the first year. Hell, maybe even before that. Turns out he was sleeping with my best friend. Maybe they did it at our wedding."

"But you stayed with him."

"I was pregnant. We had a baby." She pressed her hands against her face. "It's not easy to raise a son by yourself."

"I know."

"Oh God." Lillian got up, knotting the robe more securely around her waist. "I'm doing it again."

"Doing what?" He was dressed now. He just had to get his coat, his bag.

"Complaining about how hard it is without a husband when . . ."

"When I have to live with how hard it is without a child." He sat back down on the bed. Just another few minutes, he told himself. What difference would it make? Lillian sat down too and began stroking the hair back from his temples. But then he surprised both of them by gently enclosing her wrist with his fingers. The caress was stilled. "Lillian, what's in this for you? We've never talked about it."

"We've never talked about anything. We've been busy." She smiled. But she didn't look happy.

"We're talking now. Tell me. I want to know. What do you get from this?"

"You," she said simply. And then didn't say anything else.

"You're a beautiful, sexy woman," Rick said, choosing his words carefully. "And I'm grateful to you. But—" How would he say it to her?

"But you're not going to leave your wife."

"No, I'm not going to leave her. Not ever."

"Because of your daughter."

"That's right. Because of our daughter. Dahlia."

"What if she leaves you?"

"Naomi? Leave me? Why would she?"

"Because of me."

"You would tell her?" Rick's eyes searched her face for malice, for cruelty, but found none.

"Of course I wouldn't tell her," she said. "But even if I wanted her to know, I wouldn't have to tell her. At some point she'll just . . . know."

"What do you mean? How will she find out if no one tells her?"

"No one had to tell me about Ramon," she said. "I could read the writing on the wall."

Waiting for the train, Rick thought about what Lillian had said. Would Naomi really find out what he was doing? And if she did, would she leave him? He did not want that to happen, not at all. Yet he didn't want to stop what he was doing with Lillian either. Didn't want to and didn't plan to. He looked at his watch again; it was past eleven. He was counting on the fact that Naomi would be asleep. That way he wouldn't have to face her, not just then.

But by the time he had gotten off of the train and was walking up the hill to his house, he was already itching to see Lillian again, to squeeze her tight little ass in his hands, to push her down on all fours so he could plunge into her from behind.

The house was dark as he put his key in the lock; he closed the door behind him and locked it again. He stood for a moment looking up the stairs at the banister, whose curved shape he could just make out. Treading quietly, he made his way up to the room where his wife lay sleeping. He moved carefully, so he wouldn't wake her.

The next day there was a holiday party at Holy Name Hospital. Although he knew Naomi didn't usually go in on Saturday, she had told him she wanted to be there for that. She hadn't asked Rick if he would join her. Good thing. It would give him a day to pull himself together, without anyone around. Maybe by Sunday he would feel something like settled again.

8

Orange Juice

Estelle had not thought about how crowded the streets would be. So many people. And they were all moving so quickly. The gum-cracking young woman pulling a snowsuit-clad child along by the hand; the tall black man with the impeccably cut coat and the heavy leather case that banged his thigh as he walked; the teenage girls whose jackets were open, despite the cold, and whose electric-colored backpacks—hot pink, neon green, Day-Glo orange—seemed too heavy for their young bodies. All of them had somewhere to go, somewhere to be. So did Estelle. Her final destination—Brooklyn—and her purpose—to find Dahlia—propelled her forward, even if she wasn't certain of the actual path she would need to follow.

She moved slowly, making her way through the crowd. No one seemed to notice her hesitation though. A relief. She knew she did not look that disoriented—she was not, for instance, in her bathrobe or talking to herself. Still, she felt uneasy. She experienced periods of lucidity, followed, no interspersed really, with periods of confusion, and she could never predict when she would be able to locate herself in her surroundings or when everything would blur into an infuriating tangle of sensations.

She had managed to get herself to Broadway—she saw the green and white street sign, all the letters cooperating under her intense scrutiny. Broadway was a long street, she remembered that. It began way uptown, didn't it? And it went all the way downtown. If she continued along Broadway, she would eventually come to Manhattan's tip. To the water. And the bridge. But this was far, too far to walk, even with the comfortable sneakers on her feet. And her hands, though clenched in her pockets, were cold. She didn't think she could manage the gloves. The gloves were too much.

She kept walking at her tentative pace. The shops lining the streets were as interesting to her as the people she passed. A shoe repair place, with piles of worn shoes and boots heaped in the window, a hardware store advertising a sale on Benjamin Moore paint—didn't Benjamin have something to do with a key, with lightning? A supermarket: cardboard pictures of glazed hams and cooked turkeys decorated the big, plate glass window. She kept walking and came to a fruit stand. Pears were stacked high in one bin, lemons in another, grapefruit in a third. Estelle's stomach growled. She was hungry. She had not planned on being hungry. She had eaten her breakfast after all. But something about the effort of escaping and being outside in the fresh, cold air had caused her to feel the pangs of appetite. Now what?

She saw prices posted on the fruit—9s and 7s, 4s and 3s—but they made no sense at all. The twenty-dollar bill was in her shoe. Should she, could she go into the store, proffer the money, make a choice, and hope that she would not be cheated? Or worse, spotted for what she was: an escapee. Against the back row of the stall, pineapples stood lined up, their coarse, green stems springy and erect. Behind them were boxes of crackers, pretzels, and cookies.

Estelle hesitated before the door. A young woman, Oriental, smiled at her from behind the counter. Could it be the one from that place she was fleeing? And if so, would the woman recognize her? Her heart speeded up, *thump-thump-thump*. Estelle looked again, and the smile was still there. This decided her. She walked inside, hands still in her pockets as if she had not made up her mind to choose something, anything from the shelves. Choosing would be a decisive act, a commitment. Then she saw the bananas. Curved and yellow, they were as cheerful and benign as plastic toys. She reached for a small bunch and glanced quickly at the woman. The woman nodded her head, a small, deferential gesture. Yes, Estelle thought, I can do this. I can. She took two bananas—two would be enough, she hoped—and continued down the aisle, bananas clutched to her side. She stopped at a refrigerator case and selected a small carton of orange juice. Tropicana. There was a little girl in the grass skirt on the carton. Estelle recognized her, Tropic-Anna. She had been on the carton for years, and here she was again, like a friend waiting to greet her. Estelle was irrationally happy now. Bananas, juice. She had provisions for her journey, food and drink.

She stood in line and as she waited, she knelt down to extract the money from her shoe. It took a few seconds but there it was, moist and probably a bit smelly. No matter. Worse was that she didn't think she could get up. She remained in a crouch, her legs starting to hurt, and then her feet too. She thought she might topple over onto the floor, when a strong arm—she looked up to see that it was attached to a stocky Oriental man—was reaching down, pulling her toward him. She was up then, up and on her feet. Thank God. God and her savior, who offered her a nod much like the one the woman behind the counter had.

When it was Estelle's turn, she handed the woman the money and put her modest purchases on the counter for bagging. A look down at the candy yielded another random impulse: she added a package of strawberry gum, for Dahlia, and a bar of Hershey's chocolate for herself. She loved chocolate. Hershey's was far from the best, but it was here, it would do.

The Oriental woman handed her back several bills and some coins. Estelle was afraid to put the money in her shoe again. Next time, she might not be able to get up if she bent down. She transferred one of the gloves to the other pocket and reserved a pocket just for the money, coins first, jangling pleasantly, and then the bills, folded in half. She didn't bother to count them, because the whole process of counting had eluded her now; even the attempt would make her dizzy and sick.

Estelle left the store with the bag swinging on her arm. She reached in and snapped the bananas apart. Slowly, she peeled one and ate it. Delicious. More delicious than anything she had eaten in . . . she didn't know how long. Maybe it wasn't just the food at that place but the place itself that caused the food to lose its taste, its savor. But here, in the relative freedom of the chilly morning, she was hungry and able to enjoy what she consumed.

Eating as she tried to make her way through all those people proved difficult. She stopped at a corner and peered down a side street. There was the bright pointed turret of a tower, the shiny gleam of a slide. A playground. She could sit in the playground and eat. Estelle began walking with greater determination toward the spot, which turned out to be almost empty this morning, just a lone black woman watching as a small boy in a puffy down parka ran up and back, up and back, the whole length of the space.

Estelle sat down on one of the benches and slowly ate another banana and then opened the bar of chocolate. The sky was a weak, wintry color, somewhere between blue and gray, and she watched as a few cigar-shaped clouds moved across it. The chocolate was making her thirsty, so she attacked the orange juice container. It was hard to open, and she nearly tore at it with her teeth but finally her recalcitrant fingers were able to prize open the spout. There was a straw attached to the carton, but it was small and thin; Estelle worried that it would drop into the opening and be lost. After a minute, she realized it was meant to be poked through a special spot on the container. So it hadn't been necessary to open the spout after all; she had wasted her time. Getting the straw into the container took several jabs, more precious seconds wasted.

Such a major effort for such a minor task. But it was essential, because it allowed Estelle to drink without dribbling. Dribbling meant she was regressing, giving in to the helpless, muddled child who threatened to engulf more and more of her mind, her will, every day.

The orange juice was cold and satisfying. She sucked it up with noisy, slurping sounds, glad no one was around to hear them. When she was through, she deposited the banana peels, the empty carton, and the candy wrapper in the trash. The little boy had climbed into his stroller now; the woman was wheeling him away. Watching the boy made Estelle impatient to see Dahlia, so she got up from the bench and prepared to continue on her journey. She touched the package of gum, safe in her pocket. Thinking of how Dahlia would react to it actually made her smile, a real smile this time.

Estelle wished she could walk along one of these streets, where there were fewer people. But she didn't know where she was exactly. Broadway was at least familiar, so she made her way back to the busy avenue and kept walking in the same direction she had been heading earlier. The juice had chilled her, but the exertion of moving along and at the same time avoiding being pushed or hit—a man on a bicycle crossed right in front of her, narrowly missing her sneaker-clad feet— caused her to grow warm again. She was pleasantly sated from her meal, and up ahead she saw the big round dot that indicated a subway stop. Inside the dot was a clear white number. The number 1. The subway train might be the answer to her problem. The subway was fast, the subway was cheap. The subway could take her all the way to Brooklyn, of this she was sure.

But as easily as it answered one problem, the idea of the subway gave birth to a whole litter of others. How to manage the stairs? The fare? Which train should she take? And where would she get off? Asking to go to Brooklyn wasn't enough. She needed more information. She could see the house so clearly now, the aged bricks of the facade, the brownstone stoop leading up to the glass-fronted double doors, the tree that grew out front. But she didn't know the name of the street. And, all at once, she was aware of needing to urinate.

This realization—the uncomfortable pressure in her bladder— made her stop where she was, even though this caused the man directly behind to bump up against her back and then move around her, not with an apology but a muttered curse. She had not thought about what she would do in this event. Not thought about it at all. But here it was, a clear and pressing need to which she had to attend. She could not hope to find her way in the maze of trains and stations without first finding a restroom.

Estelle turned and made her way back to the playground. She needed a place where she could sit and think, to puzzle out what she might do next. She returned to the bench and sat down. As she sat looking blankly around at the slide coiled like a corkscrew, the few pigeons that hovered close in the hopes of some crumbs, she saw a square black-roofed building near the far entrance. What was in there? Didn't those buildings house bathrooms? Estelle got up quickly and walked over to investigate.

The black metal door was locked, but there was a small, dirty window and she was able to look inside. Two white sinks, a tile floor, two stalls. Behind those two stalls were toilets. But the door. The door was locked. Frantically, she tried the handle again. The window was shut and protected by metal bars besides. She would not be able to slip through. Not this time. The pressure from her bladder grew stronger. She imagined it expanding inside her until it began to crowd her other organs and its membrane grew dangerously thin, almost transparent. She shifted uncomfortably from one foot to the other. The pressure kept mounting.

Estelle was so frustrated she wanted to weep. But weeping would help nothing. She looked around the deserted playground once more and made her decision. Ducking around the back of the building, she lifted her coat. Pulling down her pants as little as she had to, she squatted, urinating a big puddle that soaked the ground. Urine splashed the backs of her calves and ran in rivulets around her sneakers. Disgusting but necessary. She stood up.

The immediate need had been met. But now she was flooded with shame. Even though no one had been here to see, to witness her regression, she knew. She was an old, deranged woman, reduced to relieving herself in public like a dog or a horse. She returned to the bench—her bench, as she now considered it—and sat down. Her sneakers left wet footprints behind her.

Estelle sat on the bench for a long time. She would not make it to

Brooklyn, she saw that now. She was not capable of it. She could go back to the big building, the home, that's what they called it—though anything less homelike she could not imagine—where it would be warm again, where there would be a toilet and a shower too, to wash herself. But she did not move. The light brightened and then waned. At some point, the playground was populated again by clusters of children, who dumped their backpacks by the fence and went tearing off to the jungle gym, the swings. The sight of these children aroused the ache to see Dahlia, but still Estelle did not move. The sky grew darker now, the children dispersed, but she remained on her bench, sorrowful and cold.

She would not have moved had not the policeman approached her. He was young and not very tall. She could hear the sound made by his heavy shoes in the quiet playground.

"Need some help, ma'am?" He had stopped in front of her and was looking down where she sat. Estelle saw that his dark blue policeman's cap was tilted back on his head a little to reveal the thick head of blond hair. His mother must have loved that hair when he was a child; she probably ran her fingers through its buttery smoothness a dozen times a day.

"No." She waited for him to leave, but he didn't.

"It's getting cold," he observed. "Don't you want to go home?"

"Home?" Estelle said. His eyes looked kind; the tip of his nose was pink with cold. "I don't have a home."

"No home? Then do you want me to help you find a shelter for the night? It's going down into the teens later. You don't want to spend the night here."

Yes I do, thought Estelle. This is my bench. This is my home. But she could see that he would not leave, so she reluctantly stood up. Her knees were stiff; it was hard to stand. The young policeman took her arm, and she let him lead her somewhere, anywhere, which turned out to be a rather derelict building with bright fluorescent lights and scuffed linoleum underfoot. It reminded her of the big place she had left. Maybe this was his home.

Estelle sat down on another bench, this one thickly painted with dark, clotted-looking paint, and accepted the coffee and doughnut the policeman provided for her. The coffee was not very hot, but she drank it anyway. She supposed she wouldn't have to worry about finding a bathroom this time. The doughnut was covered in powdered sugar. It got all over her hands and her coat, but it was the first thing she had eaten since the bananas and the chocolate and so she was glad to have it, messy as it was. She had just finished the last sticky bit and was brushing away the remnants of the sugar when a woman burst into the room, accompanied by the blond officer.

"Yes, that's her! Thank God she's all right!" The woman looked vaguely familiar, though Estelle could not at first place her.

"Did you want some coffee?" Estelle said, holding out her empty cup to the woman. "It's not too hot, but it's good just the same. And I'm sure they would give you a doughnut if you asked. Jelly. With powdered sugar on top." The woman worked in the home. Though Estelle could not remember the name, she recognized the face and, even more, the strident, grating voice. She had heard it in the hallways, in the big room, in her dreams.

"Mrs. Levine!" said the woman indignantly. "Where did you go? We were all so frightened. Something could have happened to you." She was helping Estelle up and talking to the officer at the same time. "Something did happen to me," Estelle wanted to say, "but you wouldn't understand what it was."

"She must have slipped out sometime this morning. After breakfast. At occupational therapy they thought she was in physical therapy and the physical therapist thought she was in arts and crafts. Jesus, the whole place was in an uproar. I had to call her daughter. She came racing in all the way from Brooklyn." The woman was shaking her head, recalling the confusion of the day.

"Did you say Brooklyn?" Estelle asked, her voice clear and firm. The word *daughter* had her confused, as it often did. Who was her daughter again? But Brooklyn was something she could latch on to;

Brooklyn she understood. "Brooklyn. That's where I was trying to go." She turned to the officer with the blond hair and the pink nose. After all, he had treated her with such respect and courtesy; he hadn't seemed to mind about the urine splattered on her shoes and legs, hadn't even mentioned it. "Can you take me there please? Now?"

9

Pink Room

Naomi and Rick met at Vassar in the late 1970s. She had been a good student in high school and was accepted by both Smith and Cornell too. But if she left New York State and went to school at Smith in Massachusetts, she would have had to sacrifice the sizable cash prize that came with her Regents Scholarship Award. Moreover, the crystalline winter day on which she had visited Smith made her uneasy. Everything was too perfect: the small wooden structures that looked more like the model homes in some artfully reconstructed historic village than actual college buildings, the impossible sheen of the waxed floors in those structures, the crisp fields of snow reflecting the sun in such an unfriendly, blinding way, the fact that all the girls and women she met—aged from seventeen to seventy—wore what amounted to a kind of uniform: black velvet hairbands; skirts and jumpers of stiff denim or corduroy; cotton turtlenecks imprinted with ladybugs, hearts, or in one case, mice. Naomi, who had chosen to wear her perfectly faded jeans with the hand-embroidered butterflies on the pockets, a black angora sweater, and her dark red cowboy boots to the interview, felt distinctly out of place.

Cornell had greater appeal; when she visited Ithaca one weekend, she loved the way the campus was tucked into the surrounding hills, the clean, vivacious character of the place. But on Saturday night, a group of rowdy frat boys had burst into the dorm room where she had been staying with a friend. Cackling and whooping, they hurled pillows and rolls of toilet paper at the frightened girls before unzipping their flies and spraying the walls, floor, and furniture. Nothing could have induced her to go to Cornell after that.

In comparison, Vassar seemed both welcoming and familiar. The campus was beautiful, with hundred-year-old trees, well-tended lawns, a Gothic-style library right across from the main building. But she saw faces in many colors, clothing in many styles; she didn't think she'd be such an anomaly here. Moreover, it was just ninety miles or a two-hour train ride away from New York City. Her escape route, should she need it, was easily at hand.

Although it had been coed for a number of years, Vassar still felt like a women's college. She had heard rumors that many of the boys who went there were gay. This bothered Naomi not at all. Her best friend all through high school, Bruce Anastasi, had come out during their junior year, and she thought he was the sweetest, most considerate boy she had ever met. She was even campaigning to get him to join her at Vassar, though he had his heart set on going to school someplace warm, like L.A. or Florida. Naomi was only mildly interested in boys in high school, although she was very interested in men. She found her male teachers, fathers of her friends, and friends of her parents more compelling than the boys she met at school, though she was sensible enough to know that nothing good could come of such infatuations, at least not then. So she was content to wait until the boys she knew grew up, lost their rough edges and their loutishness. Until then, she had friends like Bruce with whom she could hang out.

Falling in love with Rick, then, was a surprise. The first time she saw him was in the Wood Reading Room up on the library's top floor. The room was one of the only ones in the building where smoking was allowed, and although Naomi didn't smoke, she liked the seclusion and quiet of the place, and began to make a habit of heading up there after dinner at the Dining Center. Sophomore year she was taking The Russian Novel in Translation, and every night she would head for the same comfortable seat that faced the window overlooking the campus. She read steadily, with only short breaks, from eight until midnight: *War and Peace. Crime and Punishment. The Brothers Karamazov. Oblomov.* "The Overcoat."

One night, however, she climbed the narrow stairs to find that her usual seat was taken. A tall boy, oblivious to her sense of displacement, was sitting in her chair, a science textbook spread open on his lap. His wavy brown hair was abundant on the sides and back of his head, but it had already started to thin, just perceptibly, in the front. At thirty he would no doubt have a bald spot. He had very long lashes for a boy. As Naomi stood staring at him, he looked up and smiled in a curious and friendly way. She realized she was being rude and chose a seat nearby. Every now and then she glanced at him. He read with what appeared to be great concentration, shifting forward only slightly as he turned a page. By eleven-thirty, the room had emptied out. Naomi and the tall boy were the only ones left. Slouched into the chair, with her cowboy boot–clad feet propped up on the low table, she kept reading. Finally, just before midnight, she stood and stretched. He looked up and caught her eye again.

"Time to head out," he said easily.

"I know. I wouldn't want to have to spend the night here."

"There are worse places," the boy said.

Naomi said nothing, but busied herself gathering her things. " 'I cannot sleep unless I am surrounded by books.' " Naomi looked up quizzically. "Borges said that," explained the tall boy. He had a hesitant, slightly self-conscious demeanor that Naomi decided she liked. Many of the boys she had met here, the straight ones anyway, were pretty conceited. They acted like the girls should be grateful for any shred of attention shown to them. But this boy was different.

"You like Borges?" she said. He had move closer to her now; if she reached out her arm, she could have touched him.

"Borges and some of those other Latin American writers too. Cortázar. Gabriel García Márquez."

"I loved *One Hundred Years of Solitude*," Naomi said. "I've read it three times."

"If I buy you a beer at the Mug sometime, will you tell me which parts you liked best?" said the boy. He was smiling down at her now, smiling with that same open, friendly smile he had given her when she walked in.

"When?" Matthew's Mug was the bar on campus; it owed its name to Matthew Vassar, the nineteenth-century brewer who had founded the college.

"How about now?" But Naomi had already known he was going to say that, just like she had already known that she was going to say yes.

They become a couple after that, but slowly. Rick courted her patiently: a plastic pumpkin filled with candy corn at Halloween, a foil-wrapped chocolate turkey at Thanksgiving. For her birthday, he presented her with a potted gloxinia plant, its bell-shaped blossoms a deep, velvety purple edged in white, and an autographed, hardbound first edition of *One Hundred Years of Solitude.*

"Where did you even find this?" she had said, leafing through the pages reverently.

"I have my sources," he said. And smiled.

They saw movies at the Juliet movie theater across the street from the campus, studied together in the library. On Friday afternoons, when their classes were through for the week, they would stroll off the campus, along Collegeview Avenue until they reached Main Street, with its slightly squalid, post–urban renewal charm. Naomi loved the walk, on which she could glimpse the Hudson River coming in and out of view as the street rose and dipped. They passed Laundromats and bars with hand-painted wooden signs: Suds 'n' Stuff, Sit & Sip. There were thrift shops, where they shopped for vintage clothes: a tuxedo and cashmere vest for Rick; a black velvet evening coat lined in ivory satin with a matching muff for Naomi. All together, the purchases came to less than twenty dollars.

They had most of their meals together, at the Dining Center or sometimes at a local restaurant, like the Little Brauhaus, where they ate cold veal chops and sauerkraut, or the diner or the Italian restaurant with its red flocked wallpaper and generous servings of clams marinara.

It wasn't until December that they actually slept together, the first time for each of them. Not that they hadn't wanted to before that. But both had roommates and both wanted the experience to consist of more than a hurried shedding of clothes, a hasty coupling. They considered renting a room at Alumnae House, the Tudor-style inn on Raymond Avenue, where they sometimes went for Vassar Devils—slices of chocolate cake covered in chocolate ice cream and fudge sauce—but neither had the nerve. Then a friend of Rick's, a senior with a large single in Cushing Hall, was going home for the weekend and offered Rick the use of his room. When Naomi came to Cushing at the appointed time, she hesitated in front of the door. She was excited but nervous too: What if she disappointed him? Or he disappointed her? Maybe she should have stopped to get a six-pack of beer before showing up. Finally, she knocked.

"Hi," he said with his easy, sweet smile.

"Hi yourself." She was wearing the velvet coat she had bought at the Salvation Army. It was not warm enough, and her hands were icy.

"Don't be scared," he said. He locked the door once she was inside. Naomi looked around the room. The lights were out, but there were several squat, pillar-shaped candles burning brightly. She thought she detected the aroma of vanilla. Her favorite.

"Did you bring those?" she asked.

"Uh-huh. And these too." He gestured to indicate a bottle of massage oil—also vanilla scented—and a box of condoms that were waiting near the bed. Spread over its rumpled surface was an Indian print spread she recognized from Rick's room. A Bob Dylan album was playing softly on the stereo. Other albums—Linda Ronstadt, the Rolling Stones—were laid out nearby.

"Here," he said, taking the coat by the shoulders, "let me help you out of that."

Underneath it Naomi wore only a black satin slip with lace edging and thin straps. She had purchased it on another trip to the Main Street thrift store. Rick stared before reaching over to slide a finger under one of the straps. "And that too," he said softly as he leaned down to kiss her neck.

They got engaged just after they graduated, and married shortly after that. At the bridal shower, at which Naomi received two toasters, a food processor, and a bread maker, several of her friends remarked that she and Rick already seemed married. It was true. Naomi was surprised by how comfortably their lives seemed to mesh and blend. She had imagined that love was accompanied by more Sturm und Drang: quarrels, recriminations, dramatic partings, luxurious reconciliations. But none of this characterized her relationship with Rick. He was easy to please and pleased her easily. They began their lives together in Philadelphia, where he attended podiatry school at Temple and she pursued a graduate degree in English literature at Penn. Later, they moved to Brooklyn, bought the house, and began restoring it together. There were, of course, detours along the way: Naomi's disillusionment with graduate school, her repeated miscarriages. But when Dahlia came along, everything seemed to glide back into place. And then, in a single, unbelievably prosaic moment, Dahlia had died, and everything changed.

Naomi stood on the top of the stoop, looking up Carroll Street. Always there were the two church spires, stacked in neat progression as she looked up the hill. The first was the thick, sturdy tower of the Catholic church on the corner of Sixth Avenue; the more graceful and elongated of the two belonged to the Dutch Reformed church on the corner of Seventh. She had never actually gone into either of them, nor did she especially want to, but that didn't diminish the visual appeal they had for her, the rush she felt every time she looked and found them there. She loved to see them etched cleanly against the sky:

when the sun hit them brightly, the bricks and stone of which they were built seemed to warm and mellow. On gray days, the spires took on the grainy, gray cast of the light. Clouds made an appealing backdrop for them; mist could shroud them with a soft and hazy cover. Even at night she could dimly make them out, their solidity and mass smudged charcoal against the darkness. She looked at them whenever she left the house and whenever she entered it. They were both beacons, calling her home, and anchors, fixing, ordering, and organizing the world beyond her door.

Today was no different. In the waning light, the two spires appeared crisp and nearly black. Then she took out her keys and opened the door to the house.

"I'm in here," Rick called from the living room. Naomi walked in to find him sitting in the dark. The ceiling fans were on, though, and sent a pleasant breeze through the room.

"What are you doing?" she asked.

"Nothing." Naomi turned away, toward the stairs. "Naomi, wait." Rick had gotten up, was following behind her. "There's something I want to tell you."

"I'm listening," she said, but she crossed her arms, folding them in and over herself.

"Allison was here today." Naomi waited silently. "She wanted to help."

"Help what?"

"Me. You."

"Well, I don't want her help."

"But she's already done it."

"Done what?" She heard the hardness in her own voice as she asked the question. Heard it and didn't care how it sounded.

"The room." Rick took a long breath. "Dahlia's room."

"What about Dahlia's room? She didn't go in there, did she? You didn't let her touch anything, did you?"

"I told her she could."

"Could what? What did you tell her she could do?" Naomi was

yelling now; she wondered irrelevantly if Jack and Margie, the elderly couple who lived next door, could hear her.

"I told her she could clean out the room."

"Clean out the room?" Naomi's voice dropped suddenly. "You told your sister she could clean out Dahlia's room without asking me?"

"Yes." Rick paused. "I did." Naomi ran up the stairs, pulled the door open. The emptiness she saw there was like seeing her daughter dead all over again. The furniture, the toys, the clothes were all gone. Curtains, rug swept into the void.

"How could you?" she wailed. "How dare you?" Only the walls, painted pale pink, remained intact. What had they done with everything? She wanted it back, all of it. Every plastic teacup, every broken crayon. She would find out where they had taken the things, tell whoever it was that it had been a mistake. She would do this, she could do this—retrieve the remnants of her daughter's life even as she could never retrieve her.

Naomi backed out of the room and closed the door. She marched into the room she had shared with Rick since they had bought the house and began pulling books down from a shelf that stood in one corner. Here was one book with substantial weight and heft: *The Complete Works of Robert Frost*. Hadn't he bought that for her? Standing at the top of the stairs, she pitched it down. *Thwack*. It made a satisfying sound as it hit the floor. She heard Rick come out into the hall, but she had gone back to the bedroom in search of more books. The second one landed near the first. The third hit Rick in the stomach. But the blow seemed to galvanize rather than hurt him, and he came running up the stairs after her.

"What the hell are you doing?" he asked, breathing hard, as if a single flight of stairs had winded him.

"Doing? What am I doing? How about what you're doing? What you did?" She was holding two more books tightly in each hand but she didn't throw them. Yet.

"I was trying to help."

"Help? Help what?"

"Help us get through this." Naomi stood very still. She dropped the books to the floor, where they landed with a soft thud.

"Help us get through this," she repeated in a mean, mimicking voice. "Well, let me tell you something," she said in her normal tone. "I don't want to get through this. There is no getting through it. Or over it, under it, around it. Dahlia is dead, don't you get it? Dahlia is dead and you as good as killed her." There, she had said it, said the dark, hateful thing she had been harboring, brooding over, ever since Dahlia had died. She began to cry then, harsh, ragged sobs that made her shoulders shake and her chest heave.

"Don't you think that's what I've thought too? Every fucking minute since it happened?"

Naomi raised her face to look at him. She had meant for her words to wound him. But the impulse was derailed by what he had just told her. Wanting to hurt him was not the same as watching him want to hurt himself. How had she not realized how horrible all this had been for Rick? She had been so busy blaming him that she had lost sight of that.

"You've been so miserable," she murmured. There was the room, of course, the room he had let his sister destroy. She was still angry about it. What was a room, though, compared to a child? The white bed, green table and chairs. She mourned them but knew they wouldn't bring Dahlia back.

"Yes. I have." Rick sat down on their bed, and then stretched his legs out so that he was semi-reclining. He was still wearing his shoes, and his heels pressed against the coverlet. Naomi stared at him. He was such an orderly, even fastidious person; in all the years that they had been together, she had never seen him put his shoes on this bed, any bed. She sat down next to him and gently uncoiled her body so that it lay alongside his. Then, putting her face to his chest, she wept— with him this time—for Dahlia.

10

Christmas Shopping

Lillian Acevedo stood in front of the sink, washing the dishes from the night before. After Rick had left, she had been too tired to bother, so she had double-locked the door behind him, gone back into the bedroom, and almost immediately fallen asleep. She woke early the next day, refreshed, but sad too. She missed Jason, who would be with his father all weekend. She was sleeping with another woman's husband, a woman who had lost a child, no less. The day was gray and cold.

But Lillian hadn't let herself wallow. She had gotten up, showered, and dressed in her favorite tight jeans, the ones with the rawhide laces she tied tightly over her flat stomach, and her zebra-striped top. She changed the sheets, bundled the bedding and the dirty clothes for a trip to the Laundromat on Fourth Avenue later that day, ate a bowl of generic-brand cornflakes. Not as good as Kellogg's but substantially cheaper. While she was out, she would run a few errands. Maybe later she could do a little straightening up in Jason's room. Would he notice if she got rid of just a few of the plastic dinosaurs? He never played with them anymore. How about the trucks? There were so many. Feeling blue was something you could fend off with energy and activity. And she was doing just that. She finished her cornflakes and put the bowl in the sink along with last night's dishes.

Lillian washed the wineglasses first, then the plates. They were white with gold trim, her best china, given to her by her former best friend, Tiffany, when Lillian and Ramon had gotten married. Tiffany had been her friend since ninth grade; she was the maid of honor at Lillian's wedding. That she was sleeping with Ramon was a piece of information that Lillian hadn't discovered until somewhat later on. But when she did, she yelled at Tiffany, called her names. Bitch. Slut. Brouhita, which was what Lillian's grandmother had always said of any woman who crossed or angered her. Little witch. She even broke one of the plates, hurling it across the room, not to hit Tiffany but to make it clear just how angry she was. That stopped in a hurry. Bad enough she was losing a friend. Did she have to lose the dishes too?

Funny, though, that although she had ended the friendship with Tiffany, she hadn't been able to end things with Ramon. Not then. He had apologized, of course, got down on his knees, wrapped his strong arms around her thighs and pressed his face into her belly, told her that it was all Tiffany's fault, she had come on to him, begged him, un-zipped his pants, started doing all those things with her tongue, *Dios mío*, that no guy on the planet could resist. Even describing it got him all hot again, only this time he was where he belonged, with Lillian, whom he loved so much. He was crazy to have cheated on her, he'd never do it again, he swore. Pulling himself up, he faced her and pushed the straps from her top aside, burying his face in her breasts, licking first, then nipping. He made her crazy with desire, always had. So Lillian forgave him. That time, and the time after that, and third time too. Not that he was betraying her with Tiffany anymore; he had moved on, to greener pastures, brighter skies. Why confine yourself to your wife's best friend when there was a whole world of women just waiting for the sweet magic you could make on their dumb, trust-ing bodies? And hers had been the dumbest, the most trusting.

Lillian was twenty when she first met Ramon. Twenty and a junior at Hunter College in Manhattan. Not some dumb-ass business or tech-nical school, the kind that advertised on the number 4 subway train that took her from the Bronx to East Sixty-eighth Street. Hunter was the real thing: a big, important school; the best of the city schools, Doris Del Rey, her guidance counselor at Morris High School, told her.

Perfect for a smart girl like Lillian whose parents didn't happen to have a bank account that matched their daughter's intellect. But Hunter would do just fine. She could study real subjects, like philosophy and Northern Renaissance painting, not just accounting or computers. Freshman year had been a bit of an adjustment, but in her sophomore year she picked a major—political science—and by her junior year, she had hit her stride. Her professors liked her, she had a slew of new friends, the commute back and forth to the Bronx was just added study time; she made the dean's list two semesters in a row. She had been thinking about graduate school—law, international relations— and had gotten some encouragement from her teachers. Meeting Ramon had changed everything.

He was in one of her classes, Constitutional Politics, and the first time he opened his mouth to respond to the professor's query, she had swiveled completely around in her seat to take a look at the face, the mouth, the throat from which that deep, sexy voice had emerged. Tall, tight dark curls, skin somewhere between café au lait and cocoa. A dark jacket over a white T shirt; the shirt was pulled tight over the lean, muscled chest. He caught her looking, stopped whatever he was saying to the professor to give her a slow, appraising nod before he continued. He waited for her after class, and she followed him to a coffee shop where she sat, raptly, across from him, while he described his ambitions—big ones—for using his degree as a stepping-stone into grad school and then a political career. He was only two years older than she was, but he seemed so sure of himself, of his plans.

Ramon lived in Sunset Park, Brooklyn, where he had grown up, had managed to avoid the drugs and gangs on the street, and planned to be their next councilman or district leader. They had both ordered coffee, but she let hers sit, cooling, then cold. Around his neck he wore a thin gold chain, from which was suspended a tiny crucifix. She had the irrational but overwhelming urge to take it in her mouth, sucking until she extracted the liquid sweetness she was sure it possessed. It took all of two dates with him before the crucifix was dangling not far from her lips as Ramon moved gracefully above her supine body.

They were a couple from then on, meeting after classes and on weekends in Manhattan, a convenient midpoint between the Brooklyn apartment he shared with his parents and the Bronx one she shared with hers. Still, as crazy in love as she was, she had no intention of letting herself get sidetracked from her professional plans. But Ramon was both lazy and sloppy when it came to birth control and did his best to avoid the condoms that she bought and insisted he wear.

"Oh come on, baby. It's like putting on a Baggie or something. I hate to wear that thing," he said, nudging her gently with the tip of his penis. "Why can't you go on the pill? Like all the other girls?" They were both naked in his boyhood bedroom, his parents conveniently out for the evening, the posters of athletes and rock stars looking benignly down on them.

"You mean the ones who are going to get blood clots and breast cancer? Those girls?" The condom was sitting on the pillow, still in its foil package, nowhere near anyplace where it might actually do her some good.

"Lillian," he crooned, pushing his way in a little farther. "Come on, *mamacita*. Just this once. How can it hurt?"

It didn't hurt at all; in fact it was sublime. But it did result in her getting pregnant. Pregnant. Not yet twenty-one, not yet finished with college. She couldn't believe this had happened to her of all people: Lillian Consuela Hernandez, class president, valedictorian, up-and-coming attorney, international affairs adviser, or foreign correspondent.

She made the best of it, though. Married Ramon before she started to show, in a long, lace-decked white dress with a veil and a train. Moved to Brooklyn with him, set up housekeeping in a small apartment in a row house in Sunset Park. She still had her goals, planned to finish school, anyway, baby or not. Which she did, despite the fact that everything took longer than she expected. Way longer. She didn't graduate with her class but stretched things out over the summer, into the next fall. It was worth it, though, worth every bit of her effort. She had the guy, she had the baby, and she had the degree.

But she did find that her enthusiasm for the next phase—graduate school—had waned. Once she had Jason, her priorities changed, not in incremental shifts but all at once, like the radical movement of the tectonic plates her professor had so vividly described in the geology class she had aced. Jason was a big, easy baby, weighing almost ten pounds when he was born. He had Ramon's dark curls and her dimples, but his light yellow-green eyes were all his own. And how they lit when they saw her, hands and feet waving in their synchronized, frantic dance of joy when she walked into any room where he was.

She loved him so much, this plump-thighed, delicious boy of hers, loved kissing his fat cheeks, his baby tummy, his feet, his nose, his forehead, even his perfect little lips, though she worried perhaps that she should not, maybe it was too much pleasure to be coming from her, through her, to him. Still, once in a while she indulged, stealing tiny kisses, like sips of heaven, from his adorable baby mouth. How could she leave this baby to go to classes or the library? It would all have to wait. But no more babies for a while. When she was healed from the birth, she had herself fitted for an IUD. If she couldn't trust Ramon, she'd have to take care of things for herself.

It turned out she couldn't trust him about a lot of things. Oh, he loved the baby, all right, was happy to toss him up in the air to elicit that chortle of infant joy, buy him some expensive and wholly inappropriate toy, which Lillian would later have to confiscate—and then endure the baby's screams. Ramon was fine with the easy part, the photo ops. But when it came to the diapers, the ear infections, the sleepless nights, he was not much help.

She remembered an afternoon when Jason had thrown up on her six times and Ramon refused to hold him while Lillian took a quick shower.

"It's the playoffs," he said, as if that explained everything. Lillian looked at him stretched out in front of the TV, Budweisers ringed around him, a bowl of Doritos on the table. Instead of arguing, she called her mother, who made the long trek from the Bronx; during the hour that it took for her to get there, the baby threw up two more times. "Jesus, can't you do something with him?" Ramon frowned. "Do I have to go to a bar to watch the game?"

"Not a bad idea," Lillian had said, handing the squirming, whimpering baby to her mother before closing the bathroom door and stepping under the shower's hot spray. When she emerged, her mother was walking the baby up and down the room. Though the beers and the Doritos remained where they had been, the television was turned off and Ramon was nowhere in sight.

"Did he say when he'd be back?" Lillian finished toweling off her hair and reached for her son. His head rested on his grandmother's shoulder, but when he saw Lillian, he lifted his face and gestured toward her.

"What's the hurry?" her mother said, handing Lillian the baby. "With him here, you'll have two babies. Right now there's only one."

"What is it with you guys?" Lillian looked at Jason, whose dark hair was stuck to his face with sweat. "Don't you ever grow up?" Jason whimpered. Underneath his neck it was sticky and sweaty too. "Do you need a bath, *papi?*" She carried him into the bathroom, pulled out the plastic infant tub, and set it in the regular tub to fill. "Let Mama wash you off, make you nice and clean." She started taking off his clothes, unfastening his diaper. Her mother was right. Having Ramon around did make it seem like she had two babies instead of one.

What finally did it? Made her snap, pushed her to the limit, drove her over the edge? She couldn't remember, really; it had not been one single defining event but more like a steady sifting down of debris, just a little at first, and then more and more, pouring over her until she had to say, Stop! or she would be buried entirely.

Since the divorce four years ago, Lillian had moved again, into another, even smaller, apartment, on an even less nice street. She had thought of moving back uptown, to be closer to her mother, but Jason had started school by then and she hadn't wanted to uproot him. Unlike Lillian, the boy had poor concentration and couldn't seem to pay attention—letters and numbers bored and frustrated him. He cried easily and was prone to nightmares. Better to keep him here in Brooklyn, she reasoned, in a familiar neighborhood, with his father close by. If they moved to the Bronx, Lillian feared Ramon would never see Jason—the commute would just be too much trouble.

There was another reason she didn't move back uptown. Lillian had been something of a star in her old neighborhood. Everyone had known how bright she was, how ambitious. How humiliating, then, to return to her mother's house, no husband in sight, her little boy the object of speculation and pity. She would not do it, not even to make things easier for herself.

She hadn't entirely given up her professional plans, either. When she finally kicked Ramon out, she had gone to work, part-time, in a law office. She thought that the familiarity with the work would be an asset should she decide to apply to law school later on. So five mornings a week, she put on panty hose and a skirt, dropped Jason at school, and took the train in the uptown direction instead of down. When she emerged from the subway station, she joined the throng of people on the streets, all hurrying to be in their offices by nine.

Lillian's own office—cubicle really—was in a big building on Park Avenue. She rode the elevator to the thirty-fifth floor, waited for the receptionist to buzz her in, settled at her desk, and began the day. It was nonstop once she did: making the coffee, cleaning the pot; answering phones; scheduling appointments and conference calls, meetings and briefings. Then there was the firm's actual work, the trials and depositions.

Lillian was efficient and organized; she excelled at her job and was given a superior performance evaluation and a raise two years running. Still, she didn't like the work. Or, more aptly, the work was all right, but she thought the environment in which it was performed objectionable. There were so many things she didn't like about Russell, Goodrich and Blaine. She could hardly begin to list them. But she found herself harping on the clothes she saw every day in the office. All of the lawyers wore suits. The men's were mostly navy or gray; the women wore those colors too, but also camel, beige, and black. Lots of black, like they were undertakers not attorneys. Lillian did not own suits in these colors, except for a black velvet one with rhinestone buttons and a slim skirt with a slit up the back that she knew was not appropriate office attire. She didn't care about not having the right suits, because she did not want to dress like the lawyers who eddied through the halls with their quiet voices and muffled laughter. Didn't want to and didn't plan to.

She bought suits, all right, but they were in the colors she liked: red, purple, electric blue, and lime green. In the spring, she bought what she thought of as an Easter suit, made of raw silk in a shade of deep pink. She also bought white silk pumps and had them dyed to match. Her boss—Curtis Russell, with a horseshoe of silver hair surrounding his shining, sun-speckled pate—seemed to overlook her sartorial splendor, but some of the other lawyers, especially the women, who were distinguished from one another chiefly by their choice of accessories—one wore a heavy silk scarf in a muted pattern, another a strand of pearls, a third a gold brooch in the shape of a maple leaf—did not. She could feel their disdain, cool yet cutting, when she came into their offices, handed them files, asked if she could order up lunch. "Tacky," she could feel them thinking as they took in her clothes, her wrist covered in plastic bangle bracelets that clicked when she moved, her high heels. Tough luck, she mentally retorted. Tough shit.

Ultimately, the clothes were her undoing at Russell, Goodrich and Blaine. At the firm's annual holiday party, she wore her black velvet suit, only instead of a blouse under the fitted jacket, she had on only one of her favorite push-up bras, so that her smooth, lovely cleavage was clearly visible to anyone who cared to look. One of the senior associates could not keep his eyes off her. After his third scotch and soda, he stuck his hand—along with a crumpled cocktail napkin and several oily, salted peanuts—right down the front of her jacket.

Galling as this was, the reaction from Claudia Naylor, the human resources manager, was even more so.

"He's terribly sorry," said Claudia, who wore huge, hip-chick black-framed glasses that dominated her face. "But he says that he was, how did he put it"—she looked down at a typewritten sheet of paper; clearly she had taken notes when she talked to him—" 'aggressively enticed by the provocative display of flesh.' "

"I see," said Lillian, who sat across from Claudia, clenching and unclenching her fists. She had with her a small brown paper bag that she balanced on her knees. "He's a drunken idiot who can't keep his hands to himself but it's my fault. Isn't that blaming the victim somehow? Like in a rape case? I thought it wasn't politically correct to do that anymore."

"Lillian," Claudia said, stretching her arms across the desk in a conciliatory gesture, "just let it go, okay? He's one of the firm's best attorneys. Do you know how many billable hours he was responsible for last year alone?"

"That's all you have to say to me? Let it go?"

"He did apologize," Claudia reminded her, pulling her arms back and folding her hands.

"Not to me, he didn't."

"What do you expect? Flowers? A formal apology in front of the whole firm?" She sighed. "He's an attorney, remember? He's not going to put it in writing."

"So that's it? You're just going to overlook it because of his 'billable hours'?" Lillian looked beseechingly at Claudia, who did not meet her gaze. Instead, Claudia looked down as she carefully tucked the sheet of paper she was holding into a manila folder extracted from her top desk drawer. Lillian stood, holding the brown bag inches from Claudia's face.

"What's that?" Claudia looked up at last.

"The evidence." Lillian emptied the bag, dumping the balled-up, grease-smeared napkin and the peanuts onto the blotter; the napkin remained where it was, but the peanuts rolled off the desk and onto the floor. "You might as well destroy it. Or eat it for all I care."

She left the office that day, after successfully negotiating for decent severance pay, and, because she persuaded Claudia to "lay her off" in exchange for not pursuing the issue with the groping associate, she was able to collect unemployment as well. All in all, that guy's roaming hands had bought her about five months of time.

When it was nearly over, she knew she had to work, and soon. But not like the work she had done at the law firm. She no longer wanted the commute to Manhattan, didn't want the edge and bite of a fast-track job. No, she wanted to be home in the afternoons, to be the one to pick up her son from school at least on some days, to sift through his backpack for the notes from the teacher, spelling tests, and math quizzes, set out the plate of Oreos, pour the milk.

When she pressed the buzzer to Rick Wechsler's office on Monroe Place, her first thought was, Twenty minutes door to door. While she waited for Dr. Wechsler to come out and interview her, she looked around the waiting room, with its sofa, coffee table, and three chairs. She mentally cataloged the examining rooms she knew lay beyond. This was the ground floor of a brownstone; there was probably a garden out back. She thought of the many school holidays, the clerical half-days, that left her scrambling for child care when she still worked at the law firm. Maybe she would be able to bring Jason with her sometimes. He could hang out in the waiting room and do his homework or read. When the weather was good, he could go out back, maybe throw a ball a little. She was getting ahead of herself, she knew. All this would be possible only if she got the job, of course. If.

She didn't have to worry. Dr. Wechsler asked a few cursory questions about her prior employment and scanned her fresh-from-the-copy-shop résumé before saying, "You're hired. Can you start tomorrow?" Later, she learned that he and Helene had gone through three office managers in six months. There was the one with the peroxided, spiked hair and pierced cheek who said, "Whatever," when the patients asked her a question; the one who, though she vehemently denied smoking, reeked of cigarettes and left the butts underfoot, in the toilet and the plants, and in a last, memorable episode, had actually left one smoldering on her desk where it ignited a pile of bills waiting to be mailed. The office assistant who followed her didn't smoke but alternated between a manic stream of chatter and a nearly autistic silence, slammed the file cabinet drawers so hard she broke the metal frame and shattered four of the office's coffee mugs in a single day.

Now two years later, Lillian was still happy with the job, with the relative ease of it, the flexibility it provided. She was able to drop Jason off in the mornings without a frantic rush and pick him up from after-school most days before five. When she needed time off to take him to the pediatrician or to attend the reading celebration in his class-room, there was no problem. Of course, having an affair with Dr. Wechsler—Rick—was a problem, but not one she could have foreseen when she was first hired.

Lillian had liked him from the start: soft-spoken, courteous, mild. She liked the way he talked to his daughter, Dahlia, when the girl called the office or stopped by with her mother. She liked the way he talked to Naomi, his wife. She had not once thought of seduction or an affair: he was married and utterly off-limits to her. After being Ramon's betrayed spouse, she had no desire to put some other woman in that position.

But somehow her thinking shifted, imperceptibly at first, when Dahlia was killed. First she was sorry, so unbelievably sorry, that such a thing could happen, and to him of all people. She offered her condo-lences, went to the house on Carroll Street with food, watched when Dr. Wechsler returned to the office as rigid and self-possessed as an an-droid. She knew his marriage was suffering; she could hear the exces-sive politeness with which he addressed his wife, the politeness that had at its source distance, grief, and blame.

Still, none of this made her intend or decide to seduce her em-ployer. Her kiss was a competely unplanned gesture, something that had arisen out of his empathy for her, for her situation. Once she kissed him, though, once she felt him literally thaw in her arms, melt at her touch, she knew that she was as hooked as he was. She spent the rest of that day in a state of intense, suppressed excitement. Dr. Wechsler. As a lover. She found she could not stop thinking about him, the unfamiliar geography of his mouth as it had pressed against her own. Anything more than that kiss was wrong on so many levels, wrong, stupid, and cruel too. But she had not been with anyone since Ramon moved out—not that guys hadn't tried, but she was bitter, wasn't ready—and she found, suddenly, that she was as smitten with her boss's quiet, easygoing ways and slow-spreading smile as she had been with Ramon's quick confidence and bravado.

She had no plan for what would happen after that afternoon in the examining room; she only knew that she was going to do this one thing she thought was wrong, do it and let the rest just happen.

Finished with the dishes, Lillian dried the wineglasses with paper towels and put them away. Everything else she left in the dish drainer. She wanted to get to the Laundromat early, so she hurried down the stairs, the lumpy load of bedding bumping softly after her. Dropping the load off with instructions to the man who did the wash to separate the darks and lights, she headed out onto Fourth Avenue. She needed some groceries, and a few last-minute Christmas presents. She had almost everything on her list, but she wanted to find one more thing for Jason, something to help take the sting out of his father's disappointing news about their canceled trip. She had told him a few days ago, expecting the worst: shouting, tears, a full-scale tantrum. Instead, he had become very quiet. After a minute or two, he went to his room and gathered up all the things she had bought—the bathing trunks, the fins, the plastic mask for seeing underwater, the inflatable raft with the Yankees logo in the center—and dumped them on the floor of the living room.

"I need a garbage bag," he announced.

"Garbage bag? For what?"

"All this." He prodded the raft with the toe of his sneaker. "It better be pretty big."

Lillian gave him the bag and helped him put everything inside.

"Are you sure you want to do this?" she asked, pulling on the handles and tying them shut. "You could use those things another time.

The raft. The trunks. In the summer, maybe. If you go to sleepaway camp."

"I don't want them," he said, and the finality in his voice hurt her more than any tears, any tantrums could have. She thought of all the money she had spent buying this stuff. Then she looked at his sad face.

Let him, she thought, lugging the bag down the stairs and out to the curb. Just let him.

Walking down the busy street, she studied the store windows for inspiration. Not another action figure; he already had a chess set, checkers, Monopoly, and Parcheesi. Besides, he didn't even like board games that much; he once told her that trying to figure out a chess problem made him mad, "Like I got sand in my eye, Mom." Sports equipment was always an option, but much as she didn't like to admit it, she relied on Ramon to pick out this sort of thing; otherwise, she always got it wrong, the bat too heavy, the ball too hard, the glove the wrong shape, or size, or color. Sports. Who could understand the pull it had on guys, anyway, even the youngest ones?

The stop at the Laundromat had given her an idea. In the window there had been a sign offering kittens for adoption. Not a kitten though. A puppy. Jason had wanted one for the longest time but had heard "no" so often he had stopped asking. She was well aware of the annoyance a puppy would entail: the whining, the chewing, the inevitable accidents on the apartment floor that she would be obliged to clean up. Still, she was going to do it. For her boy. For him.

Lillian hurried along, stopping at the necessary stores but with her mind already on the next task, breaking it down into the various steps, plotting out her strategy. She would call the North Shore Animal Shelter, get her cousin Maria to drive her out there. She'd find a dog with a sweet disposition, keep him at Maria's until Christmas Eve, sneak him back home when Jason was asleep, and have him there when Jason woke up on Christmas morning. How happy it made her to make these plans, to imagine Jason's surprise. It was only when she was back in her apartment again, putting away the apple juice and the eggs that she thought of Rick. Rick, who would not be with her on Christmas morning, and for whom, somehow, she had not managed to buy a single thing.

She checked the kitchen clock. Still early. On impulse, she grabbed her coat and her bag, quickly locking the door behind her. As she hurried back down the stairs, she thought of the row of stores and businesses along Fourth Avenue: Dee Dee's Donuts, where the *D* in the first word of the sign had been missing for the last two years, the 99 cent shop, the video store, and the Laundromat where she'd left off her own laundry. There wasn't a single place where she could imagine finding something for Rick. Instead, she caught the R train and then changed for the D. She was at Thirty-fourth Street, and Macy's department store, in less than thirty minutes.

The ground floor was decorated with hanging garlands and enormous wreaths; Lillian had to push her way through the crowds into the store. She hadn't been here in at least three years, maybe four. The last time had been when she had taken Jason to see Santa on one of the upper floors. Lillian had been delighted by the simulated train ride to the North Pole, the motorized penguins and polar bears set up to entertain the long line of children waiting for their turn, the cottage— decorated with plaid chairs and stenciled reindeer on the walls— where they actually had their audience with Santa.

"And what would you like for Christmas?" Santa had asked Jason, then six or seven. Lillian immediately liked the guy dressed up in the red suit and white beard. No effusive ho-ho-hoing and false cheer marred his performance. Instead, he'd perfected a calmer, more low-key manner. To Lillian he was perfect.

"I'd like my dad to come live with us again," Jason said without any hesitation. "And for my mom to stop cursing whenever he calls on the phone."

Lillian's cheeks flamed as Santa's eyes met hers in a worried gaze.

"I'll see what I can do," he told Jason, who hopped down and walked off without looking back.

Today, Lillian wasn't on her way to Santaland, however. She headed for the men's department, where she planned to buy a gift for Rick. It turned out that the men's area was on the ground floor, and it was as mobbed as everywhere else in the store. She was jostled as she examined sweaters and shirts, socks and ties. She didn't want to buy Rick any of those things and continued looking.

Now here was something with more possibility—a bathrobe. Hadn't he worn hers last night? She'd buy him a robe and he could leave it at her place—it would be like having a small bit of him when he wasn't there. The thought pleased her. She looked at a wool robe but decided it was too scratchy. Terry cloth was more comfortable, but there was something so dull, so neutered about terry. Like you were buying it for a four-year-old. Cotton was always nice, and some of the cotton robes were even on sale. But no, wait, here was the perfect thing: a dark silk paisley robe, in rich tones of midnight blue, brown, and black.

"Are you going to take that?" asked a young woman in an ugly quilted coat.

"I'm not sure," Lillian said, hand possessively on the garment as she spoke.

"Well, if you're not, could I see it?"

"All right." Lillian wished the woman would go away so she could make her decision in peace. But the woman remained there, watching as Lillian examined the garment more carefully. The fabric felt smooth, even luscious to the touch; the lapels and pockets were trimmed with dark brown piping. So elegant. Lillian heard the woman sigh, clearly annoyed by the time she was taking. Brouhita, she thought as she checked the price tag. Expensive. But wasn't she looking for something different, something special? Wasn't that why she had come here? "I'm taking it," she announced. The woman in the ugly coat—Lillian saw that even the bullet-shaped buttons on the coat were ugly—made a face and then huffed away. Too bad for her, thought Lillian, gripping the silk robe even tighter in her hands.

As she stood on line at the register, she imagined herself giving Rick the robe, and the pleasure he would take in receiving it. Lillian knew he was someone who appreciated a gift, the effort and expense that went into the choice.

"Will you be having it wrapped?" a harried-looking salesman asked her; she hadn't realized it was her turn.

"Yes," she said. "It's a gift."

"The wrap desk is upstairs." The salesman was busily punching numbers into his computerized register. "I'm sure the gentleman will appreciate it."

"Fiancé," Lillian blurted out.

"Excuse me?" He glanced up, fingers momentarily suspended.

"The robe. I'm getting it for my fiancé. We're going to be married in the spring." Now what made her say all that? Lillian felt foolish and even guilty for uttering the lie, but the salesman just touched his bow tie lightly and smiled.

"Congratulations," he said as he slipped the boxed robe into a large shopping bag. "And Merry Christmas."

"Merry Christmas to you," Lillian said. Clutching the bag tightly in her hand, she headed toward the exit. She decided to skip the wrap desk after all. Ramon would be bringing Jason back soon, and she didn't really have the time. Anyway, she suddenly had a strong need to get back to Brooklyn, where she could carefully, lovingly wrap the silk robe—her fiancé's silk robe—all by herself.

11

Gone

On the Wednesday before Christmas, Naomi was just finishing her fifth round of tic-tac-toe with Jamal Jones when Pat Ryan walked into the room.

"You have a phone call," Pat said.

"Can it wait?" Naomi wrote an X in an empty square.

"I don't think so." She looked anxious in a way Naomi did not recall having seen.

Naomi made her final X and waited for Jamal's grin as he supplied the winning O. Then she got up. "I'll be back."

"Tomorrow?" he said.

"Friday." She put her hand lightly on his head. "Promise."

Naomi hurried to keep up with Pat. "Sorry to put you to all this trouble."

"It's okay." Pat pushed the button and the elevator doors opened. "You're worth it."

Back in Pat's office, Naomi took the phone and heard the news about her mother's disappearance.

"Gone?" she said to the nursing home administrator who was falling over herself apologizing.

"Yes, Mrs. Wechsler, gone. We're still not sure how she got out or if she's even left the facility. But she missed both physical therapy and arts and crafts. No one has seen her since breakfast."

"I'll be there as soon as I can." All the recrimination and accusation—What do you mean she's gone? Why isn't she being watched better?—could be put off until later. Why spend time fighting with this fool when she could be on her way there? She put in a quick call to Rick. He was with a patient; the woman who worked in his office, Lillian, wanted to know if she should interrupt.

"No, that's all right. Tell him I'll call him later."

"Is everything okay?" Lillian said. Naomi heard a strange catch in her voice, as if whatever it was Naomi was calling about somehow concerned her too.

"It's my mother. She's missing from the nursing home."

"Oh, I'm so sorry." Again that tone.

"I'm on my way there now. I've got to go."

She hung up. Whatever it was that was nagging her about this conversation would have to wait. Naomi was hurrying down the hospital corridor once more, one arm in the sleeve of her coat, the other fumbling with her scarf, when she ran into Michael.

"Please let me know what's happened," he said. "I'll give you my cell phone number." He wrote it on a piece of paper and handed it to her. It was only when she was standing on the subway platform, anxiously waiting for the number 1 train that she paused to consider what this information, this new intimacy, might mean. But then she was swallowed up with concern for her mother and she didn't think about it anymore.

Estelle had still not been located when, almost two hours later, Naomi arrived in Riverdale. The facility had been searched thoroughly and now people were checking the grounds. A shrill woman with heavily made-up eyes and a chunky silver necklace was sent to "counsel" Naomi, but the only counsel Naomi wanted was her own. Until her mother was found there was nothing that would give her any comfort. Trying not to glare at the woman, Naomi asked to use the phone so she could call Rick. This time, Lillian put her right through.

"Missing? For how long?" he asked.

"Since this morning."

"Jesus." He let his breath out. "Do you want me to come there? I can cancel the rest of my appointments. I'll come right now."

"Not yet," Naomi said. "Let me call you again a little later, okay?" She put down the phone and thought of the slip of paper Michael had handed her, which was now folded and tucked into a zippered compartment in her purse. Why was she thinking of him now? Did it have something to do with her having told Rick not to come, to wait until she asked? Or did it have something to do with Lillian? Naomi opened her purse and took out the paper. She wanted to call Michael, to receive whatever comfort he might offer. But before she could, the three men assigned to searching the grounds had come back in.

"Nothing," said the taller of them, a custodian, from the looks of his navy blue uniform. "Not a trace." The other two men just nodded solemnly.

The nursing home's executive director, a short, powerful-looking man named Leonard Reingold, strode into the room following this announcement. He ran his hand through his abundant gray hair and stared at Naomi.

"I've been in charge here for thirteen years and nothing like this has ever happened before," he said in lieu of a greeting.

"I think we should call the police," Naomi said, not even bothering to respond. She was angry, furious even, but had decided before she arrived that she would save it, save it all, until she knew what had become of her mother. This was not out of desire to spare anyone's feelings, but out of consideration for her own: she knew she had to marshal what strength she had to deal with what had happened to Estelle, whatever that turned out to be.

So the police were called and more staff members dispatched, some by car, some on foot, to local stations in the neighborhood. Naomi decided to go with one group that was walking; it would be better than waiting at the home. She traipsed through the darkening streets of Riverdale like a pilgrim, carrying her guilt as if it were an offering. Why hadn't the home taken better care of her mother? Why had Naomi consigned her mother to them? It was late in the afternoon, almost five, when a cell phone call came in: Estelle had been found near the 241st Street subway station. A policeman on the beat had discovered her at a playground and brought her back to the station house a few blocks away. When Naomi saw her mother, Estelle was seated on a bench, hands and face smeared with traces of a mysterious white substance.

"Mom!" Naomi moved closer and saw that the white was nothing more than powdered sugar. "Are you all right?"

"I suppose so," Estelle said and then added, "I need a bath."

"You can have a bath as soon as you're back at the home, Mrs. Levine." This from a loud woman with jet-black hair pulled into a bun and a wide, exceedingly mobile mouth. Naomi ignored her and sat down next to her mother.

"Why did you leave? Was the home that bad?"

"Home?" said Estelle. "Whose home are you talking about? Not mine. Not yours, either."

"I'm sorry you were so unhappy there, Mom."

"She never said she was unhappy. Not once." The black-haired woman looked from Estelle to Naomi and back again, as if daring her to challenge this.

"Happy." Estelle sniffed. "Who's happy?" She turned her gaze on Naomi. "Being happy has nothing to do with anything. I didn't leave because I wasn't happy."

"Then, why?" Naomi lowered her voice, as if trying to avoid the intrusion of the social worker who insisted on remaining nearby.

"It was because of Dahlia," Estelle said. "I was trying to get to Brooklyn to see her. I haven't seen her for so long. Why don't you ever bring her with you?" Her voice dropped, as if in concert with Naomi's, but Naomi could hear the accusation in it. "You should have brought her today."

Naomi had to close her eyes for a second. In the blackness behind her eyelids, she saw the white scrap of paper with Michael's cell phone number written on it. Now she knew why she had it, why it was so important. She needed him to help her, help her utter the thing she had been dreading and anticipating for all these months. He would know what to say, how to frame it. He would help her choose the words, soften the blow.

But when she opened her eyes, the slip of paper was gone, the telephone way across the room, and her mother—alert, focused, impatient, annoyed—was looking at her, expecting an answer.

"Dahlia is dead, Ma," Naomi croaked more than said. "Dahlia is dead."

12

Merry Christmas

No one ever started out in life wanting to be a podiatrist. Certainly Rick hadn't. As a boy growing up in Great Neck, Long Island, his fantasies had strayed into typically boyish realms. Dreams of becoming a fireman or a policeman gave way to those of basketball player, astronaut, and paleontologist. By the time he reached college, he was sure it was some form of science that would occupy him, though his goals had changed. He thought about and rejected medical school on the basis of its competitive climate, which didn't suit his retiring and somewhat reticent nature. Instead, he veered toward dentistry, and started preparing for the dental boards. There was some shame in this, as he came from a family of doctors: his father was a gastroenterologist; one brother was an oncologist, and the other, to their father's unending pride, was the head of endocrinology at a major hospital in Atlanta.

Only Allison, his baby sister born so many years after the rest of them, was exempt from the familial pressure. Indulged, delighted in, fussed over, Allison zipped through Brown in three stellar years, spent a miserable semester at Columbia journalism school, and then found her truest and most congenial home working for a glossy women's magazine called *Now!* Allison didn't have to compete with his brothers the way Rick did. But even though they ribbed him and goaded him, he had decided somewhere along the way that he was just going to let his brothers win. It was so much more important to them anyway.

The idea of podiatry school came to him one morning of his senior year in college. He had woken early; Naomi was sleeping next to him. They each had singles in Main Building that year and spent every night together, in his room or hers. In the gray light of dawn, he saw her foot poking out from the blankets. It was a small, delicate foot, with traces of pale, iridescent nail polish, mostly chipped off now, on the toenails. What color was it? Hard to see.

Rick sat up to observe her foot more closely. His hair was matted to his head from sleep, his mouth dry and slighty pasty. He wasn't wearing a pajama top and the room was cool, so goose bumps started to rise on his shoulders and chest. But still, he continued to stare at Naomi's exposed foot, finding in it the answer to a question he hadn't known he was asking.

Her instep was high, and he could make out the slight roughness of a callus on her heel. How humble, and literally, how earthbound. He controlled an urge to take it in hand, to feel its weight, the texture of her skin, because he didn't want to wake her. What linked Naomi— or anyone—to the ground more firmly and emphatically than their feet? Even more essential than teeth, more rudimentary than hands, feet were what kept you planted here. Feet, he suddenly realized, were worth knowing, and worth caring for. He switched course and began preparing for the MCAT, which would allow him to apply to medical, podiatry, or osteopathy school. Later, when he told his brothers he had been accepted to all the podiatry programs to which he'd applied, they had laughed.

"Of course you were," smirked Mark, the oncologist. "How many applicants were there? Three?"

"Come on, give him a break," said Scott, the endocrinologist. "There must have been at least ten."

Even his father, though less openly derisive, had said, "Are you sure it's going to be enough of a challenge for you, Richie?" The use of his childhood nickname made Rick seethe, but he answered calmly enough, "Don't worry about me, Dad. I'll be challenged plenty." And he was.

The courses he had been required to take those first two years—anatomy, physiology, histology, pharmacology, pathology, pediatrics, neurology, orthopedics—mirrored those he would have taken in med school. His father and brothers were thinking of the old days, when the field was less evolved, less medical. Chiropody, that's what they had called it, and it was basically some guy with a razor, scraping and cutting. But things were different now. Rick would be able to prescribe drugs, administer injections, perform surgery. He went through the four-year program at Temple, did an internship at Cornell, and then settled in Brooklyn. He hadn't regretted any of it.

Rick liked his work, his patients, the flow and hum of his days. He appreciated the chance to make a difference, without having to deal, in any immediate or pressing way, with mortality. In all his years of practice, he had never lost a patient. Not true of his father or brothers. Or that guy McBride at Holy Name. How many patients—kids—did a doctor like that watch die? Rick didn't even want to guess.

But despite the lack of imminent danger and of threat they faced, Rick's patients stayed on his mind. He remembered their ailments and the particular stories behind them. Mr. Baumgarten, an eighty-three-year-old diabetic, had come in with two badly ulcerated toes. Rick knew it would have been easiest—and perhaps the most cautious—to have recommended amputation. He knew of other podiatrists who wouldn't have risked the gangrene, who would have done it immediately. But he also knew that Baumgarten, who already used a walker, would be incapacitated without those toes. Lose the toes, lose the mobility. Lose the mobility, shorten the life.

When Rick saw the state of Baumgarten's feet, he reached for the phone himself, called a vascular surgeon, and made sure the patient was seen that very day. The operation to restore the circulation took place the next afternoon. It was Rick's quick diagnosis and response that saved the toes. Mr. Baumgarten still mailed holiday greetings—his latest one was displayed on the office mantel, where Lillian had arranged the cards the patients sent—and was planning, he told Rick during his last visit, on taking a cruise to Aruba.

Then there had been the young woman, a ballerina with the New York City Ballet, who'd traveled to Brooklyn all the way from the Upper West Side on the strength of a recommendation. God, the deplorable condition of that girl's feet. But she was quite stoic, even unconcerned, about the corns, calluses, and blisters. She hadn't come to see him for any of that. Instead, an aggressive case of tendonitis in her left foot was making it impossible to dance without severe shooting pain. One doctor she had seen wanted to give her a cortisone shot, but she had heard how cortisone could weaken a muscle, causing it to "pop." So Rick began a course of anti-inflammatory drugs, ice packs, taping, and sustained elevation. Within a few weeks, the pain had subsided.

She was so grateful that she'd sent three tickets—first ring, center—to *The Nutcracker*. He and Naomi had taken Dahlia, and they were all transfixed watching the young dancer as the Sugar Plum Fairy, supple feet in their pink satin shoes moving with such ease, such grace, he could not reconcile the vision of them with what he'd seen in his office. Later, they had gone backstage to her dressing room, also at her invitation, where Dahlia was permitted to touch her costume, her feathery, long-handled makeup brushes, the jeweled tiara she wore on her head. And later still, she had sent along new patients, other dancers from the company, to his office. Valentine, that was her name. Virginia Valentine. He had loved her feet. And Morris Baumgarten's. He loved them all.

Christmas came. Rick and Naomi stayed home, which was what they usually did. Years before, he had pointed out that December 25 was always a little melancholy for Jews. "It's like everyone else in America is having a party and we're not invited," he told Naomi, who agreed. So they did their best to make it a pleasant day for Dahlia, renting movies with holiday themes—*How the Grinch Stole Christmas,*

Belle's Enchanted Christmas—and made cookies or played cards. Now that Dahlia was gone, there seemed no point in trying to manufacture the festive feeling. Instead, Rick got up late, read the paper in excruciating detail, took a walk up Carroll Street and into Prospect Park, then took a long nap that left him feeling disoriented and grumpy when he awoke.

"Want to go out to eat?" Naomi stood by the bed as he stretched, rubbed his face with his hands.

"I guess." He sat up. "Where did you have in mind? Chinese? There's that new Asian-fusion place on Fifth Avenue?" He figured places like that would be open and not too obsessed with the holiday he did not celebrate.

"Chinese would be good." Naomi sat on the bed. "But not in Park Slope. Let's go to Sunset Park. I hear there are good places there. Like a mini-Chinatown."

"Who told you that?" His voice came out sounding more contrary and irritable than he intended; this was what guilt did, it made you mean and small. But Sunset Park was where Lillian lived. Even though he was not likely to run into her today—he knew that she and her son were spending the day in the Bronx with her parents—the thought of even being in the neighborhood where he had betrayed Naomi made him feel testy and anxious. He didn't think he could sit in a Sunset Park Chinese restaurant with her, study a menu, pretend to be interested in whether he ate noodles or dumplings, talk about her work at the hospital or his at the office.

"Someone at Holy Name," she said quietly, but he could see she was hurt. No surprise. His tone was hurtful. Lillian had said that somehow or other, Naomi would find out about what he was doing. He had not wanted to believe her then; he had insisted on thinking that if no one told Naomi, she wouldn't find out. But suddenly he realized that he didn't have to worry about Lillian or someone else telling Naomi. He would end up telling her himself, whether he meant to or not. Maybe it was better to do it directly, once and for all, and not in nasty little increments, as he'd been doing for weeks.

"I'm sorry," he said. "I know what a jerk I sound like."

"You do. But at least you're my jerk," she said. He heard her trying to keep her voice light, her tone easy. Heard, too, what a struggle it was. He stood and Naomi stood too.

"Let's go out," he said. "Anywhere you want."

The light had already started to fade; the streets were quiet and the air not all that cold. He and Naomi walked down Carroll, turned the corner and headed toward the subway.

"There's this place on Twenty-second Street that's supposed to be really good."

"The trains will be slow."

"We're in no rush." They waited on the platform for over fifteen minutes before an R train pulled in.

The restaurant, more than twenty blocks from where Lillian lived, was surprisingly crowded. Apart from the small plastic wreath on the door and the few lights strung haphazardly around the room, there were no other concessions to Christmas. Tiny tables covered in flowered oilcloth were pushed close together, and the waiters and waitresses had to sidle between them.

Rick and Naomi took off their coats and sat down. Rick looked at her. Here, in this unfamiliar setting, he could see her better, more clearly than he had in a long time. She wore a ribbed wool sweater the color of oatmeal and jeans that were faded to a muted, almost pastel blue. Her smooth dark hair was pulled back in a tortoiseshell clip. She looked, as she somehow always did, finely drawn and utterly self-contained. He glanced down at the menu then, its myriad offerings. He didn't want to eat anything, but they were here to eat after all. He might as well try.

"You can order," he told Naomi. And she did. When the food came—fragrantly spiced dumplings with delicate crimping around their edges, noodles, a whole steamed fish—he found it was surprisingly appetizing, even delicious. He had not been this hungry in a long while, and certainly not while eating with Naomi. He ate second help-ings of everything; she offered food from her own plate, transferring it to his with the aid of her chopsticks. Perhaps buoyed by the new tastes or the unfamiliar surroundings their conversation here was dif-ferent too. Naomi didn't once mention Dahlia or anything related to her; she didn't even talk about her mother, who had escaped from the nursing home not long ago, and who had been, finally, told about Dahlia's death. Instead, she regaled him with stories about volunteers and staff—not patients—from the hospital. He found himself laugh-ing, really laughing at one of her imitations—the intonation, the ges-tures she added. She smiled back, and took a big gulp of her water.

"Mmm, I'd love a glass of wine." She put the water glass back down on the table.

"I know," Rick said. The restaurant had no liquor license and they hadn't thought to bring a bottle. "Maybe I could run out and get some-thing. Isn't there a liquor store across the street?"

"Would you?" She looked up at him. "That would be great."

Rick shrugged on his jacket and hurried out. There was an open liquor store across the street, and though there weren't many choices, he came away with a decent bottle of white. Before he crossed again, he saw an open drugstore, where a rotund, turbaned man stood be-hind the register. Rick felt an immediate sense of camaraderie. Here was someone else for whom Christmas was just the day sandwiched between December 24 and December 26.

The store had its requisite shelves of antacid and aspirin, of tooth-paste and shaving cream. But a glass display case near the front held a few cheap watches and alarm clocks, a paltry assortment of perfumes. Rick recognized the unadorned white box with its simple black letters as Chanel No. 5. Hadn't he bought that once, years ago, for Naomi when they were still in college? He remembered how she had loved the squared-off bottle with its faceted stopper as much as she had loved the scent.

"I'll take that," he said to the man with the turban, pointing at the box.

"You want wrap?" His accent was thick, but his manner exceedingly courteous.

Wrapped. Yes. It was a gift.

"Please," said Rick as he counted out the money. The man produced a small square of silver paper and a silver bow. Rick was out the door in what seemed like seconds.

Naomi had ordered another dish in his absence, a plate of seasoned rice flecked with vegetables and shrimp. She was serving him some when he sat down, bringing the cold with him. The waiter saw the wine and hurried over with a corkscrew and glasses. Rick poured, first for Naomi, then himself. He couldn't quite bring himself to make a toast, however, and simply raised the glass to his lips. Not bad. He watched as Naomi took a long, deep swallow. Then he took out the silver-wrapped package.

"For you." He raised his glass again and watched her over the rim.

"Why?" She held it in both of her hands but didn't open it.

"Hey, Merry Christmas, right?"

"Merry Christmas," she said, and there was a break in her voice that made him think he had miscalculated, made a mistake, but then she gained control again. Opening the paper carefully, she looked at the box, then at Rick. "Thank you," she said. "Very much." She took out the bottle and unloosened the stopper, touching it lightly to her wrists, holding it under her nose.

On the way home, he put his arm around her shoulders and held her tightly against him. He smelled the perfume, sweet and heady. But it was less an erotic embrace than a fraternal one. So he was surprised, shocked even, when they were in bed together later that night and her hand—still small, still soft—began traveling up his thigh in the direction of his crotch. For a few seconds he lay very still, thinking that this must be a mistake, maybe she was half asleep, not fully aware of what she was doing. But then she reached for him, stroking intently, seriously. Her touch was very gentle, gentle and hesitant. Rick remained frozen, inert under her fingers. Jesus Christ. Hadn't he been dreaming of this, hoping for this, for months? But that was before Lillian. Lillian, who started out being just the antidote and who had become his reason for getting up in the morning. How had he let this happen? He sat up, put his face in his hands.

"Rick?" The caress was suspended; her hand had dropped back down to the mattress. "Are you okay?"

"I'm okay." Though he sure as hell didn't sound it.

"Is it that you're not ready for this yet?" He felt her shift onto her side. "Is it too soon?" Look at that, she was giving him the perfect excuse, the perfect alibi. He could say, Yes, yes that's it, too soon, not ready, still grieving.

Instead, he blurted out, "I've slept with someone else," into the darkness of their room.

"It's that woman, Lillian, the one who works for you, isn't it?"

"How did you know?" He was stunned. Lillian had been right. The writing on the wall. It had been there all along. And tonight, just now, in fact, Naomi had read it.

"What difference does it make how I know?" she asked before getting up, groping for her bathrobe, her slippers. "Does it really matter?" She crossed the room in the dark and stood by the door. Rick switched on the light.

"I'm sorry," he said, knowing how inadequate his words were. Still, they were true.

"Why?" Naomi remained by the door, hands stuffed deeply into the pockets of the robe.

"Why am I sorry? Or why did I do it?"

"Either. Both. I just don't understand."

"I'm not sure I do either. It was something that . . . happened."

"Once? Twice? Ten times?" She hadn't moved from where she stood but leaned lightly against the door frame.

"A few times."

"How many?"

"Why are you asking me that?"

"I want to know what it means to you. What she means."

"I really don't know."

"That's just great. You don't know how many times you slept with her, don't know why you slept with her, don't know what it means to you. What were you thinking? That you could just keep on doing it . . . indefinitely?" Her voice was quiet but savage. "Do you love her?"

"Not the way I love you." This at least he knew for sure. She stared at him, not saying anything for a moment. Then she moved back across the room and picked up the sweater and jeans she had worn earlier that night.

"I'm going out now," she said, clutching the clothes tightly to her. "I'll be home in the morning. I want you out of here by the time I get back." She left the room and Rick strained to hear the sounds she made dressing, putting on her boots. He could hear her on the telephone, calling the car service down the street, and a little while later, he heard the car pull up outside the house, the door open and then quietly close again.

When he was sure that she had left, he too got up and dressed, put a few things in a canvas overnight bag. He looked at his watch as he strapped it on. Midnight. Where was he going to go at this hour?

Rick went down the stairs quietly, as if he were trying not to wake someone who was sleeping above. He left his bag by the door and curled up on the sofa, gripping his own body tightly, trying to ease, or at least contain, the sharp and sudden pain.

13

Accounting

The morning after Christmas, Michael sat on the honey-colored leather sofa in his living room, engaged in a desultory game of Scrabble with his daughter Brooke. The deluxe Scrabble set—board perched on a lazy Susan, dark wooden tiles instead of the pale blond ones—had been one of his Christmas gifts from the girls. But no one else in his household shared his enthusiasm for Scrabble, and though Brooke was doing her best to appear interested in the game—she had just made the pedestrian word *jet,* a real waste of the letter *j* in his opinion—he could see that despite her good intentions, her attention was dwindling. At least she tried, he thought fondly. Her sister had been nowhere to be found when the lid to the cardboard box was lifted off and the cellophane bag containing the letters sliced open. Naomi Wechsler had told him that before the stroke her mother had been an avid Scrabble player, but that no one else in her family had enjoyed the game either.

He was just totaling up Brooke's points when he felt the vibrating of the cell phone—against his chest. He slipped it out of his pocket and answered tersely, "McBride."

"Michael? I'm sorry to bother you at home." He had just been thinking about her and here she was: Naomi Wechsler.

"That's all right," he said. Brooke looked at him with mild interest, and he composed his face into what he hoped was an expression of polite professionalism and tempered concern.

"I know you must be busy with your family and all," Naomi continued. "But I wanted to see you. Today, if I could."

"Today is fine, yes, I can do that." He looked away from his daughter's eyes. Everybody knows everything all the time, he could hear his mother saying. "I can meet you in my office. Can you be there in half an hour?"

"I'll be there," said Naomi and then she hung up. Michael replaced the cell phone and stood up. "That was someone at the hospital, princess," he said to his daughter. "I'm sorry, but we'll need to postpone our game. Hope you don't mind."

"That's okay, Dad." Brooke looked visibly relieved. "We can finish it later. Or even tomorrow. Tomorrow's cool." She stood now too, tall and lovely, and moved toward the door. "Too bad you have to work today, though, huh?"

"Well, that's a doctor's life," Michael replied. "I chose it."

Michael left the room and hurried upstairs. He had grown up in this house, he and his sisters and brothers, all squeezed together on the fourth floor, the third floor reserved for his parents and his grandmother, who had lived with them until she died at the age of ninety-seven. Park Slope was a name he didn't hear back then; the area was just called South Brooklyn and their neighbors were civil servants, garbage collectors, grocery store owners, the occasional salesman or schoolteacher, not the hedge fund managers and corporate lawyers who surrounded him now, the only people who could currently afford the street and the neighborhood's million-dollar-plus prices. Years later, after his parents had died and he and his siblings had inherited the house, Michael was surprised to find that he was the only one who wanted to live there again. The rest of them—Kevin, Tommy, Stephen, Kathleen, Maud—had scattered: to Bay Ridge, Staten Island, Long Island, and New Jersey. But Michael had wanted to resume life in his boyhood home, and Camille enthusiastically agreed. Of course, once they were actually in the house, she had done a lot of tearing up and out, reconfiguring and rearranging, so that the spaces no longer resembled those of his youth.

But not everything had been altered. Some of the things he remembered still remained, like the tall windows on the parlor floor, the ones that let the light spill in on summer mornings, and the curved niche just off the second-floor landing, where his mother had always kept a painted statue of the Blessed Virgin. Even now, when Michael ran his hand along a certain spot on the banister, he could feel the series of nicks he and Kevin had gouged out when they were still in grade school, part of some arcane ritual whose exact meaning he could no longer recall. Tears had filled his mother's eyes when she discovered those grooved lines, but she didn't punish the boys. Didn't matter, though. Her lingering, reproachful disappointment was worse than any punishment could have been.

Upstairs, he pulled on a sweater over his shirt, used his hands to smooth his hair. Naomi. Naomi had called him. She had sounded upset. Tense. It must have been something important to have rated a call at home on the cell phone. She hadn't ever used the number before. He wondered if the reason for the call had anything to do with her mother. Well, he would find out. He loped back down the stairs, nearly colliding with Camille, who was carrying a small stack of freshly washed sheets in a basket. They smelled good.

"Are you going out?" she asked. He knew she thought he worked too hard, took on too much. But she also understood his need to do these things. Understood and seldom complained.

"Just down to the office."

"Today? The day after Christmas?"

"I know." He shifted his weight on the step, impatient to be on his way.

"There's a hole in your sweater."

"Is there?" Michael looked down. She was right; a hole the size of a quarter sat just to the left of his navel. "Can you fix it—darn it or something?"

"Right now?" Camille looked amused.

"No," he said, poking a finger through the opening. "It doesn't matter, does it?"

"I suppose not." She shifted the basket of laundry to the other hip so she could lean over and lightly kiss his cheek.

"I won't be long," he said, giving her arm a squeeze.

"Promise?"

"Promise." He continued down the stairs, reached for his coat, and pulled open the door. There. He'd done it. Out the door in five minutes, he'd be at his office in another ten. Waiting for her if he could. "Fools rush in," his mother's voice echoed again, this time with another of her favorite expressions. But was he foolish, really, to want to see this woman who so clearly needed him? Wasn't that part of who he was, what he had chosen for himself?

Back at Downstate, where he'd gone to medical school, no one would have predicted that Michael would have ever become a department chair. He was too hands-on, too involved, too emotional. Private practice for sure; that was the way he'd go. Or so his teachers and classmates had predicted. But it turned out that Michael had an affinity for the academic side of medicine as well. To him, it was not at all separate from the human side. His specialty—infectious diseases— brought him into contact with the continually shifting immigrant landscape of New York. Malaria, tuberculosis, encephalitis—who was getting these illnesses and why—these questions were the mainstay of his research. And reseach, he discovered, was not sterile, not without a context. It always contained a narrative, a direction.

A family came from Guyana, a woman with her two grandsons from Haiti, another woman with an infant daughter from New Delhi. With them came a particular set of diseases, each with its own winding trail of symptoms and causes. Tainted water, corrupt govenments, civil unrest, cows, flies, mosquitoes, rats—all these can and did provide the origin of illnesses that traveled and spread from one country to another, adapting and mutating as they went. It was as if everyone on earth was connected by a vast and complex system of microbes, germs, antibiotic-resistant bacteria. Illness was passed along, like love, like prayer. There was no real stopping it; only tracking, decoding, diverting. Herpes simplex, chicken pox, rheumatic fever—each had its own story to tell, written, indelibly sometimes, on the flesh and organs of the children who were afflicted.

He'd had a private practice alongside the research too, and most of the paraphernalia in his office dated from those years when he was growing it. But Michael also showed himself adept at handling the occasionally volatile climate of interhospital politics. Eventually, he moved out of research and into administration. Dealing with the head of the nurses' union—a difficult, perpetually aggrieved woman—the cadre of subspecialists in the pediatric department as well as the general residents who reported to him came easily. The morning meetings with the senior residents, themselves a mini–multicultural seminar, with doctors from India, Africa, China, and elsewhere were usually calm affairs; listening to the cases as they were described—the broken bones, tonsillectomies, and ruptured appendixes—Michael liked the feeling of being the captain of this particular ship, prudently steering all the members on board toward recovery, toward health. For there was something fundamentally hopeful about pediatrics: children had the most amazing recuperative powers: most of their kids got well. Doctors knew this and depended on it.

Of course, Holy Name was not a level-one trauma center like Kings County; they didn't see the worst cases and did not often lose a child. Which made it all the worse when they did. There was something particularly excruciating about the death of a child—the life cut short, the anguish of the parents. But it was also as if the doctors were testing the limits of medicine itself, asking, With all we can do, why can't we do that much more? Naomi's daughter, Dahlia, for instance. It had seemed so galling that the ER doctors who'd been on duty at the time, the cluster of nurses who stood futilely aside, could have done nothing, nothing at all, to save that child.

As he walked quickly along Eighth Avenue toward the hospital,

Michael watched his own breath—slightly labored; he needed more exercise—emerge in curled, white wisps. He thought about Naomi, waiting for him at the office. What could it be that pulled her from her house to meet him? Her mother, whom she had said could not seem to absorb or understand Dahlia's death?

On Sixth Street he turned and headed inside the building. Once upstairs, he saw that Naomi was already there and waiting for him, her small figure dark in the wide, white hallway.

"Hope I haven't kept you," Michael said, unlocking the door and ushering her inside.

"Just a minute or two." Naomi stood in the center of the room, looking around. "It was sweet of you to come." She smiled at him, and he could see she had been crying.

"Sit," he said, gesturing to the pair of chairs that were poised in front of his desk. She sat down. He didn't take the chair behind the desk, because he didn't want to be that far from her, but sat on the desk itself, pushing aside a pile of folders and a Lego tower to make room.

"The reason I called you—" she began, then stopped. "It's Rick." She looked down at her fingers, which were interlaced in her lap. "He said, he told me that—" Again, she stopped but this time didn't resume speaking. Michael said nothing at first; he had learned to wait. The silence between them continued to stretch, then sag.

"He told you . . ." Michael finally prompted, seeing that she needed assistance.

"He told me he had slept with someone else." The words came out quickly and were followed, yet again, by her silence. Michael didn't have an immediate response. Infidelity after a child's death. Not so uncommon, maybe not even, ultimately, so damaging to a marriage, particularly if it had been a good marriage. But so much depended on what had gone on before. Had it been a habit, a pattern? Or an aberration in response to the wholly aberrant nature of losing his daughter?

"And you didn't know?" he asked.

"Not until last night. I wanted to call you then. But it was late. And it was Christmas."

"Christmas," he said, thinking of his own family, the girls, the tree, the meal, the houseful of guests who had arrived in the afternoon and stayed until late in the evening. He looked over at Naomi and saw that she was crying. Not with any force or vigor, just slow tears leaking, as if she didn't have the energy to brush them away. "Do you have any idea how long it's been going on?"

"Not very long. But that's even worse somehow. That he could have done it after . . ." She paused. "I didn't get all the details. I was so angry I couldn't even look at him. I spent the night with a friend. I told him I wanted him out by the time I got back."

"And was he?"

"He was. There was a note saying he'd be staying with his sister." She paused again. "Have you ever been unfaithful?" Naomi was not looking at him as she spoke, but down at her fingers, still trapped in their own intricate embrace. "To your wife?"

"No," he said. His voice was firm, unhesitating. But that was not the right question, the one whose answer was caught in his throat like a sharp little fishbone: Had he ever wanted to? To which the answer would have been, Yes, oh yes. With you.

He hadn't really known, not fully, that that's what he'd wanted. Hadn't known until she had told him about Rick and he'd felt the first shameful flush of something like happiness, not at her distress, never that, but at the sense of what? Permission, that was it. Permission that Rick Wechsler's faithlessness suddenly granted. For if her husband were doing it, why couldn't she? Naomi looked up.

"Would you though?" she asked, very softly, and reached out a hand to stroke his hair. Michael felt the spot where her fingers had touched heat up, as if with fever. Would he? Did she have to even ask? His mother's favorite child, his grandmother's too, altar boy, Catholic school, Catholic college, medical school, the grueling residency, married over twenty years, and never had there been anyone else. Would any of that even matter when this moment, and all that would follow, was totaled and reckoned with? God was a precise and exacting accountant, of that much Michael was sure. Still, as Naomi continued the gentle caress, he cupped her face within his own two hands and leaned his lips down to hers.

14

The Lady Eve

Dead. Estelle kept repeating the word over in her mind. Dahlia was dead. It made no sense to her. Dead was for old people like Milton. Or like her. But Dahlia. How could this be? Estelle could see her jumping on the bed, clattering down the stairs, pumping the swing at the playground so hard that Estelle was sure she would go flying off and be pitched forward, over the chain-link fence and into the matted grass beyond. "A real *vilde chaya*," she would say to Naomi with a kind of grudging respect. A wild thing. Estelle was proud of her, this fearless granddaughter, the one who argued back and talked loud and just might end up getting anything, everything, that she ever wanted. She hadn't been so bold as a child. Neither had Naomi. Naomi had been a truthful girl, finding it hard to lie, hard to deceive her mother or anyone else. And now Naomi had said that Dahlia had died, been killed in a car accident, except no one had been speeding, no one else had been hurt, even the car was fine. So Estelle had to believe this was true, unbelievable as all the facts seemed to be.

Gazing out of her window at the water, Estelle saw that it looked almost black. But now the inky color felt satisfying and correct, a fitting reflection of her inner state. Had the water been the exquisite turquoise of her Florida vista, she didn't think she could have endured the sight. She pulled down the book about Hollywood from her shelf, tried to find solace in the old faces, the old names, but somehow, even this beloved book failed to provide her with a means of escape, a safe haven, an exit. The faces, formerly so filled with expression, seemed blank and vapid now; the eyes didn't shine. Estelle was too aware of being watched and monitored to meld effortlessly into the world that the book evoked.

Ever since she attempted to leave this charmless place and go to Brooklyn, it seemed there was someone—nurse, aide, orderly, social worker—hovering about the periphery of her presence at all times. She closed the book again, let it slip from her lap and fall to the floor. So what if it got dirty or the spine was weakened? She wanted to destroy it. Estelle was angry with the people assigned to her care, her captors, prying and spying all day and all night too. And she was angry with herself, for not having had the foresight, and the fortitude, to have made her way to the row house in Brooklyn, where at least she could have seen for herself that Dahlia no longer lived there. She badly wanted, no needed, to do that. Naomi wouldn't have lied to her, but maybe there had been some mistake. A mistake that perhaps only Estelle could identify and maybe, just maybe, miraculously right.

In the mornings, one of those big, strapping girls—she didn't even try with their names anymore—came in to help her dress and wash. Then she would be escorted to her various activities—physical therapy, arts and crafts—where she would become the responsibility of whoever was in charge. She was aware of the murmured conversations, the looks in her direction. She could imagine what was being said: "That one tried to get away. You've got to watch her like a hawk." And that's just what they did: watch her, watch her, watch, from the moment she opened her eyes to the moment, long hours later, when she closed them again. Someone came in to check on her at night, too, when the lights in her room were extinguished. Lying there in her bed with her eyes closed but not sleeping, she heard the door open, felt the oblique shaft of illumination from the perpetually lit hallway, heard the sounds of someone shifting their weight, peering through the darkness to make sure she was there. The door closed again, and then the cycle repeated four or five times during the night.

In the mornings, she was even more grumpy and disoriented than usual. She was like a penned dog, restless and seething with spite. What if she were to act out the part, run in circles around her room, yelp, urinate, not discreetly on the ground as she had that day when she actually had managed to get free, but right out in the open, a spreading, stinking puddle on the carpeted floor? Years ago, before she came to this place, she remembered reading a newspaper article about prisoners who had flung the waste from their bedpans onto the heads, into the faces even, of their jailers. At the time, reading about this act had frightened and horrified her. But now, as she recalled it, she felt a new sense of kinship with those incarcerated, with their crude, useless rage.

Even as she entertained such fantasies, she knew she would not act them out, not today or tomorrow or ever. Not because she wasn't angry enough, but because her work, such as it was, remained unfinished. She had left these walls once, setting out toward Brooklyn. She had not gotten there. That did not mean, however, that she could not try again. Only this time, she would ask for help. And such help would only be forthcoming if she could prove, once more, that she was harmless, cooperative, docile, obedient. That she had earned it, she thought bitterly.

With difficulty, Estelle bent down to retrieve the book of Hollywood photos from the floor. There was a small tear in the dust jacket, but otherwise it seemed intact. She opened the book again, hoping for the magic contained within to reach out from the pages, place a hand on her cheek, beckon her inside. Look at Mae West, such a card, that one. And Merle Oberon. What a *shana punim*. Estelle was once more soothed, calmed by her friends, the pictures. So much so that when one of the orderlies stuck his head in the door—an alarming jack-in-the-box sort of face, with a pointy nose and predatory-looking teeth—she only glanced up from the book and smiled sweetly.

Later that evening, she asked for assistance in calling Naomi. Her daughter's voice sounded peculiar to her, but maybe everything seemed peculiar to her now.

"I want you to take me there," she told Naomi.

"Take you where?"

"To your house. To Brooklyn." Estelle waited for what seemed like a long time.

"What for?" Naomi asked finally.

"Does a mother need a reason?" Estelle was irritated. The girl was smart. She had gone to that good college, hadn't she? Two of them, in fact. Why did she sound so stupid?

"All right, Mom." Naomi said slowly, as if she were translating the words from another language, one at a time, in her mind. "I'll come and get you."

"When can you come?" Estelle wanted to know. "Can you come now?"

Naomi, however, could not come to Riverdale until the following Saturday. Estelle had a calendar on her wall, one with big, sappy pictures of kittens and puppies that Naomi must have sent, as if age had rendered her mother incapable of appreciating some well-executed Vermeer reproductions or at least some acceptable views of the New York City skyline.

Today was only Monday. She would have to wait nearly a week. The days passed slowly, and by Friday morning, she didn't think she could tolerate another minute's delay. Still, the day had to be gotten through—meals, therapies, whatever had been decreed for her. At least there was a movie in the afternoon, *The Lady Eve*. Just the thought of Barbara Stanwyck in that one—so young, so effervescent—made Estelle, well, if not happy, at least some reasonable approximation of it.

But after lunch—slices of dense yet curiously wan meat loaf, carrots as flavorless as they were garishly colored, mashed potatoes again!—she felt a headache coming on. She asked for and received two blue Extra Strength Tylenol tablets, and went to the movie anyway. Just at one of her favorite parts, though, where Stanwyck, now impersonating an English aristocrat, meets Henry Fonda again, Estelle's headache flared. She returned to her room shakily and took to her bed. Her chest hurt as if someone were pressing down on it and there was a little rasp to her breathing.

"Bronchitis," said the doctor who was summoned and came to see her after dinner.

"Will I be better in the morning?" Estelle almost whispered; her throat hurt too.

"You mean will you be feeling better? I think so; we'll start the antibiotic right away."

"No, I mean can I go out tomorrow? I was supposed to visit my daughter." And my granddaughter, Estelle wished she could say but didn't.

"I'm afraid you won't be going anywhere tomorrow," said the doctor, not unkindly. "Maybe in a few days."

A few days! Estelle was so disappointed. More waiting. And she had missed that delightful movie, one of the only pleasures she had here. Later on, an aide appeared with her antibiotic and she swallowed the pills eagerly. She had to get better, so she could go to Brooklyn. She would have no peace until she climbed the stairs, stepped over the threshold to Dahlia's room, and faced whatever it might be that she found there.

15

Palm Court

On Dahlia's seventh birthday, Rick had brought home the three Chinese dwarf hamsters. They had identical black eyes, identical silvery-brown coats and identical dark stripes outlining their delicate, crushable spines. Dahlia had loved these creatures with her typical immoderate devotion; she crooned to them, petted them, cupped them in her hands and let them settle their bodies across her nose and mouth, where they stretched out, appearing to enjoy the warmth of her breath. She groomed them with an old toothbrush, cleaned their cages faithfully, shredded bits of lettuce to add to their dishes of seed, bestowed countless kisses on their small, furred heads. She thought about them, drew pictures of them, worried over them as if they were the offspring she would one day have.

Once, while Naomi was preparing dinner, Dahlia had come bursting into the kitchen, her hands raised and flapping wildly. "Mommy! Rosie's in the piano!" She was crying hard as she spoke.

"The piano? Why is she in the piano?"

"I wanted to play hide-and-seek with her. I didn't know she'd disappear!" Then Dahlia described how she'd placed the hamster on the piano keys and closed the lid. When she opened it, the hamster was gone. Naomi turned off the water and followed Dahlia into the living room.

The lid to the piano was still open. Naomi closed it and then opened it again. The hamster must have slipped into the seam where the lid, when folded, had fit. She tried looking into the dark space of the seam but saw nothing. There was a slight scratching noise emanating from somewhere in the center of the piano's fruitwood body: Rosie, tucked into its recesses. "What are we going to do?" Dahlia wailed. "We have to save her!"

Rick wasn't home, so Naomi got the toolbox and tried to take apart the piano. She was able to get the top portion unscrewed and set onto the floor, but Rosie, sensing the commotion, responded by finding her way deeper into the piano and was now scampering back and forth—they could hear her tiny nails on the wood—across the bottom. Naomi was stumped. The piano lid was still on the floor; the hamster, still in the piano. How to lure her out? She offered Dahlia a chocolate-dipped yogurt pop to distract her while she continued to think. Food. Now there was an idea. The hamster would need to eat.

Naomi was able to fashion a kind of maze out of some empty paper towel rolls, connecting the maze to a cardboard box she set on the piano bench. In the box, she put some of the bedding from Rosie's cage, a handful of seeds, a minced carrot, and the lid of a jar, in which she had put a little water.

"She'll be hungry, and she'll smell the food," Naomi explained. Dahlia nodded gravely, her face a canvas of smeared chocolate and dried tears.

"We have to hope she'll feel comfortable in the box and decide to stay."

That night, as she put Dahlia to bed, Naomi could feel her daughter's sorrow, keen as a blade.

"I just want her to come back," Dahlia said. Her earlier hysteria was spent, and now she sounded depleted and sad.

"I know, sweetie. We all do."

"Mommy?"

"Yes, honey?"

"If something happened to Rosie, I really don't think I could stand it." The blanket was pulled up around her shoulders; in the dark room, the small, pale oval of her face seemed to hover above it. Naomi had not replied, only bent her head to kiss Dahlia's hair.

It took two more days, but eventually Rosie did venture out of the piano; it was Rick who saw her early one morning in the kitchen; he was able to trap her and return her to her cage before Dahlia had gotten up. Oh, the joy that reigned on Carroll Street when Dahlia awoke to find Rosie spinning contentedly in her wire wheel, oblivious to the pain her absence had caused! But despite the happy outcome, Naomi remained unsettled. What if something did happen to one of the hamsters? Even barring accidents, disasters, and escapes, their life spans were not known to be long. Dahlia's grief would be so enormous; Naomi didn't think she could encompass it.

"What if Rosie had disappeared for good?" she had asked Rick later that night, after Dahlia was asleep. "Or if she had died?" They were lying together in bed; she moved closer to him as she spoke, nudged one of his feet with her own.

"That's the risk of loving anyone or anything." Rick put down his book and turned to face her. "The loss is devastating. But you have to be able to take it."

"Could you?" she had asked.

The weeks after Rick left, the weather turned bitterly cold, colder than it had been in years. The wind whipped up the streets of the neighborhood, tangling the branches of the trees, yanking some up out of the ground entirely. Snow fell, froze, and fell again, leaving treacherous icy patches under the fresh whiteness of each new accumulation. Naomi hurried up the hill to her job at the hospital, shivering and cursing; it was hard not to feel each tug of the wind against her coat as a personal affront, each drop of stinging, frigid rain, as an attack.

She limped through the first weeks of Rick's absence, hardly able to believe he was really gone. Even though she was the one who had told him to go, she still felt abandoned and bereft. First Dahlia, and now Rick. She had been so angry with him, she hadn't realized how his leaving would affect her: it was like losing Dahlia all over again, because he was the other person on earth to feel Dahlia's loss as deeply as she did. Why had he cheated on her? Because she had lost interest in sex, in the pleasure of her body joining with his? Was that all it was? Couldn't he have waited, been more patient? She would have come out of it, had he just given her the time.

But she still missed Rick's presence in the house, which suddenly felt unfamiliar, even foreign to her. At night, alone in what had been their bed, she lay awake, listening to the various sounds: the hiss and clank of the steam as it came up through the pipes, the wind rattling a window in its frame, the light tapping of the rain on the skylight in the hall. None of these noises were strange in and of themselves. But without Rick and Dahlia to help absorb them, they seemed to reverberate too loudly. She had bought herself earplugs, and when they didn't help, she pulled up a small table fan from the basement and turned it on, facing the wall. It wasn't the breeze she needed; it was the steady, comforting sound.

To counteract her sense of discomfort in her own house, Naomi started cleaning it. When she had started teaching, the mountain of chores suddenly seemed unending, and so she had hired Henryka, a sturdy, cheerful Polish woman with gray-blond braids wrapped around her head, who came once a week to mop the floors and scrub the bathrooms. After Dahlia had died, Naomi kept her on for a bit but finally decided that she could resume the cleaning herself; it seemed somehow wasteful and indulgent to ask someone else—even someone she paid—to clean up after her when she had no job and no child. Once immersed, she found she didn't mind doing it at all; in fact, the predictable, repetitive nature of the tasks—the dusting, the polishing, the sweeping, the washing—helped keep her own sorrow at a manageable distance.

In the weeks since Rick left, though, the cleaning assumed a new and almost religious significance. In addition to the regular maintenance of the house, she did what she thought of as "deep cleaning," one room every week. This meant burrowing in and getting down to scrub and scour everything, even things she might normally omit or forget. She hauled out the ladder and climbed its metal rungs to wipe down the moldings that ran around the room's upper perimeter; she washed the windows, moved furniture, and rolled back rugs to clean underneath them. You never really knew a house until you had cleaned it in this way, she decided. Cleaning allowed you to understand the house's skeleton, its inner workings; cleaning exposed all the weaknesses, the strengths. The way the southern exposure at the back of the house illuminated the dining room, for instance. It bathed the room in a soft haze of yellow, but it also revealed every mote of dust she'd missed on the furniture or in the corners.

Her goal was order, and even more essential, purity. She assigned herself a finite job, like the linen closet or the medicine chest. Getting rid of old, faded sheets, frayed towels, and outdated prescriptions seemed to ease her joints, her very bones, as if she were shedding a skin and uncovering a lighter, more flexible version of herself underneath.

One Sunday, she tackled the basement. Things were, predictably, more dusty and haphazard down here. A deflated basketball, an inner tube with a hole, an old chair that needed caning. Finding the lidded plastic boxes where she had stored Dahlia's baby clothes was hard; she pressed her face into the tiny hooded garments, the pajamas that snapped up along the legs, and let the soft, slight mildewed material sop up the tears she did not even try to stop. When the boxes were gone, the clothes washed and bagged for giving away, she felt wrung out, but better.

When Naomi wasn't cleaning, she was at the hospital, where she could let herself become immersed in the routines of the day. She was there full-time now, and she was even getting paid. Pat Ryan and her girlfriend, Claire, had decided to move to Seattle; before she left, Pat wrote a recommendation for Naomi that left all the other candidates for the job far behind.

The new job suited her. Naomi was still involved with the pediatric ward, but she was now responsible for overseeing volunteer activities throughout the hospital, like the St. Saviour's girls who came in one afternoon a week and the bookmobile. She was able to initiate some new things too, like enlisting a local Brownie troop to sponsor a magazine drive and to make tissue-box covers that went into the patients' rooms. She found a beauty school on Dekalb Avenue willing to send students onto the wards; patients could get their hair cut and colored, receive manicures and pedicures, even the occasional facial. There was some deep, instinctual connection between health and grooming, Naomi believed. She thought of the methodical way cats licked their own fur; even Dahlia's hamsters had had their own tidy ritual of rubbing their faces with their minuscule paws.

Naomi still frequently saw Michael at the hospital, though after that day in his office—there had been nothing more than a prolonged, astonished kiss—they were both somewhat shy and off balance with each other. What was supposed to happen next? For Naomi, married to the same man all those years, the thought of committing adultery was like trying on a strange new garment, one where the armholes had been moved and the zipper was in an unfamiliar place. Rick had done it first, but that didn't make it easy or natural for her. Instead, Rick's transgression seemed to disorient her, throwing so many of her assumptions—they would always be together; he would never betray her; they would watch their daughter grow up, get married, start a family of her own—into a nervous and jangling disarray. Then there were Michael's wife and his daughters, thoughts of which paralyzed her. She was a wife wronged; how could she willfully inflict the same pain on another woman, another, for all she knew, blameless wife?

There were also practical issues to consider. Where and when would a meeting take place? Naomi could have coffee with Michael in his office, chat with him when they met in the hospital corridors, but there was no place to go, no place to be alone. They both knew meeting, or even being seen together, in the neighborhood was a mistake; Naomi had lived here for nearly fifteen years; Michael, even longer. Too many people knew them, would recognize them; it would never work. They could have gone to Manhattan or somewhere else farther away. But when would this happen? Michael's time was almost entirely accounted for. And Naomi was unwilling to bring him to the house she had shared with Rick. Despite the fact that the first violation of their marriage had been his, that was still something she felt incapable of doing.

Then, in late January, Michael told Naomi about the infectious disease conference he planned to attend early the following month. This year it was in New York City, at the Plaza Hotel. Although he certainly could have gone back to Brooklyn to sleep, Michael always stayed at the hotel where the conferences were held; that way, he was free to have a late drink or early breakfast with his colleagues from around the country. There were always lots of people at these events he needed to see. But it would be an easy matter for Naomi to come to the hotel one night and visit him in his room. Almost no one else from the hospital would be attending; it wasn't likely she would be spotted or recognized.

"That is, if you want to," Michael had said to her, as they sat in his office one morning, coffees cooling together on his desk.

"I want to," Naomi said steadily, though she was not at all sure that this was what she wanted. There had been something sweet and chaste about that kiss, the one that had no prior history and, until now, no future. A tender, isolated moment that would yield no consequences, commit her to nothing.

"I'll call you when I get there," he said. "Give you the room number and a time. And you have the cell phone number, of course." Naomi nodded. Ever since that day after Christmas, she had not used it. She still didn't feel she had a right to.

By the beginning of February the worst of the cold seemed to have passed, and the night Naomi found herself traveling uptown, toward the Plaza, the air was bracing, not bitter. As she walked down Carroll Street toward the subway entrance on Fourth Avenue, she looked up at the sky; it was a rich, deep blue color she had not seen in a long time. She had dressed casually, in a clean pair of black jeans, black boots, a black ribbed sweater, as if telling herself that nothing illicit might really happen tonight; she was going to see Michael as a friend, because he was, in fact, her friend.

But she did put on a pair of silver hoop earrings, and she secured her hair with a silver clip purchased the day before at The Clay Pot, a shop on Seventh Avenue that sold handcrafted items. A swipe of lip gloss—she was not one for makeup really—and a few drops of perfume at the base of her throat, her temples, and wrists. But not Chanel No. 5, as much as she liked the scent. She had taken the bottle Rick had given her on Christmas and put it way up on the top shelf of her closet, a place she only looked once or twice a year.

The train was slow in coming and stopped many times between stations. It was after nine when Naomi emerged from the subway. But despite the hour, the Plaza's lobby was crowded, and she stood there for a moment, just looking. On the surface, the hotel still seemed to brim with opulence and privilege, but Naomi knew the place had slipped from its exalted status of decades earlier. The conference, for instance. There would have been a time when the Plaza never would have hosted a conference.

She had brought Dahlia here once, shortly after reading her Kay Thompson's *Eloise*, and Dahlia had predictably been taken with the trappings of luxury: the enormous crystal chandeliers, mirrors, thick rugs, extravagant urns of flowers everywhere they looked. Even the ladies' room had a small vase of yellow roses near its entrance, as well as marble-topped sinks and tightly rolled hand towels secured by ivory grosgrain ribbons.

They had eaten in the Palm Court, where a man with a toupee and a tailcoat dramatically flourished a bow over a somewhat battered violin. Loving the music as she had, Dahlia failed to notice that the man's coat was too small and ripped under the arm, or that his playing was just barely passable. The surface had bewitched her sufficiently, even if the substance had become ersatz and threadbare. The plate stacked high with its tower of tea sandwiches elicited fresh delight; she had methodically opened each of them, eaten their contents daintily with a fork, and put the discarded triangles of bread into a neat pile on her napkin. When the dessert cart appeared, she picked a raspberry tart, which she ate slowly with her eyes closed.

"Do you like it?" Naomi had asked, watching her daughter, who seemed serious, even solemn, as she chewed, then swallowed. Maybe the tart wasn't quite fresh; her own dessert, chocolate mousse, was only a small step above pudding.

"Like it?" Dahlia's eyes popped open again. "Mommy, it's heaven."

Remembering all this made Naomi almost decide to turn around and go home again. Almost, but not quite. Instead, she went to the desk and in a low voice asked for the room of Dr. Michael McBride.

"And whom shall I say is calling?" asked the uniformed young man behind the desk.

"Naomi Wechsler," she said.

"Fourteenth floor. Room 1402," the man replied, gesturing toward the elevators.

Naomi rode up in an elevator with a young couple—both tall, both fair, both heavyset—and a pair of frail, elderly women who seemed weighed down by their furs. She was the first to get off, and when she did, she tried to shake the feeling she had of being watched. Judged. She walked down the wide, elegantly proportioned corridor until she came to the right room.

Michael answered her knock immediately. Standing in the open doorway, he looked even more disheveled than usual. His shirt was wrinkled and had dark smudges on the cuffs; his pants seemed wrinkled too and were lightly flecked with something white and crumbly. Naomi spied his suit jacket hanging from the back of a striped chair and his tie, stretched out like an eel, on the bed.

"You came," he said, as if he hadn't expected she would.

"Yes." She fiddled with the strap of her handbag, fingered the lapel of her coat.

"I'm so glad." He took her arm gently and brought her into the room, which was spacious though somewhat generic in feeling. There was another, albeit smaller, crystal chandelier up here, a patterned carpet, a sofa covered in peach brocade, an ornately carved wooden desk on which there were stacks of papers, folders, and an open laptop. In one corner was a round table where a bottle of white wine and a pair of glasses had already been set up. And although she tried not to look directly at it, there was the huge—it must have been king-size—bed with its smooth white sheets, pillows in their embroidered cases, quilt already folded back, dominating the space.

To avoid the bed's mute reproach, Naomi walked over to the windows. Even in the dark, she could make out the undulating lines of Central Park laid out below her. Here, in this view, was the grandeur the room itself lacked.

"Something to drink?"

Naomi turned. Michael held the bottle in his hand.

"That would be nice." She sat down and tasted the wine, which was fruity and smooth, without taking off her coat or setting down her purse. She could have a drink with him, and then leave. Nothing would have happened, she would have nothing to regret. But then she thought of the empty house back in Brooklyn, her daughter dead, her faithless husband gone. Why not have the small bit of comfort, of pleasure this night was offering her?

"Are you all right?" Michael was standing above her, looking down at what must have been her tense, anxious expression.

"I'm all right." Naomi set down her purse and stood up. Slowly she began unbuttoning her coat, letting it slip down to the chair. Her sweater came off in an easy gesture, though it pulled the silver clip out of her hair. It dropped to the carpet, where Michael knelt down to pick it up. When he handed it to her, his fingers reached for hers, and together, they let the silver clip drop again.

It was nearly nine when Naomi awoke the next morning. Michael was gone; he'd left her a note on the pillow, though, and she brought it closer to her face so she could read it. But her eyes didn't want to focus yet; she'd had a lot to drink the night before and realized, from the heave and lurch of her stomach as well as the throbbing of her head, that she was badly hung over. A trip to the bathroom and a hot shower seemed to improve things, though only marginally. She called her office at the hospital to say that she wasn't feeling well and wouldn't be in until later that day. She was rubbing her hair dry with a towel when a light knocking on the door caused her to freeze. Where could she hide in this room? In the bathtub? Behind the desk?

"Naomi? It's me." She recognized Michael's voice and hurried over to the door.

Before saying anything else, he kissed her. Naomi was still reeling from last night, the utter strangeness yet comfort with this new body, the revised image of herself: a woman, still married, who had slept with another man. Who was himself married. God. Yet she responded to the kiss instinctually and stood there letting it settle in and around her for what seemed like several minutes. Finally, she pulled away.

"Aren't you busy? With the conference?"

"There was a break. Instead of having coffee with the infectious disease people from Boston Children's, I came up here to see you. To make sure you were all right. You were pretty looped last night."

"Was I?" But she knew the answer to that already. "I hope I didn't humiliate myself."

"Not a chance," he said, eyes still watching her face, still watching all of her.

"I should go." Naomi turned away from the intensity of his look. What would he see if he kept looking? That same intensity reflected on her own features? She put the towel down, ran a comb through her hair. Her clothes were strewn on the floor; she gathered them quickly and put her hand on the door to the bathroom. Michael looked at his watch. "I've got a little time. I can walk you to the sub-way."

"You don't have to."

"I know." He smiled. "I want to."

Her hair was still a little damp when they stepped out onto Fifth Avenue a few minutes later. There was sunshine, weak but still percep-tible, and Naomi felt oddly comforted by it. Across the Fifth Avenue was FAO Schwarz, another of her stops with Dahlia on the day they had gone to the Plaza. But Naomi didn't want to be reminded of that now and crossed the street instead, drawn by a slice of color she saw in the window of Bergdorf Goodman.

This wasn't a store where she usually shopped—too expensive, too exclusive, too rarified for both her taste and her budget. But the color—it turned out to be a scarf—had caught her attention. It was a long, simple but thick rectangle of cashmere, in a robin's-egg blue. The window was filled with cashmere scarves in different, brilliant col-ors: lemon, scarlet, fuchsia. There was even a black one, which would have ordinarily been Naomi's choice. Something about that particular blue color, though, pulled her closer. She wanted to touch it, sniff it, wind it around her neck, her hair.

"You like it, don't you?" She turned. She had momentarily forgot-ten Michael was with her.

"It's not a color I usually wear. But I think it's so beautiful. Like the blue that heaven would be. That is, if heaven existed."

"How do you know it doesn't?" His voice was light, but suddenly, Naomi was crying. If there actually were such a place, then she had foolishly squandered her chance of ever going there, of ever being re-united with her daughter.

"Naomi," he said, and took her in his arms while she wept. "I'm so sorry. What did I say?"

"It's nothing." She shook her head, scattering teardrops on the pavement. Then she looked up, put her hand on his chest. "Let's go in. I'm going to buy it."

"No," said Michael as he steered her toward the revolving door. "I'm going to buy it for you."

"Why would you do that?" Naomi knew this was a kind of rude thing to say, but she didn't seem to censor herself with him. That was so much of what she liked about being with him; she could say whatever came into her mind, unedited.

"Because I want to." Inside the store, though, he looked momentarily dazed. The elegant women dispensing their mists of perfume, the men with their expensive, imported shoes, the color of chocolate, of cognac, of tobacco. She knew he didn't belong here any more than she did. But all at once he seemed to get his bearings and directed her, as if by instinct, to the counter where the scarves were displayed. The robin's-egg blue scarf poured from a brass hoop like a lush, cashmere waterfall.

"We'll take this one, please," he said to the saleswoman, and he handed her a credit card. Naomi watched as the transaction was completed and the scarf shrouded first in tissue, then a paper bag, and finally the lilac shopping bag with the store's name and logo imprinted on it. Then back through the revolving door and out onto the street again.

"Thank you," she said, clutching the bag to her chest. She had the thought that if she dipped her hand inside, it would be like dipping it into a tropical ocean—warm, tranquil, blue.

"You are most welcome." He touched her cheek softly. His fingers, without gloves, were cold, but she didn't care. Then all at once, she saw his expression metamorphose into one of shock and horror. She turned to see what it was he was seeing. A young girl, standing a few feet away, was looking at them with an equally horrified expression on her face. His daughter.

"Brooke," Michael said, as if to confirm what Naomi had seen. And then he dropped his hand, as if her skin had scorched him.

16

Driven Snow

"*I cannot believe what* an asshole you are," said Rick's sister, Allison. He was sitting behind her in the small bedroom of her Yorkville high-rise watching as she applied her mascara with a careful hand.

"That thing you're using?" Rick said, pointing in her direction.

"What thing?" Her hand, momentarily suspended, seemed raised in some sort of greeting.

"That little curled thing? Isn't it called a wand?"

"So what if it is?" Allison resumed the application of her makeup. "You're changing the subject."

"I guess I am. It's not fun to have your little sister call you names."

"I'm sure it wasn't fun for Naomi to find out that you've been screwing your office manager." She finished with the mascara, put the wand back into the tube from which it had emerged. "As I said, you are an asshole, big brother. First-class. No doubt about it."

"Did I ever say I wasn't?" He crossed his legs and then uncrossed them again. He wasn't comfortable in this apartment; he felt perpetually squeezed and fettered by its low ceilings, its boxy little rooms. He'd come here when Naomi had asked him to leave, although Allison had not been home then; she'd been on a photo shoot in Paris. Rick had her key and the doorman knew him, so he'd been able to use the place in her absence. But now that she was back, she was making up for all the things she'd been unable to ask or say when he'd first arrived.

"No." Allison turned away from the mirror so she was facing Rick. "You didn't. But I still don't understand why. Why would you do something like that . . . so soon after Dahlia . . . died. That's all."

"I was dying too," Rick said. "Every minute of every day."

"And you think Naomi wasn't?"

"I know she was. But she couldn't help me, Allie. And I couldn't help her."

"So your answer was to start fucking the office manager?"

"It wasn't like that." Rick tried shifting his long body back in his chair but it too felt small and cramped. Was everything in this apartment doll-sized or was he just imagining it? "She came on to me first," he added in a low voice. There was something particularly humiliating about being grilled and then excoriated by his baby sister. When had she become such an authority on love, sex, and marriage anyway?

"And you couldn't have said, like, no? Or how about, Sorry, but I'm married?"

"Look," Rick stood up so that he was now standing over her. Better, this was a much better vantage point from which to have this conversation. "If you want me to leave, I will. Just say the word. I'll go peacefully, I promise."

"I don't want you to go." Allison leaned over and took out a pair of dangling earrings from an enamel box she kept on the dresser. "You may be an asshole, but you're still my brother. My favorite brother." She slipped them through the holes in her ears—how the hell did she do it without looking?—and then picked up her hairbrush. Although it was already after nine, she was going on a date; first drinks at a bar downtown, then dancing. She wouldn't be home until early the next morning.

The downstairs buzzer rang, and when Allison picked up, the doorman made some garbled announcement.

"Grant's here," she said, combing her hair out with her hands and reaching for her shiny black coat, her spangled black bag. Allison somehow managed to give the color black all the variety and pizzazz of a rainbow, Rick observed with affection. "Don't wait up."

The apartment was quiet again when she had gone. Youth, thought Rick, but not at all bitterly. He didn't even want to be out drinking and dancing until dawn anymore. Though he couldn't have said right at that moment where it was he actually did want to be.

Ever since the day when he had packed a bag and walked out the door and down the brownstone steps of his house, he had not known where, precisely, he was going or what he was going to do when he got there. That first morning, he had walked through the cold and quiet streets to his office, although he had no patients, and sat with his hands folded and his head down on his desk as if he were praying. But he was not praying, he was just thinking about how he had reached this place in his life: no daughter, no wife, no home. No single act or moment could be held wholly responsible for where he was now; instead, it was a series of small, seemingly random dots on a map that, when connected, put him in this particular location.

He had stayed like that for a long time, until at some point, he'd heard a key in the outer door of the office, and then a small slam. Naomi, he thought, she's reconsidered, she's come to get me, to tell me to come back. He got up, went into the waiting room. Instead of his wife, he saw it was Lillian, wearing a fur-trimmed parka and holding a puppy on a leash.

"Rick," she said, clearly surprised, pulling down the hood of her parka and shaking out her hair. The puppy whined, and strained on the leash trying to get free. "I wanted to catch up on a few things before the office reopened. I wasn't expecting to see you."

"I wasn't expecting to be here."

"Is there something wrong?" The dog was still whimpering and Lillian reached down to pat his head.

"You can let him go," Rick said, and when she did, the puppy came bounding over and placed his big paws on Rick's chest. Then he licked his chin. "Friendly, isn't he?"

"And a little nuts. But Jason loves him." She smiled indulgently.

"Who wouldn't?" Rick stroked the dog's smooth black head. Must be part lab, he thought. The dog responded by rolling on his back in canine bliss. "I'm surprised Jason would even let him out of his sight."

"He had to. His dad picked him up today."

"Your ex doesn't like dogs?"

"He likes them all right. But his new girlfriend is allergic. So no dog at the apartment." She looked at the dog rolling around on the floor. "Her loss." Then she added, "So, what are you doing here anyway? You never answered the question."

"Naomi kicked me out. I didn't have anyplace else to go."

"She found out, then? About us?" Lillian took off her parka, hung it on a hook, and sat down on one of the waiting room's chairs. Rick sat too. "I told you before, honey: the wife always finds out."

"But does the husband always tell her?"

"You told Naomi? Why?"

"I don't know. I suddenly couldn't take not telling her anymore." The dog thumped his tail on the floor, demanding the attention Rick had let stray.

"And she asked you to leave?"

"Last night. I slept on the couch until it was light, though. Then I came here." He reached down again, stroked the dog's belly.

"So what will happen now? Where will you go?"

"I can probably stay with my sister. She lives in Manhattan. She'll be furious with me, but she'll let me stay anyway."

"I feel terrible," Lillian said. "It's my fault, you know."

"No, it's not." Rick was certain, at least, of that much. "You didn't have to coerce me, remember? I was willing."

Lillian didn't reply. She called the dog, who ignored her. She tried again, this time more sternly. The dog gave her a baleful look and then walked over to where she sat.

"How late will you be here today?" she finally asked.

"I'm not sure." Rick stood. It didn't feel right to be here alone with her. Not anymore.

"I'll see you on Monday, then," Lillian said, moving toward her desk.

Rick watched her. She was as desirable as any woman he had ever seen, ever fantasized about. But wanting her, having her, meant losing Naomi. How had he gotten himself into this? And how the fuck would he get himself out?

That had been more than two weeks ago. More than two weeks since he'd seen or talked to his wife, though he'd been sending her daily e-mails, to which she had not yet replied. More than two weeks since he'd been in his house, walked up the stairs, stood at the door in the dining room, looking out at the small yard, the pleasing arrangement of the neighbor's windows, the handful of squirrels making their nervous, agile way up the trunk of the tree in the yard's far corner.

Since that time, he had been sleeping at Allison's, first in the queen-size bed that took up nearly her entire bedroom and later, after she'd returned, on the fold-out sofa in the living room. He had gone to his office, where he had administered to a host of infections, ingrown toenails, and four bunions—all on women—at least two of which would require surgery. It was the shoes women wore—with their admittedly sexy high heels and pointed toes—that exacerbated the condition; when a man had a bunion, it almost never required the knife.

He had operated on a woman whose tight Achilles tendon was giving her pain and on another, a diabetic with a flaccid, mournful face, whose big toe he had to amputate. Rick didn't like doing the amputations, even when they were necessary and done in an effort to stave off something worse, like amputating the entire foot or, in some cases, the leg. But the patients rarely saw it this way; instead they felt like something was being taken from them and he, Rick, was doing the taking. This one wept as she was wheeled into surgery, and Rick had to steel himself against the tide of emotion—frustration, pity, anger—that he felt rising inside. Don't look into her eyes, he told himself. Think about the foot you're going to save. Think about the leg.

But afterward, when she came to, she couldn't stop talking about her toe. "It was part of me," she kept saying. "I can't believe it's really gone." Rick was grateful he didn't have any surgeries scheduled for the next couple of weeks; patients like this one rattled him, made him feel, irrationally, like a thief. Whereas, in fact, he was not a thief; he was only an adulterer, and not even a very active one at that.

Though there was now greater opportunity for him to see Lillian—the nights her son spent with her ex-husband left her alone in her apartment—Rick found himself reluctant to suggest coming over. And Lillian did not invite him. He still tracked her progress through the office, still remained hyperaware of her throughout the day, the sound her shoes, always heels, made on the floor, the smell of the lotion she rubbed on her hands after she had washed them. His fantasy life about her was as rich and active as ever. But he couldn't reconcile those fantasies with the reality of his situation: Naomi, alone in the house on Carroll Street, while he camped out at Allison's, trying to get comfortable on the fold-out bed's thin mattress.

Lillian seemed to sense it too, this barrier that had suddenly risen between them, and though he often caught her looking at him, she offered nothing in the way of further intimacy, no opportunity to get closer to her than their workday allowed.

So his nights were spent mostly with Allison or, if she had a date, alone. He loved his little sister, though she puzzled him. Allison, who had zipped through school in record time, becoming fluent in French during her semester abroad and in Italian during an extended summer she spent in Rome after graduation. She taught herself Spanish too, just for the hell of it, she said. But even though she could have been a successful academic—"Think of the perks, the benefits," wheedled Scott and Mark—or even a translator, she claimed not to want such a life. Instead, she gravitated toward the fashion magazine, where she claimed that her facility with languages was useful in her work.

"Yeah, you can order some brainless, anorexic model her latte in Italian," said Scott. Mark agreed. "Or order her kir royale in French."

Rick held off from sharing his own thoughts on the subject—he knew how irritating it was to be heckled by their two high-achieving, perpetually competing siblings—but he too had to wonder. Was there something Allison was avoiding with her amusing but admittedly lightweight magazine job? Or did the work have some pull, some depth, even, that he simply could not fathom?

Rick was awakened the next day by the sound of Allison dropping her boots by the apartment door. Not that she was being excessively loud; he hadn't been sleeping too well ever since he had left his house. And of course the foldout couch was not too comfortable.

"Have a good time?" he asked, propping himself up on his arm so he could look at her. Her coat was open and he could see a slice of bare midriff where her shirt had ridden up. Last night, when she'd left, it had been tucked in. He tried not to consider the implications of that. The sex lives of his siblings was possibly the most unerotic subject on earth. Though God knows Mark and Scott used to discuss their own conquests in the most graphic of terms—"Tits like melons, man! I couldn't believe the size of them!"—even they had shied away from the subject of Allison's love life, as soon as she had grown old enough to have one.

"Mmm," she said, sitting down on the bed and shrugging off her coat. "I did. Grant's a good dancer."

"Uh-huh." Rick was stretching, thinking about getting up and making some coffee or, even better, going out for some. It was Sunday. Nowhere he had to be.

"Good kisser too." Allison looked down demurely at her fingernails. He noticed then that they were painted a pale metallic color, somewhere between silver and blue.

"Thanks for sharing," he said. Now he really was going to get up. He wasn't in the mood for this.

"What, all of a sudden you're a prude?"

"Not a prude. I just don't need all the gory details."

"There aren't any more. End of story."

"Good." He swung his legs over the side of the bed.

"What's your rush?" She hadn't moved from where she sat, but was staring at him with that imploring look of hers. That look she'd been perfecting since she was, oh, about three. Still, he couldn't resist it.

"No rush." He sat back down. "I just wasn't sure what I was going to hear."

"Something that will surprise you."

"Oh?" he asked. "And what would that be?"

"I'm a virgin." She waited, clearly wanting his reaction.

"A virgin? What do you mean, virgin?"

"What you usually mean when you use that word. Pure. Innocent. Untouched as the driven snow." She was teasing him, that was it.

"But how about a minute ago? When you said Grant was a good kisser?"

"I didn't say I had never kissed anyone. I just said I was a virgin."

"I see." But he didn't, not really.

"It's not that I don't like guys, kissing them, all that. But I haven't— what was that term we used in high school? Gone all the way?"

"Why not?"

"I don't know. I just haven't met the right person, I guess. Or if I have met him, the timing hasn't been right. I just don't want it to be another ordinary thing I've done. I still think it should be special." She lay back on one of the pillows, crossed her ankles.

"Sounds reasonable." He lightly touched her chin with his finger. "Why are you telling me this now?"

"I wanted to apologize, I guess. For calling you an asshole last night."

"That? Forget it." He smiled. "Anyway, I am an asshole."

"The thing I'm trying to say is, maybe I had no right to say that, because I don't know what it's like. To sleep with one person for all those years. And then to sleep with someone else."

"I told you: it's okay."

"But still. I didn't mean to make things worse."

"You didn't make anything worse." Rick found himself remembering that when Allison was sixteen, she had badly wanted a nose job. She begged their parents, who weren't sure how to respond. His brothers, already deep in their respective medical grooves, had been ready to call on the plastic surgeons they knew, set her up for a consultation. Rick was against it though. He did his best to convince her to wait. She listened to him, and in the end had decided she liked her profile well enough to leave it alone. Years later, she was grateful, calling him her nose's savior. "I'm the one who makes things worse."

"Well, you can change that, can't you?"

"What do you mean?"

"Get in touch with Naomi. Tell her you're sorry."

"I've been in touch with Naomi."

"You have? What does she say?"

"Nothing. I've been sending her e-mails. She doesn't answer."

"E-mails aren't good enough. You have to call her. Go to see her."

"Allie." She really was so young, wasn't she? "Naomi doesn't want to see me. At least not now."

"Do you want to see her?"

"Yes. No." He scratched the back of his neck. Why couldn't he end this pointless conversation and get that cup of coffee?

"It can't be both, Rick."

"Why not?"

"It just can't. You have to know what you want."

"What I want," Rick repeated as he stood and stretched, "is coffee. Really strong. I'll see you later." He disappeared into the bathroom to pull on his clothes and waited for a few more minutes before emerging again. When he did, Allison was gone from the fold-out couch; he could see that the door to her bedroom was now closed. Good. Taking advantage of her temporary absence, Rick picked up his wallet and his coat and stealthily made his escape. The fact was that he did want to see Naomi. He missed her, he missed their life together, even if it had become in recent months a fugue, an elegy.

Rick decided to move out of Allison's apartment. He could see that it was time to go. The only thing was that he didn't know where. He had friends, like Jon, who would have put him up. But he didn't want the questions, even those that were not spoken, and the judgments, even though they might have been well deserved. What kind of guy starts screwing around on his wife after their daughter has been killed? That's what Allison thought, and that's what Jon would think too. Though he hadn't defended himself when Allison was giving him hell, he'd had enough. What right did she have to judge him? How could she know what it was like to have been driving the car that day? Did she or anyone know how it felt to hold your daughter's limp body in your arms, knowing even as you raced her into the emergency room that it was too late, that no one and nothing there could help her?

The office. The answer came to him suddenly. That's where he would go. It had once been an apartment and so had a bathroom with a shower, a small kitchen with a microwave, minifridge, and coffee-maker. He could sleep on the couch in the waiting room or bring over a sleeping bag and set it out on the floor. He tried it for a couple of nights and found it curiously soothing. He didn't tell Helene or Lillian or, of course, any of his patients. He didn't even tell Naomi.

Rising before six, he would put on his sweatpants and sneakers and go for a run along the Promenade. He'd been a fairly serious runner in college, though he hadn't done it for years. Still his legs, his lungs, and indeed his whole body quickly adapted themselves to the requisite rhythms. The slight stiffness when he began, then the heat of his own exertion thawing and warming him. The puffs that his breath made in the cold morning air, the easy movements of his arms, urging him on. The early-morning light hitting the water, the impressive dense clutter of Manhattan's skyline, seen just across the East River.

As he ran, he felt the weight of the past months—thoughts of Dahlia, of Naomi—not ease so much as shift. He had been desperate and crazy in allowing himself to succumb to Lillian. But that was over now. He ran as if he could run toward penance, toward salvation. He ran as if running long and fast enough could carry him back, to his house, his wife, to some semblance of a life that he could really live once more. Now, if Naomi would only ask him to come home and live it with her.

17

Rubber Soul

She saw them. Saw them. Saw them, saw them, saw them. The words beat a nasty refrain in her head. They summoned an even nastier picture: her father with that woman. His fingers lightly touching her face. Not fucking her, not even kissing but simply touching. Still, Brooke recognized, inchoately, the unequivocal sexual valence of the gesture. It meant that they had been kissing, they had been fucking. And not that long ago, either.

Brooke remembered her too: she had met her before Christmas, when she and Mackenzie had been shopping for their mother's gift. Her father had introduced them. Naomi. That was her name. And now here she was, fucking Brooke's father, and Brooke's mother didn't know a thing about it. Brooke didn't know how she was so sure of all this, but she was. The certainty of this knowledge, awful as it was, somehow comforted her. At least she knew something. Lately, it had seemed as if she didn't know anything at all. Or worse: what she thought she knew had changed so radically, without her even understanding how or why such transformations had taken place.

It had started months ago. She would suddenly see something or someone in a completely different way, as if all of what she had believed about them before had become like some extraneous crust, just so much debris that was easily brushed away. Stephanie Conners, for instance. How was it that two months ago she would have said

Stephanie was her best friend in the world and now Stephanie seemed to her to be shallow and vacuous, capable of no thought more penetrating than the impending purchase of a new blow-dryer at Rite Aid pharmacy. Not that Brooke didn't care about blow-dryers or how she looked and all of that. Of course she cared. But she had some detachment from it too. A sense of irony that Stephanie was utterly lacking. Stephanie, for instance, believed all that stuff they printed in the magazines about what brand of blush or foundation the model wore.

"They get paid for endorsing those products," Brooke had explained more than once. Stephanie, however, refused to believe her. No, Stephanie was without any critical faculty whatsoever, Brooke decided. Stephanie was, in fact, a moron. How had Brooke missed it all this time?

Various teachers of hers at St. Saviour's had been subject to the same mental revision. Why had she thought Mrs. Remson was so funny? Miss Craine so sophisticated and smart? Even the nun who taught religion, Sister Ursula, seemed completely devoid of inspiration and faith. She recited the prayers as if she were reading pages in the phone book, not as if she believed the words she was speaking. Maybe she didn't. Maybe none of them did.

It was around this time, when everything began to look and seem different, that Brooke had started cutting school. Just a period or two here and there so she wouldn't get caught. She'd always been a good student, a good girl, so she was able to get away with her little excursions up to Prospect Park when she was supposed to be in English class or down to Seventh Avenue when she should have been in gym. Nothing serious of course. Nothing that was going to really count. There were times when she felt like there wasn't enough air in the classroom, and when she felt like that, she knew she had to get out, at least for a little while. So she would take a quick walk up to the park and wander around for a little while, maybe sit on a bench and stare at the sky. Or she would go in the other direction, to Barnes & Noble, where she could slip downstairs and pick out a book to read. Not that she couldn't have bought a book; her parents were generous with money and always encouraged the girls to read, to buy books. But once she had made a purchase, Brooke felt it was no longer her own: her mother might ask to see what she'd chosen, her father would ask her opinion of it. A book that she looked at in a store, however, was entirely, completely hers. So far, Brooke had been successful in avoiding detection. She was careful, she was circumspect. The only one who knew what she was up to was Mackenzie, but Mackenzie wouldn't tell. Brooke knew she could count on that, even though she and Mackenzie hadn't been as close as they had once been.

Lately, Brooke's reevaulation of everyone in her life had come to include her twin sister as well. Mackenzie was too good, too passive, too eager to be the perfect daughter. But there had been years when they had been each other's best friend, strongest ally, most trusted confidante. She could remember Mackenzie sitting behind her in the room they had insisted on sharing, brushing her hair while they talked. They had had their own private language—a series of odd, syncopated syllables punctuated with a series of winks and hand gestures—that drove their mother crazy. Mackenzie had helped her ace her geometry exams, taught her how to dive, never revealed to any of their bunkmates at summer camp that Brooke sometimes still sucked her thumb. Even if things had cooled between them, Brooke knew that she could still rely on her sister's discretion.

The morning she had seen her father with that Naomi person, Brooke had ventured further than she'd ever dared before: she had decided to skip the entire morning and head into Manhattan. Now, that really was serious; she risked getting caught. Which made it all the more compelling a thing to do. She didn't have a clear idea about what she would do when she got there; she just wanted to walk around the thronged, noisy streets, absorb some of their energy, their pulse as she walked. She had taken the F train to Rockefeller Center; her parents had taken her there when she and Mackenzie were little. They'd see the Christmas show and the big tree; they would watch the skaters on the rink and then walk uptown along Fifth Avenue. They had not done this in a while; both she and Mackenzie had decided these activities were beneath them now, too much like the activities of tourists.

"What's wrong with acting like a tourist in the greatest city in the world?" Camille had countered. "There's always something to see in New York. You should be glad you've got the chance to see it." But still, she hadn't been able to persuade them. So it was odd that of all the neighborhoods she could have chosen to wander—the Village, Soho, Chelsea, the Upper East Side—she should have picked this one. Maybe she was just starting with something familiar, before she went off someplace new. Only then she had seen her father and the whole day, no, not just the day but her whole life, had been ruined.

She didn't stop, didn't stay to hear whatever pathetic excuse he might have offered her. She saw them and then she fled, turning around and heading south, back downtown, from the direction in which she had come. With her long stride, she was back at Rockefeller Center in minutes. The Christmas tree was no longer in evidence, but there were still several skaters gliding around on the rink. She stood by the railing, watching but not seeing. How could her father be doing such a thing? What would her mother say when she found out? That is, if she found out. Was Brooke supposed to be the one to tell her mother what she had seen? Just the thought of this made her want to vomit, without fanfare, into a garbage can or right onto the pavement. She willed herself to pay attention to the skaters, and the urge subsided.

After a few minutes, she realized she was cold, and she started walking again, down Sixth Avenue. Pretty soon she came to Twenty-third Street and then Fourteenth, both places she could have caught the F train back to Brooklyn. But Brooke had no intention of going back to Brooklyn anytime soon. Her father was at that infectious disease conference; he wouldn't be home for another day, maybe two. Was that woman staying with him the whole time? Didn't she have a job? And a husband? Brooke knew she was really asking for trouble by skipping an entire day of school. Maybe Mackenzie would cover for her. In any case, she didn't care. There was too much else for her to deal with now. School could wait, certainly, until tomorrow.

She veered east, and when she reached Astor Place, she decided to stop. It was past noon and she was hungry. There was a big coffee shop near the subway station, and she went inside. The tables were all filled, but she saw a lone stool at the counter. She sat down, ordered a cheeseburger and fries, and then discovered that the sight of the meat—she had ordered it medium, but it appeared before her rare and slightly bloody—again made her want to throw up. Her appetite effectively killed, she picked at the fries and nursed her Coke. Back in the street again, she continued walking, but this time east, toward the part of the city called Alphabet Town.

She wasn't allowed to go here, not really. Her father had made that clear when she and Mackenzie started taking the train into the city by themselves last year. In the past, she had always listened to him. Always wanted to listen. When she was little, she had thought him perfect, without a single flaw. On Career Day at school, he'd come into her class and talked to the restless, fidgety fourth graders about what it meant to be a doctor, how seriously he took his mandate to heal and, failing to heal, to do no harm. He'd come with posters illustrating the hidden mysteries of the human body: the intricate map made by the veins and arteries, the surprisingly graceful configurations of the bones, the improbable shape of the organs. When the posters proved insufficient, he resorted to drawing on the board with colored chalk. Throughout the presentation the kids were rapt and silent; at the end, they started clapping all at once.

Even as she grew older and understood that he was of course not perfect, she still found so much to admire in him: she'd seen the way people at the hospital looked up to him. Seen the way he, in turn, looked at them: never down, but as equals, eye to eye. Her father. With his perpetually messy white hair, his deep blue eyes, his strong shoulders that had carried both her and Mackenzie at the same time. And now this.

Here she was at Avenue B. She stopped in front of a store whose psychedelic-looking sign made the lettering hard to read. Finally she deciphered the single word: *Vinyl*. She went in. There, wooden bins housed what looked to be hundreds of old records: pop, jazz, soul, rock. The Grateful Dead and Joni Mitchell. Louis Armstrong and Ella Fitzgerald. Posters from long-ago concerts and tours—torn at the edges, yellowing—hung on the walls; photographs of singers and musicans were tacked up on top and around them. How did people even listen to records anymore? Did record players still exist? Hanging from the ceiling on wires and string, Brooke saw a number of Christmas ornaments. They must have been leftovers from the holiday. These too looked old; they were made of glass and were dusted with that flaky white paint that was supposed to resemble snow. Some were decorated with pictures of bells; others with stars of Bethlehem. She had seen things like this in boxes in her grandmother's basement. Somehow, they wouldn't have looked the same if they had been hanging at her grandmother's house, though she couldn't have said why.

Brooke lifted a Beatles album out of a bin. *Rubber Soul*. Never heard of that one, though she of course knew about the Beatles. Her father used to sing their songs when she and Mackenzie were little—loudly, exuberantly—until they grew old enough to beg him to stop, please, please stop. "She Loves You." "Twist and Shout." "I Want to Hold Your Hand." She remembered the tunes, the lyrics even. Though right now, the memories stabbed her, as if they were part of some innocent, earlier life she had only hours ago found out she no longer had any claim to. Was this just the beginning? Of the before and after into which things would now and forever be divided?

"Hey, want to hear it?" asked the red-headed guy behind the counter. He had been reading a book when she'd walked in—she was the shop's only customer—but now he looked up.

"Oh, that's okay." Brooke took in his long red hair and the odd, intriguing amber color of his eyes.

"It's no trouble." He came out from behind the counter and reached for the album. Brooke handed it to him and watched as he opened a big, boxy-looking case near the cash register, and then

Brooke saw the turntable, the plastic arm with its quaint needle. "There are some great songs on this." He pulled the record from its cardboard cover, careful to handle the black shiny disk only by its rim, and placed it on the turntable. Then he fiddled with a knob or two. Brooke listened to the scratchy sounds of static before the shop was filled with music—tender and, at moments, melancholy. "Isn't it good, Norwegian wood?" crooned one of the Beatles, though which one she couldn't have said. Her father had never sung this song. Maybe he didn't know it. But she didn't want to think about her father now. He was still uptown somewhere, while she had found her way down here, to this store with the records and the sweet, unfamiliar music. She liked being here. It almost made her forget about what she had seen, what it meant. Almost. But not quite. Forgetting was going to take more work. She would have to try harder.

"You don't find this one too often," said the red-haired guy when the song ended. "And when you do, it's almost always scratched. This copy is in great shape." He picked it up again and blew on the surface before returning it to the jacket.

"I've never heard it before." Brooke shook a lock of her own hair out from behind her ear so that it partially covered her face. She thought it made her look better. Older. More cool. "I like it."

"You've got good taste." He grinned. His teeth, though a little crooked, were very white. She saw a glint of silver, momentarily, in his tongue. When he closed his mouth again, it was gone. She felt obscurely disappointed. She wanted to see it again, ask him questions, maybe even touch it. Did it hurt to have to put in? All of a sudden, she wanted one of her own. No, not one, but several: tongue, eyebrow, nostril, navel. She wanted this beautiful boy to take her by the hand and show her where, how, such things were done.

"Do you think so?" She stepped a little closer to him now. "Do you really think so?"

"It's a great album," he repeated. "Early Beatles is the best. The later stuff"—he made a face, indicating his scorn—"that's all trash. The early stuff is what's pure, you know?" He was studying her now, she could see it. Brooke wondered what he saw when he looked at her. Under her open coat, she was no longer wearing her St. Saviour uniform, or at least not all of it. Before getting on the subway train that morning, she stopped into the Purity Diner and, within the tiled safety of a ladies' room stall, peeled off the maroon-and-gray plaid skirt and the maroon V-neck sweater and stuffed them both into the large slate blue canvas bag she had bought recently at Pearl Paint in Manhattan. She loved the bag, loved thinking that it might be just the kind of thing an art student, one who went to Cooper Union or Pratt Institute, would carry. She replaced the uniform's skirt with her favorite jeans and the sweater with a gray hooded sweatshirt that completely hid her white, school-issue polo shirt with the SSH logo on the front. She had also applied some sooty-looking eye shadow and a coating of a dark, berry-stained color to her mouth. Did he notice all these details? Did he care?

"Maybe I should buy it," she said, though she didn't have much money with her. Ten dollars, fifteen at the most.

"It's pretty expensive." He flipped over the album to check the price on the back. Brooke got a good view of the Beatles' faces on the album's front cover, slightly elongated, pulled out of shape. *Rubber Soul.* She got it.

"How much?" She did the thing with her hair again, staring all the while at his, pulled back in the ponytail, not a strand out of place. Most boys she knew weren't so neat. But most boys she knew didn't have long, red-gold ponytails either.

"Seventy-five. And that's cheap. I hear it can go for over a hundred on eBay." He held it out, ruefully, as if he knew she could not afford it.

"You're right. Too steep for me." She took the album from him and put it back in the bin where she'd found it. Besides, even if she had bought it, how would she have played it?

"What's your name?" he asked.

"Brooke."

"Nice to meet you, Brooke." He held out his hand, like an adult would have done. She took it, surprised by its strength, its fineness. He had clear, pale skin, well-tended nails, and he wore a ring with a jet-black stone at its center. "I'm Otter."

"Otter?" Brooke heard the way her voice scaled up. Heard and hated it. But Otter? How strange a name was that?

"Well, it's Chris actually. But I'm changing it. To Otter."

"Otter." Brooke tried it out again, this time without the squeak. "So, um, Otter, do you, like, work at this store all the time? Or do you go to school too?" She realized that they were still holding hands.

"I'm a freshman," he said. He let go of her hand with some reluctance, or so it seemed to her. "At NYU."

"Oh." It didn't seem like a good idea to tell him she was still in high school. And only a sophomore at that. But he didn't ask.

"I'll be getting off from work soon," he said, glancing up at the clock on the wall. The clock was another artifact from the past, with flamelike tendrils sprouting from around the edges of its face and a thick, slightly grimy cord that ran from its bottom to an outlet on the wall. "If you want to wait, we can go out somewhere. For coffee. Or a beer."

"A beer?" Brooke could hear the squeak again. Better try to control it. Still, she knew this guy wasn't old enough to drink beer legally. Not in New York State, anyway.

"I know a place where they don't bother to card you." He smiled, and again she caught the gleam of silver.

"Where did you have it done?" she asked. God, she was such a geek. But he seemed to like her anyway. And she really, really wanted to know. "Your stud, I mean."

"You like it?" He stuck his tongue out so she could see it more clearly.

"Yes," said Brooke as she leaned closer to peer down at the small bit of silver that perforated the surface. "I really do."

"I can take you to the place where they do it." His tongue retreated back into his mouth. Brooke wanted to follow it.

"Really? Would you?"

"Sure thing," he told her, eyeing the clock again. "Why don't you just have a seat over there until I can go?"

Brooke sat on a wooden folding chair that looked like it had spent the last fifty or so years developing moss and odd strains of fungus under the porch of a crumbling summer house. There was nothing in this store that wasn't old. Nothing except Otter. He was fresh and young and unlike anyone she had ever met. Now how perfect was that?

18

Puppy Love

The dog was taking up all of her free time, but Lillian didn't mind, she was grateful, actually, for all the attention he demanded. Jason helped and he was great about playing with the dog, whom he'd decided to call Yankee, and feeding him and walking him too. She was proud of how well her son was handling the responsibility. But Lillian had to help with the training, the walking, the bathing, the trips to the vet. Still, taking care of a frisky puppy was better than thinking about Rick and the impossible place he had come to occupy in her life.

Hadn't Lillian been the one to point out that Naomi would, inevitably, find out about them? Though she hadn't expected Rick to be the one to tell her. But it didn't matter how Naomi had found out. The point was that she had. What had Lillian thought Naomi would do with such information? Give them her blessing? Say, "Oh, that's just fine, you can sleep with my husband on Tuesdays and Thursdays, and on Saturdays too if I happen to be out of town"?

No, Lillian had been guilty not only of sleeping with another woman's husband, but also guilty of lying to herself about its consequences. For Naomi had done what she herself had when the knowledge about Ramon had finally sunk in: she'd kicked him out. Lillian couldn't find a way to rationalize or explain her own behavior. That first afternoon in the office had just been an impulse. But the impulse, once satisfied, had not led to satiation. Instead, it had created its own demand. She had always liked Rick Wechsler. He was a great boss. A great guy. And somewhere along the line, she had fallen in love with him. So now here she was, guilty as sin, guilty as charged, guilty, just plain guilty.

But guilty was not the same as sorry, not quite. For as guilty as she was, she also saw, in Naomi's knowledge, a new opening. She had asked Rick to leave. Maybe she would ask him for a divorce. And if that were to happen, what would prevent her from being with Rick again, this time in a more legitimate way? Her thoughts circled around and around each other, none of them leading anywhere in particular, all of them making her feel tired and stressed. She had never even had the chance to give him the silk bathrobe she'd bought as a Christmas gift. It remained under her bed, wrapped, beribboned, and covered with plastic bags she had saved from her dry cleaning.

Days in the office were hard. She felt him looking at her all the time, and when she thought he wasn't aware of her, she was looking back. It would have been so easy to invite him over on a Saturday night when Jason was with his dad, or to go into Manhattan some Sunday morning to meet him. But she didn't. She had already done enough. If it was going to continue with him, it had to be on different terms.

Instead, she totally revamped the office's filing system, devised a better method of follow-up for their patients, taught her son to play poker—he seemed to have an affinity for cards—and signed Yankee up for an obedience training course that met on Saturdays in Park Slope. If Jason was home, he accompanied her to the class; if he was at his father's, she went by herself, and afterward, walked Yankee up the hill to Prospect Park.

She had bought him a red collar, and when she let him off the leash—risking a fine, she knew, but she couldn't resist—she liked to see the flash of red as he streaked across the snow. With the dog at her side or running just a little ahead, Lillian walked from one end of the park to the other, past Long Meadow, which was ringed with trees whose thick, dark branches held snow that was whiter, more pure than the grayed slush underfoot. She made her way past the skating rink, the duck pond, and the new Audubon Center bird sanctuary. With the hood of her parka drawn tightly around her face against the cold, she headed for the exit near Ocean Avenue and then looped around until she reached another, near Grand Army Plaza and the central branch of the Brooklyn Public Library. She wanted all this walking to tire her out at night, so that she could sleep without thinking of Rick Wechsler, and what would happen next, to him, to her.

One weekend when Jason was away, she invited her cousin Maria to join her. Maria wasn't at all keen on the idea of walking in the park. "It's too cold," she complained. "Why can't we drive?"

"I want to let Yankee have a good run," Lillian replied. "He needs the activity." She didn't add, "So do I."

"All right," Maria said. "But not for too long, okay?"

They entered the park at Third Street. The day was sunny and there were children in the playground, though not many. Most of them seemed to be scattered on the surrounding hills, pulling bright plastic sleds up gentle inclines before they could slide down, or throwing snowballs at each other. She had taken Jason there too, sometimes, after his team had finished their ball game in the park, but lately he hadn't wanted to go anymore. "It's too babyish," he explained. And she supposed it was. It made her a little sad to watch him grow up and away from her, especially when she doubted she would ever have another child.

"Jesus, I almost slipped!" said Maria. Lillian looked down at her cousin's ankle boots, which were stamped with a faux alligator pattern and had three-inch heels.

"We'll stay on the road." Lillian didn't want to point out that those heels were hardly the best choice for walking in the snow. She felt lonely when Jason was away and glad of her cousin's company—no need to antagonize her. "It's all shoveled there."

They walked in silence for a while. Maria took a package of cigarettes from her pocket and offered one to Lillian.

"No thanks." Lillian was tempted—she had smoked when she was younger, though had stopped when she became pregnant with Jason.

She remembered how she and Maria would go upstairs to the roof of Lillian's apartment building with a handful of cigarettes Maria had filched from her mother. Sitting on the tarred surface, they would smoke and spin their plans: Maria was going to be a singer or actress, Lillian the lawyer who would negotiate all her contracts and movie deals. Now Maria lived in the Bronx with her mother; her husband had walked out, leaving her with the kids—there were three—and had neglected to provide a forwarding address. Lillian's own situation wasn't much better.

"Let me know if you change your mind." Maria lit a cigarette and took a deep drag. Lillian missed it, the nicotine rush, the way the cigarette punctuated the little events of the day: the first cup of coffee, a sandwich from Subway, talking on the phone to her best friend, sex. The last cigarette of the day she had loved sharing late at night, on the roof with Maria, or Ramon, a hundred years ago.

She turned away from Maria and the ribbon of smoke that rose up from the glowing cigarette. Yankee was a little ahead of them; he had spied another dog down the road and loped off to investigate.

"Yankee!" Lillian called. "Come!" The dog looked in her direction but was too excited by the prospect of sniffing the brindle-coated boxer to obey. Even from where she stood, she could see that his tongue was hanging out as he circled the boxer and attempted to interest it in a game of chase.

"Yankee!" Lillian's voice rose, and Yankee, deciding her displeasure was not worth the risk, reluctantly left the boxer and began walking back to where Lillian and Maria stood waiting.

"Good boy," Lillian called. She wanted to reinforce his decision to return to her side. At the sound of her pleased tone, he broke into a run. He ran up alongside Maria and, in his excitement, knocked her down into the snow.

"Jesus!" Maria stood up and wiped snow from her knees, her coat. "Can't you train him or something?"

"That's what I'm trying to do," Lillian said, offering her arm to Maria. "He didn't mean it, you know."

"I guess I'm not a dog person," Maria said. "Can we go inside now? Please?"

They went back out at Third Street and headed down into the heart of Park Slope. This was one of the prettiest streets. Houses— many limestone, a few brownstone, and a few brick—sat well back from the sidewalk. The trees were big and old; in the spring, they arched overhead, forming a canopy through which the dappled light played. Lillian liked this neighborhood; she always had. Too expensive for her to live in though. No way she could have afforded these rents. Even people who made a good living might have had trouble. Rick had told her that he and his wife would not be able to afford the area now, but they had bought fifteen years ago, when things were different. Well, that was the way of cities. Things changed, sometimes for the better, sometimes not. Maybe Sunset Park would become a more expensive, desirable place to live one day. Of course, if that happened, she and Jason would probably have to move elsewhere.

Yankee, confined to his leash, trotted briskly alongside her. Occasionally, he looked up into her face, as if trying to reassure himself that she was still there. Good dog. She made a woofing sound and he woofed back.

"Was that you?" Maria asked. "Or him?"

"Both," Lillian admitted.

"Girl, you are nuts," said Maria, but she was smiling. "Talking to dogs. What's next? He'll tell you what he dreams? Ask you out for dinner?"

"Hey, I've known him for just over a month but already I can tell that he's more loyal than most guys I've met."

"Oh, that's great. Lillian finally stumbles on a terrific guy. Only problem is that he's four-footed."

"Picky, picky," said Lillian. She hadn't told Maria about Rick, hadn't told anyone. But suddenly she wanted to unburden herself to her cousin. She just didn't want to do it there, in the middle of the street. "Want to stop? For a coffee or something?"

"Definitely. I'm wet, I'm cold, and I'm hungry."

They slowed when they passed Dizzy's on Ninth Street, but there was a long line and Maria didn't want to wait. Instead, they continued along Seventh Avenue until they reached the Barnes & Noble at the corner of Sixth Street.

"Let's go in here," Lillian suggested. She tied Yankee to a parking meter and firmly told him to stay. She'd be able to watch him from the window. The dog looked up, as if he were going to protest, but then he settled back down on his haunches to wait. Lillian walked into the store and Maria followed her.

There were only a handful of people in front of them, and at first, Lillian was busy scanning the offerings—hot chocolate, that's what she wanted—and didn't pay attention to the small, dark-haired woman standing slightly ahead of her. Then she realized that the woman was Naomi Wechsler. Rick's wife.

"Come on," she said, grabbing Maria by the arm and pulling her toward the store's wide front doors.

"Hey, what are you doing?" Maria tried shaking her off, but Lillian's grip was too strong.

"Quiet. I'll explain when we're outside." They left the store and rounded the corner onto the avenue. Lillian quickly turned away, so that Naomi wouldn't see her if she happened to look through the large, plate glass window. Yankee barked an enthusiastic greeting. But before Lillian swiveled her head around, she had noticed something. She couldn't have said what it was, but she had suddenly registered the fact that Naomi was not alone; she had been with someone, a white-haired man standing in front of her. She stepped off the curb and concealed herself slightly behind the cab of a delivery truck.

"What are you doing?" Maria came over to where Lillian stood, planting herself right in front of Lillian's view.

"I'll explain in a minute. Now could you please move?"

"That's what you said when we were inside," Maria said grumpily, but she moved aside so that Lillian had an unobstructed view into the Barnes & Noble café. There was Naomi Wechsler, still waiting on line. In front of Naomi was the guy: tall, kind of sloppy looking. As Lillian watched, Naomi reached up and flicked something—lint? a piece of thread?—from his arm. It was the kind of casual, even thoughtless gesture that nonetheless bound you intimately to its recipient. For this was absolutely an intimate relationship: Lillian had no doubt about that.

As Maria waited and even patted Yankee—gingerly, as if she expected him to knock her over again—Lillian looked more carefully and saw that under his open coat, Naomi's companion wore the white smock of a doctor; though she couldn't read it from where she stood, she was also able to pick out the chain with the laminated ID around his neck. Holy Name. That must be where he worked. And so did Naomi, Lillian realized. Rick had told her about his wife's volunteer work.

Rick's wife was on intimate terms with—sleeping with—a doctor from Holy Name Hospital? Did Rick know anything about it? Lillian didn't think so. But here she was feeling so guilty over what she had done, what she had enticed Rick into doing. It had never occurred to her that Naomi Wechsler also might have had something to feel guilty about.

"Aren't you finished yet?" Maria said. "I'm still freezing, still hungry, and still wet. And you haven't even told me what the hell you're doing."

"Come on," Lillian said as she untied Yankee from his post and linked arms with her cousin. "I'm going to let you in on everything."

19

Sand

Estelle sat in the passenger's seat of the car, dividing her attention between Naomi, who sat next to her driving, and the view out of the window. Her daughter looked tired, with dark shadows under her eyes and a new, unfamiliar pinch to her mouth. The view out the window was even better than she remembered or imagined. When they reached the Brooklyn Bridge, Estelle felt tears rising in her eyes, so beautiful, so expansive was the sight of the grayish green water—finally, finally!—all around her. The day was cold and gray, and a fresh layer of white covered the soiled remnants of previous snowfalls.

After pelting her with the usual barrage of questions—How are you feeling? Did you eat today? Are you warm enough?—Naomi lapsed into a preoccupied silence. Estelle could tell she neither saw nor had any interest in what was outside the window; instead, she seemed totally absorbed with some inner drama of her own. Not that Estelle blamed her. She must still be thinking, as Estelle was, of Dahlia. Though she had had a longer time to absorb the information than Estelle had. Last summer, that's what Naomi had told her. Estelle strained to remember what she had been doing, thinking, back then. It had been hot, she supposed, but the place—she still couldn't bring herself to think of it as a home of any sort—was always reversing the temperatures, just, it seemed, to confound her. In the summer, the air was always chilled, frigid even, requiring sweaters and long pants although outside it was baking.

Once over the bridge, they had to drive more slowly and stop often; the traffic was heavy. Only a single block separated Atlantic Avenue from Pacific Street, a puzzling proximity that set Estelle's mind scurrying in a futile direction, trying to process the information. Weren't the Atlantic and the Pacific oceans very far apart, at opposite ends of the country? Or was this another of the ways her mind was betraying her, becoming, day by day, a hostile presence, unreliable and touchy when she needed it most? She decided not to say anything about this to Naomi, who was looking ahead, still with that preoccupied expression on her face. But the words *Atlantic-Pacific, Atlantic-Pacific* began to assume an unnerving rhythm in her head. She forced herself to think of something else.

The traffic began moving again, and soon they were driving down Fourth Avenue. Plumbing supplies, car alarms, gas stations—these were the businesses lining the wide street. Further down, though, just past the entrance to a subway station, Estelle saw what looked like a new apartment building going up. Naomi was driving too quickly for her to make out the cross street, but she knew they were nearing Naomi's house; she could feel it.

"What's that?" she asked, pointing at the redbrick structure. It was taller than any of the surrounding buildings. She saw that some of the windows were actually doors, opening onto terraces.

"Condominiums," Naomi said, without even looking. "I hear they're going to be pretty expensive. Right here on Fourth Avenue. Who would believe it?" But she didn't sound especially interested or concerned with what was going on around her, right in her own backyard as it were. Estelle caught a last glimpse of the building—big, a bit hulking, but imposing nonetheless—and then shifted her attention to Carroll Street, as Naomi made the turn and drove up the block.

"Look at that," Naomi said. "Almost at the front door." She was looking in the rearview mirror as she maneuvered her way into a parking space. In Florida, Estelle had driven. She couldn't imagine now how she had ever done it. The judgment it required, the speed of the reflexes that was necessary. But she was not going to dwell on that now. She was here, in Brooklyn, and only minutes away from entering Naomi's house. When Naomi had parked and helped her unfasten the seat belt, Estelle opened the car door herself and stepped out into the street. The house was on a hill, she had remembered that, the feeling of looking up the street, toward the trees, church spires, and ultimately the park, and then down, in the other direction, toward the water.

Naomi took her arm as they climbed the stoop. A key appeared, the door opened. Estelle followed her daughter through the arched inner double doors into the hallway and through another wide arched double doorway into the living room. She looked around, remembering. The last time she had been here Milton had been with her. The room looked the same—cream-colored walls, big mirror over the mantelpiece, a pleasing collection of comfortable-looking chairs and a sofa. But some ineffable thing was altered, different. It wasn't just Dahlia, though Estelle knew, of course, that Dahlia's absence would account for some of the strangeness she was feeling. This was something else. She struggled to find it in herself to give a name to what was not there.

"Your husband." This was the best she could do. His name was not in a place where she could reach it.

"Rick?" Naomi was taking off her coat, reaching for Estelle's. "He's at his office. He goes to work during the day."

"How about at night? Does he come home at night?"

"Why are you asking?"

"Why shouldn't I ask? I want to know. Rick. Your husband. Does he come home, here, to this house at night?"

"No," Naomi said very quietly. She did not look at Estelle, but down at the two coats she clutched in her arms.

"Ah," said Estelle. She sat down, suddenly tired. "Why not?"

"It's a long story." Naomi was moving away from her now.

"So? I'm in no rush."

"Let me hang these up," Naomi said, still with the coats. "And I'll make us a cup of tea."

"All right." Estelle looked around some more. There was a celadon-colored vase, tall and graceful, that she didn't remember, and a lamp that she did. It had been given to her by her own mother and she had later given it to Naomi. "I want to see Dahlia's room anyway. I'll go while you're making the tea."

"Can you make it up there all right? Do you need help?"

"I can walk up a flight of stairs," said Estelle, slightly offended. Her mind might wander, but she had not become infirm or feeble. Not yet.

"It isn't her room anymore," Naomi said in a pained voice. "We got rid of her things. It's even been repainted."

"Things," said Estelle. "Things are only what's left behind. They don't matter. Believe me, I know." There was some reason that Naomi didn't want her to go upstairs. She could sense it.

"What do you mean?" Naomi looked interested now.

"Right after your father died, I wouldn't get rid of anything. Not his clothes, even coats and suits he hadn't worn for years. Not his bathrobe or his razor. Not his old slippers. I kept it all."

"And?"

"And?" repeated Estelle. "And nothing. Nothing came of it. I didn't feel closer to him. It was just so much stuff."

"So you got rid of it? Of everything?"

"Pretty much," Estelle said. "Maybe I have some cuff links. His wedding ring."

Naomi said nothing, and went into the kitchen. Estelle heard the sound of water running. Tea, she had said. Slowly, Estelle moved back through the room and up the stairs. When she got to the top, there were several doors, and looking at them, she felt disoriented. The right one, she thought. Which is the right one? Then she realized it didn't matter, she would open them all, look inside each room.

The first door she opened was a bathroom. All right. Nothing astonishing there. The next was a light-filled room that faced the small yard in back. Hadn't this been Naomi's room? Estelle was fairly sure it had. And look, here was a dresser, no two. A chair with a blouse thrown casually across its cushion. A pair of shoes, heels neatly together. But there was no bed here, just an open space in the center where a bed should have been. She retreated, opened another door. Here the windows faced the street. The room was painted a fresh, new-looking white and was bare except for a mattress set in the middle of the floor. It was made up with sheets, a quilt, and pillows. Now here was a puzzle. A room without a bed, another room with only a bed.

Estelle opened another door. Behind it was a small room with a desk and a computer; a bulletin board hung above the desk. Apart from a few silver tacks, it was empty. Cardboard boxes lined the walls, though they appeared to be empty too. The last door opened onto a room that was equally small, though this one was packed with things: a man's overcoat, piles of sweaters and shirts, a knitted vest, a tangle of ties. Books were piled in one corner; a tennis racket and pair of skis in another.

She could make no sense of this arrangement: who lived where, slept where, was beyond her understanding. What she could understand, though, was Dahlia's absence. The girl with the brown limbs and brown hair was nowhere to be found. Estelle buried her face in her hands, waiting for the flood of tears—she had not cried, not once, since Naomi had told her—to release itself, and then to pass. When it did, she went back down the stairs in search of her daughter.

In the dining room, Naomi had set out mugs for the tea, a plate filled with cookies. Estelle sat down, reached for a cookie. It was crisp and thin, tasting of butter, of ginger. She chewed it thoughtfully as she looked at her daughter.

"You've been crying," Naomi said, almost accusing. She didn't take a cookie, just held her steaming tea close to her face.

"Your daughter is gone." Estelle swallowed quickly and her hands went up to her eyes. Wet again.

"I told you what happened. Dahlia died. In a car accident."

"And your husband? Did he die too?"

"Mom!"

"Well, he isn't here. You told me so yourself."

"I said he wasn't living here. I didn't say he was dead."

"So where is he?"

"At his sister's apartment. In Manhattan." Naomi took a sip of tea, set the mug down.

"We drove through Manhattan. To get here." Estelle sipped her tea too. It tasted better than what she had been drinking in that place. So much better.

"Yes, we did."

"But you haven't said why he's living in Manhattan. With his sister."

"Because I asked him to."

"You asked him to leave you?"

"He was sleeping with someone else."

"Sleeping?" Estelle thought again of the bed upstairs, which she guessed was her daughter's. Did Naomi move it around from room to room? And did this have anything to do with what she was saying about her husband?

"You know what I mean." Naomi looked exasperated. She looked down at her mug, then pushed it away.

"No," said Estelle. "I don't."

"Having an affair. Sex."

"Sex? Like a boy? Or a girl?" Estelle knew she should know what Naomi meant. But it was so frustrating, this retreat and advance of her thoughts, her memories, her comprehension.

"Shtupping, Ma. He was shtupping someone else."

"Oh." This word she knew. "Is that all?"

"Is that all?" Naomi's voice rose as she repeated her mother's words. "Isn't that enough?"

"I don't know. They all do it, you know. They can't help it." Estelle reached for another cookie. This one was shaped like a crescent moon and had a sprinkling of nuts on the top of it. Estelle liked nuts.

"Not all," muttered Naomi. "Not Daddy."

"Oh yes. Even your father." Estelle bit delicately on the cookie. Delicious. Maybe Naomi would give her some cookies to take back with her.

"You're kidding." Naomi stared. "I'm not sure I want to hear this."

"Years ago, your father used to sell textiles." Estelle ignored her and launched into the story. This was one she knew well. She could tell it, no breaks, no confusion in her mind. She took a breath, continued. "He had a briefcase full of samples. Gabardines, meltons, worsted wools, tropical weights. Tweed. Plaid. Herringbone. And some really expensive blends too. Cashmere and alpaca. Vicuña. He sold them to men's clothing manufacturers—companies that made suits and topcoats."

"Yes, I know all this," Naomi said. Estelle could detect her impatience.

"Every day he went out with that briefcase." Estelle would not let herself be deterred. "Dressed in a suit, with a vest no less, sewn from one of the fabrics he sold. He had to, you know. Had to show the prospective customers how well the suit would look when it was all made up. He wore a tie too, and always had a clean handkerchief sticking out of his pocket. I would press a week's worth on Sunday night, so he would always have a fresh one. Shined shoes. A hat. The handkerchief was only a little piece, but it was important." She stopped, remembering. "He was a looker, your father. Really."

"Mom, I know all about Daddy's life as a salesman. He was very good at it. I remember."

"You don't remember this though," Estelle said.

"Remember what?"

"The time I found one of those handkerchiefs stuffed way down into his jacket pocket. It was covered with lipstick. Pink lipstick. I didn't wear pink lipstick. Not then. Not ever."

"I had no idea," Naomi murmured.

"It was like in a movie. An old one. Remember George Bailey wiping off Violet Bick's lipstick?"

"George Bailey? Violet Bick?"

"The movie." Still no look of comprehension. Now it was Estelle's turn to be impatient. *"It's a Wonderful Life."*

"Oh," said Naomi. "Right. Of course." But it didn't sound like she had any idea of what Estelle was talking about.

"All I had to do was show it to him. He told me the whole story. One of the secretaries at a company he sold to. A flirty little thing. I met her once at some holiday party they invited us to. She had on that pink lipstick and pink nail polish, and she was wearing a pink dress with red cherries all over it. She told me how when people asked her what she did, she would say, 'I'm in men's pants.' Then she laughed, ha, ha, ha. She sounded like a donkey. As if that were a funny thing for a young woman to say. Well, she was in men's pants, all right. Your father's pants."

"So what happened?"

"Happened?"

"I mean, what did you do then? Tell him he had to leave?"

"Leave? Why would I have done that?"

"Mom, most women don't like it when they find out that their husbands have been unfaithful to them." Naomi paused, ran her finger around the rim of her mug. "I know I didn't like it."

"You have to look at the whole picture. Daddy and I loved each other. We were happy. We had a home. We had you. That girl, the one with the lipstick and the cherries. She was something that happened once. He lost his head. Was I going to throw out a marriage, a life, just because of a mistake he made?"

"We're different, then. When Rick told me about what he'd been doing, I asked him to leave. And he did."

"That was foolish. He belongs here. With you."

"If he belongs with me, why was he sleeping with," she paused, "—shtupping—someone else?"

"He lost his daughter." Estelle could feel the sadness rising up again. But no, she would have to control herself. For Naomi's sake. Naomi needed her, she could see that. "He was looking for something, anything, to make him forget that."

"So you're excusing him? Rationalizing?"

"No." Estelle wiped her mouth with a napkin. It was made of cloth and it felt good against her lips. "Explaining him. He did a bad thing, yes. But he's your husband. The father of your child."

"My child is dead, remember?"

"That doesn't matter. The person you are, the person he is—none of that disappears, whether Dahlia is here or not. She changed you. Both of you. And because of that, you belong together."

"I don't know." Naomi's shoulders slumped, and Estelle resisted the impulse, virtually automatic, to tell her to sit up straight. "I don't think I can forgive him."

"So you think this is better? Being alone in this house? Sleeping around?"

"Sleeping around?" Naomi actually smiled. "I'm not sure that's what you mean."

"Upstairs." Estelle persisted. "The bed is in one room. The clothes are in another. Your husband's things are somewhere else."

"I didn't want to sleep in the room we used to share. It didn't feel right."

"But you left the rest of the things there. Clothes. Shoes."

"I just haven't had the energy to move everything in there. Besides . . ." Naomi trailed off and Estelle waited. "The room where I'm sleeping now—it used to be Dahlia's."

"Dahlia's room," said Estelle. "I remember now." Then she added, "Your life is too confused. You're all over the place."

"That's true," Naomi said. "That's what I am: all over the place."

Estelle wanted to say more, to tell her, show her, how to gather herself up again, make her life of a piece, not these fragments. But she didn't know how and suddenly felt too weary to try.

"I'm tired," she announced abruptly. This trip, the effort required of her to have this conversation, had worn her out. The strain of paying attention, marshaling her thoughts all day, remembering, making connections. She had come here in search of Dahlia, or Dahlia's absence. But what she had found was even worse. Dahlia had gone and

Naomi's family had gone with her. Estelle looked over at the sofa, where several plump pillows and a fringed throw folded over the arm made it seem an inviting and comfortable oasis. "Do you mind if I lie down for a little while?"

"Of course not." Naomi got to her feet and took Estelle's arm. "Maybe you want to go upstairs. You could stretch out on my bed."

"No," Estelle said. "I'll rest down here. You go up. You have things to do up there."

"Nothing that I need to do right now."

"I wouldn't be so sure," said Estelle before walking over to the sofa and sitting down. She eased off her shoes. "I wouldn't be so sure of that at all."

Estelle dreamed that she and Milton were young again and on their honeymoon, which had been in Bermuda. The dream was particularly vivid and textured; she was aware of the sensation of the sand, superfine, palest pink, under her feet, the moist, salty taste the sea left in her mouth. She and Milton walked together hand in hand along the shore. But then Milton dropped her hand and began walking faster. Soon he was a good distance ahead; in a minute she would lose sight of him altogether. "Wait," she wanted to call out. "Don't go so fast." But when she tried to speak, no sound came out.

Instead, the wind blew the sand into her parted lips. She stopped, brushed it away, even tried spitting to get it out. But the wind blew harder, and the sand was everywhere. It coated her tongue, stopped up her ears, made her eyes burn then close. Soon she would be buried in the sand, buried alive. She flailed her arms around, trying to push the sand off her and away. She awoke and found she was pushing at a pillow that had slipped from the back of the sofa to rest gently on her cheek. Naomi was nowhere to be seen.

Estelle struggled to sit up, and as she did, she again took in the room, the windows with their wooden shutters, the intricate pattern of the rug on the floor. Her heart, which had been beating frantically, slowed down. "A dream," she said aloud, as if she were comforting a child. "Just a bad dream."

There was a tapping out in the hallway, on the stairs, and Naomi entered the room.

"Did you sleep?" she asked. "You looked like you were really out."

"I was dreaming," Estelle said. But she didn't elaborate. It was too much effort. She could see from the way the light entered the room at a slanted angle that the afternoon was fading. Soon it would be dark. "You should probably drive me back."

"All right," Naomi said. But she didn't sound happy about it. "I'll make us another cup of tea first. Then we can get going."

"Promise me you'll call your husband." Estelle could not, even now, summon his name. But it didn't matter. She knew who he was, what he was. That was the main thing.

"Why should I?" Naomi asked.

"Why not? It couldn't hurt."

"Mom, you are such an optimist," Naomi said. She knelt by the sofa and felt around under it until she located Estelle's shoes, and pushed them in her mother's direction.

"Better than being a pessimist." Estelle stood, slipped her feet into the shoes. "Let's have that cup of tea," she said. "I'm thirsty."

"From the nap," said Naomi, moving toward the kitchen.

"Or the sand."

But Naomi didn't hear the remark, and Estelle did not repeat it.

20

Mea Culpa

Michael did not attempt to follow Brooke down Fifth Avenue, but instead watched her march away—long, light brown hair swishing angrily from side to side as she receded—without moving from where he stood. Sensing his momentary paralysis, Naomi led him away. They walked, briefly in Central Park, and in a zoo he remembered visiting with Camille and the girls.

Then he walked her to the subway station at Sixtieth Street and Fifth Avenue. When they said good-bye, he turned and crossed the street without waiting for the light to change. The driver of a black Mercedes honked furiously and shook his fist. Michael jumped onto the curb, sweating and still in a mild state of shock.

Back at the hotel, the conference room was overheated and dry. He thought he could feel his skin tightening, his pores shriveling. He slipped into a seat and tried to look attentive, even interested as the next speaker—the infectious disease guy from Boston Children's, as it happened—began sifting through his heavy sheaf of papers and clearing his throat. Fortunately, Michael's own paper—a study about the troubling resurgence of pertussis in children whose parents had refused to have them vaccinated—had been delivered yesterday. He did not think he would have been up to doing it now.

Brooke. Brooke had seen him with Naomi Wechsler. Had seen him and understood all that it meant. He had only to think of the expres-

sion on her face—horrified, disbelieving, betrayed—to know everything that she knew. To feel everything that she felt. He had not
stopped her, because for the first time since becoming her father, he
had nothing to say, no explanation to give. So he had let her walk away.
Where would she go? What would she do?

He had an urge to leave this conference, his colleagues, his world, and
rush back to Brooklyn. He wanted to run up the stoop of his house, fling
open the door, make sure everything was still intact, still standing. Had it
all disintegrated in that instant when Brooke saw him, turned to smoldering, black ash as he stood there in the street, he wouldn't have been
surprised. There were always consequences for what you did. Wasn't
that yet another thing his mother was always pointing out?

Michael resisted the impulse, forcing himself to remain where he
was, at least for the time being. This was the last day of the conference; by this afternoon, everything would be winding down. It would
be easier—that is, less noticeable—to leave then. But he found he
couldn't sit still. He crossed and recrossed his arms, his legs, first at the
knees, then the ankles. Scratched his head, sending a fine sprinkling of
dandruff down, to settle on his shoulder, where he brushed it away.
Fiddled with his tie. Finally, he got up and went quietly to the back of
the room. Cans of soda had been set out, along with plates of tired-
looking sandwiches, cookies, and pastries. He picked up a danish,
cheese from the look of it, and bit down, not because he was hungry,
but because it gave him something to do with his hands, his face.
Though it was stale, he continued chewing. After a few bites, though,
it turned waxy in his mouth. He discreetly spat out what he'd been
eating into his napkin and threw it, along with the rest of the pastry,
away. Brooke had seen him and for all he knew, had gone home to tell
her mother what she had seen. What would happen then was something that Michael could not imagine.

Michael and Camille had been married for over five years before
the twins were born. Five years was a long time to wait, especially for

practicing Catholics. Camille had always wanted a big family; when she tried, and failed, to become pregnant, she began to pray. First it was Mass three times a week, then every day, and sometimes, on Sundays, twice a day. She went to confession too, dredging up sins from her childhood, holdovers that she thought might have caused God to punish her in this way. It got so that she couldn't bear to look at pregnant women in the street. The sight of a newborn, swaddled and held by its mother, brought her to tears. Michael was puzzled but not despairing. He was a physician after all, with a physician's faith, not only in God, but in the power of his profession. He persuaded Camille to consult doctors as well as priests, and eventually to undergo the IVF treatments that were deemed necessary.

The treatments were not easy. First the constant monitoring of temperature and secretions. Then the drugs that coursed through her system, making her cry, making her swear, making her feel like she never wanted to get out of bed again. And then the disappointment when the treatments failed too. Three separate times, with three separate but equally dismal outcomes. The first time, it failed altogether. The second time, she became pregnant but miscarried. The third time, an ectopic pregnancy that had cost her a fallopian tube.

She finally decided to give up. "It's God's will," she told Michael, but he could see she wasn't reconciled at all. This business about God was just something she was saying, not buying. He worried about her, how she would accept what for her was not acceptable. How would they go on living together, as husband and wife, when she felt so cheated, so bereft? She would blame herself, blame him—it didn't matter because in the end, blame of that kind, ongoing, corrosive, would ruin any marriage.

And then, one day she conceived. Just like that, when they had given up, stopped trying, stopped hoping. She had started talking about adopting and was already contacting Catholic charities that had access to children in Brazil, in Peru, in Guatemala. Somewhere out there, she told Michael, there was a baby for her. Her job was to find it. Instead, she found herself pregnant with twins.

"Can you believe it?" she had whispered, rubbing her midsection that had only just started to swell. "It's like we're being given an extra one. To make up for what we lost."

Michael wasn't at all sure about this, but he was happy, simply, to see Camille so happy. That was enough. The fetuses gained weight and volume; the ultrasound revealed a tangle of limbs, a forest of tiny, webbed hands and feet. They were born at Holy Name, just a week shy of their due date. Michael's good friend in Obstetrics, Inge Vang Olsen, delivered first one, and then seven minutes later, the second baby girl. Michael had hoped to give his brand-new daughters the kinds of names he was familiar with: Mary Grace, Kathleen, Bridget. Instead, Camille came up with Brooke and Mackenzie.

"But those sound like last names," he had pointed out. "And not even the last names of anyone we know." They were still in the delivery room; Camille's hair, dark with sweat, was glued to her scalp.

"That's the point," she replied. "They sound so elegant. So patrician."

"Patrician?" Michael was not sure where she had gotten such an idea or even such a word. Still, she had longed for those babies, carried them, given birth to them. He supposed, with all she had gone through, that she should get to name them too.

There were no other miracles after that; no other children. But Camille was grateful for the ones she had, and let them fill her, completely and to the brim. Years before, she had been a nurse at Downstate; that's where he had met her, pretty little Camille Casseretti from Bensonhurst. He remembered her busily moving through the corridors, emptying a bedpan with the same casual grace that she arranged flowers in a vase. Shiny brown hair streaked blond in places, a tiny mole near the corner of her mouth. He had courted her, won her, married her. And now, he was going to lose her. He knew it, he could tell.

Although the physician from Boston Children's had not finished delivering his talk—he gulped down some water before starting up with the slides he had brought—Michael left the lecture. He walked purposefully to the men's room as if really needing to go, and as long as he was there, stood by the urinal for a minute. Afterward, he washed his hands for a long time with hot water and a generous squirt of liquid soap. He then dried them with great care. His reflection in the mirror was its usual disheveled self, but this time, he minded. He looked the way he felt: as if he, and the life he had led, were literally falling apart.

Somehow, he managed to force himself back into the conference room, whose lights had been dimmed for the slide presentation. He was able to pretend to absorb the substance of the talk, to make sense of the images on the slides—hugely magnified clusters of spores, of bacilli, of streptococci—although they all swam unpleasantly in his head, a sea of abstract shapes, multiplying and swirling before his eyes. He couldn't look anymore. Instead, he was transported back to an incident that must have taken place fifty years earlier. They were all—Kevin, Tommy, Stephen Kathy, Maud, and their parents—at a movie theater on Flatbush Avenue. His father had brought them to see Walt Disney's *Dumbo*. Michael had loved the movie, and although he wouldn't have let his brothers know, the plight of the baby elephant being separated from its mother set off a fearful thrum of anxiety in his own heart. But it was the sequence in which Dumbo accidentally gets drunk and hallucinates that actively terrified him.

"Make it stop," he said to his father, pulling on his sleeve. "Please, Dad."

His father looked down at him, clearly annoyed. He couldn't believe Michael was actually frightened. His brothers and sisters turned away from the movie, preferring instead this real-life drama that was unfolding right in front of them.

"For the love of God, Mikey, it's just a cartoon," his father had said, exasperated. But Michael wouldn't be calmed. When his father returned to watching the movie, Michael got up from his seat and hurried down a long aisle—it had seemed to go on and on—toward the slivers of light that outlined the swinging doors. He wouldn't watch the rest of the movie, but would wait, beyond those doors, until it was over and his family was ready to leave. On the way he collided with an usher—they still had ushers in some of the bigger theaters back then—who took him by both shoulders and stopped his headlong flight.

"Whoa, where's the fire, little guy?" whispered the usher. To Michael's extreme humiliation, he burst out crying. The usher led him out into the brightly lit lobby and sat him down on a high stool behind the candy counter. There, he offered tissues, a delicately fizzing soda with pebbles of ice that Michael could crunch, and a large box of Milk Duds. Michael had never before had such a big box of candy all to himself; he was torn between trying to eat the whole thing now, before he had to share with his brothers and sisters, and finding a way to hide it so he could eat the Milk Duds a few at a time and draw out the pleasure. When his brothers and sisters emerged from the movie, he decided, he would offer the Milk Duds. Sharing the candy would deflect the questions—and the inevitable teasing that would accompany them—about why he'd needed to leave. He opened the box of candy and pulled out a piece. It wouldn't hurt to eat a few while he waited, he reasoned. His mouth filled with the lush taste of the chocolate, and his fear, at least for the moment, subsided.

That was it. He couldn't stand it anymore. He got up from his seat yet again, strode into the lobby. His things were still in his room, and he took the elevator up to the fourteenth floor to retrieve them. He would invent some excuse for why he'd left early, some family emergency. God knew, it was true.

The bed had been made, but otherwise the room was the same as when he had left it. Bending down to pick up the socks he had left lying on the floor, he found the silver clip that had been in her hair when she'd arrived the night before. Though he knew it was hardly a smart thing to do, he deposited the clip in his pocket, a tangible piece of her that he would keep with him. For despite everything that had happened and everything that was still waiting to, he wanted her, this woman who had let him touch the place in her that would never be healed. He wished he could explain to Brooke, to Camille, that what he felt for Naomi had nothing to do with either of them. But they would never believe it. Neither, if he was in their place, would he.

His packing completed, he returned to the lobby and managed to check out without running into anyone else. From the street, he pulled out his cell phone to call Adelaide at the hospital, telling her that he'd left the Plaza and wouldn't be back in the office until the next day. Then he descended into the subway station at Fifty-third Street and took the F train back to Brooklyn.

Traveling at that hour was a novelty. The train was populated, not packed, and it seemed that there was an overabundance of teenagers. Michael looked at his watch; it was just after three. School was out. What had Brooke been doing in Manhattan this morning anyway? He knew she had school that day. He also knew that Camille was unaware that their daughter cut classes. Any problem, any issue with the girls, she shared with him, even when it seemed that to do so would have been compromising a confidence.

"Does she really want me to know this?" Michael had asked the night that Camille told him that Brooke had started menstruating.

"No, of course not," Camille answered.

"Then it's not necessary to tell me," Michael said gently.

"How can you say that? She's your daughter. You have to know what's going on with her. That's your right. No—your obligation."

Michael gave up trying to convince Camille otherwise, but he was careful not to let on or suggest to his daughters that he had any information about them that they had not offered directly. Where was Brooke now, he wondered for the hundredth time. The train had just stopped at Twenty-third Street; not even in Brooklyn yet.

To distract himself, Michael focused on a short kid with gelled hair and a leather jacket. He was talking to a girl whose pretty face was compromised by the reddish, angry-looking blemishes scattered across it. He thought of the excellent dermatologist at Holy Name, and had to restrain himself from giving this girl his name. The urge to help was as strongly ingrained in him as the urge to breathe.

Although his usual stop was Seventh Avenue, he was too antsy to wait and jumped off the train at the preceding stop, Ninth Street. He hurried up the stairs, not at all weighed down by the overnight bag he carried. He was on his way to the florist—yep, that old cliché, flowers for the wife when you wanted to make amends—when he remembered the church. St. Thomas Aquinas; he'd passed it often enough. Not that he and Camille ever came down here. Good. He was less likely to run into anyone he knew.

He didn't really expect the church to be unlocked, but a sign advertising afternoon bingo made him decide to try; when he did, the heavy wooden door opened easily. Signs pointed the way to the bingo game downstairs, but Michael ignored them and went into the church itself. Inside, it was massive, empty, and dark; even the altar lights were off.

Michael approached a railing, set his bag down, and bent his head. Nothing would come, though, none of the prayers he'd been reciting since he was a kid, no words at all. He stood there anyway, until a noise made him turn around. A priest with a pink bald head and a silver crucifix Michael could see even from this distance was crossing the church. Michael left his bag where it was and walked toward him.

"Hello, Father," he said.

"Can I help you?" The priest spoke pleasantly.

"Would you hear my confession?" Michael was surprised by the words, but there they were, he had said them.

"Now?" The priest seemed unsure; he touched the crucifix lightly with a finger that seemed painfully bent with what Michael guessed was arthritis. He wondered if he should tell him about the arthritis clinic they ran at Holy Name. "I usually hear confession on Saturday. At four. Can you come back?"

"I don't think it can wait, Father."

"All right then." The priest touched the crucifix once more, with more authority this time. He walked to the back of the church, where the confessionals were, and gestured for Michael to follow him. Stepping into the small booth and closing the door, Michael was transported back to his childhood, the weekly ritual he had both dreaded and loved.

"Forgive me, Father, for I have sinned . . ." Michael began the familiar litany, learned decades ago. It didn't matter that he had fallen away from the easy faith of his youth; somewhere inside, he was and would always be a Catholic. When he uttered the words "Impure in word, thought, and deed," he thought he detected a sigh from the priest.

"Were these impurities committed with someone else?"

"They were."

"Someone who was not your wife?"

"Someone who was not my wife," Michael repeated.

"And on how many occasions did they take place?" In my mind or in fact, Michael wanted to ask, but didn't. He gave an answer and received first a brief if lackluster lecture on the sanctity of marriage and his job to uphold it, and then the penance, the Our Fathers, the Hail Marys he had to recite. When he came out again, the priest would not look him in the eye.

Michael was left not with the fresh, buoyant feeling of childhood, cleansed of all sins, secure in God's love, but with a murky, unsettled kind of gloom. There would be no peace for him here, or anywhere, until he got home and faced whatever it was he was going to have to face.

He fairly ran up the hill, stopping briefly at a florist on Fifth Avenue to buy a large bouquet of tulips, roses, speckled lilies—what Camille would make of this gift he didn't even contemplate—and then continuing on until he reached his house. There it was, four solid stories, with its stoop and its wrought iron gate, its planters and its glass-paned double doors. Lace curtains hung in those panes, a pattern of vines and trellises that Camille said was a reproduction of a traditional pattern found in the south of France. House-proud, that's what his mother always said about her. But why not, when it brought her—all of them, really—such pleasure?

His hand was shaking as he put the key in the lock. Inside, it was quiet. "Camille," he called out. "Camille, I'm home."

"Michael?" Camille had been in the kitchen, which was downstairs on the garden level. "You're back so early. Is the conference over already?"

"Just about," he said, setting down the bag but still clutching the flowers. She didn't look angry or alarmed, just mildly curious. "I was exhausted though. I had to come home."

"You work too hard." She came closer and gave him a quick kiss on the cheek. Then she looked at the bundle he clutched to his chest.

"Flowers?"

"Why not?" He handed them to her. "I just wanted to get them for you."

"Well, aren't they pretty? Thank you." She pressed her face into the lush blooms, which had, as Michael knew, no scent at all. Damn hybrids. At least they looked good.

"So where are the girls?" There, he had said it and his voice hadn't given him away. At least he didn't think so.

"Mackenzie's at basketball practice. Brooke has choir."

"Oh." He turned away, afraid to let her see the relief that had flooded his eyes, his face, his entire being. But it would be short-lived, he knew.

". . . wasn't expecting you for dinner," Camille was saying. "Not sure what I have in the freezer."

"We can order out." Michael began unbuttoning his coat. "Or even go out if you like."

"Flowers. A restaurant. And both on a week night," Camille said. "What's all this? Are you feeling guilty about something?"

Michael felt his mouth go dry and his head begin to throb. But her tone was light, easy; she was teasing him, that was all.

"Don't be silly," he said, still unable to look at her. "What in the world would I have to feel guilty about?"

21

Falling

Her bottle of beer tasted terrible—sour and vile. How come guys were always making such a huge deal about chugging them down? But Brooke liked the mellow, I-don't-give-a-damn feeling it kindled in her and so she was willing to endure it. She would have ordered wine, but she didn't know much about it and didn't want to embarrass herself by revealing her vast ignorance. And hard liquor was too risky. She was aiming for pleasantly, blurry-around-the edges drunk, not plastered or passed-out drunk.

"Want another one?" said Otter.

"Sure," Brooke said. "Why not?" She watched as he walked over to the bar—a long, highly polished slab of some dark, hard stone—and asked for two more. His ponytail caught the light and swayed a little as he moved. She thought about his tongue stud. What would it be like to kiss a guy who had that in his mouth? Would the stud be cold? Or because it had been nestled there, inside his mouth, would it be warm? She hoped she would get a chance to find out. Earlier they had gone to the tattoo and piercing parlor, but the place was closed, so Otter suggested that they come here instead. Which had been fine with Brooke. Turning her attention away from him, she gazed into the mirror that hung above the booth where she sat. She thought she looked pretty good, with her hair sweeping across her face and her flush cheeks. Who cared about her father and that woman now? Not Brooke. Not a bit.

Otter returned and set a glass down in front of her. At least she didn't have to drink it from the bottle; when she did that, she always took in too much air and then had to burp—loudly, too—to get rid of it. She didn't want that to happen tonight. In a practiced, fluid movement, Otter poured the beer into Brooke's glass. When it had been filled and the foam subsided, he raised his own glass and she did the same.

"To John and Paul," he said.

"And Ringo and George," she added. Then she touched her glass to his, sloshing the beer just a little, so that the foam bubbled up and over the side.

Three—or was it four?—beers later, they left the bar, which was on Avenue D. It was dark by now, and Brooke had not a clue as to where they would go next or what would happen when they got there. She didn't care either, though somewhere, in the part of her brain that remained stubbornly sober, she knew that her parents would be wondering what had happened to her. Wondering and worrying too. She could imagine her mother, looking at the clock, then pressing her lips together and expelling her breath through her nose in that tense, exasperated way she had. She would kiss her index finger and touch it to the St. Christopher's medal she still wore, even though St. Christopher wasn't the patron saint of anything anymore. Brooke felt an ache when she thought of her mother; she didn't especially want to hurt her. But the ache hardened when she thought of her father. He would be worrying too, and not just because she was late getting home. He knew what she had seen, and had to be wondering what she would say—to Camille, to Mackenzie, even to him—about it. Well, let him wonder. Let him worry too. He deserved it.

"Ouch." Otter stopped to rub his finger and put it to his mouth.

"What happened?"

"Whacked myself on that mirror," he said, gesturing to a car parked at the curb. Brooke had noticed how he swung his arms when he walked; she liked that about him, as she seemed to be liking so many things.

"Can I see?"

He held out his hand and she turned it over in hers. Here were his pale, long fingers, the silver ring she had noticed earlier. She could see where he had hit himself; the finger was red and might have even started to swell slightly. Without thinking, she brought it to her lips and kissed it. Damn. Now he was really going to think she was dorky.

But instead he gave her this big, even goofy, smile—he must have been more than a little drunk too—and used that same hand to lightly touch her cheek. Brooke would have loved this had it not reminded her of her father and that Naomi Wechsler person this morning, and her face settled into a scowl.

"Hey, no offense," Otter said and withdrew his hand. He started walking again, and Brooke, momentarily stunned by what had just happened, remained where she was, watching him go. Then she snapped out of it and had to trot a little to catch up.

"There you are," he said, smiling again. "I thought I made you mad or something."

"It wasn't you," Brooke said. "It was—" But she didn't finish. She wanted this night to obliterate her day, not rehash it.

"Anyway," Otter was saying. "It's kind of late. Shouldn't you be getting home?"

"Yeah, late," Brooke agreed. She had told him, while they were in the bar, that she was still in high school, and at the time it hadn't seemed to bother him. Now she wished she had lied. It was over, her great adventure, unraveling before it even began.

"Where do you live?"

"In Brooklyn. Park Slope."

"Cool," said Otter. "I know a couple of people who live there."

"It's okay." Brooke was still feeling deflated.

"I'll take you home." Otter put his hand on her shoulder. This time Brooke stayed still. "You shouldn't be on the train by yourself. It's not safe."

"You don't have to," Brooke said, but inside she thought, Yes, yes, yes. Maybe once they got to the subway, something else might happen. Something different and exciting. Maybe they would decide to head out to LaGuardia Airport and watch the planes land. Or get off the train at Manhattan's tip and together walk across the Brooklyn Bridge together.

"I know. I want to." He paused. "But your parents. Aren't they going to be angry you were out so late?"

"They're away," she improvised on the spot. "They went to this conference together. My dad's a doctor."

"Well, that's a relief. I don't have classes tomorrow, so I'm okay. Come on, let's find the train."

They walked together in silence for a while, and when they came to Second Avenue, stopped, waiting for the light to change. When it did, Otter took her hand in his and kept it there. Brooke was thrilled but did her best not to show it. Guys didn't like girls who gushed, who looked too starry-eyed. She was in control though; she could rein it in when she had to.

They came to the subway station at Astor Place. She had already been there today, hours ago, but it seemed much, much longer, as if the time that had unspooled since she had sat at the counter and picked at her food, had been days instead. It was like the sensation of being little and going to the beach—when a day seemed to stretch on for so long, it could have been divided into chapters: arriving, setting up the blanket and the umbrella, running into the water that first time, looking for shells with her sister and getting mad that Mackenzie seemed to find the best ones, the peanut butter and jelly sandwich that always held the crunch of sand, the sunburned shoulders you only noticed when it was too late, more swimming, the drip castle their father helped create, the trip to the ice-cream stand, the sleepy ride home at the end of it all with sand still in her hair, between her toes, and chafing her skin underneath the still-damp bathing suit.

Right now, the station was as busy as it had been at noon. People hurried down the steps or up them and out into the street. You'd think it was rush hour, not midnight. But Manhattan was different from Brooklyn; Brooke had figured that out by the age of ten. Otter might think Park Slope was cool, but it was nothing compared with all this activity, this animation. Brooke suddenly understood that this was where she belonged, here in the city, as they called it, not back in boring Brooklyn with her clueless mother, her lying, hypocritical father.

Otter pulled out a MetroCard and swiped for both of them. A train—it must have been the number 6—had just pulled out of the station as they descended; Brooke could see its lights retreating into the tunnel. Now they would have to wait, but Brooke didn't mind at all; she was in no hurry to get home.

They sat down, the only occupants on a wooden bench. Down at one end of the platform, Brooke could see a couple kissing. Somewhere at the other end stood a guy with a huge suitcase around which several lengths of rope had been tied. She looked up at Otter, who was reaching into his pockets. From one, he pulled out a harmonica; how retro was he? But she liked that about him too.

"Do you play?" she asked.

"A little." He put it to his lips and by running it across them, created a pleasing melodic wheeze. The couple didn't stop kissing, but the guy with the suitcase looked in their direction. Otter took the harmonica away from his mouth and popped something between his lips. Brooke couldn't see what it was but guessed it might have been meant to mask the beer on his breath. Candy? Gum?

"Want one?" Otter extended his hand. Brooke reached down, expecting to find a breath mint. Instead it was a small blue pill.

"What is it?"

"Something to take the edge off."

"The edge?" Brooke had no idea of what he meant.

"The edge," he said patiently. "You know. It just helps you get over whatever's bothering you." How had he known anything was bothering her? She hadn't said a word about what she had seen this morning. But maybe he could sense it, the thing that was trailing her like a cloud of black smoke or a bad smell.

"All right." She downed it easily. "To take the edge off."

Otter put the harmonica to his mouth again, and a jazzy, bright sound emerged. This time, even the couple stopped kissing to look. Brooke found herself made unreasonably happy by this small series of events: the music, the liquor, the boy, and maybe even the pill, though she doubted it could have worked so quickly.

"Here we go." Otter stood and Brooke did too. A train pulled into the station and opened its doors. Within minutes, they were at the Brooklyn Bridge Station. "Last stop," called the conductor. "Last stop on this train."

"We'll have to change here," Otter explained. "Get the number 4 to Brooklyn."

"Whatever," Brooke said, and though she knew how people used that word constantly, she really did mean it. The pill, whatever it had been, really was working now, and it made her feel even more dreamy and disconnected than before. Where was she going, anyway? Home? And what had happened this morning that had made her never want to go home again? Something, she could remember that. Something having to do with her father. But the exact details were vague, breaking up and dissolving in her mind even as she tried to reconstruct them.

They sat on another bench, waited for another train. Maybe they would go on switching trains and waiting for yet another one all night long. Brooke smiled at the thought. Otter took out the harmonica and once again began to play, something mellow and balladlike. This time, Brooke stood up and began to sway in time to the music. She wasn't dancing, not really. There were no steps she performed, no pattern to which she adhered. But she loved the feel of moving to the music. This must, she thought languidly, be the pill. Without it she would have been too inhibited, too concerned about how she looked, what Otter would think. But she had taken the pill, which in turn had taken, as he said, the edge off. And oh, how good it felt. She suddenly thought of edges, sharp, cutting edges, that sliced to the quick when you touched, or even looked, at them. But her edge was gone tonight, blurred and buffed by the music and the beers and the magic little pill.

Otter continued to play, and Brooke took a few steps away from him, toward the edge of the platform. There it was again, that word, *edge*. This edge was bordered by raised, skidproof dots and highlighted by a thick stripe of yellow paint, now somewhat dirty but still clearly visible. She was drawn toward it, and moved in that direction until she had reached it. Then she began walking along the edge of the platform with her arms outstretched, like a tightrope dancer. Despite the beer, despite the pill, she felt calm and centered. She moved slowly, cautiously, along the yellow stripe, the music snaking around her, urging her to keep going, keep on course, keep steady. Then, in a wholly unremarkable moment, she fell, tumbling heavily onto the tracks. She landed in what felt like a heap, her ankle twisted painfully beneath her. The music stopped.

"Jesus fucking Christ!" Otter rushed over. She looked up at him, confused. Her first thought was how dirty it was down here: wrappers from McDonald's; flattened beer cans; a thick, unimaginable kind of filth, greasy but at the same time dustlike, covering everything. She saw something move: a large, glossy insect, like a roach only bigger. She watched it, repelled but weirdly fascinated at the same time. The insect's body had a crisp, almost shellacked appearance; the movements of its legs were surprisingly graceful as it scurried away. Then she understood where she was, why Otter was yelling. The tracks. She had fallen onto the subway tracks. She had to get up. And fast.

"Brooke," Otter called, and she saw his hand reaching out over the platform edge. "I'll pull you up." She grabbed the hand and tried to hoist herself up. But her ankle gave way instantly, and for a second, the pain of trying to stand on it made everything disappear.

"Are you okay?" Otter looked like he was crying.

"I hurt my ankle." Brooke thought her voice sounded faint, a whisper. Could he even hear her?

"Let me get help." Otter got up.

"No!" Brooke's voice was loud now; loud and clear. "Don't leave me here!"

"Okay," soothed Otter. "Okay." He knelt again, and once more stretched his body out on the platform. This time, he extended both of his arms. "Use the other foot to stand on."

"I don't know if I can," Brooke said, but she grabbed his hands anyway, this time steadying herself on the other foot. This ankle seemed fine, but she would have to use the other, hurt one to brace herself so that she could haul her body up and out. Gingerly, she raised her injured foot up to the wall, applied a little pressure. A swift slicing pain made her drop it immediately.

"It's hurts too much," Brooke whimpered. "I can't do it."

"Brooke, you have to! I have to pull you out!"

"Hey, what are you kids doing? Are you crazy?" A black man in a brown uniform towered over her; from where she was, Brooke could see the looping white script that adorned the pocket: Edgar.

"She fell onto the tracks and hurt her ankle," Otter said. "I'm trying to pull her out, but she can't put any weight on that foot."

"Fuck the foot," Edgar said, getting down on the platform alongside Otter. "We'll both just reach down and pull her up."

"Do you think we can?"

"We better try," Edgar said.

Brooke felt the ground tremble before she could even see the lights. A train. A subway train was heading down the tracks. She looked up at the four hands, two pale and two dark, and the four arms all reaching for her. She let them grab her wrists, her forearms, and they began to pull. The lights from the train were painting the tiles of the subway walls gold; she could feel their heated, merciless glow. Would the driver see her? And even if he did, would he be able to stop in time?

"Pull," hissed Edgar, and they did. Brooke felt her torso elongate and stretch, she felt the rough, abrasive surface of the wall as her stomach scraped along its surface. The train was closer now, so close, its powerful sound amplified to a roar in her ears, blotting out everything else, but they were doing it, they had done it, pulled her up and over the side as the train came pounding along the rails, arms, breasts, belly, thighs, all pulled from the pit, safe on the platform, one foot, the good one, kicking free of its shoe, the other, the one she tried not to move because of the pain, as still as she could keep it.

"Goddamn, we did it!" she heard Edgar say.

"We did it!" Otter echoed. The train exploded into the station, the roar no longer just in her ears but lodged in her mouth, her throat, her eyes. In its urgent, headlong rush, the roaring train struck her foot, the one she had hurt, the one that was still hanging, just the smallest bit, over the edge. Brooke felt her body smacked then yanked along the subway platform by the force; she twisted once, then again, enveloped in a blaze of white, incandescent pain. Then the savage, blinding white was snuffed out as everything went abruptly and mercifully black.

22

House on the Hill

"What the hell do you mean, Naomi is sleeping with a doctor from Holy Name Hospital?" Rick was raising his voice in public, something he never did. But he was doing it now, and he didn't even care who heard. "Is this something you've made up? To hurt me?"

Rick and Lillian were sitting in a Chinese restaurant in Sunset Park, the same restaurant he had gone to with Naomi on Christmas Day. Earlier that afternoon, Lillian had said she needed to talk to him, somewhere away from the office. But she hadn't invited him to her apartment; instead, she had suggested a restaurant she knew, although until they walked through the door he hadn't connected her suggestion with the place he had been before.

"I told you: I saw her, getting coffee at Barnes and Noble. This guy was standing in front of her."

"So what made you think that they were together? That she had any connection to him at all?"

"She brushed something off of his coat. Lint. A thread. I don't know. I couldn't see. But I could see what it meant. It meant they were—"

"Sleeping together?" He still couldn't, wouldn't, believe it. "How can you infer that?"

"I just knew, that's all. You don't do that to someone unless you're close to them. Really close."

"Holy Name," Rick said, lowering his voice. "She works at Holy Name now, you know. Not just volunteering anymore. She's got a regular job. She knows people, must have made friends by now. What you saw," he paused to consider it again, "doesn't have to mean what you think it did."

"Maybe," Lillian conceded. "Maybe I'm wrong."

The waiter appeared with a pot of tea, which he poured into the thick, handleless mugs on the table. He handed them a pair of menus, which Rick took and then put aside.

"Why are you telling me this?" He pressed his hand around the white curve of the mug. The heat felt good.

"I thought it would make you feel less guilty." Lillian looked down at the table. "That if she were doing it . . ."

"Then it wasn't so bad for me to be doing it too. Is that it?"

Lillian lifted her head and nodded. He could see the tears in her eyes. She wasn't trying to hurt him; no that wasn't it at all. She was guilty too, as guilty as he was. Or was there something else?

"So who was the guy, anyway? Someone young?" Rick took a sip of the tea. Black, hot, strong. He took another sip, and then another.

"No, not young. White hair, all in a mess, standing away from his head. I saw he was wearing an ID tag, I just couldn't read the name."

It took a moment to register, but when it did, Rick wondered why he hadn't seen it before. That doctor. The one from the summer. He knew and, at the same time, rejected the knowledge.

"McBride? Naomi and McBride? Is that what you're telling me?" His voice got loud again. Someone turned around to stare. Fuck you, he thought. Fuck me. It all made sense though, didn't it? That's why she had been hanging around the hospital, that's why she had gone ahead and taken the job there. How had he not noticed it?

"Who's McBride?" Lillian looked confused.

"The head of the pediatric unit. At Holy Name."

"Oh." She still didn't get it, but why should she?

"He's the one—" Rick stopped. "The one who told us that Dahlia had died."

"Rick!" Lillian reached over and ran her fingers over his wrist. He looked down at her hand on his flesh and suddenly stood up. The mug of tea tipped over, and a pool of dark, steaming liquid puddled on the table and began dripping on the floor.

"Sorry," he said. "I'm sorry." He reached into his pocket and handed Lillian two tens. "Get yourself something to eat, okay? I'll see you in the office tomorrow."

"Where are you going?" she asked, mopping at the wetness with a napkin but not taking her eyes off his face.

"I don't know," he said. He meant it.

Rick left the restaurant and headed for the subway. Without really planning it, he took the R train to Union Street, and when he found himself in the street again, he walked up the hill on Carroll, toward his house. Or what had been his house. He hadn't been here since Naomi had asked him to leave. He hesitated before climbing the brownstone stairs, but then once he began, took them quickly. Though he had his key, he rang the bell. Once, twice, three times. There was no answer. She was out. With him? McBride, the poacher, the prick?

Rick let himself in, called her name anyway, just in case. "Naomi?" God, he sounded pathetic. What a wimp, what a wuss. "Naomi?" he called again, louder, more imperative this time. Still nothing. The rooms were all dark, and he flipped on a light. Nothing different down here, nothing had changed, at least not that he could see. He turned back into the hall, mounted the stairs.

He hesitated before walking into the bedroom he had shared with Naomi. When he did, he was puzzled by the big open space in the middle of the room. Puzzlement turned to suspicion when he found the mattress and boxspring, sans headboard, in what had been Dahlia's room. Did she have that McBride guy over to the house? Is this where she let him fuck her? The thought made his chest constrict and his stomach burn. He closed the door, not bothering to look in the other rooms.

He walked heavily down the stairs again, went into the dining room, and stood there. He didn't know why he had come or what he expected to find. But he did know that while he had walked in the door tentative and questioning—he cringed a little to think of how his voice had sounded calling out Naomi's name; he was glad she had not been home to hear it—he would walk out in a wholly different frame of mind. He was angry, that's what he was. Angry at Naomi, at McBride, at himself for setting all this in motion. Rick knew that he was at fault; he assumed the first transgression had been his, and he was prepared to accept both the blame and consequences. But the idea that Naomi should betray him with a doctor from Holy Name—no, not *a* doctor, but *the* doctor who had been so woven into the story of Dahlia's death—well that was something else. Something that made everything he had done seem very different.

He tried to remember McBride, who had come to this house, stood in this very room, and told him how truly, deeply sorry he was that their child had been killed. Sorry my ass, Rick thought bitterly. He had come sniffing around the home of a bereaved couple, looking for a way to put the moves on the wife. What kind of doctor did a thing like that? What kind of man? Rick didn't know, but he wanted, suddenly, to find out.

He went to the shelf in the kitchen where the phone books had always been kept and began flipping through the Brooklyn white pages. His hands were actually shaking. Get a grip, he told himself sternly. Get. A. Grip. *H, I, K*; here it was, *M*. There were several McBrides but only two Michaels. One was on East Seventh Street, in Kensington. The other was on Ninth Street. Number 530, which would be right up by Prospect Park. He would bet on that one. Rick looked at his watch: eight-thirty. Late enough for the scumbag to be at home, but not late enough to be asleep. Not that Rick would have cared if he had woken him.

He put the phone book away and turned out the lights. Then he hurried from the house, long strides taking him up the hill, toward the park, where he turned and began walking along Prospect Park West. He stayed on the side of the street that bordered the park most closely, so there were few cross streets to impede his progress. He walked quickly, fueled by shock and rage, his legs extending and stretching,

stretching and extending, bringing him closer and closer to his destination.

It seemed that he was at Ninth Street in no time at all. Standing on the corner, Rick stopped, waited for his breathing to slow down. The night was clear and frigid; looking up he saw the pale, lifeless moon, a hunk of deadened rock that was millions of miles away. Then he turned and headed down the street.

McBride's house was a nice one—four stories, brownstone, good condition. The shutters, original no doubt, were closed, but he could see narrow stripes of light shining through their tight slats. It was a nicer house than his, way nicer, but hey, the guy was a doctor, a real doctor, as his brothers, even his father, had he been alive, might have said. They had never stopped ragging on him about being a podiatrist, not even all these years later. Well fuck them, and fuck McBride too, who had the chutzpah, the balls, to nail his wife. Rick's wife.

Now that he was here, he was no less angry, but he was at the same time strangely calm. Dahlia was dead, Naomi had exiled and betrayed him. What did he have to lose? He could say what he wanted—anything. Yell at the guy, call him names. He tried a few of them out loud: Motherfucker. Asshole. Dickbrain. None seemed sufficient to convey his fury.

He rang the bell. The door opened almost immediately, as if the white-haired guy—yeah, it was McBride all right; Rick recognized him easily—had been waiting just behind it. Rick saw his features working, registering surprise, disappointment, recognition. Clearly, McBride had been expecting someone, only that someone wasn't Rick. Yet Rick could tell McBride knew him from somewhere, he just couldn't place him. Rick watched all this silently, with a kind of detached, even faintly amused interest. But before McBride could settle the pieces into their proper configuration and solve the puzzle, Rick had drawn back his fist and then let it explode, wham, right in McBride's startled face.

23

Mail

Naomi sat with the letter unfolded in front of her. She had read it three times now, and each time, the words were the same. "Due to an unforeseen and potentially hazardous asbestos situation in key areas of our facility, we are required to temporarily close down certain wings while the necessary cleanup and containment measures are taken. Every effort has been made to reassign the affected residents locally, but we were unable to obtain a local placement for your mother, Estelle Levine. Instead we have found a spot for her at our sister facility, the Jewish Home for the Aged in Bridgeport, Connecticut. Of course, we understand that this may represent an upheaval for her and for your family, and we are sure that you will want to familiarize yourself with the facility before making any decision. For that reason we are inviting you and your mother to join us for a guided tour through the facility on . . ."

So Estelle was to be moved. Again. Naomi refolded the letter, resisting the impulse to crumple it and hurl it into the trash. She didn't know what her mother would think of this plan. She wondered whether she had even been told, or had those in charge decided to wait, to feel out the families first before informing the residents. Naomi didn't think Estelle was going to be happy about living in Connecticut.

She looked out the window at the darkening sky. She had come into work late today; after her morning at the Plaza with Michael, she took the train back to Brooklyn and headed to the hospital without stopping home first. There were a number of phone calls to be returned and several e-mails requiring immediate reply. Late in the afternoon, she met with a group of high school volunteers, the St. Saviour's girls. Wasn't that where Michael's daughter went to school?

All day long, Naomi had relived the horrible moment when she had watched Michael's face turn into a pained gargoyle of itself. She had turned to see the girl, but had gotten only a fleeting look before she had pivoted and strode away. Naomi and Michael had stood there for a few seconds. When it was clear that he wasn't going to try to follow his daughter, she led him into Central Park. They came to the entrance to the zoo—now it was called the Wildlife Center—and Michael pulled out his wallet to pay. They walked in silence for a few minutes.

"Are you all right?" Naomi asked finally.

"No." He stopped in front of a glass-sided pool that was home to a quartet of seals. A single seal was visible under the water's surface, its supple body spiraling effortlessly as it swam. The others were congregated on a pile of rocks, their wet, shining fur reflecting whatever pale sunlight there was. "I'm not."

"I'm so sorry," Naomi said. Their roles had somehow reversed; now she had to find it in her to comfort him.

"And to think I was worried about someone from the hospital seeing us."

"I know." She reached out to take his hand. "It's awful."

"Thank you," he said.

"For what?" Naomi was puzzled.

"For not saying, 'It's not so bad' or 'It could be worse.' Because it is that bad. And it couldn't be any worse."

Suddenly the relative silence of the pool was broken by a group of schoolchildren, whose feet made loud, stamping sounds on the pavement. They burst into excited squeals when they saw the animals. Naomi guessed that they were about ten—older than Dahlia had been, younger than Michael's daughter was. She watched them for a moment before turning back to Michael. He had been watching too.

"She'll be all right, you know." Naomi felt impelled to share her sudden conviction. The girl, Brooke, would be wounded by what she had seen, but somehow the incident, painful as it was, would be incorporated into her life. Because she still had her life.

"Do you really think so?"

"I do. Not that it will be easy. She'll tell your wife. And she'll be furious, call you names. She'll think you betrayed her. And maybe you have. But the fact is, you've been a good father to her all these years. A wonderful father. That doesn't vanish in an instant. Even an instant like . . . that."

"Maybe you're right. God knows I want you to be right."

"I am, Michael," she said, urgent in her need to have him believe her. "I know I am."

The school group was clustered about the pool now, and one of the Wildlife Center workers appeared with a bucket of fish. Naomi was momentarily diverted by the sight of a seal—sleek, agile—jumping up to claim its prize. Just for a second, she got a look at its face—compact, rounded head sloping down to a gentle snout; bright, preternaturally intelligent eyes; thick, quivering whiskers on either side of its nose—and she was gripped by a fierce longing to hold the dark, slippery body in her arms. Water baby. Ghost child. The seal splashed into the pool and the moment was over.

"We'd better go," Michael said. "I'll walk you to the subway."

She somehow managed to endure the rest of the day and was grateful to be home at last. And now this. Naomi stood and went into the kitchen. It was time for dinner, though she didn't have much appetite and even less inclination to cook anything for herself. A can of lentil soup and some crackers would be enough. A hot bath. And sleep, if sleep would come. She noticed the shopping bag from Bergdorf Goodman still sitting in the middle of the room where she had left it along with her coat, and she went to put both away. Her coat went on its customary hook in the hallway. She looked down at the bag. The scarf was such a beautiful color. And it had felt so soft. But she didn't think she could wear it, not now.

What had she thought last night when she climbed into bed with another woman's husband? That whatever happened between them could remain a private and isolated act that affected nothing and no one else? Maybe Rick had thought the same thing when he began sleeping with that office manager of his. And look, he had been the one to tell her; she might not have found out about it for a long time. Or perhaps she wouldn't have found out at all. Some men were better at covering their tracks than her father had been. Yet such speculation was beside the point. He had told her. Maybe it was because he had felt guilty. Or maybe it was because he wanted it to end. She hadn't thought about it quite that way before. But somehow, the whole experience must have changed Rick, changed him enough so that he himself confessed. Once you were married, had a child—or lost one—there were no isolated acts anymore. Everything you did affected someone. She ought to have known that.

Naomi left the shopping bag in the hall, near the coat. For now, she just needed to get through this night, and the next one, and the one after that. She wished she could call Michael, find out where his daughter was, if she had come home, what she had said. But that might actually make things worse. Instead, she heated the soup and pitched the crackers, which were stale. Afterward, she settled down on the sofa to read the paper but found herself unable to concentrate.

She thought of how she had driven Estelle out to the house and remembered the sight of her mother's slight, aged body asleep on this same couch. She hadn't known, wouldn't have ever dreamed, that her father had been unfaithful. Yet Estelle had known about it, kept quiet about it, and had gone on with him and their life anyway. She had urged Naomi to do the same. It was different, though, wasn't it? Her parents still had a daughter worth staying together for: her.

"I don't think I can," she whispered aloud, to her mother and to herself. But she no longer felt so certain or so self-righteous about it. Maybe she hadn't sufficiently understood the extent of Rick's grieving. Maybe she had pushed him away often enough to make him turn to someone else. Maybe she shouldn't have been in such a hurry to tell him to go, or to have thrown herself into Michael's arms. Maybe, maybe, maybe.

The phone rang and she jumped, scattering the newspaper all over the floor in her haste to answer it. When she did, she was disappointed to find the recorded voice of a telemarketer on the other end, announcing that she had just won a deluxe getaway package to— She replaced the receiver quietly before she heard the destination.

The letter from the nursing home was still on the table. Naomi unfolded it again, prepared to read it a fourth time. Then realized she didn't have to. She wasn't going to send her mother to Connecticut— Riverdale had been far enough and look at how that worked out. Estelle had been miserable there. Miserable enough to have tried escaping. Looking and sounding worse each time Naomi saw or spoke to her.

But on the day Estelle had come to Brooklyn, she had seemed better. More lucid, more like her old self. That story she had told, about her father and the secretary. She had been able to do that, in coherent sequence, with very few hesitations or gaps.

The first time Estelle had been found wandering the streets of her Miami Beach neighborhood dressed in a slip and a straw cowgirl hat she had worn to a costume party in 1967, Naomi had flown down to Florida in a panic. Her father was dead, her mother poised on the narrowest ledge of sanity. After Estelle had recovered from the "petticoat episode," as she had called it, she assured Naomi that she was fine, everything was fine, her behavior prompted only by an outpouring of grief and longing for her dead husband. Reluctantly, warily, Naomi had returned to Brooklyn, only to be summoned to Miami again a mere week later. This time, Estelle had gotten as far as the supermarket dressed in the same hat, although she had decided to exchange the slip for her beaded satin wedding gown. Surprisingly, it still fit, and she had wandered the aisles of the Winn-Dixie in a regal, even haughty manner, scolding the stockboys for the high prices of the laundry detergent, the sloppy displays of potato chips. Norma, one of Estelle's friends, had been in the supermarket at the time and had called Naomi to tell her about the incident.

Naomi had not known what to do. The nursing home in Riverdale seemed, at the time, the best of her options, and despite the waiting list for the place, one of Rick's odious brothers had managed to pull a few strings and secure a spot for Estelle right away. In her own mind, Naomi had always considered the decision a provisional one; they would wait and see how Estelle adjusted to her new situation before deciding that it was, in fact, what was best for her. But after Dahlia's death, Naomi had not revisited the issue and instead had been grateful that it was something she didn't have to think about, or deal with, at least not then. Until today, and the arrival of the letter. She got up and reached for the telephone again. She might not be able to do a damn thing about Michael or his daughter. But she could do something about her mother, and she could do it soon.

She reached for the phone and quickly punched in the number of Rick's cell; she didn't want to give herself time to change her mind. She and Rick had not actually spoken since he'd left, though he'd been e-mailing her and there were the checks that he sent on a regular basis. So there had been no opportunity to talk about what would happen next: Would she file for divorce? Would he? If that happened, who would get the house? Or would they sell it, split the proceeds? Even thinking in this way made her feel unbearably sad. She had been betrayed by Rick. But the thought of resolving their impasse through legal means brought no sense of satisfaction or even relief. Still, she wasn't calling to talk to him about any of that. At least not tonight.

Rick didn't answer, and she didn't want to leave a message. Instead, she steeled herself for the call to his sister, Allison. Allison might know how to reach him. He had been staying there. Or at least that's what he had told her. The phone rang a couple of times, and Naomi was ready to hang up when she heard the young female voice—her sister-in-law—at the other end of the line. Although Allison had apologized—profusely—for her role in what Naomi considered the desecration of Dahlia's room, Naomi nonetheless harbored a glowing coal of anger against her: small yet potentially incendiary. Still, if she wanted to reach Rick—and Naomi did want to reach him, badly—she would have to get through this.

"Allison? It's Naomi." There, that was a start.

"Naomi! How are you?" She stopped. "I'm sorry. What a dumb question."

"It's okay," Naomi said, aware of how cold she sounded. "Really, it's okay."

"Well, it's good to hear your voice. I've been thinking about you."

I'll bet, Naomi thought but instead said, "I was trying to reach Rick." This was hard, harder than Naomi had anticipated. "Is he there? I'd like to talk to him."

"That brother of mine." Allison made a snorting noise into the phone. "He hasn't been staying here."

"Do you know where he is then?"

"No," Allison said after a pause. "I don't."

"Oh." Naomi had nothing to say to that.

"But if I hear from him, I'll have him call you. Right away."

"Sure," said Naomi. She was disappointed, she really was. She had understood, suddenly, what she needed to do about her mother. And Rick was the first person she had wanted to tell. "Thanks."

Naomi hung up and stared at the phone for a few seconds. Okay, she told herself, okay. So he's not living there. Maybe he's living with her. Maybe not. Naomi gathered up the newspaper to put in the recycling pile. There was the page with the crossword puzzle still blank, untouched. She never did the puzzle, but Rick did, every day. Seeing those small, empty squares suddenly made her miss him very much.

Maybe she would suspend delivery of the newspaper. She didn't seem to read it very consistently, and when she did, it so often filled her with despair. Looking around the room a last time before she went up to bed, she thought that no matter what happened, she didn't want to leave her house. Especially not now, when she had decided that she wanted to bring Estelle there to share it with her.

24

The Prodigal

It turned out that Camille had a tray of eggplant parmesan in the freezer, which she heated in the microwave. While she was washing some lettuce for a salad, Mackenzie came in, dropping her heavy backpack—what did his girls keep in there, bowling balls? hand weights?— and called out, "I'm starved. What's for dinner?"

"It's almost ready," Camille called. "Go wash up."

"Hi, Daddy." Mackenzie kissed Michael's cheek. Her hair was pulled back with a shirred white headband, and her lips were still cold.

"Hi, yourself. How was practice?"

"Exhausting. The coach was a total maniac. Everyone was complaining."

"Oh?" He was making the appropriate queries but having trouble listening to the answers. Brooke. Where was Brooke? That was all he could think about. When Camille put the food on the table, she looked at Brooke's empty seat and asked the question Michael had not trusted himself to say aloud.

"Where's your sister?" She put a big portion of eggplant on Mackenzie's plate. "Shouldn't she be home by now?"

"Maybe choir ran late," Mackenzie said between bites of the eggplant. "Mom, this is so-o-o good."

Camille served Michael a more modest helping. "She knows she ought to call us if she's going to be late. That's the rule."

Mackenzie pulled off a piece of bread from a loaf in the center of the table and began to mop up the sauce with it.

"Can I have some more? Please?"

"Yes, you may," Camille said with a sigh. "And Mackenzie, honey, let's try not to talk with a mouthful of food, okay?"

When they had finished eating and Mackenzie was helping to clear, she stopped by her sister's empty, untouched plate. "Should I leave this here, Mom? For when she comes in?"

"All right." Camille paused, staring down at the plate. "But she's going to be in trouble when she does."

Michael wandered into the kitchen, where the flowers he had brought earlier were sitting in a vase on the counter. The warmth of the room had caused them to open, and the fat, lush blossoms seemed to crowd each other for space.

"You really have to talk to her," Camille said. "Missing dinner without calling. And on a school night." The refrigerator door closed with a sound like a kiss. "It's getting so that I can't say anything to her anymore. She's so touchy."

"Teenagers," Michael said, trying to keep his voice light. "You know how they are."

"I know, I know," Camille said. She covered the remainder of the eggplant with aluminum foil and began loading the dishwasher. "But she's always been closer to you. Even when she was little."

"I'll try talking to her, okay?"

"Thanks." She looked up at him, quizzically, he thought. But then Mackenzie's voice floated into the kitchen.

"Mom? I need a bar of soap. There's none left."

"Soap? What about your homework?" Camille walked out of the kitchen and leaned over the banister to call up the stairs.

"I'll do it after I shower, I promise. I just feel so sticky and disgusting. From practice."

"All right." Michael heard her going up the stairs. He was alone in the room. It was only seven-thirty. Still, nothing to worry about, not really. Of course, he was the only one who knew that Brooke had not been at school this morning, so the likelihood of her being at choir practice was pretty slim. He looked at the flowers again, touched a soft petal. Then he thought of his cell phone, which he'd turned off hours ago. Maybe Brooke had tried to reach him. He dug it out of his pocket and was just checking his messages when Camille came back into the kitchen.

"There was a fresh bar of soap right on the sink. She didn't even see it. What's with them, anyway? They want to be so independent, and then they can't seem to do the least little thing for themselves." Before Michael could reply, the phone rang.

"That must be Brooke," Camille said and reached for it. As she listened, Michael watched the hopeful look in her eyes fade and go out. "Yes. Okay." She wiped down the countertop as she spoke, squeezed out the sponge. "No, I didn't tell him." A pause. "All right. I will." She set the sponge in the holder by the sink. "Thanks for calling." She hung up. "Just someone from the parents association," she said to Michael.

"I gathered." Michael felt her looking at him again, in that puzzled, critical way. Or maybe he was just imagining it. "Well, I'm sure she'll be home soon." He didn't think he could stand this anymore and turned to leave the room.

"She'd better. She's already grounded this weekend. I'm working on next weekend now."

"Camille," Michael said, hesitating on his way out. "Don't be too hard on her."

"How about telling her not to be so hard on me?"

Michael sat in the living room, or parlor, as his grandmother had liked to call it, pretending to read the paper. The phone rang two more times, and each time, he closed his eyes behind the shield of the newsprint and uttered a small prayer. Mackenzie wandered into the room, wearing clean sweatpants and a white St. Saviour's T-shirt.

"We've got a big project due in biology," Mackenzie announced, sitting down in a chair across from him and putting her feet, in their pink, fluffy slippers, up on the sofa, despite Camille's numerous admonitions about that very thing.

"Project?" Michael peered out from behind the paper.

"It's not due for about a month. But I was wondering if you'd help me."

"Of course I would." Slowly, Michael lowered the paper to look at her. Her hair was wrapped in a big towel. Through the thin fabric of the shirt, her breasts—small, pointed—were clearly visible and the sight made his throat ache. How had his daughters, those little girls, gotten to be this age? And how had he?

"Thanks, Daddy." She leaned over to kiss him again; this time, her lips, her whole body, seemed to emanate warmth.

"What's a father for, anyway?" He picked up the paper again and watched her walk away. Camille was still in the kitchen, on the telephone again. A quiet, ordinary evening at home, except, of course, that it was anything but ordinary. He was so tense that he decided to have a drink—that's what his father would have done—and got up to pour himself a strong one.

On his way to the liquor cabinet, Michael was halted by the ringing of the doorbell.

"I'll get it," he said eagerly. Now this, surely, was Brooke. It had to be. She had a house key, both girls did, but they often rang the bell anyway, another childish habit to which they continued to cling. "I'm right here."

Michael yanked open the door in a great, dramatic gesture, prepared to enfold this child, this weary prodigal, in his arms. He didn't care where she'd been, what she'd seen, what she thought. All he wanted was the chance to hug her, let her know that despite everything he loved, no, adored her. That much he knew was true.

But it was not Brooke standing there in the dark rectangle of night framed by the open door. It was a man—tall, tense looking, vaguely familiar. In the instant before Michael could place him, the man's fist suddenly and without warning shot out and landed in his face.

The blow forced Michael to stagger backward and hit the painted ceramic umbrella stand that Camille had bought in one of the antique stores lining Atlantic Avenue. The umbrella stand teetered and then crashed. Michael put his hand to his lip, now starting to swell. But he was momentarily more concerned about the broken umbrella stand that Camille had loved than with the blood coating his fingers.

"Michael, what is going on—" Camille came running into the hallway. Michael was leaning against the wall, while the man who had hit him stared down at him, breathing heavily with his mouth open, like a dog.

"Who are you?" Camille demanded.

The man continued to look at Michael. "You tell her," he said quietly. "Go on. Tell her who I am."

"Do you know this person? What happened? You're bleeding!" The pitch of Camille's words reached Mackenzie, who came running down and stopped in the middle of the stairs, terrified when she saw her father's bloodied face and the strange man standing in the doorway.

"Mr. Wechsler," Michael said with some effort. It felt like one of his teeth might be loose. Naomi's husband. He recognized the man now.

"I don't understand," Camille said. But her voice was quieter now that Michael had identified his assailant.

"Mr. Wechsler's daughter was brought to the hospital last summer. She had been in a car accident. A fatal car accident." Gently, Michael probed the tooth with his tongue, sending a shiver of pain through the left side of his face. Goddamn, it really was loose.

"That still doesn't give him the right—" Camille started to say.

"Rights," said Wechsler. "Let's talk about rights, okay? Yours. Mine. My *wife's*."

"Michael, this man is crazy." Camille went to stand next to Michael, who had by now moved away from the wall. His mouth was still trickling blood, and he reached into his pocket for a handkerchief. There wasn't one, so he used his sleeve.

"Do you think I'm crazy?" Wechsler leaned close to Michael. "Do you?"

"Don't hit him!" Mackenzie remained on the stairs, looking from one adult to the other, trying to sort out what was going on. "Please don't hit my father again."

Wechsler looked up at Mackenzie, whom he seemed to just notice. His bottom lip, then his whole lower jaw started to tremble, as if he might cry. Quite suddenly, he turned, ran down the stairs and up the hill, toward the park. Camille just stood staring at Michael, the jagged shards of pottery littering the floor around them. It was left to Mackenzie to hurry down and close the door behind him. As soon as she did, Camille was propelled into motion, bending down to pick up the larger pieces of pottery, sending Mackenzie into the kitchen for the broom. Mackenzie hurried back into the hallway, holding the broom and dustpan in one hand and a roll of paper towels in the other.

"Do you want me to do it, Mom?" she asked. "I could wet the paper towels and go over the floor when I'm done." She looked anxiously over at Michael but did not speak to him. Maybe she was afraid to.

"Yes, sweetheart," Camille said. Michael could hear the gratitude in her voice. "That would be really helpful." Then she turned to Michael. "I know you're going to tell me what all this was about. But first I have to know if you're okay."

"I'm okay," Michael said, amazingly calm considering what he was preparing to say next.

"Are you sure? Maybe I should run you down to the ER just to be safe, because it looked like he hit you pretty hard—"

"No." Michael found his strength, his confidence growing. He began to feel the way he did when he had to deliver the news to parents about the child they loved and were about to lose—or had already lost. Profoundly sad, but steady too. It was his job to do this. And he did it well. "I—I mean we—have to stay here."

"Because—?"

"Because of Brooke."

"What does Brooke have to do with all of this?" Camille asked. Michael could see the apprehension settle over her face, weighing it down and instantly aging it. He had seen this look on women's faces before but had never imagined he would be seeing it on Camille's. Or that he would be the one to cause it. Buck up, he told himself. That would be his father's advice right now. You made your bed, now lie in it. That would be his mother's. Mackenzie was still sweeping, but she was looking down now, at the floor.

"Let's go inside," Michael said, gently taking Camille's arm and steering her toward the living room. He wasn't bleeding anymore, but the whole side of his face still throbbed. There was something almost welcome in the pain. "It will be easier to hear if you're sitting down."

Later, much later, the phone call came with news of Brooke. Michael and Camille left a detailed note for Mackenzie before they headed into Manhattan—barely any traffic, the ride smooth and seamless—to be with their daughter.

25

Salvation

Estelle knew that they were planning to send her to Connecticut. They thought they were being so careful, didn't they? So discreet. But she was shrewd, more shrewd than they were, and she had put it all together—the conversations, the memos, the phone calls she wasn't supposed to be listening to, or understand. What else did she have to do here anyway? Glue feathers to a square of felt and call it art?

At first, she told herself that it didn't matter. Riverdale, Connecticut, it was all the same. The halls, the rooms, the meals, the imbeciles with whom she was surrounded. But this indifference subsided and was replaced by a fierce if not wholly comprehensible resistance. She didn't want to be moved—again. It was hard enough for her to remember where she was at any given time. Little as she liked this place, she had come to know it: the smells in the air, the dismal view out the window. That day when she'd walked down Broadway, toward a train she would never catch, had nonetheless helped locate and ground her. And she badly wanted that grounding; limited purchase as it was, it was all she had.

Connecticut was also farther from Brooklyn, farther from her daughter and her son-in-law and all the troubles they were having. It would be even harder for Naomi to come and get her and bring her back to that row house she lived in, the row house in Brooklyn.

These thoughts, though, were futile, a circular track that went around and around, with no discernible exit or escape. What could she, Estelle, in her present condition do about any of it? Talk to the social workers? No one would listen to her or take her seriously. "Yes, we understand you'd rather stay in Riverdale, Mrs. Levine, but it's not possible because . . ." Estelle tuned them out. Not to be trusted, not one of them. And she couldn't depend on Naomi for anything either. Her daughter had worries enough of her own. That much was clear. Estelle was going to have to figure this out by herself.

For several days, this took the form of brooding. She refused to get out of bed, refused to eat—no great loss there—refused to attend any of the classes, workshops, or therapy sessions for which she had been scheduled. She relented only when it was movie time, and then only because they were showing *Stage Door*, one of her all-time favorites. She was entranced as she watched it, even reciting some of the snappier lines right along with the actresses; that's how familiar she was with the screenplay. But when the film ended and she was reminded, once again, of where and who she was, she started to cry.

"Now Mrs. Levine, it's not such a sad movie, is it?" said Belinda, the attendant who helped her up from her seat and back to her room. "I thought it had a kind of an uplifting ending, didn't you?" But though the woman was kind enough, Estelle didn't even bother explaining. What was the point? What was the point of anything, when you thought about it? She allowed herself to be led back to her room, where she spent the rest of the evening sitting without the lights on, staring out the window. Darkness inside, and darkness out. It was all darkness, and in the end, darkness was all you could reasonably hope to expect.

The next morning she was no less gloomy, but she had a thought that put her gloom at some kind of distance, in some new perspective. She could end her own life if she wanted to. This was a strangely liberating, even intoxicating thought. If they really were going to send her away, and in so doing cause the quality of whatever life she had left to deteriorate so radically, she could opt out, make a different, wholly unexpected choice. This thought carried her through the morning and well past lunch. Though not a religious woman, Estelle had some faint belief in an afterlife; she yearned to be reunited with her husband, her parents, her older sister Gloria, who had died suddenly from a burst aneurysm in her brain. And Dahlia. How she longed to see Dahlia again.

Even the thought of taking her life was fraught with complications. The what, where, when, and how of it stymied her. She didn't want to feel any pain; she wanted to go gently into that good night. How was this to be accomplished in an environment where she was watched and monitored virtually all the time? It would take some thinking about.

Nothing that involved a weapon. Estelle had no desire for a brutal end, which ruled out guns, knives, and blades of any kind. Hanging frightened her—it was known to be unreliable, sometimes resulting in a slow, painful death. Gas would be good, her head in the oven like that poet, Sylvia something, all those years ago. But that would not be easy to accomplish. Jumping from someplace very high might work; she thought of the bridge, the Brooklyn Bridge, which she had crossed not long ago on the way to Naomi's house. Then she remembered her aborted subway trip to Brooklyn and decided against that particular plan. Too hard to find her way there; too many obstacles. And it would be cold. So very cold.

Pills, clearly, were the answer. There were so many of them in this place, dispensed freely to all the residents several times a day. Big, small, round, flat. Some shaped like shields, others, like eggs. She had seen tablets in blue, white, gray, yellow, and pink; capsules in amber and black, and sometimes filled with tiny multicolored granules, like the candies she had been fond of using to decorate the birthday cupcakes when Naomi was a little girl.

There might be a way to obtain some of them, even those intended for other people. Estelle knew that many residents refused their medications, pretending to swallow them and then sending them down drains or tossing them out windows later on. She would have to start paying better attention to who took what, and when. That shouldn't be too hard. Most of the people here were only too happy to blab; she had merely to extend herself, just a little, and all the things she needed to know would come flocking to her, like pigeons home to roost.

She began with her neighbors in the dining hall. The fat lady and the trembling, skinny man. The woman was a veritable fountain, babbling information, advice, warnings all mixed together. She took medicine for her heart, she happily confided, medicine to control her high blood pressure, medicine to help her sleep. It was the sleeping pills that were of most interest to Estelle, but it didn't sound like her voluble companion would part too easily with these.

The man was somewhat morose and taciturn, but when Estelle asked about his grandchildren, the floodgates came pouring open. How he missed them, his *shain kinderlech*, how he wished he could kiss their foreheads, their fingertips, every day, no, every minute of every day. He was on several different medications but distrusted all of them. "The doctors," he warbled. "Little *pishers*. What do they know? I make like I'm taking the pills they give me, but when they aren't looking, *phut*." He made a spitting gesture into his hand. "I throw them away."

"Maybe you would consider saving them for me next time?" Estelle said. "Since you don't want them anyway?"

"Sure, sure." He smiled, a baring of his teeth that looked more pained than mirthful. "What will you do with them though? Sell them as day-old, at half price? You've got to give me a cut if you do." His laugh quickly dissolved into a cough, and she waited patiently until he had got his breath again.

Encouraged by her success with her tablemate, Estelle once again returned to the arts and crafts room and to her various forms of therapy. There had to be other residents who were not taking their medication; it was up to her to find them.

Then something happened that made all her careful plans wholly unnecessary. It was an innocuous enough incident: one of the women from arts and crafts had loaned Estelle her sweater when Estelle complained that she felt cold. Usually the room was way too hot, but today for some reason—was the heat malfunctioning?—the room was cool, even chilly. It wasn't until she was back in her room later that day that she discovered a bottle of sleeping pills in the pocket of the sweater. Where had they come from? Estelle couldn't believe that the answer to her dilemma had lain, dormant, in that small fold of cloth all afternoon. There was the owner of the sweater, however, whom she would have to deal with. But that could wait until arts and crafts, which wouldn't happen again until later in the week.

Estelle studied the bottle carefully in the brief intervals she was alone in her room. An over-the-counter brand in a plastic bottle, the label written in bold, black letters that were easy to read. Estelle fretted over how strong they really were, but reasoned that the whole bottle—she shook it to confirm its contents—ought to work, especially if she took them at night and was not found until the morning. She was small, she was thin. They just might do the trick. She hid them in her closet, poking a hole in the lining of a white eyelet bathrobe that she wouldn't wear for months. No one would look there; she was certain of that.

When it was time for arts and crafts again, she brought the sweater with her, nervous that its owner would question the missing pills. But when she found herself in the big, open room with the paper-covered tables, the owner was nowhere to be seen. The room was hot again; whatever had been wrong with the heat had been fixed. Estelle's inquiries yielded the information that the woman had gone into the home's adjacent hospital, for surgery. It was unclear when or even if she would return to arts and crafts. Estelle hung the sweater up in her own closet, carefully, considerately, smoothing out the material.

It was shortly after this that she was told officially about the move to Connecticut. It had something to do with asbestos. What that was Estelle could not remember. But anything they told her would be a lie, so really, did it matter?

"It won't be for another couple of weeks, Mrs. Levine," she was assured by the social worker. "And of course you'll get a chance to visit the facility first, see if everything is to your liking."

Her liking. What would be to her liking would be to exchange this deteriorating body and this uncertain mind for the vigor, the confidence, of youth. No chance of that, now was there? Instead, she went back to her room, groped around in the closet until she found the white robe. She hadn't noticed how yellowed it had become; the sleeves, the hem were all discolored with age. Like her. But then she felt for the lining, ran her hand along the bottom, and yes, there was her bottle, her escape route, her salvation if she so required it. Just knowing that the bottle was there made her feel secure and peaceful. She had found the exit, and could use it if she had to.

Outside her window, the wind whipped and blew the branches of the trees back and forth. Estelle watched and waited. Fridays came, her own silver heaven, with the movies she had loved as a girl, and loved still. *Some Like It Hot. Citizen Kane. You Can't Take It with You.* She didn't need the bottle, not yet. She would hold out until the move to Connecticut became a certainty. There would be plenty of time then. All the time in the world, and it would all be hers.

One morning, she woke to bright, winter sun. The light on the water sparkled and the naked trees looked black against the intense blue of the sky. Belinda came in to help her dress.

"So I hear you're looking at a change, Mrs. Levine," she said as she ran a comb through Estelle's hair.

Estelle didn't say anything. So much for taking a look at the facility, making sure it was to her liking. They had just gone ahead and decided without her approval or consent. Even Naomi hadn't bothered to call. Well, who cared what an old woman thought or wanted? No one here. No one anywhere.

At breakfast, Estelle intentionally littered the floor with crumbs from her toast and smeared margarine—she never saw butter here, not once—under the table. She dropped used tissues in the hall, tried to scrape the paint on the wall in her room with a screw she had found lying on the floor. In arts and crafts, she made a collage that was composed entirely of scraps of black—black paper, black fabric, black ribbon. It was Friday and there was a movie, but it was a Western and she didn't much like Westerns. Still, she sat through it because it was better than being alone with her thoughts. The bottle, she reminded herself. I still have the bottle.

Friday evening she decided to attend services in the home's small chapel. If she were really intending to carry out her plan, she felt she ought to have a little spiritual solace or guidance to help her on her way. The chapel was a small and unattractive room on the basement level, so that there was no natural light anywhere. And the services— in English; the prayers sounded like those uttered by Episcopalians— were led by a woman. Estelle supposed there was nothing wrong with having a woman as a rabbi—this one was young, with tightly curled hair and a very loud voice—but it felt so strange to her. She didn't have enough years left to acclimate herself to this change, she thought. This change or any other.

She listened as best she could, though mostly her mind wandered to the religious training, such as it was, of her childhood. She remembered being taken on the High Holidays to a shul just off Avenue M, she and her sister both in their matching princess-style red coats with the black velvet collars and buttons. Estelle and Gloria would grow bored and fidgety during the long service, but her bubbie, who always accompanied them, would slip the girls sweets from her patent leather clutch—a butterscotch candy wrapped in gold foil paper, a striped peppermint, a sour lemondrop—and let them bury their faces in the soft plush of the sheared beaver coat she wore. Maybe that's all old age ever was—an ongoing contest between the past and the present. Usually the past won, hands down.

After dinner, Estelle pulled the bottle from the lining of the robe and slipped it under her pillow. She would take the pills later on, before she got into bed. She wanted to be comfortable, to make it all as easy as she could. She thought again of her sister, her parents, her husband with whom she hoped to be rejoined. She thought of Norma, who had died of breast cancer after all. And she thought of Dahlia, her only granddaughter, who never had the chance to grow up or grow old. It was Dahlia, she decided all at once, whom she would seek out first.

Estelle put on a clean flannel nightgown, got a glass of water, arranged her slippers by her bedside out of habit. It was only when she was in bed, the bottle a small but perceptible bump beneath her pillow, that the phone rang. At first the noise startled and even confused her; she had forgotten momentarily what the phone was and somehow thought the loud ringing was an alarm of some sort, but what? Clock? Burglar? Fire? Finally her eyes settled on the telephone. She picked it up.

"Mom?" It was Naomi. "Mom, are you all set for Monday?"

"Monday?" Surely they weren't planning to move her so soon. Not that it would matter anyway.

"Yes, Monday. Didn't they tell you I was coming?"

"You can't come tomorrow instead?" Maybe tomorrow would be better. Let Naomi be here when they found her.

"Well, I could if you want me to. But we can't talk to the social worker or any of the doctors until Monday, so I thought I'd wait until then. If that's all right."

"Talk to the social workers? Doctors? What for?"

"About the move, Mom. Didn't they tell you?"

"Oh." Estelle let the word sit for a few seconds. "Yes. The move. To Connecticut."

"No, no. Not Connecticut. I want to bring you back here. Bring you home."

"Home," Estelle repeated, her mind darting around wildly before alighting on one of the flickering associations the word held. "Which home do you mean?" The one she and Gloria had lived in, with the chenille bedspreads in their shared room? Or the ones—there were more than one, after all—that she and Milton had made?

"Home to Brooklyn, Mom. Home to our house."

"I didn't know," Estelle said. "They didn't tell me." Although

Naomi was still talking, she set the receiver down and reached under her pillow for the bottle. She carefully slid her feet into her slippers and padded into the bathroom. Opening the bottle, she dumped all the pills into the white porcelain bowl of the toilet. Then, pressing the lever as hard as she could, she flushed.

26

Lucky

Opening her eyes, Brooke felt as if they had been stabbed. Quickly, she closed them again. One of her arms was wrapped with gauze and bandages; its weight felt heavy, even painful against her body, so she moved it slightly. That hurt too. She tried to move her legs, her feet, but it hurt too much. Oh God, everything hurt.

"Brooke?" She heard a voice. Her mother's voice. Brooke wanted to see her, but didn't think she could stand that stabbing sensation again, so she reached out instead. There it was, her mother's familiar hand: warm, a little dry, nails short but smooth and buffed. She felt for the wedding ring on her mother's finger, and the engagement ring with its trio of diamonds above it. She and Mackenzie used to beg to try it on when they were little.

"Mom," she said, her voice hoarse and whispery. "Mom, I'm glad you're here."

"Me too, honey." Her mother's hold tightened, and Brooke could hear the hiccupy sounds of her weeping. "Me too."

Tentatively, Brooke tried opening her eyes again, just a little this time. It hurt, but she kept them open anyway. She looked around at the unfamiliar room, trying to take it in. A hospital, but not Holy Name. Her mother, sitting by the side of the bed, gripping her hand. Her sister, sitting a little farther away. Her father was nowhere in the picture. Was this a good thing or not? Brooke couldn't decide, and rather than try, she closed her eyes. There was an IV attached in the arm without the bandage. What were they pumping into her anyway? She wanted to ask, but it felt too hard to talk. And her arm had begun to itch, though she was too weak to scratch it. She thought of being in the subway station with Otter, the silver gleam of the harmonica, the pill. She remembered falling onto the tracks, being pulled up just in time. But that was all. Memory stopped right there.

"She's woken up," her mother was saying to someone who must have just walked into the room. Her father? Cautiously, she opened her eyes once more. It hurt just a shade less this time.

"That's great." A doctor, but not her father. This one was on the short, pudgy side and had a thin, vaguely comical mustache hovering above lips full and pink as a girl's.

"How are you feeling?" He addressed the question to Brooke.

"Not so great." She shifted in the bed and looked down at her hands, one of which her mother still held. The gauze on her arm was no longer white; something brownish red and yellow had begun seeping through. "Looks like it's time to change the dressing."

"Let me see," said the doctor, inspecting her arm. He turned to a nurse, issued some instructions. Then he turned back to Brooke. "You're a lucky girl, you know."

"Lucky?"

"The force of that train pulled you along the entire length of the platform. If you had hit the wall going at that speed . . ." He left it for her imagination to supply the rest.

"But I didn't."

"No." He looked down at the clipboard he was carrying. "You didn't."

"Thank Jesus, Mary, and Joseph," her mother said. She was still crying. "Somehow you turned and instead of hitting the wall, you rolled into the center of the subway platform. You hit the bench instead. That boy. That boy you were with. He and the man who helped pull you out—they told us what happened."

"Otter," said Brooke. "And Edgar." She could see the white, looping letters, floating in the space before her eyes.

There was a window across from the bed; outside it was almost dark. Was it dusk or dawn? Brooke didn't know. She winced while the bandage on her arm was removed and the wound cleaned. The doctor's pager beeped and he excused himself. Brooke waited until both he and the nurse had left before she spoke again.

"Mom?"

"What is it, sweetheart?"

"Where am I?"

"At Bellevue Hospital, darling."

Bellevue. Wasn't that were they took crazy people? But it was also a major trauma center. She knew because her father had once told her that. Her father.

"And where's Daddy?" Her mother quickly looked away, at Mackenzie, before looking back at her.

"He's in the cafeteria. Getting some coffee. We've been up all night."

"I want to see him." Her mother and Mackenzie looked at each other again. Though it made her head ache, Brooke could not stop the anger from rising up in her, a nasty little wave cresting and ready to break. What did they think, she was an idiot or something?

"All right," her mother said somewhat tentatively. "Mackenzie, honey, would you go find your father? Tell him Brooke woke up."

Left alone with her mother, Brooke tried to sit but found that much of her body was also covered with bandages. What about her face, she thought in a panic. What had happened to her face?

"Do you have a mirror?" she asked her mother.

"Yes, but I don't think—"

"I want to see myself," Brooke said clearly. Her mother reached for her purse and pulled out a mirror. Handing it to Brooke, she compressed her lips until they were just the merest line, but she remained silent.

"Oh God." Brooke took in the swelling around her eyes, the cuts that scored her chin and cheeks. It looked like she had applied sandpaper to her skin. "Pretty bad, huh?"

"We're just so grateful you're alive," her mother said. She took the mirror and stuffed it back in her purse. "We could have so easily lost you."

There was a sound at the door and Brooke looked up to see her father. Mackenzie had brought him back, but she had not returned.

"Jesus, Daddy, what happened to you?" Brooke saw the split, swollen lip and almost forgot her fury at him. Almost.

"It's a long story," her father said. Looking at her, his eyes filled with tears. Had she ever seen him cry before? If so, she couldn't remember it. And it couldn't have been anything like this: standing in the center of a room, burying his face in his hands and sobbing. "I'm sorry," he said, words slightly muffled by his open palms, but she managed to hear them anyway. "Brooke, baby, I am so sorry."

"Mom knows, then." She looked over at her mother, who was not crying anymore. She returned Brooke's gaze with a grim, steady look of her own. "You told her about how I saw you with that woman? And how I just wanted to get away? From her. From both of you."

"She knows," her father said, raising his wet face from his hands. "Your mother knows everything."

"Well, I don't know everything. Maybe you'd better fill me in." It was so hard to talk, to say any of this, to say anything. But she struggled on.

"Fill you in on what?" Her father took a couple of steps closer to the bed. "What is it you want to know?"

"What you were doing with her." Brooke's voice dropped. The words felt jagged and sharp, pieces of bone, of broken glass. No words had ever hurt so much to say. But still, she had to ask, had to try to understand. How he could have done it. What he was planning to do now.

"Brooke, I wish to God you hadn't seen me—us. What I did was wrong." He wiped his face with his hands and pulled up a chair close to the bed. "Your mother and I—" He stopped and looked at Camille. But Camille was no longer looking at either of them and instead sat twisting her rings—the wedding band, the engagement ring—around and around her finger. "Your mother and I will work this out."

"I don't believe you," she said, defiantly looking from one parent to the other. Now she was angry at her mother too. Her father had lied to them, deceived them, and yet it looked like her mother was just sitting there. Like she had decided to roll over and play dead. God, were all the adults in her life so totally full of shit? She turned away from both of them and noticed an envelope sitting on the bedside table. The handwriting was unfamiliar, but it was clearly addressed to her. Maybe someone from school? It was close enough to reach.

"What's this?" She spoke to her mother, ignoring her father for the moment.

"It's from that boy. He came to the hospital with you. He stayed for quite a while, but then he had to leave. He asked me to give you that."

Brooke opened the note and scanned the few lines it contained. He was sorry—seemed like everyone was sorry, didn't it?—about what had happened. He hoped she didn't hold it against him. Brooke supposed he meant the beers, the pill. Well, he hadn't forced her to do any of it, had he? Still, the note seemed to be more about him than anything else. What he'd done. What he hadn't. She let it slide from her hand to the floor.

"Anyway, I don't care about him, I—" Brooke stopped when she saw the doctor reappear in the doorway. He nodded to her and to her mother. Then he looked directly at her father.

"Have you told her?" His voice was low.

"Told me what?" Brooke couldn't believe that this guy was talking about her in the third person, like she wasn't even there. Did her father talk like that about patients, even if they were kids? Somehow she didn't think so. The doctor's chubby face flushed as pink as his lips, but he didn't answer her question. "I'm sorry. I thought that's why you came up. So you could tell her together."

"Tell me what?" It hurt to raise her voice, but she wanted them to pay attention.

"It's true, there is something we haven't told you," her father was saying. To her amazement, her mother got up and went over to where he sat. She reached down for his hand and laced her fingers tightly through his. It looked like she was going to start crying again.

"Maybe I'd better leave now," the doctor said. "You let me know when you want me to come back."

He would not look at her. God, another shithead adult. What was it, something in the water, the air?

"What?" Brooke was frightened. What had they kept from her? "You have to tell me. You have to."

"The train," her father began. He stood up, still holding her mother's hand. "Do you remember the train?"

Brooke tried hard to summon the memory. It had come into the station, she felt it, heard it. But they had pulled her up and away from it, hadn't they? Otherwise, how could she be lying here and talking about it?

"The train pulled in. But I was on the platform. I know I was."

"They did pull you up," her father said. "You were mostly on the platform, and we are so thankful for that."

"Mostly?" Brooke's heart began to beat faster and the bandaged arm throbbed along with it. "What do you mean, mostly?"

"The train did hit you. It dragged you along the platform." It seemed he was speaking more and more slowly. Or was it that her hearing had speeded up?

"But I'm all right!"

"Yes and no." How calm he seemed, how calm and centered. This must be how he was when he talked to people when he had to tell them about the terrible things that had happened to their kids. This is how he must have been when he told that woman, Naomi whatever her name was, that her daughter had been killed. "The train hit your foot and essentially pulverized it. They tried to save it . . ." Suddenly his calm facade disintegrated, just like that. His voice cracked, and when it did, Brooke felt a cold, awful kind of knowledge seeping into her blood, her bones. "They tried all they could, sweetheart. You were in the OR for hours. But they couldn't do it. They just couldn't do it."

Then he began to cry again, this time not shielding his face but leaving it exposed, a terrible wound. Had she thought that seeing her father touching that Naomi person was the worst day of her life? Well, she was wrong about that. So wrong. Nothing could be worse than this, watching him cry, totally break down and sob, not once but twice in the same day, the same goddamned hour.

"Show me," she said. Her father disengaged his hand from her mother's and gently turned back the blankets that until now had covered her lower body. Brooke saw her legs, both wrapped and bandaged in several places. But one leg, the one whose ankle she had twisted in the fall, was several inches shorter than the other. Though it was swathed and covered by the white bandages, she understood the meaning of that difference, the absence it mutely conveyed. She knew what she would see when the bandages came off: a stump, a place where her foot had been, and was no longer.

27

The Doctor's Daughter

Rick had never slammed anyone in the face before, and for hours afterward, it seemed like his hand was trembling, even glowing. Though he'd spent his childhood defending himself from his big brothers, he'd never launched such a direct hit. Punching, yes, but in the stomach or arm. A smack on the head or cheek. Also pinching and even biting. But a sock in the kisser—no, that was beyond the pale. Until the night when he'd been so crazed, so out of his mind with jealousy and rage that he'd gone to McBride's house and done just that.

Later, he'd loped around Prospect Park, trying to burn off the anger, the newly opened stream of grief. He'd half hoped someone might try to mug him. Then he could punch that guy in the face too. But the park was cold and deserted. He saw no one, only a white and blue patrol car, which, had the policeman inside actually seen him, would have stopped and picked him up because he sure as hell looked guilty of something.

As he ran, his thoughts ran with him. That he'd cheated on Naomi was bad, he knew that. That she should respond—no, it was retaliate—by sleeping with Michael McBride made some kind of sick sense to him.

He could understand what motivated Naomi: the desire to hurt him, to have her justified revenge. But what could McBride's motive have been? Didn't the guy have any professional ethics? A basic sense of decency? It was as if he had found out they'd been fucking on Dahlia's grave. He slowed down, felt the cold seep into his feet, his hands. When he got back to his office, he took the hottest shower he could stand and sat waiting for the next day to happen to him.

In the morning, when Lillian told him that Allison was on the phone, he went into his office to take the call, shutting the door behind him.

"Where have you been?" Allison asked without bothering to say hello.

"Hey, what's this? Has Mom been reincarnated and started channeling through you?"

"Naomi's been trying to reach you. She's been calling your cell, calling the office, calling me." Odd that Lillian hadn't mentioned Naomi had called.

"All right, so you've reached me. What's up?"

"I don't know, she wouldn't tell me. But she just said to tell you to please get in touch with her, immediately."

"All right, then. I'll call her now." Allison had already hung up. He dialed his number on Carroll Street. Naomi answered on the first ring.

"What's gotten into you? I heard you were at Michael McBride's last night. He could have you arrested, you know. Maybe he should."

"How do you even know about that?" Rick found that he was sweating as he spoke, reliving the moment when he punched McBride out and not feeling in the least bit remorseful.

"Michael told me," she said in a low, dangerous voice.

"Well, good for him. I've got nothing to hide from him. That loath-some, lying scumbag. Lillian was one thing, Naomi. But you and McBride—" He didn't finish.

"I'm going to tell you something else about Michael now. Something I think you should know." Was she crying? It sounded like she might be.

"What's that?" he said gruffly. Little as he cared about McBride, he still hated to hear her cry.

"He has a daughter. Two actually. They're twins."

"So he has two daughters. Big deal." McBride and his brats. "Who gives a fuck?"

"You will when I tell you what's happened to one of them." And then she did.

He didn't know how he'd managed to see the next patient Lillian had set up in his examining room, but as soon as the exam was over, he walked out, into the street, without even bothering to put on his coat. He could tell it was cold from the way the wind swept the litter around on the streets, but he felt nothing, not a thing. Her foot, he kept thinking. She had lost her foot. Rick walked to the promenade, looked out at the water, which was rippled and gray.

The irony of this was horrifying. That he should be a podiatrist and yet somehow be implicated in the loss of this child's—and that's what she was, a child—foot was the worst thing he could have imagined. For he was implicated: he could not escape it. Had he not slept with Lillian, he did not believe Naomi would have slept with McBride. And if that had not happened, McBride's daughter would not have seen her father with Naomi on that day, an incident which had ended in the ghastly accident Naomi had described.

Rick tried to imagine the brief meeting on Fifth Avenue: McBride, Naomi, the girl. The first two he had a handle on; the third eluded him entirely. Who was she? Tall or short? Slim or voluptuous? Dark or fair? Not that it mattered. She was a kid, McBride's kid, and no doubt she had loved him the way that girls love their fathers, the way Dahlia had loved him. Finally the cold began to penetrate, and Rick turned in the direction of his office.

He walked quickly, hands stuffed in the pockets of his pants to garner what little warmth he could. Amputations. The lopping off of a diseased digit or extremity to preserve the integrity—the life—of the whole. He had performed many in his years as a podiatrist and quite a number of them on feet. But none on a girl as young and healthy as that one was. What would life be like for her now? He thought about the prosthesis, the physical therapy she would need. And what about life for her parents? McBride. Jesus. He still wasn't sorry he'd hit the guy, but he was sorry for what faced the shit-eating bastard now. Okay, so you screw someone else's wife, the mother of a dead kid who was brought to your facility. And as a result, you pay, not with your life but with your daughter's. Or a piece of it. When he arrived at the office, he told Lillian to cancel the rest of his patients scheduled for that day. Then he picked up the phone again to call Naomi. "I'm coming over," he said. "Wait for me. Please."

28

Fielding

Spring had come early that year. Lillian peeled off her wool sweater and tied it around her waist. It had been cool when she left her apartment this morning, but now, at four o'clock in the afternoon, the air had turned mild. Lillian walked the short distance from the subway train until she reached the stone wall and the wide, inviting entrance. Poly Prep Country Day School, read the wooden sign posted in the grass. She turned and went inside. Jason had told her where the game was scheduled. Reluctantly, he had agreed to let her watch, but only if she swore she would not do anything to embarrass him, like cheer or squeal when he joined the bat to the ball or made a terrific play out in the field.

There they were, the bunch of boys in their loose-fitting shirts, their caps that kept the sun out of their eyes. Jason had his back to her, unaware that she was there. She had resisted the impulse to pick up a bottle of Gatorade for him. Not that he wouldn't have guzzled it down happily. But she knew that being handed a drink by your mother was totally, completely uncool. And she did respect the tyranny of cool, at least in kids his age. Time enough to take him out for pizza later. When they were alone, she could make as big a fuss as she wanted; he liked it, in fact. He just didn't want anyone else to know that he did.

Lillian settled herself on the bench behind the outfield. This was not an official school game, but just a practice. Still, the fact that the coach wanted Jason there was an indication of the kind of attention Jason would get next September, when he was actually a seventh-grade student here. She still had trouble believing it.

But it was true. The coach from Poly had seen Jason play when his own team had been pitted against Jason's and lost, and he'd noticed her son's undeniable prowess on the ball field. He'd been so impressed that he'd come back to see him several more times and to talk to Jason's old coach. Together, the two men arranged for Jason to try out for Poly's team, and when Poly's coach had really seen what Jason could do, he'd made sure the boy was offered a scholarship that would pay his entire tuition. Just knowing that the coach, and the school behind him, had such confidence in him had changed something in Jason. His concentration, his schoolwork, his grades had all improved dramatically in the last months. It was as if he knew he had to stretch higher to reach the bar, and he was doing it.

Waiting for the coach, who had not yet shown up, the boys started horsing around. A tall, husky black kid grabbed the hat of a short, wiry boy. Seeking to up the ante, the smaller boy retrieved his hat, and then grabbed and tossed the black boy's hat even farther, over the fence. Jason ignored all this, and instead practiced his stance, his swing. He had a habit of touching the tip of his bat to the plate before he swung, the way a horse might paw the ground, impatient to be on its way. She never mentioned it to Jason—it was the sort of thing that would make him mutter self-consciously, "Ma, you look at me too hard"—but she did find it endearing. Jason's coach from the previous season had told her, "He's the most focused kid on the team." Watching him now, she could see it was true. She was glad she had been able to leave work early to get to see him play. Had she known the weather would be so mild, she would have skipped the subway and walked to Poly instead. Her new office was on Seventy-seventh Street in Bay Ridge, easy walking distance on a gorgeous spring day.

Lillian no longer worked for Rick Wechsler. After that horrible business last winter with that doctor's daughter, she no longer felt she could. She had gone over and over it in her mind—had she been right in telling Rick about his wife? He had been so hurt and so angry. She hadn't meant to hurt him; that wasn't it at all. There was a selfish motive involved, but that had not been it. She had wanted Rick to see that his wife was hardly so perfect or so pure. Maybe they would split up. And she and Rick could be together. Because that's what she had wanted. She had fantasized about it, dreamed about and finally confided in Maria about it.

"You think the Jewish doctor is going to dump his wife and marry the office manager? Who happens to be Puerto Rican besides?" Maria was sitting with her legs crossed on Lillian's couch, eating from a carton of Vietnamese takeout.

"Why not?" Lillian had answered. "What if he loves me?" Her own carton of food remained, for the moment, unopened.

"Loves you? What, you actually believe that shit they play on the radio? Are you still thirteen? Maybe you still believe in the tooth fairy too. And the Easter Bunny."

"Don't get any of that sauce on the couch," Lillian had replied sulkily. "It'll leave a mark."

"You just don't like what I'm saying." Maria finished the glass noodles she had been eating and reached for a beer.

"No," Lillian had conceded. "I don't." She picked up her carton of noodles and pulled open its neatly tucked flaps.

"Honey, I understand. You love the guy."

"Yeah." Lillian put the carton down. "I do."

But loving someone and being able to make a life with them were two entirely different things. Lillian saw that as clearly as she saw Rick's pain over his wife's infidelity and his desire, despite everything that had happened, to remain married to her. She was simply not going to get this man, much as she wished she could have him. He was not in a position to marry her, be a stepfather to her son. And she wanted those things. Whatever they had going back last winter, well, it was over now. It was over the minute he told his wife. Somehow, there was never enough room for three in these things, was there? Even Ramon would break it off with whoever he was screwing once

Lillian found out about it. Then there would be the promises and the pledges. He was so sorry . . . How could he . . . He would never . . . And she would believe him—until the next time rolled around and it would start all over again.

So she had started looking for another job, circling the want ads in the paper, making the rounds to employment agencies. She had taken the position in the Bay Ridge dentist's office even before the business with Jason and Poly was settled. Now that it was, her new job would be only that much more convenient. Slipping out to see a ball game or have a meeting with one of his teachers would be easy, a piece of cake. She was doing it, she realized. Raising this kid, helping him thrive. She didn't need Ramon and she didn't even need Rick. Though she knew she was going to miss him. She already did.

They had had a farewell drink on her last day in his office. They'd stopped into one of the older Irish bars on Montague Street and ordered martinis.

"Who drinks a martini anymore?" Lillian asked when hers arrived. She impaled the olive with a toothpick and held it up in front of her.

"I guess I do. You too." Rick was reserved, quiet. But he was almost always like that. She wanted to ask him so many things: How's your wife? Is she really taking you back? What happened to that doctor? Is his daughter all right? Instead, she ate the olive, which tasted rubbery and old.

"Have you found a replacement yet?" Lillian knew that Rick had listed her position in the newspaper.

"Not yet. But a couple of people have called. I'll be interviewing next week."

"That's good." But she didn't think so, not really. It should be me, she wanted to tell him. I'm the one that you want. She sipped her drink. Strong. That was okay though. Strong was just what she needed.

"I'll miss you, Lillian." Rick took a sip of his own drink. "I really will."

"I know," she said. "Me too."

"But it's always been Naomi first. And it always will be." He finished the drink, looked around for a waiter.

"I envy her." She felt a rush of embarrassment, and to conceal it, she took a long gulp of the drink, finishing it off. It was very cold and seemed to numb something inside her.

"Envy." He looked down, peering into the empty glass. "Huh."

I am not going to cry, Lillian thought. I am not. She stood, a little uncertainly, and reached for her coat. He didn't try to help her.

"Good-bye, Rick," she said. And she forced herself to walk to the door without looking at him again.

That was on a Friday; her new job started the following Monday. She was the office manager for a pair of married dentists, Sam and Tess Ordan. With their short, brown hair, full cheeks, and snub noses, they were one of those couples that seemed more like brother and sister than husband and wife. They showed up for work in the morning together, left together in the evenings. In between, they saw everyone from three-year-olds getting their first checkups to octogenarians still proudly hanging on to their own teeth. Once again, Lillian applied her skills to the tasks she was assigned: filing, billing, scheduling appointments and follow-up visits. Everything ran more smoothly under Lillian's direction. Tess Ordan was delighted with the change.

"We love how you've reorganized things around here," she told Lillian one day as they were both getting ready to close the office. "You've really got a gift."

"Thank you, Dr. Ordan." Lillian turned off the computer and watched the screen go dark.

"But we don't think you should confine it to office management."

"I'm not sure I understand." Lillian got up, straightened the papers on her desk. Was this some sort of prettily worded dismissal? A pink slip in a fancy envelope?

"Have you ever thought of becoming a dental hygienist? Sam and I both think you'd be a natural."

"Me? A dental hygienist?" Lillian had to stop to consider this idea. It was not one she had ever entertained before.

"The pay is excellent and there's always a demand. Sam and I can't seem to find a really good one. Or if we do, she always leaves."

"I'd have to think about it." Lillian reached for her coat and her bag.

"Of course. But we can talk about it more. You can start the training while you're working here. I know what programs are around; if you are interested, I'm sure I could point you in the right direction."

Lillian surprised herself by enrolling in the program. Even more surprising was how well it suited her. Her classes met in the evening, so she was able to keep her job. Some of the coursework could even be completed online; the Ordans had given her their blessing to stay late and use their computer. She worried about leaving Jason, but Ramon had recently broken up with his girlfriend and so he seemed to relish his son's company on the nights she was busy. Now if Lillian could just finish the training before he got serious with someone else.

She learned to prepare the basic tray setups, mix the materials, maintain the massive and forbidding equipment. She found she especially liked exposing and processing the dental X-ray film, watching as the underlying dental bone—dense, black, primal—emerged before her eyes. That she was learning how to handle the array of bright and refined instruments that were housed in the neat, shallow drawers gave her a pleasing sense of competence. And she had a kind of natural empathy for the patients. So many of them were nervous when they arrived at the dentist's office; they expected pain. She understood that expectation, and she found she was good at dismantling it.

Out on the ball field, the coach—Lillian had learned his name was Pete Showalter—had his arms around Jason's, positioning his hands on the bat. She couldn't hear what Pete was saying, but she could see that Jason was absorbing the information with that unswerving attention he showed to every aspect of the game, whether he was watching or playing it. Pete took his hands away and stepped back. Jason stepped up to the plate and readied himself for the pitch.

Lillian watched as he lowered the tip of the bat and dipped it down, tapping lightly. Overhead, the sky had turned a liquid blue; there wasn't a cloud to sully it. A few gulls flew by, squawking, on their way to the water under the Verrazano Bridge. The ball came whistling in Jason's direction, but he let it pass once and then twice. He looked at Pete, who looked back at him and nodded ever so slightly. When the ball came toward him a third time, he hit it hard and sent it flying across the field in a wide, beautiful arc. The player in right field scrambled after it, and Pete turned to give Jason a thumbs-up sign as Jason ran to first base, then to second, to third, and all the way home. Remembering her promise, Lillian wedged her hands under her thighs to keep from clapping. Way to go, Jason, she silently cheered her son. Way to go.

29

Blue Room

The big room on the ground floor of Naomi's house on Carroll Street had been freshly painted, a pale, cool shade, the color of an April sky. The windows had been washed so that their panes sparkled and the floors had been recently sanded, giving the wide pine planks a muted amber gleam. Estelle recognized several pieces of furniture—a loveseat with a fleur-de-lis print, a bow-front mahogany dresser, a tufted footstool—but from where she could not remember. Naomi explained that the pieces had come from Estelle's condo in Florida and had recently been liberated from the limbo of storage.

Sitting on the loveseat, Estelle looked out the back window at the yard. No water, unless she counted the birdbath with its fluted column in the center of Naomi's minuscule yard. But the birds came several times a day: sparrows, blue jays, doves, cardinals, and robins. It amazed her to think that she could identify and name them all. Sometimes she said the names aloud, spelling out the letters when she could. She thought that if she did this, she wouldn't lose them, not ever again.

Most days were peaceful. Naomi brought down breakfast—toast or a muffin, sometimes cold cereal with a banana sliced on top—and often sat with her as she ate. Afterward, Estelle watched the birds or the television.

Naomi had given her a machine that allowed her to play all the old movies she loved. The movies came on silver disks, like records only smaller and shinier. Estelle was intrigued and had an urge to bite into one. Would the taste be metallic? Sugared? Minty? She refrained, though, and instead tried to fathom how those disks became images she could see and hear. It stymied her, but no matter. She could plan her day around the movies, watch them over and over, in any order she chose.

The men who danced—Kelly and Astaire—were good for a whole week, maybe more. Then there were those two willowy girls she liked so much, Katharine and Audrey. Both slender, both classy. And both with the same last name. Were they mother and daughter? Sisters? Estelle couldn't be sure.

Sometimes there were visits from a social worker or from a physical therapist, but these things didn't happen so often, and when they did, Estelle minded them less. On days when the weather was nice— and there were more of these now that spring had come—she and Naomi might go for a walk or a drive: to the big park up on the hill or the museum that was not far from it. Often they went to what had become Estelle's favorite place, the Brooklyn Botanic Garden. The last time they were there, the lilacs had been starting to bloom. Estelle had wanted to press her face into the sweet purple flowers, only Naomi reminded her it wasn't permitted to touch things here. Estelle remembered taking Naomi here as a child. Now she was the one being led around by the arm, told what she could do, what she couldn't. The thought depressed her momentarily. But then she just let herself feel glad to be here, with the flowers and the sun. Later, they stopped at the store on the corner and bought two big bunches of lilacs, which Naomi then put in a vase on Estelle's table. The heady scent was everywhere, and if she closed her eyes, she could be inside one of the blossoms. The bottle of pills seemed very far away.

Of course, she had her bad spells, even here. One afternoon, she went into the downstairs bathroom and in the medicine chest she found several small metal tubes—some gold, some silver. Their function eluded her, though she knew she ought to recognize it. She took a gold one, held it in her hands, sniffed. Nothing. She moved it from one palm to the other and noticed after a while that the top came off easily. Inside was a stick of a vibrant color, like crushed peach blossoms mixed with ground glitter. She could swivel the bottom up and down to make it rise or make it hide. How amazing! Did all these tubes contain such treasure? She tried them all and was delighted by the sticks of creamy pigment hidden inside, waiting for her to release the secret.

Tentatively, she tried marking the back of her hand with the one whose color looked like that of a poppy. She liked the feeling as it moved along her skin—so easy, so fluid. She had to do more of this. But where? Not the walls, with their fresh blue paint. And the floor was too rich a color on its own—none of the pigment showed up very well when she attempted it. In the end, she covered the white tiles in the bathroom—squares on the walls, hexagons on the floor—with shapes and colors. Dots, big and small, long undulating stripes, waves, webs. She ran a color stick around the lip of the sink and along the borders of the mirror. Marvelous. Truly marvelous.

When Naomi came later, Estelle took her daughter's hand and led her into the bathroom.

"There," she said proudly. "What do you think?"

"Mother!" Naomi exclaimed. She picked up one of the tubes. "What have you done? All your good lipsticks. Ruined. And you've made such a mess." How ashamed Estelle had felt then. Ashamed and stupid too. Lipsticks, that's what those tubes were. Nothing but lipsticks. She thought of Milton, the smeared handkerchief. She ought to have known. Estelle offered to help her clean up, but Naomi just waved her away, like a child.

The next day, however, Naomi came downstairs carrying a flat tin box and a spiral-bound pad.

"For you," she said, and opened the box to reveal a whole bevy of colors: blue and pink, orange and red. Then she flipped open the pad, thumbing through the creamy white pages.

"For me?" Estelle liked the colors, but was hesitant about using them. Look at what had happened before.

"To draw with." Naomi picked up a stick of color—a rich, nutty brown—and put it to the paper. A line, first thick, then thin. "Here," she said, handing Estelle the stick. "You try."

Estelle began drawing, timidly at first, and soon with greater confidence and abandon. Slashes of color, bands of color, blobs of color, blocks of color solid as this house. She loved the easy way the color would glide, almost flow, onto the paper. She couldn't get enough of the sensation.

"Oil pastels," Naomi had explained.

"Oil pastels," Estelle repeated happily. Indigo and violet. Moss green and primrose. She loved the names Naomi read to her as much as she loved the purity of their hues. Estelle continued to draw, only now she tried to make things to which she could attach words: rainbows and raindrops, flowers and stars. Naomi suggested that they pull out the pages, hang them in frames on the blue walls. But Estelle said no. She wanted to keep the pictures safe within the pad. That way, looking at them gave her the feeling of reading a book. Only this was a book of her own creation—her hand, her eyes. Who ever would have thought?

The drawing, the movies, the company of her daughter brought solace. Yet Estelle still mourned Dahlia, and Milton too. That was to be expected. She didn't shrink from it. But Naomi was young. She should not mourn forever. It should be different for her, or at least Estelle hoped and wished it could be. It was hard for her to read Naomi. Instead, Estelle felt like her daughter had erected an invisible yet palpable barrier around herself, so that she was shielded and protected from her mother's scrutiny. At least her husband—what was his name? How was it that the names of the birds, the colors, would stick but not this?—was back in the house now. Estelle had insisted on it, as the condition on which she would move in with Naomi. Naomi had been surprised and not at all eager to comply.

"You want me to take him back? After what he's done?" They were at the nursing home when they had this conversation; Naomi had come early, before the appointments with the doctor and social worker.

"Yes," Estelle had said. "I do."

"Why?" Naomi had asked. "Why is it so important to you?"

"I don't want everything falling to pieces. At least not while I'm still alive and here to see it." Estelle had then thought briefly of the bottle she had hidden away, her hedge against what she could no longer bear to tolerate. It was gone now, but she was not. And as long as she was still here, she would do what she could to help her daughter.

"All right, then. He can move back. I'm not saying I'm taking him back, but he can live here. If he wants to, that is." Estelle remembered that tone well, and the sullen teenage Naomi who had used it so frequently. So what? She had endured Naomi's adolescence; she would endure this too. Estelle didn't let her daughter's resistance deter her; she just plowed on through it. So the husband had come back, and Estelle was glad. She had always been fond of her son-in-law, his gentle, easy ways with her daughter, her granddaughter. None of that, it seemed, had changed.

"It's really good to see you, Estelle," he had said when they first met again at the house. He took her hands in his, kissed her on both cheeks. "I've missed you." Estelle believed him too.

Now that she was living here, he came down the stairs every morning, tapped on her door to say good-bye. In the evenings, when he returned home, it was the same. He brought her those shiny disks she liked—DVDs, they were called, she remembered now—from a place up on Seventh Avenue, and hung a shelf near her television where she could store them all. So he had shtupped another woman in a moment of mourning and madness. Was that a reason to get rid of such a man? Estelle thought not.

Sometimes, Naomi invited Estelle upstairs to have dinner with them. On those occasions, Estelle could see, plainly, that her daughter had still not totally forgiven her husband. Naomi was living with him, but at the same time seemed determined to remain aloof from him too. The pair of them seemed to circle around each other, alert and wary as the birds who settled on the rim of the birdbath in the mornings.

Once, after dinner, Estelle had gone up to the third floor of the house, to use the bathroom. The doors to the bedrooms were open and what she saw only confirmed what she had suspected: large beds in two of them. Clothing—she recognized the husband's slacks and Naomi's skirt—in each. So he was living with her, but not sharing a bed with her. All right, Estelle had thought. All right. It's going to take more time. And she might well be here to see, even encourage it, to happen. That was something, she reminded herself. For now, it would have to be enough.

Outside in the backyard, a pair of gray-brown doves perched on a telephone wire. Estelle watched as they shifted themselves a couple of times before they fluffed out their bodies, lowered their heads into their chests, and settled down.

30

Lakewood

The Web site showed about eight different kinds of prosthetic feet that were currently available. There was the Mercury DB Foot with its "individually selected composite heel and toe springs that are independently mounted onto a lightweight carrier." Reading the description, Brooke learned that the springs provided a high level of elastic strain energy to ensure a smooth transition from heel strike, mid stance, and toe off through the gait cycle. It sounded good, but how did it compare with the Patient Adjustable Multiflex Foot? And then there was the Endolite Stellar Foot, featuring a unique heel cushion adjuster and an integral titanium pyramid, and the new Dynamic Response Foot, ideally suited for playing tennis, jogging, or just walking to the office.

Brooke sat in a chair in her bedroom, scrolling through the options before leaving the site. A pair of lightweight aluminum crutches was within easy reach; she had gotten rather good with them over the last few weeks, at least in the house. Camille had been nagging at her to go out more often, to "conquer her fear." As if it were something she could do in a single, swift motion, like slamming a door or swatting a fly.

Camille had also been pestering her about getting an artificial foot, and to placate her mother, Brooke was checking them out online. She didn't see any point in mentioning that even looking at the Web sites made her feel dizzy with indecision. No need to share that particular nugget of information with Camille or anyone else.

For the first few weeks of her recovery, she wouldn't even consider a prosthesis, no matter how much her mother cajoled or badgered. She ignored the suggestions of the social worker who came to visit her at the hospital, and those of the doctors too. She heard them say, more than once, that she was not ready to deal with the fact that she had lost her foot in the accident and would need to get an artificial one if she were to resume a normal life.

But what none of them understood was that she hadn't wanted to pretend that she was going to have a normal life, because she wasn't, not ever again. Nor did she even want one. All that was over now. And as for not dealing with the lost foot, well, what did they know? Had any of them been there when she'd locked the door to her room, taken off all her clothes, and stood supported by the crutches in front of the full-length mirror on the back of her closet door? She had looked at her reflection, the long torso, the high, small breasts, the leg with its clean, abrupt ending—it looked sort of like a round of bologna—dangling uselessly, inches off the floor. When—or did she mean if—anyone else looked at her like this, what would they see? The leg and its hideous deformity? Would that render the rest of her peripheral, even invisible? And that asshole social worker thought she was in denial. It was a joke, a sick joke. She wanted to let someone else in on it, but couldn't think of whom. Her mother and sister seemed perpetually terrified around her, like she was made of glass and in danger of cracking any second. Her father was barely there. Although no one had come out and told her, she knew that he had moved out of the house on Ninth Street and was living elsewhere. When she confronted Mackenzie with the question, her sister had confirmed her suspicion.

"So where is he now?"

"He said he's staying with Aunt Kathleen."

"But she lives on Staten Island."

"He commutes."

"Oh." Brooke let her eyes wander around her room. It was still cluttered with the dozens of cards she had received wishing her a speedy recovery, along with teddy bears, bags of jelly beans, and now-deflated Mylar balloons. Seemed like everyone in the whole school had sent her something. Ditto for everyone from church and the choir too. She suddenly wanted it all out of here: gone with an imperious snap of the fingers. "That's a drag."

Her father had come to see her daily at the hospital, though not while her mother was present. He had been the one who was with her when they unwrapped the bandages from her leg and she saw, for the first time, the place where her foot had been. The amputation was a clean one, ending just above the ankle. There was a lot of scarring around the stump, which was dark pink and wrinkled looking.

"Some of that will fade," her father had said. "The redness will get paler over time."

"Oh, that's really something to look forward to," Brooke had said bitterly. "I can hardly wait." Her father had made a tight fist and brought it to his lips. It looked like he would start crying—again. Brooke was sorry. Her anger toward her father moved in and out, sometimes blowing off easily, other times settling heavily like a fog all around her. But as angry as she was, she couldn't have devised a worse punishment for him if she had tailored it to order. She thought of those medieval flagellants she had read about in her church history class: the hair shirts, the stones in the shoes, the whippings. God, he would have fit right in back then, wouldn't he? He seemed at home, somehow, with his suffering.

Still, those comments would just pop out from time to time, like gremlins, unbidden, from her lips. She remembered a fairy tale in which an obnoxious, rude girl discovered that every time she opened her mouth to speak, something horrible—a snake, a toad, an insect— would emerge. Sometimes, Brooke kind of liked that image of herself, strewing venom with her words. Other times, it disgusted her.

When she'd come home from the hospital, her father still visited her, though her mother arranged not to be at home when he did. One thing she was really grateful for was that he had taken her side when she said she did not want to return to school. Though her mother thought she should go back as soon as she was physically able to, Brooke refused. She was not going to endure the gossip, the speculation, the combination of pity and revulsion that she was sure was waiting for her back at St. Saviour's. Her parents, she knew, must have argued about it plenty, but at least she hadn't had to hear them. And in the end, she got her way. Her teachers sent home her assignments and tutors her mother hired administered the tests. Soon she would be finished with her sophomore year, and, if she could just get her way again, with St. Saviour's for good.

Leaving St. Saviour's was her new goal, the one she had not shared with her parents or her sister. She wasn't ready to tell them, at least not yet. But when she clicked off the Web site for the prosthetic devices she now realized she would need to get, she logged on to another, much more compelling site: the home page for the small coed boarding school in the Maine woods she had found.

"The Lakewood Academy, located amidst a plethora of natural flora and fauna, offers its students a unique combination of stimulation and solitude. Class sizes, which are small, are supplemented by one-on-one tutorials with members of our committed and caring teaching community . . ." Brooke kept reading, about the honors track, the courses in Russian and Chinese, the interdisciplinary programs that students could create for themselves. She looked at the pictures of the campus, tinted gold and red in autumn, lavender, pink, and white in spring. Staring at the digital images, she knew she wanted to leave not only St. Saviour's but Brooklyn, and the wreckage of her family life, behind. Now she had only to convince her parents to let her go.

So Brooke started her campaign, subtly at first. Pushing aside the nausea it seemed to engender in her, she had been dutifully considering all the prosthetic options available. She agreed to the sessions of physical therapy—only not at Holy Name—she would need to build up the strength necessary to use the prosthesis. She would go for a fitting, maybe as soon as next week. She did well in her schoolwork and tried not to curse so much, at least within her mother's hearing.

Brooke even agreed to see the therapist her mother had consulted about her, whose office on First Street was filled with all kinds of dolls—Barbie, baby, and everything in between. She asked the therapist if she could play with them, and when she was told yes, proceeded to cut the hair of the Barbies and gouge the eyes out of the baby dolls. The therapist had picked up one of the shorn Barbies.

"I like her new look," she said. Brooke studied the woman. Unlike all the other adults in her immediate circle, this one was not full of shit.

"Yeah, new look," Brooke repeated and smiled a cold, hard smile.

But despite all Brooke's efforts at cooperation, she knew that it was not going to be easy to convince her parents, especially her mother, to let her go. After the accident, it seemed that her mother would now be worried every time she left the room, much less the state. Camille's face had been transformed in these last months. She looked both older—the lines around her mouth and eyes seemed deeper, and since she was no longer going to the hairdresser's, her drab, gray roots had started to come in—yet younger too. There was a broken look in her eyes that made Brooke think of an abused child, and it hurt her to think she had caused it. Still, she felt she had to go. She was choking here. Gasping for air.

Downstairs, she heard the front door slam. Mackenzie, home from school, no doubt. Brooke wondered briefly what her day had been like. Girls from school had called, e-mailed, sent more dopey cards; she responded to none of them, not even Stephanie, whose simpering, stupid voice she never wanted to hear again.

"Hey, you're up." Mackenzie stood awkwardly in the doorway to Brooke's room, waiting to be asked in.

"Yeah. Well. It is after three."

"I know, I just thought you might be . . . resting." She pulled on a strand of hair, wrapping it around a finger and letting it go. It was an irritating habit. But it showed that even Mackenzie was uncomfortable with her now. And why not? She was a freak, a gimp, a unipod monster.

"You might as well come in." Brooke knew she was being bitchy, but she couldn't help herself. Some days it was just like this and she went with it. It was hard enough to open her eyes, look down to the stump—her father had been right, some of the redness had disappeared—and not want to walk out an upper-story window. Being nice on top of it was just too much to expect.

"Okay. Thanks for asking me." Mackenzie sat down on the bed, and Brooke turned back to the screen so her sister wouldn't see her scowling. God, where did she think she was? At tea with the queen of England? Having an audience with the pope?

"What's that?" Mackenzie was looking at the picture of Lakewood, the one that showed a lone student sitting in a canoe, paddle poised above the glassy surface of the water.

"Nothing." She clicked off the page and turned to face her sister. Something in Mackenzie's face, so much like her own, broke through her defenses. This was her sister after all. Her twin sister. They had shared time in the womb, had the same fucking DNA. Brooke had an urge to scream, "We're not alike anymore, you dumb bitch! Don't you get it?" But Brooke couldn't afford to let her rage—which sometimes, when she was alone, erupted in satisfying episodes of smashed eggs and entire boxes of tissues that she shredded—into this conversation. She needed Mackenzie as her ally, not as an informer, running off to tell their mother that she, Brooke, had snapped, gone over the edge. So she bit back her anger and instead simply said, "I need you to help me."

"Help you? How?"

"Can you keep a secret?" Brooke asked.

"What do you think?" Mackenzie glared at her.

"Relax," said Brooke. She was amazed—and relieved—that Mackenzie dared to show any irritation with her at all. Now at least they were on familiar ground. "I just had to be sure." Brooke looked at the open door. "Close it, okay?" Mackenzie got up to close the door and then returned to the bed. This time she sat even closer to Brooke. "I'll show you what I was looking at." Brooke went back to the site and let Mackenzie read along with her.

"Lakewood prides itself on the respect accorded to each and every student, for we believe that it is the uniqueness and individuality of our students that is our greatest resource. Because of the emphasis on personal achievement and independent growth, Lakewood students avoid the kinds of pressure to conform found in so many of today's educational environments . . ."

"So what about it? Someone you know going there?"

"Me." Brooke let the word sit for a minute. It was the first time she had voiced this particular wish out loud and she wanted to see how it felt.

"You? But this school is far away. It's in . . ." Mackenzie's eyes roamed the screen. "New England, somewhere, right?"

"Maine," Brooke said.

"Maine," echoed Mackenzie, still gazing at the screen. "Mom will never let you go. No way."

"You have to help persuade her, then." She reached out and took one of Mackenzie's hands. It had been a long time since she had done that. "I have to go. Have to, do you understand?" Brooke felt the tears rising in her eyes, and she reached up angrily to brush them away. Fuck all that self-pitying shit anyway. She would get out of here. Say good-bye to her ruined parents, her guilt-ridden sister. In Maine, no one would know about the life she had led before, the one in which she'd had two feet, like everyone else. In Maine it wouldn't be, "Poor Brooke, did you hear about what happened . . . ?" It would just be, "Brooke McBride. You know. The girl with one foot." Take her or leave her.

"Okay," said Mackenzie. "Okay." They sat together for a few minutes, hands still clasped, until Camille called from downstairs and Mackenzie stood up to leave.

"Mackenzie? Are you up there with Brooke? Ask her if she wants something to drink. A Sprite. Or lemonade. I can bring it up on a tray." Both girls looked at each other as their mother's words carried up-stairs.

"She's trying to be nice," Mackenzie said. "You know she'd do any-thing for you."

"That's just the point." Brooke clicked off the Lakewood home page and shut down the computer. "She'd chew my food and breathe for me if I let her. And if I let her, what happens to me?"

"Mackenzie? Is everything all right?" Camille's voice had taken on a familiar tinge of anxiety. "Should I come up there?"

"We're fine, Mom." Mackenzie looked back at Brooke. "I'm com-ing right down."

"Don't forget," Brooke said. "Promise me you won't forget."

31

Snapshot

God never gives you more than you can bear. This was another one of those trite little sayings of which his mother had been so fond; she faithfully trotted it out when describing the misfortunes of anyone she knew and loved. But Michael, who had long doubted this bit of maternal wisdom, now knew it to be entirely false. God had given him something he truly could not bear, and he was being crushed, ground down daily, as he tried to shoulder the burden. One night, he told himself, one night where he had strayed and slipped. But one night was all it had taken to completely undo his life, yank it apart by the seams. And now here he was, not even trying to keep it together, but holding the rent pieces in his hands and thinking, Now what? Where do I go from here?

Although Camille had not asked him to, he moved out of his house and went to stay with his sister on Staten Island. It was agonizing to leave, but he no longer felt he was entitled to stay. Leaving was his form of penance, his sacrifice, and he accepted it with resignation. At least it was something he could do.

Walking the streets of his sister's neighborhood, he was reminded of how much quieter it was here, almost suburban in feel; he watched as spring erupted with a painful, even excruciating beauty all around him. He took the ferry to Manhattan every morning, then caught the subway to Brooklyn. It was a long trip there and a long one back, but he didn't mind, or not enough to matter. At least it made him tired at night, tired enough to get some sleep. Looking out over the water and feeling the fine, mistlike spray on his face, he thought of all the stricken, bereaved parents he had ever seen or talked to, all the comfort he had ever tried to offer. Children who had leukemia and brain tumors; children who had drowned, been hit by speeding cars, died in fires, fallen from windows. He had spoken gently and quietly, held hands, dispensed hugs and tissues, attended funerals. And despite all that, there was not a shred of consolation or redemption available to him; there had been none from the time he had been told by the ER doctor at Bellevue that Brooke's foot was beyond saving. That was a decisive moment, the one from which there was no going back. In some ways, Michael felt his old life had ended there and a new one began. He was still trying to orient himself in this strange new world he had wandered into; still trying to find his bearings.

Now, on weekday mornings he arrived in Brooklyn early and walked from the subway to the hospital. The ordinary trees on Seventh Avenue were enjoying their brief moment of splendor, lacy blossoms adorning the branches. An involuntary reflex caused him to slow down when he came to Barnes & Noble; he couldn't help looking into the window of the café, hoping he might see Naomi standing in line for coffee. A ridiculous idea, this. Naomi no longer worked at the hospital. They had spoken briefly a few times, and she had told him about her decision to bring her mother to live with her. And to ask Rick to come home. He had not wanted to tell her about Brooke, but there was no avoiding it; she had asked him and he couldn't lie.

The night he spent with her was as sweet and exquisite as anything he had ever known. Running his fingers, then his lips, along the unfamiliar peaks and hollows of her small body, feeling the shudder, the luxuriant release of breath as she came—these were the things Michael relived, his tender sorrow, his private joy too. He had had the sense—unreasonable, grandiose—of a healing more profound than any he had ever been able to accomplish before. Naomi had wanted something from him, some knowledge, some answer. And he had felt as if he had given it to her.

But the price for that gift was Brooke: her trust, her future. All ruined, destroyed now. Brooke spoke to him, endured his visits, but he knew it was all changed between them. She veered from sarcasm to tears, frustration to rage, all in a matter of minutes it seemed. It was like having a toddler again, only she was that much bigger, that much more angry, more hurt. And he was responsible for all of it.

He had just sat down at his desk and looked over at the stack of papers Adelaide Peters had set out for him to review—thank God for Adelaide, her patience, her loyalty—when the phone rang. It was five after eight. No one was in the outer office yet, so he picked up.

"Daddy?" Mackenzie's voice was low, as if she didn't want anyone to overhear. "Can I come up and see you? I'm in the lobby."

"Of course, honey. Come right now. Tell the security guard to call up."

Minutes later, Mackenzie was stepping out of the elevator doors; Michael was there to greet her.

He kissed her forehead. She smelled of something floral. Perfume. He looked at the school uniform, the pleated skirt, the white blouse, the cardigan tied around her shoulders. A girl, still. But a woman soon. "On your way to school?"

"Yes. I have a few minutes though." She let him take her arm as they walked down the corridor to his office. When they arrived, he sat down in a chair next to hers.

"Anything wrong?"

"Why do you think that?" She was playing with her hair, always a sign of nervousness.

"Just a hunch. Here you are, bright and early. You needed to tell me something. Something that couldn't wait."

"Not tell. Ask." She stopped pulling on her hair and let her hand fall to her lap.

"Okay then. Ask me. Ask me anything." He even managed a smile.

He had to work to earn her trust back too. Brooke and Camille were not the only ones he'd hurt.

"It's about Brooke. She wants—" Mackenzie stopped, her gaze falling on a photograph of the three of them—Mackenzie, Brooke, Michael—taken out in Montauk a few years earlier. "She wants to go away. To boarding school. And she wants you to persuade Mom to let her go."

"Boarding school." Michael sat back in his chair, feeling the breath knocked out of him. "Why?"

"She just can't stand it here anymore, Dad. You can guess the reasons."

"I suppose I can." Michael looked at the photo. Camille had taken it; he remembered her standing back, wanting to make sure they were all in the frame. How tan the girls were. How happy. "Has she asked Mom herself?"

"She's kind of afraid to. She doesn't want her to get, you know . . ." Mackenzie rolled her eyes.

"No. I don't. What?"

"Let me put it another way. Do you think that Mom will agree to Brooke going anywhere, ever again?"

"Well, she's had a bad shock, she's still recovering."

"She'll be recovering when Brooke is forty, Daddy. You know I'm right."

"And if you are?"

"You'll talk to Mom. Make it okay."

"I need to think about it." Michael couldn't bear to look at the picture anymore. He averted his eyes and reached for a stuffed gorilla that was holding court on his desk.

"Okay," she said, standing up. That perfume again. Like a cloud around her. "I should be going," she added. "I've got math first period."

"I'm glad you stopped by."

"Me too."

"Love you, honey." Michael squeezed the gorilla hard now, its plush body yielding easily to his fierce grip. She didn't say it back. After she was gone, he returned the gorilla to his desk and picked up the photograph again. Brooke wanted to leave home and he was supposed to stand back and let it happen. Camille was not the only one who lived in dread of letting this child go. He had to remind himself that she would be off in a couple of years anyway. Her desire was just accelerating the course of events, not determining or significantly altering them. Still, he didn't know if he could do it. Once she left, he didn't believe she would come back. She wanted to leave them all behind. And who could blame her? He thought about Camille. What would he say to her and how would he say it? But he understood, as well as he had ever understood anything in his life, that Brooke needed to go and he needed to help her do it. He ran his finger over her golden, smiling face. Let God go with you, he thought. Now and always.

32

Cycling

Now that it was warm, Rick had started riding his bicycle again. Not just to and from work or along the promenade and the park. He continued to take those rides, but he also began taking longer trips to neighborhoods he seldom visited: Ditmas Park. Midwood. Sheepshead Bay. Bensonhurst. Brooklyn, as he pedaled through it, was vast and mysterious, its enclaves well shaped and solid. The names of the streets—Marlborough Road, Argyle Road, Mermaid Avenue, Surf Avenue—reached as far and wide as the borough's borders, revealing the aspirations and the longings of its planners and its residents. He asked Naomi if she would join him on one of these rides but she demurred, saying that her bike was in need of repair or that she wasn't up to it.

Without telling her, Rick pulled her bike out from its home in the basement. It was dusty and the tires were flat. He noticed some rust around the chain. But all these were minor things, easily repaired. He walked the bicycle over to Dixon's Bike Shop on Union Street. Three days later, he retrieved it, shined, spiffy, and ready to ride. He had asked for new pedals, a new cushioned seat, cushioned handle grips, and a wide wire basket. He imagined Naomi riding this bike up to the farmers' market at Grand Army Plaza, returning home with melon and berries, zucchini and lettuce. Food for their table, for the meals they now shared together again.

She'd asked him to move back late last winter. Now it was May and he was once more living on Carroll Street, coexisting, if not cohabiting, with Naomi. His mother-in-law occupied the two rooms downstairs; Naomi had told him that Estelle wouldn't agree to live there unless he did too.

"Is that the only reason you're asking me to come back?" he had asked.

"Not the only one. But it's right up there."

Rick didn't care. He wanted to go back, to his neighborhood, his block, his house. He slept in their old room, by himself. Naomi had moved into what had been Dahlia's bedroom. When they both went upstairs at the end of the day, he could hear her moving around and he imagined her taking off her clothes, securing the sash of her bathrobe around her slender waist, getting into bed. He wanted to be there with her, but this time he was willing to wait, no matter how long it took. He thought of Lillian, hoped everything was going well with her son, her job. But though he still wanted her, it was in a wistful, even melancholy way, without the ravening hunger of last winter.

Rick led Naomi downstairs to the basement early one Saturday morning and showed her the refurbished bicycle. She didn't say anything at first, only ran her fingers along the newly bright handlebars, gave the seat a gentle squeeze.

"It looks great," she said finally. "Thank you."

"Why not take it out for a spin?"

"Now?"

"Sure. I'll bring a bagel down to your mom. Sit with her for a while."

"All right," she said. "Let me get dressed."

Naomi had hired Winifred Peters, Adelaide's sister, to help care for her mother, but she didn't come in on the weekends. Apart from the incident with the lipstick—Rick had spent over an hour helping Naomi scrub down the bathroom—Estelle had been doing well since she'd been with them, but clearly they could not leave her alone for long.

While Naomi was gone, Rick toasted a bagel, spread it with cream cheese, and presented it to Estelle on a plate.

"You're a nice boy," she said, taking a bite of bagel. There was cream cheese on her chin, but she dabbed at it with her napkin and it disappeared. "But then, you always were."

"Not a boy anymore, Estelle. I haven't been one for a long time." These bagels were good, but not as good as the ones he used to get when he drove out to Avenue Z with Dahlia. He had never been back there since. He never would.

"Oh, but you are. A mere cub. A pup."

"Nobody who's lost a child is a boy." Jesus Christ, why had he said that? Now she would get upset and Naomi would be angry with him. But to his surprise, Estelle looked more like her old self than at any time in his recent memory. Sad, yes, but not devastated.

"I know." She laid her hand over his. "It almost killed you. Naomi too. But it didn't. You're here. She's here. You'll get through."

"Really?" He found there were tears in his eyes.

"Really."

Later, he heard Naomi come in, and he got up to help her carry the bike back downstairs. Estelle was watching *Roman Holiday*.

"No, let's leave it upstairs," Naomi said.

"It was fun?"

"It was great," she said, gathering her hair off her neck into a pony-tail. "I rode all the way out to the end of Ocean Parkway. Almost to the beach." The sight of her exposed throat suddenly made him want to kiss that naked, vulnerable spot. "I want to start riding more. Next time we should go together."

"You think so?"

"I do."

He put Naomi's bike next to his on the downstairs landing. The handlebars were touching and the wheels stood close together.

When the doorbell rang the following Saturday, Rick was surprised to see Winifred Peters standing there. Naomi appeared right behind him and ushered her in.

"Estelle's having a nap," Naomi told Winifred as she set down her bag and took off the wide-brimmed cotton hat that she wore. "But I told her you'd be here today."

"I'll give her a tuna melt for lunch," Winifred said. "She says she loves my tuna melts."

"We'll be gone for a few hours," Naomi said. "But Rick will have his cell phone. I'll give you the number."

"Have I missed something?" Rick listened to this exchange without understanding it. "Are we going somewhere?"

"Yes," Naomi said, turning to him. "For a bike ride. Remember?"

Naomi wanted to repeat the ride she'd had the week before, so they rode along the bike path on Ocean Parkway. In Midwood, they passed religious Jewish families, young women with long dresses and wigs, holding the hands of tiny children while older ones walked or skipped beside them. One woman, visibly pregnant, pushed a toddler in a stroller; she couldn't have been more than twenty. As they got closer to the ocean, the population changed. Now the young women wore high heels and tight low-rise jeans; their vividly colored hair—copper, raven, platinum—was elaborately styled. When they spoke, it was in Russian.

Finally, they came to the end of the bike path, but they continued on anyway. Naomi didn't want to go to Coney Island—they had taken Dahlia there too many times—but to Brighton Beach. They locked their bicycles on the boardwalk and walked down the steps toward the water.

"Let's take off our shoes," Naomi said, kneeling down to untie hers.

"Okay," Rick agreed.

He carried both pairs, with one arm. Naomi reached for his free hand as they walked along and he enclosed her fingers tightly in his. The beach was neither crowded nor empty. They saw lean, vigorous couples in their sixties and seventies, with browned, leathery skin; a

Hispanic family whose darkly beautiful kids were tossing a Frisbee. They saw plenty of cigarette butts and candy wrappers—but still, there was sand, there was sea, and there was sky.

"Who could believe this is New York City?" Rick said.

"Brooklyn, to be exact." Naomi looked up at him. She didn't smile, but it looked as if she might any minute.

After a while, they sat down. The sun was bright but with the breeze blowing, it felt fresh, not hot. Naomi leaned her head against his shoulder.

"I'm glad you suggested this," Rick said, not wanting to move for fear of dislodging her.

"So am I." Her head remained where it was.

"I never wanted to hurt you, you know." They hadn't ever really talked about Lillian since the night he had confessed. She had asked him to leave, and when he returned, he had felt a tacit sense of decorum governing their behavior; things that could not be broached because they were just too painful. Somehow, though, he intuited that this was a moment when the decorum might safely be broken.

"But you did."

"And so you wanted to hurt me." He watched as a long, thin cloud edged its way across the sky.

"No, it wasn't so much that. It was more that I wanted to comfort myself."

"With him."

"Yes, with him. He was . . ." She moved away then, and Rick instantly missed her weight. "He was my friend."

"I see," he said, keeping his eyes on the horizon, trying hard not to look at her. "And what does that make me?"

"My husband," she said simply. He didn't know why this comment should make him want to weep with relief, with something almost like happiness, but it did.

She stood and gave him her hand again. Slowly, they walked back in the direction from which they had come. On the boardwalk, there was a vendor selling pirogi from a cart. They each bought a portion and stood there eating with plastic forks, from the red-and-white-checked paper containers.

The sun had sunk lower in the sky when they biked down Carroll Street and stopped in front of their house. Naomi went in first, and Rick stayed outside to put the bicycles away. Later, she made dinner—a big salad, a cold shrimp and buttermilk soup, rhubarb crumble with vanilla ice cream for dessert—and Estelle came up to eat it with them.

"You both got some sun," she observed as she glanced back and forth from Rick's face to Naomi's. "It looks nice."

33

Spires

If the stunning cold of winter had been a physical attack, the limpid beauty of spring was a psychic insult, cutting and cruel. How dare the sky have that molten blue appearance? How could the buds open and burst out, the daffodils and the tulips, the hyacinths all dazzle the window boxes and planters and small front gardens with their radiant color? On the first few warm, beautiful days of the nascent season, Naomi walked through Park Slope with tears tracking her cheeks, just as they had in the days right after Dahlia had died. Then Rick fixed her bicycle, and pedaling along the same streets and avenues, she found herself freed from the immediate weight of her mourning, the velocity giving everything she passed a slightly blurred and altered look.

Despite her sorrow, Naomi's days were full. She devoted herself to caring for her mother in the way that she would have cared for a child, had she still had one. She couldn't do it all alone, of course, and was extremely grateful for the help provided by Winifred Peters. Her mother had liked Winifred right away, and their bond solidified over their shared appreciation for the old movies that both women liked to watch. Now Estelle had a companion for her film festivals; Winifred would make lunch and bring it down to Estelle on a tray. Then she'd close the blinds and turn off the lights, so that they could sit together, watching and nodding, in their peaceful simulacrum of a joint place of worship: a movie theater.

Naomi had to admit it was strange, living with her mother again after all these years. She'd left home for college at eighteen; by the time she had graduated, she was already living with Rick and hadn't gone home again. Apart from the times spent with her parents in Florida—vacation, totally outside the realm of daily routine—she had not spent a night under the same roof as Estelle. Now they were both at home here, in this house on Carroll Street. Strange, but somehow totally natural too. She didn't know how long she would be able to keep her mother with her, but she had promised herself to do it for as long as she—and Rick—felt they could.

It was also strange having Rick back again. She had told him it was Estelle's prodding that had prompted her to ask. But that wasn't the whole truth. And he knew it too, though he hadn't yet said what it was that he knew. If he had asked her again, she might have given him the more complete answer. She might have told him that she had had to spend the night with a man who was not her husband and woken up the next day to find out that it was her husband whom she had wanted all along. Her husband who had hurt her, and whom she had wanted to hurt. But look who had gotten hurt instead. Just look.

There had been a day when Naomi was cycling along Prospect Park West—she never went on Seventh or near the hospital if she could help it—and she saw Michael's daughter Brooke. She was flanked by a woman who must have been her mother and a girl who looked just like her—her twin sister. Naomi had to stop or else she would have crashed. But she didn't want them to see her; she was afraid the girl would recognize her, the way she had before.

Quickly, she got off the bicycle and wheeled it into the park, where she would be hidden by some large flowering shrubs. But her worry was unfounded; they didn't notice her at all. They moved slowly, sister and mother hovering close by as Brooke made her tentative way down the street. She must have been fitted with a prosthetic foot, but did not look altogether comfortable with it. Maybe she was just getting accustomed to it; her mother and sister were along to offer their help, their moral support.

Naomi waited until they passed before venturing out of the park again. Her breath came in tiny, shallow gasps and she could smell the sweat—from her forehead, her underarms—with its rank, unmistakable odor of guilt. She knew herself to be indirectly responsible for what had happened to this girl, and by extension, to the people who loved her. Knowing this made it easier to forgive Rick. He had acted heedlessly and hurtfully. As had she, she reminded herself. As had she.

That Brooke had not been killed when she had fallen onto the tracks that night was something Naomi gave thanks for each and every day. She did not think she could have endured the vicarious grief—Michael's, his wife's—she would have felt had the girl actually died. But thank the living God she hadn't. She was damaged, she was crippled, but she was still alive, walking, haltingly, in the spring sunshine. And Naomi had the proof: she had seen her.

Back on the bike, she pedaled down to the fish store and then on to the bakery before heading home. She took her bicycle in downstairs, but to enter the house, she had to walk back outside and up the stoop. Further up the hill were the two church spires she loved, one Catholic, the other Protestant. Neither belonged to her, and yet somehow, they both did.

The glorious spring light turned the stone rosy and, in some places, gold. Seen from this distance, the spires looked as if they were practically right on top of each other. It was only when you walked closer that you could see the distance—not much, a block was all—actually separating them. Which was it? She thought about this as she turned the key, let herself into the house where she would prepare a meal for her mother and her husband. Was the optical trick by which they were joined somehow meaningful? Or was it just that, a mere illusion obscuring the fact that they were and would always remain two distinct entities?

The question continued to engage her as she put away her groceries. Halibut went in the refrigerator, baguette on the counter. Then she stopped. The dinner preparations could wait for just a moment longer. Naomi went to the door, opened it, and stood for a moment on the stoop, regarding the spires. The shorter one was more grounded and earthbound; the taller, thinner one particularly haunting as it pierced the sky. Separate or together, she asked herself again. Maybe there was no definitive answer. It was all relative, depending on her vantage point. Together, Naomi decided all at once. Then she quietly closed the door.

Acknowledgments

The writing of this book was often an uphill climb; for encouragement, inspiration, and sustenance along the way I would like to thank Judith Ehrlich; Catharine Dubois Fincke; Patricia Grossman; Amy Koppelman; Constance Marks; Paul, James, and Katherine McDonough; Sally Schloss; Kenneth Silver; and Marian Thurm.

Additionally, there were several people kind enough to share their experience and expertise with me and these are: Dr. Jason Feit, Dr. Susie Feit, Maria Friedlander, Dr. Bryanne O'Conner, Dr. Ida Santana, Dr. Christopher Toth.

For various combinations of technical assistance, efficiency, and all around good cheer, I must thank Dianne Choie and Rachel Pace at Doubleday; Anne Merrow, formerly at Doubleday; and Erin Malone at the William Morris Agency.

Finally, I wish to express my deepest gratitude to my agent, Suzanne Gluck, and my editor, Deborah Futter, for their ongoing support and faith.